Praise for the Novels of Karen White

The Memory of Water

"The enduring ties between two estranged sisters drive the darkly engaging latest from White....Careful plotting, richly flawed characters, and a surprising conclusion mark this absorbing melodrama."

—*Publishers Weekly*

"In this moving novel, White explores the bond between sisters, the link between artistic genius and mental illness, and the keen hold a place can have on a person. She vividly describes the Lowcountry and the pull of the sea. A chilling revelation, a love story, and a bittersweet ending add to this gripping tale." —*Booklist*

"This story is as rich as its South Carolina Lowcountry setting and filled with sympathetic, endearing characters that resonate. It's an engaging, deeply moving story." —*Romantic Times* (4½ stars)

"Beautifully written and as lyrical as the tides. *The Memory of Water* speaks directly to the heart and will linger in yours long after you've read the final page. I loved this book!"

—Susan Crandall, author of *Pitch Black*

"Karen White delivers a powerfully emotional blend of family secrets, Lowcountry lore, and love in *The Memory of Water*—who could ask for more?" —Barbara Bretton, author of *Just Desserts*

Learning to Breathe

"White creates a heartfelt story full of vibrant characters and emotion that leaves the reader satisfied yet hungry for more from this talented author."

—*Booklist*

continued...

"A can't-put-it-down book by Georgia novelist Karen White."

—*Southern Lady*

"One of those stories where you savor every single word . . . a perfect 10."

—Romance Reviews Today

"Another one of Karen White's emotional books! A joy to read!"

—The Best Reviews

Pieces of the Heart

"Heartwarming and intense . . . a tale that resonates with the meaning of unconditional love." —*Romantic Times* (4 stars)

"A terrific, insightful character study." —*Midwest Book Review*

The Color of Light

"[White's] prose is lyrical, and she weaves in elements of mysticism and romance without being heavy-handed. An accomplished novel . . ."

—*Booklist*

"A story as rich as a coastal summer . . . dark secrets, heartache, a magnificent South Carolina setting, and a great love story."

—*New York Times* bestselling author Deborah Smith

"As lush as the Lowcountry, where the characters' wounded souls come home to mend in unexpected and magical ways."

—Patti Callahan Henry, author of *Between the Tides*

More Praise
for Karen White

"The fresh voice of Karen White intrigues and delights."
—Sandra Chastain, contributor to *At Home in Mossy Creek*

"Warmly Southern and deeply moving." —Deborah Smith

"Karen White writes with passion and poignancy."
—Deb Stover, award-winning author of *Mulligan Magic*

"[A] sweet book...highly recommended." —*Booklist*

"Karen White is one author you won't forget....This is a masterpiece in the study of relationships. Brava!" —Reader to Reader Reviews

"This is not only romance at its best—this is a fully realized view of life at its fullest." —Readers & Writers, Ink

"*After the Rain* is an elegantly enchanting Southern novel....Fans will recognize the beauty of White's evocative prose." —WordWeaving.com

"In the tradition of Catherine Anderson and Deborah Smith, Karen White's *After the Rain* is an incredibly poignant contemporary bursting with Southern charm."
—Patricia Rouse, Rouse's Romance Readers Groups

"Don't miss this book!" —*Rendezvous*

New American Library Titles by Karen White

The Color of Light
Pieces of the Heart
Learning to Breathe
The Memory of Water

THE HOUSE ON TRADD STREET

KAREN WHITE

NEW AMERICAN LIBRARY

New American Library
Published by New American Library, a division of
Penguin Group (USA) Inc., 375 Hudson Street,
New York, New York 10014, USA
Penguin Group (Canada), 90 Eglinton Avenue East, Suite 700, Toronto,
Ontario M4P 2Y3, Canada (a division of Pearson Penguin Canada Inc.)
Penguin Books Ltd., 80 Strand, London WC2R 0RL, England
Penguin Ireland, 25 St. Stephen's Green, Dublin 2,
Ireland (a division of Penguin Books Ltd.)
Penguin Group (Australia), 250 Camberwell Road, Camberwell, Victoria 3124,
Australia (a division of Pearson Australia Group Pty. Ltd.)
Penguin Books India Pvt. Ltd., 11 Community Centre, Panchsheel Park,
New Delhi - 110 017, India
Penguin Group (NZ), 67 Apollo Drive, Rosedale, North Shore 0632,
New Zealand (a division of Pearson New Zealand Ltd.)
Penguin Books (South Africa) (Pty.) Ltd., 24 Sturdee Avenue,
Rosebank, Johannesburg 2196, South Africa

Penguin Books Ltd., Registered Offices:
80 Strand, London WC2R 0RL, England

First published by New American Library,
a division of Penguin Group (USA) Inc.

First Printing, November 2008
20 19 18 17 16 15 14

LIBRARY OF CONGRESS CATALOGING-IN-PUBLICATION DATA:

White, Karen (Karen S.)
The House on Tradd Street/Karen White.
p. cm.
ISBN 978-0-451-22509-2
1. Real estate agents—Fiction. 2. Single women—Fiction. 3. Haunted houses—Fiction.
4. Historic buildings—South Carolina—Charleston—Fiction. 5. Charleston (S.C.)—Fiction.
I. Title.
PS3623.H5776H68 2008
813'.6—dc22 2008025926

Set in Bembo
Designed by Alissa Amell

Printed in the United States of America

To Theresa White,
my wonderful mother-in-law and ardent supporter

ACKNOWLEDGMENTS

As always, thanks to the usual suspects: Tim, Connor and Meghan for your cheerleading and your acceptance of an empty kitchen and pizza for dinner. To my editor, Cindy Hwang, and my agent, Karen Solem, for working tirelessly to help me create the best books possible, and to the rest of the well-oiled machine at Penguin, who do such a fabulous job of creating gorgeous covers and getting my books in stores everywhere.

Thank you to Pam Mantovani and Dianna Love for the initial brainstorming for the idea behind this book and for your enthusiasm that encouraged me to write it.

Thanks also to my critique partner, Wendy Wax, whose wisdom and support I simply couldn't do without. To Nancy Flaherty, my lasting gratitude for her unflagging support and her graciousness in allowing me to use her name and golf habits. And a huge thanks to Robin Hillyer Miles, a Charleston native and tour guide extraordinaire who was kind enough to read this manuscript and point out facts that I didn't have "quite right." Any errors regarding the city of Charleston and its geography are entirely my own!

And no acknowledgment would be complete without thanking my readers. You make worthwhile every moment I spend in the solitude of writing.

CHAPTER 1

Pewter reflections of scarlet hibiscus colored the dirt-smudged windows of the old house, like happy memories of youth trapped inside the shell of an old man. The broken pediments over the windows gave the house a permanent frown, yet the leaf-filtered sun against the chipped Tower-of-the-Winds columns lining the side piazzas painted the house with hope. It was almost, I thought, as if the house were merely waiting for a miracle.

I studied the house, my Realtor's mind trying to see past the wreckage. It was a characteristic Charleston single house, turned perpendicular to the street so that its short side abutted the sidewalk. The entry door, with an ornate cornice and Italianate filigree brackets, opened onto the garden-facing piazza, where I knew I would find the main entryway into the house. I wrinkled my nose, already smelling the inevitable decay I would encounter once I'd entered the house. Despite the enviable south of Broad location, any potential buyer for this property would have to be blind or incredibly stupid. In my vast experience at selling historic real estate in the city, I would bank on the latter.

The rhythmic pulse of rope against tree trunk punctuated the muggy Charleston morning air, catching my attention and drawing me to the peeling wrought iron fence to peer into the side garden. I wasn't sure if it was curiosity that made me stop or just reluctance to continue. I hated old houses. Which was odd, really, since they were my specialty in the realty business. Then again, maybe not so odd, considering the origins of my dislike. Regardless, old houses gave me plenty of reasons to dislike them. For one thing, they smelled of lemon oil and beeswax mixed with mothballs. And always seemed to accompany the slow gait of an elderly person too old to keep up the house yet too stubborn to let it go. Like the owner had exhausted all hope of finding something in the future that would ever be as good as the past. Depressing, really. It was all just lumber and plaster in the end.

Seeing nothing, I pushed open the stubborn gate covered with climbing Confederate jasmine, the rusted hinges reluctantly giving up ground. I picked my way carefully over the cracked walkway of what must have once been a prized patterned garden, my high-heeled pumps avoiding cracks and tall weeds with prickers that would tear at my stockings and silk suit with little provocation.

A fall of shadow from the rear of the garden caught my attention. Ignoring the drops of perspiration running down the front of my blouse, I gingerly stepped across the weeds to get a better look.

An overgrown flower bed encircled a fountain where a cherub in the middle sat suspended in the perpetual motion of blowing nonexistent water from stone lips. Thick weeds as tall as my hips crept into the fountain, grasping at the cherub's ankles. A gecko darted out from the chipped cement edging the fountain and ran along the side. Clutching my leather portfolio, I followed it to the back side of the statue, not completely sure why. Sweat trickled down my nape, and I raised a hand to wipe it away. My fingers felt icy against my skin, a sort of warning sign I had begun to recognize when I was still very small. I concentrated on ignoring the pinpricks that raced up my spine and made me listen to things I didn't want to hear and that other people couldn't.

I was eager to leave, but I stopped at the sight of a splash of red while my beautiful and expensive Italian leather heels sank into thick mulch. A small kidney-shaped area had been cleared of weeds and there, sprouting from fresh cedar clippings, grew four fat bushes containing the most vibrant red roses I had ever seen. They were like brightly dressed young girls sitting in the back pew of a crumbling church, and even their scent seemed out of place in the forlorn garden. I turned away, feeling an abiding sorrow that seemed to saturate the air in this part of the yard.

The heat that pressed down on me seemed to have a cold center to it, and I felt out of breath, as if I'd run a long distance. Jerkily, I stumbled to the shade under a live oak tree. I leaned against the tree trunk and looked up, searching for my breath in a garden that seemed to be soaking up air and even time itself. Spanish moss draped shawllike on the ancient limbs of the tree, its massive branches testifying to its years on this earth, its roots reaching out toward the house. The sound of the swing continued to reverberate throughout the overgrown garden, and when I turned my head, I again caught a movement of shadow from the corner of my eye. For a moment, I thought I could see a woman wearing an old-fashioned dress pushing an empty board swing suspended by rope from the oak tree. The image was hazy, the edges of it dim and fading.

The pinpricks invaded the back of my neck again, and I abruptly turned toward the piazza and marched across the garden, unconcerned now about my panty hose or anything else except getting my errand over with.

I crossed the marble-paved piazza, then pressed hard on the front doorbell and then again as I willed somebody to answer it quickly. It took forever before the slow, shuffling steps could be heard behind the closed door. I saw movement through the beveled-glass window in the door, etched in the pattern of climbing roses, the pattern deflecting light and color and separating the person on the other side of the door into a thousand fragments.

I sighed, knowing that it would take another five minutes for the old man to unlock all the dead bolts and another twenty for him to allow me to get to the point of our meeting just as surely as I knew that if I turned around to face the sound of the swing, I would see nothing at all.

The door swung open, and I took a surprised step backward as I found myself staring up into large brown eyes magnified by what looked like the bottoms of Coke bottles stuffed into wire eyeglass frames. The man had to be at least six foot three, even with the hunched shoulders beneath the starched white oxford cloth shirt and dark jacket, and he wore a linen handkerchief neatly tucked into the coat pocket.

I whipped out one of my business cards and held it out toward the old man. "Mr. Vanderhorst? I'm Melanie Middleton with Henderson House Realty. We spoke on the phone yesterday." The man hadn't made a move to take my card and was still staring at me through his thick glasses. "We made an appointment for today so that we might discuss your house."

He acted as if he hadn't heard me. "I saw you in the garden."

He continued to stare and I rubbed my hands up and down my arms, feeling as if it were thirty degrees outside instead of ninety-eight. "I hope you don't mind. I wanted to get a good look at the lot."

I turned to face the garden as if to illustrate my point and realized that the sound of the swing had stopped the moment the door opened. The lot itself was large by historic district standards, and I couldn't help but think of the wasted space the house was occupying and how much more useful it would be as a parking lot for the nearby shops and restaurants.

"Did you see her?"

His voice startled me. It was deep and very soft, as if it didn't get much use, and he was unaware of how much breath he needed for each word.

"See who?"

"The lady pushing the swing."

He had my full attention now. I looked into his magnified eyes. "No. There was nobody there. Were you expecting somebody?"

Instead of answering, he stepped back, opening the door farther, and made a courtly sweep of his hand. "Won't you come in? Let's sit in the drawing room and I'll get us coffee."

"Thank you, but that's really not necessa . . ."

But he had already turned away from me and was shuffling through a keystone arch that separated the front hall from the stair hall. A faded yellow Chinese paper covered the walls, and I had the fleeting impression of elegant beauty before I looked closer and saw the buckling and the peeling and did a mental calculation of the cost of restoring hand-painted wallpaper.

I stepped through a pedimented doorway into the room Mr. Vanderhorst had indicated and found myself standing in a large front drawing room with tall ornamented ceilings capped with elaborate cornices circling the room. A dusty crystal chandelier dominated the room, its remaining crystals seemingly held in place by thick cobwebs. An intricate plaster medallion on the ceiling above the chandelier finalized my initial impression of the room as a wedding cake that had been left out in a warm room too long.

Smelling the old beeswax, I wrinkled my nose again, comparing my surroundings to my brand-new rented condo in nearby Mt. Pleasant complete with plain white walls, wall-to-wall carpeting, and central air. I would never understand people who felt privileged to pay a great deal of money to saddle themselves with a pile of termite-infested lumber like this, and then continued running themselves into bankruptcy from supporting the horrendous upkeep such an old house demanded. I shuddered, thankful that my own military-brat upbringing had never fostered any root-growing tendencies or warm and fuzzies toward ancient architecture.

I looked around the room, careful not to touch anything that would get dust on my hands and clothes. Sheets covered most of what looked like antique furniture except for a faded *grospoint*-covered Louis XV armchair and matching ottoman as well as an enormous mahogany grandfather clock. A small black-and-white dog lay curled on the ottoman and looked up with large brown eyes that strongly resembled those of my host. The thought made me smile until I spotted the huge crack in the plaster wall that snaked up from the baseboard to the cracked cornice in the corner of the room. My eyes drifted from the large water spot on the paint-chipped ceiling to the buckled wood floor underneath. I felt exhausted all of a sudden, as if I had somehow absorbed the age and decay of the room.

I moved to one of the floor-to-ceiling windows, hoping daylight might perk me up. Pushing aside a faded crimson damask drapery panel, and almost choking on the smell of stale dust, I paused, wondering if the small etchings I saw on the wall were actually hairline cracks in the plaster. I leaned forward and squinted, wishing I'd brought my glasses. A pale gray line stretched from the top of the baseboard to about four feet from the floor. Small markings bisected the line at approximately one-inch intervals, and tiny numbers were written in a delicate handwriting next to each demarcation. Squatting to see better, I realized I was looking at a growth chart, with the initials MBG written alongside the vertical line along with the age of MBG starting at one year. Tracing my finger along the line, I saw that it stopped at MBG's eighth year.

"That was mine."

The voice came from directly behind me, and I jumped, wondering how he had managed to move so quietly.

"But the initials . . . aren't you Mr. Vanderhorst?"

His eyes focused on the pencil marks on the wall, and I noticed that an antique writing desk had been pulled away from the wall to expose the marks and now stood almost in the middle of the room. "MBG stands for 'my best guy.' My mother used to call me that."

The soft tone of his voice reminded me of my own little-girl voice pretending to speak long distance on the phone to my absent mother. I looked away. A tray with delicate china teacups and a plate of pecan pralines had been laid on an uncovered side table. Moving toward it I spotted a large frame set on the table holding a sepia-toned portrait of a young boy sitting on a piano bench.

Again, Mr. Vanderhorst's voice sounded right in my ear. "That was me when I was about four years old. My mother was an amateur photographer. She loved to take my picture." He shuffled behind me and pulled off a dusty sheet from a delicate Sheridan armchair and indicated for me to sit.

I sat, placing my leather portfolio on the floor by my feet, then leaned forward to spoon four cubes of sugar and a splash of cream into my coffee, noticing the rose pattern on the teacups. I had expected the ubiquitous antique blue-and-white Canton china found in most of the houses in Charleston's historic district. The roses on this set of china were bright red with large blooms of layered petals, nearly identical to the roses I'd seen in the neglected garden. I took a praline and placed it on a small rose-covered plate, then took another, aware of Mr. Vanderhorst watching me. Nervously, I sipped my coffee.

"Those are Louisa roses—my mama's hybrid and named after her. She cultivated those, you see, in the garden. They were famous for a while—famous enough to have magazines coming from all over to photograph them." His eyes fixed on me behind the thick glasses, studying me as if to gauge my reaction. "But now the only place in the world you can find them is right here in my garden."

I nodded, eager to move on to the subject at hand.

"Are you a gardener, Miss Middleton?"

"Um, no, actually. I mean, I know what a rose is, and what a daisy looks like, but that pretty much covers all of my gardening terms." I smiled tentatively.

Mr. Vanderhorst sat down across from me in a matching chair and picked up a teacup with slightly trembling hands. "This house had beautiful gardens when my mother lived here. Sadly, I haven't been able to keep them up. I can just find enough energy to keep up the small rose garden by the fountain. That was my mama's favorite."

I nodded, remembering the odd little garden and the sound of a swing, then took another sip of coffee. "Mr. Vanderhorst, as I mentioned on the phone yesterday, I'm a Realtor, and my real estate company is very interested in obtaining the listing for your house." I set my cup down and reached inside my portfolio to pull out the information on the property values in the neighborhood, as well as brochures that explained why my company was better than any of the other dozens of real estate companies in the area.

"You're Augustus Middleton's granddaughter, aren't you? Your granddaddy and my daddy were at Harvard Law together, you know. They even started out clerking in the same law firm, and Augustus was best man at my daddy's wedding."

My arm felt awkward and heavy as I kept it extended in Mr. Vanderhorst's direction while he ignored it. Finally, I leaned across and placed the information on the table between us, then picked up my coffee again. "Ah, no. I wasn't aware that our families knew one another. Small world." I took a quick sip of my coffee. "So, anyway, as I mentioned, my company is very interested—"

"They had some kind of a falling-out when I was about eight. Never spoke to each other again. Saw each other occasionally across a courtroom but never exchanged another word."

I focused on swallowing without choking and breathing slowly, and made a conscious effort to still my leg from twitching. *Damn.* Had Mr. Vanderhorst brought me out here just so he could tell me about my grandfather Gus? Was he about to ask me to leave? And couldn't he have just told me this on the phone to save me the trouble?

"Despite their disagreement, my daddy always thought him to be one of the most honorable men he'd ever met."

"Yes, well, he died when my father was only twelve, so I can't really say."

"You favor him a great deal, you know. Your father, too, although we've never met. I've seen pictures of him and your mother in the paper every once in a while. You don't look a thing like her."

Thank God. If he started talking about my mother, I'd have to leave. There was only so much sucking up I was prepared to do to get this listing. "Look, Mr. Vanderhorst, I've got another appointment I need to get to, so I'd like to go ahead and discuss—"

Once again he interrupted me as if I hadn't spoken. He glanced down at the two pralines on my plate and seemed to grin. "Your grandfather had a legendary sweet tooth, too."

I opened my mouth to deny it, but Mr. Vanderhorst said, "Do you like old houses, Miss Middleton?"

For a moment, I wondered if there were hidden cameras pointed on me to be replayed later on one of those stupid reality television shows. I felt my mouth working up and down as I tried to figure out how truthful I should be. As if not wanting to hear outright lying, the little dog jumped off the ottoman, gave me a withering look, then ran out of the room.

"They're, um, well, they're old. Which is nice." *Brilliant.* "What I meant to say is that old houses are really popular right now in today's real estate market. As you probably already know, prices and interest in historic real estate have increased dramatically since the nineteen seventies when the Historic Charleston Foundation sponsored the restoration of the Ansonborough neighborhood. People are buying old houses as investment properties, fixing them up, then selling them for a nice profit."

I risked taking another sip of coffee, hoping he wouldn't steer the conversation away again. I eyed the pralines, still untouched on my plate, and decided that eating one would give Mr. Vanderhorst too much of a chance to change the conversation again.

"As I said on the phone, your lawyer, Mr. Drayton, contacted us about possibly listing your house. I understand that you're thinking about moving into an assisted-living facility and have no relatives who would be interested in owning the home."

While I spoke, Mr. Vanderhorst left his untouched coffee and pralines and walked to one of the tall windows that looked out into the garden. I could see part of the old oak tree from where I sat. I paused, waiting for him to confirm what I had just told him and took the opportunity to bite into a dark chocolate praline.

His voice was soft when he finally spoke. "I was born in this house and I've lived here my entire life, Miss Middleton. As did my father, and grandfather, and his grandfather before him. This house has been lived in by a member of the Vanderhorst family since it was built in 1848."

The chocolate stuck in my throat. *Here it comes. He's not selling the house and I've just wasted an entire morning.* I swallowed and waited for him to continue, my conscience tugging at me, reminding me of almost identical words my mother had once said to me. But that had been a long, long, time ago, and I was no longer that girl who had listened with so much hope in her heart.

"But now I'm the only one left. All of those generations before me who worked so hard to keep this house in the family. Even after the Civil War, when things were tight, they sold their silver and jewelry and went hungry just so they could hold on to this house." He turned to face me, as if remembering that I was in the room. "This house is more than brick, mortar, and lumber. It's a connection to the past and those who have gone before us. It's memories and belonging. It's a home that on the inside has seen the birth of children and the death of the old folks and the changing of the world from the outside. It's a piece of history you can hold in your hands."

I wanted to add, *It's an unbearable weight of debt hanging around your neck, pulling you down until you land face-first into insolvency.* But I didn't say anything because Mr. Vanderhorst's face had lost its color, and he seemed to be swaying on his feet. I jumped up and led him to his chair, then handed him his cup of coffee.

"Can I call a doctor for you? You're not looking well." I put the coffee on the table next to him and took his hand, remembering what he'd said about his house. It might be just brick and mortar to me, but it was his whole life—a life nearing its end with no family left to refurbish the garden or enjoy the rose china. It saddened me and I didn't want it to, but I held tight to his hand anyway.

He ignored the coffee. "Did you see her? In the garden—did you see her? She only appears to people she approves of, you know."

I was torn between answering him and calling his doctor. But something he had said I had heard before and once, a million years ago, I had believed with all my young and gullible heart. *It's a piece of history you can hold in your hands.* I looked into his eyes and allowed myself to see his need and understand his pain.

Taking a deep breath, I said, "Yes. I saw her. But I don't think it's because she approves of me. I . . . seem to see things that aren't there on a kind of regular basis."

Some of the color returned to his face, and he actually smiled. He leaned over and patted me on the leg. "That's good," he said. "That's very good news." He leaned back and drank his coffee in three big gulps before standing as if nothing had happened.

"I hope you don't mind me ending our nice meeting so abruptly, but I have a few things I need to do this morning before my lawyer arrives." He pulled a clean linen napkin off the serving tray and put the pralines, complete with the rose-covered china plate, into it before twisting the napkin into a knot on top and handing it to me.

I stood, stunned, his actions again rendering me speechless. Finding my voice, I blurted out, "But we haven't even discussed . . ." I took the napkin-covered plate as he shoved it into my hands. "And I can't take your plate. I don't know when I'll be back this way to return it."

He waved his hand in dismissal. "Oh, never you mind about that. It will be back amongst the other plates sooner than you'd think."

I wanted to be angry over wasting my morning for a pointless visit. But when I looked down at the plate in my hands, all I could feel was a peculiar regret. Over what? *It's a piece of history you can hold in your hands.* Once again, I was seven years old and standing hand in hand with my mother in front of another old house. I felt in my bones what Mr. Vanderhorst was talking about, no matter how much or how long I wanted to deny it, and I allowed a foolish tenderness toward the old man to shake my heart loose.

Mr. Vanderhorst leaned across and gently kissed my cheek. "Thank you, Miss Middleton. You've done this old man a world of good by your visit today."

"No, thank you," I said, surprisingly close to tears. It had been a long time since anyone had kissed me on the cheek, and for a moment I wanted to ask if I could stay for a while longer, eating pralines and drinking coffee while chatting about old ghosts—both the living and the dead kind.

But Mr. Vanderhorst had already stood, and the moment passed. Mechanically, I hung my portfolio over my shoulder and clutched the loaded napkin carefully as Mr. Vanderhorst led me to the front door.

We passed a music room dominated by a concert grand piano, and I remembered the photo of the little boy sitting on the bench.

I didn't have time to linger as Mr. Vanderhorst's surprisingly strong hand on my back propelled me toward the front door. For a man who shuffled, he seemed determined to get me out of the house. Which was fine with me, really. I'd wasted enough of my day.

I stepped outside onto the piazza and turned back to say goodbye. He was beaming now, his eyes bright, shiny pennies behind the thick glasses. "Goodbye, Mr. Vanderhorst. It's been a pleasure meeting you." I was surprised to find that I really meant it.

"No, Miss Middleton. The pleasure was all mine."

I walked down the piazza toward the door leading to the sidewalk, feeling his gaze on me. When I got to the door, I remembered the plate I was holding. I turned and saw Mr. Vanderhorst watching me from the doorway of the house, as much a part of it as the piazza columns and leaded-glass windows. "I'll bring back the plate as soon as I can." I even imagined I'd look forward to a return visit.

"I have no doubt that you will, Miss Middleton. Goodbye."

I opened the door, then shut it behind me, feeling him watching me through the garden gate until I disappeared from his view. I didn't once turn toward the garden, where the sound of a rope swing against old bark had once again begun to punctuate the muggy morning air.

CHAPTER 2

The jarring ring of my phone two mornings later jolted me awake. I peered groggily at my clock, then cursed under my breath as I reached for my glasses so I could read the time. I hadn't quite reconciled myself to the fact that I actually needed glasses, much less wore them, so most of the time they remained in their case in a drawer. I squinted at the clock: six thirty. Damn! How could I have slept so late? I normally set my alarm for six o'clock each morning so I could get a head start on my day, and I'd already wasted half an hour sleeping in.

I slapped my hand on the receiver, castigating myself for staying up so late the previous evening and forgetting to set my alarm. But I'd been so engrossed in alphabetizing my bookshelves in the living room that the time had gotten away from me. "Hello?"

"Hi, Melanie. Sorry to be calling you so early, but Mr. Henderson said it was important that I reach you ASAP. Not that I can figure out why he didn't call you directly and let me sleep, of course, except that he knows I keep an early tee time every Saturday morning." The soft twang of my office secretary's voice seemed particularly jarring at six thirty on a Saturday morning, but the mention of my boss's name helped part the fog currently residing in my head. She cleared her throat. "Did I wake you up?"

"No, Nancy. I had to get up to answer the phone." I waited to see if the secretary noticed my sarcasm. Nancy Flaherty was very good at the rudiments of her job, but it was no secret to anybody that most of her concentrated efforts remained on her next tee time and practicing her chip shot. Ergo, most sarcasm was completely lost on her.

"That's good. Because Mr. Henderson has scheduled a meeting with you and Mr. Drayton for nine o'clock this morning, and he doesn't want you to be late. It has something to do with Mr. Vanderhorst's estate."

I blinked, then sat up fully, waiting for the words to stop swirling around my head like water in a sink. "His estate? You mean he . . . ?"

"Yeah. Seems he died in his sleep." There was a brief pause and the sound of a soft grunt of breath, and I pictured Nancy in her bedroom with a phone headset on as she practiced putting. "That's a very peaceful way to go, you know."

"But I just saw him two days ago." I couldn't explain the sudden sadness I felt at the old man's passing. I pictured him as I'd last seen him, staring out the window in his faded drawing room, looking at the oak tree that had been there before his birth and remained there still.

"I don't understand—did he mention why Mr. Drayton needed me?"

"You know that if I had that kind of information, I'd tell you, right?"

"Yeah, right." I swallowed, surprised to find a lump there. "But it's Saturday—why couldn't this wait until Monday?"

"I don't know, Melanie. All I know is that Mr. Henderson expects you to be there today."

Wearily, I sat up. "Can you tell me where we're meeting?"

I wrote down the information Nancy gave me, then hung up the phone and stared at it for a full five minutes before walking away.

After quickly showering and dressing in a suitably conservative skirt and blouse for a meeting at a law office, I made the quick drive over the new Cooper River Bridge from Mt. Pleasant and parked in my reserved space in the lot behind my office on South Broad Street. I then stopped at the corner bakery, purchasing two doughnuts with a large latte, whipped cream on top. The owner, Ruth, had already started bagging the doughnuts when she'd spotted me through the front window and had the latte machine whirring by the time I came inside.

"Morning, Ruth."

Ruth smiled, showing off a gold front tooth highlighted by her café au lait skin. "One of these days, Miss Melanie, I'm going to make you a healthy breakfast. You just need to give me more than two minutes, you hear?"

I put the money on the counter and picked up my bag. Smiling, I said, "I don't have more than two minutes or I'd let you." I grabbed my latte, licking the whipped cream off the top as I backed up toward the door.

"You're just skin and bones, missy. That ain't right, considering what you eat. You need some greens and some fruit. A bit of meat and eggs to fatten you up right."

"Maybe next time," I said as I pushed open the door. "Have a good one."

The law offices were several blocks away on King Street, but I had decided to walk them to clear my head and prepare myself for whatever was in store. I headed north, past the modern parking garage and office building in the first block—two buildings I'd heard described as "brutalistic" and "bleak," respectively, by a good number of Charlestonians. Despite a small nagging tug in the back of my brain, I refused to see anything except functionality and a good use of space.

As was my habit, I avoided looking at the historic buildings along King Street, arranged neatly in what has been called "the handsomest shopping street in America." Yes, I supposed the buildings were beautiful in their own antique, money-sucking way, but it was what I saw sometimes peering out at me from old shop windows that kept my eyes focused straight ahead. It was the same with hospitals. I had to wear earphones just to block out the sounds of the voices from people only I could see.

As I walked past a narrow piazza with stairs leading up to what was once the residential part of the building when it was used as a shop, a pale young girl stood on the bottom step, almost hidden by the climbing hibiscus that clung doggedly to the peeling paint. I had almost walked past her before I realized that her skin was nearly translucent and that her clothes were from another century. By the time I turned back, she was gone, only the slight sway of a large red hibiscus bloom to tell anybody of the girl's presence.

Focusing once again on the sidewalk in front of me, I passed the new Judicial Center—recalling the furor that had surrounded its architectural conception—and found the law offices of Drayton, Drayton, and Drayton in the next block. Since it was a Saturday, the grand reception desk in the front foyer sat vacant. I stood there, wondering what to do when large double doors off to the side of the reception area opened and an egg-domed head popped out. The middle-aged man was frowning as he caught sight of me and I felt the two doughnuts and large latte roll over in my stomach.

"Ms. Middleton?" He stuck out a well-manicured hand and we shook. "I'm Jonathan Drayton. Thank you for coming. Please come in."

Giving my mouth a surreptitious wipe in case there were any lingering powdered sugar remnants, I followed Mr. Drayton into the conference room.

There were several people sitting around the table, most of whom appeared to be office support staff. I recognized the eldest Mr. Drayton from previous business dealings near the head of the table. He sent me a tight smile before standing.

"Ms. Middleton, so good to see you again. Won't you sit down?" He indicated the chair at the head of the table.

Hesitantly, I approached, suddenly wary of my presence there and why I would be sitting at the head of the table. Was all this excitement about me obtaining the listing for the old house on Tradd Street? I sat down, crossed my legs at the ankles, and folded my hands in my lap. I pressed down hard on my hands to keep my legs from doing their normal impatient jiggle.

Mr. Drayton sat again while Jonathan Drayton sat down across from him. The room fell silent, and I began to have a very bad feeling.

Mr. Drayton spoke first. "Ms. Middleton, I apologize for bringing you in here on a Saturday. But this situation is highly . . . irregular, and I didn't think it in anybody's best interests to wait until Monday."

"This situation?" I clamped down hard on my teeth to keep them from chattering.

"Yes. You see, Mr. Vanderhorst, God rest his soul, was not only an old client of this firm—he was also a dear friend."

I looked back at him without speaking, not comprehending at all and trying hard not to look like a deer caught in the headlights.

Mr. Drayton cleared his throat and spoke again. "I understand that you went to see Mr. Vanderhorst two days ago to discuss listing Mr. Vanderhorst's house—is that correct?"

I nodded, feeling like a child sitting at her father's kitchen table and getting ready to be scolded.

"Did he give you any indication that he was willing to sell his house?"

"To be honest, I don't think the thought ever crossed his mind. I had no idea why he even brought me out there. I figured he was just lonely and wanted company." I looked down at my hands, remembering the china plate and how it had belonged to his mother. "He seemed to be a really nice man."

"Do you remember what you *did* talk about?"

I thought about the woman with the swing in the garden and how Mr. Vanderhorst had known she was there, too. I said, "He mentioned that his father and my grandfather were close friends and had attended Harvard Law School together. I believe he also mentioned that my grandfather had been the best man at his father's wedding."

Both men suddenly glanced at each other as if in understanding. I uncrossed my ankles and raised my hands to clutch the sides of the conference table. "What's this about? Did he decide to give me the listing anyway?"

Jonathan Drayton spoke this time. "Do you like old houses, Melanie?"

The second time in two days somebody has asked me that. I felt a bubble of laughter form at the back of my throat, but I clamped it down, afraid it would turn into a primal scream. "No. Actually, no. To be honest, I've always thought they were a huge waste of money and space."

Mr. Drayton leaned toward me. "But didn't your mother grow up in the Prioleau house on Legare Street?"

"Yes, but . . ."

"And didn't she sell it after your grandmother died and after your mother left your father?"

"Yes, but . . ."

"Didn't that cause resentment in you? That you had somehow missed out on your entitlement?"

"Entitlement? What . . . ?" I stood, my chair scraping the carpet, suddenly feeling as if I'd been transported into some kind of fun house of mirrors. "What is going on here? I have no idea why getting this listing has anything to do with my mother or her house."

Mr. Drayton plastered what I assumed was supposed to be a calming smile on his face. "I'm sorry, Ms. Middleton. Please sit down. I do apologize for what must seem like the third degree, but I'm still in shock at the sudden passing of my friend, and I do want to make sure everything is clear. After you hear the reason why we brought you in this morning, you'll understand why we wanted to make sure that there was no coercion on your part."

"Coercion?" I nearly laughed. "Despite my reputation in the business, I'm not in the habit of twisting the arms of potential clients, especially the elderly, if that's what you're thinking." I glowered at him as I lowered myself into my seat again and looked at the two men expectantly. "So, do I have the listing?"

There was some throat clearing and glances between the two men before Jonathan Drayton spoke. "Not exactly. It would appear that Mr. Vanderhorst has left his house and entire estate to you."

I leaned forward, sure that if I listened closely enough I could hear the theme from *The Twilight Zone* being piped into the suddenly claustrophobic office. "No."

"Actually, yes."

"This is a mistake. He wasn't in his right mind or something."

Mr. Drayton leaned toward me. "No, there's no mistake. I personally oversaw the writing of Mr. Vanderhorst's will shortly after you left him Thursday morning. He was perfectly sane." He glanced over at his son for a moment before concentrating again on me. "Well, except for the fact that he said that his mother would approve. And, to be honest, I fully expected to visit the following week to get him to change his mind. As I mentioned, all of this is highly irregular."

I rubbed my temple, which had begun to throb. "His relatives will contest the will."

"He doesn't have any."

"Find some."

The two Draytons stood in unison. Jonathan stepped forward. "Ms. Middleton, I know this is a bit of a shock—it was to us, too—but Mr. Vanderhorst was adamant that his property should go to you."

Mr. Drayton slid a sealed envelope across the table towards me. I saw my name scribbled across the top complete with my middle initial "P"—just like on the business card I'd given Mr. Vanderhorst.

"Ms. Middleton, Mr. Vanderhorst suspected you might need some sort of explanation, so he gave me this letter for you to be handed over in the event of his death. I just didn't expect for it to happen so soon."

I stared at the letter for a long time before sliding it toward me across the polished surface of the mahogany table and picking it up. I held it in my hands, feeling the heavy crisp linen stationery, but didn't open it.

Looking up at the two men, I said, "I don't want this. There's nothing in this letter that could possibly change my mind."

"Melanie—may I call you Melanie? You're just in a state of shock right now. Once you have a chance to examine the house more closely, you'll realize what a treasure you've inherited." Mr. Drayton gave me what probably passed for a warm smile to him.

"Mr. Drayton, I've seen the house. It's a dump. I'd just as soon send in a wrecking ball and end its misery."

Mr. Drayton looked alarmed. "Oh, no, Ms. Middleton. You can't do that. The entire historic district is protected."

"But it's barely habitable! I'd have to start panhandling in the hopes of not starving to death after I've paid to make the house safe enough to sell."

Mr. Drayton cleared his throat. "Actually, money shouldn't be an issue. Mr. Vanderhorst is, er, was a wealthy man. Not having any family, he had no use for it except to save it."

I felt a glimmer of hope. "So I can just abandon it until it falls down and move somewhere else to live in luxury?"

Mr. Drayton cleared his throat again, looking decidedly uncomfortable. "Um, not exactly. You see, Mr. Vanderhorst established a trust to ensure that money is spent on the restoration of the house. You will, of course, be able to draw an amount for living expenses as long as you live in the house. The exact amount will be left to the discretion of the trustee. The trust will remain in effect until your death."

I blinked hard, trying to stop my mind from spinning. "How about selling it as is? I'd have to list it way under market because of its condition, but there are lots of crazy people out there who would jump at the chance."

"Actually, you could," said Mr. Drayton. "Except a stipulation in the will states that before you're allowed to put it on the market, you have to have lived in the house for the period of one year. Ditto for all the furnishings inside the house."

I sighed and leaned back in my chair. "So, what you're basically saying is that I'm screwed." I stared down at the envelope in my hand and thought hard. "Could I just refuse it all and walk away?"

"I suppose that's your prerogative." Mr. Drayton leaned forward and tapped the envelope in my hand. "But read this before you make any decisions. I don't think Mr. Vanderhorst made his decision lightly. This house was the child he never had, and he's left it in your care."

I gripped the envelope tightly, remembering Mr. Vanderhorst standing in front of the growth chart marked on the drawing room wall. *MBG. My best guy.* Standing again, I grabbed my purse and headed for the door. "I need to be alone for a while. I'll let you know what I decide by Tuesday."

"You can take longer, Melanie."

"No. I don't want this hanging over my head any longer than it needs to. I'll let you know by Tuesday."

I didn't wait to hear their response. I'd already fled from the room and was running down the outside steps before I even realized where I was heading.

∞

When I rounded the corner onto Tradd Street, I heard the sound of the swing again. A brewing storm whipped dirt across the sidewalk and around my ankles, making me shiver despite the heat. I noticed the cracked blue-and-white tiles in the sidewalk in front of the gate, *55 Tradd.*

I looked up at the darkening sky as I pushed open the gate, making my way quickly to the piazza and to the peeling white wicker rocker I'd spotted on my first visit to the house. I'd never been a porch sitter, could even think of about ten derogatory terms I'd probably called porch sitters in the last year, but I suddenly felt compelled to sit there now and read my letter from the dead.

My dear Miss Middleton,

I know you must be reading this with some shock. I apologize for this, but do know that I don't doubt for one moment that I made the right decision. This house is meant for you.

I hope you are sitting someplace calm while you read this—perhaps a chair on the piazza. During the hour of our acquaintance, you didn't strike me as the patient sort. Your crossed leg was always twitching, and while it could be as a result of the sugar you consumed, I somehow didn't think that was it. As the old adage says: you should stop to smell the roses every once in a while. And your new house has some beautiful roses.

I am leaving you this house as a father would leave his child in the care of a guardian. One can't really own a house such as this; we are only asked to be caretakers for the next generation. I saw you looking in dismay at the restoration work needed. I have not had the energy or the good health these last years to see to it myself. But I do have the funds, as I'm sure Mr. Drayton has explained to you, to restore this house to the way I remember it growing up here as a child.

Before you reach any conclusions, you should know something of the history of this house. Yankee officers were quartered here after the fall of Charleston during the Civil War. You can still see their saber marks on the banister in the front hallway. The house was also used as a hospital during several of the yellow fever epidemics that swept through the city in the 1800s. The Vanderhorst women were too strong to succumb, and nursed strangers and dressed the dead for burial in the front foyer. They sent men off to war and kept food on the table long after money ran out. They camped out on the front porch during hurricanes and after the earthquake of 1886, armed with whatever they could find to protect what was theirs for their family. They were like the foundations of this house—too strong to be swayed by little matters such as war, pestilence, and ruin.

You are like them, you know, whether you realize it or not. I think this is why my mother approves of you being the new mistress of the house. You remind me of her a great deal. She was a beauty, too, but never relied on her looks and instead used her keen mind to get her way while never allowing her opponent to know that the fight was over before it started. There is an unease in you, too, which I sensed. You remind me of an anchor searching for a spot to latch on to. We all must have roots, Melanie, or we are like the weeds in the garden easily plucked and discarded. Unlike the rosebush, which clings to the soil and lasts for generations.

My mother loved this house almost as much as she loved me. There are others who disagree, of course, because she deserted us both when I was a young boy. But there's more to that story, though I have failed to discover what it is. Maybe fate put you in my life to bring the truth to the surface so that she might finally find peace after all these years.

I know this doesn't sit easily on your shoulders, and must feel like more of a burden now than a gift. But one must be patient, dear, for all good things will be revealed to she who waits.

God bless you, Melanie. All of my final hopes rest with you.

Nevin Vanderhorst

I looked up from the letter, aware again of the sound of the rope swing. I stood and slowly walked down the steps to where I could peer around the overgrown hibiscus and into the garden.

The woman was there again, pushing the swing, except this time the swing wasn't empty. Holding tightly to the rope arms sat a small boy, his mouth open in laughter, the sound like soft air brushing against my cheeks.

A hot, prickling sensation on the back of my neck made me tilt my head upward toward an upstairs window. I could detect a dark shadow behind the uneven glass, with penetrating eyes staring down at me. I could barely breathe, the malevolence of the presence in the window seeming to suck the oxygen out of the air.

Backing away, I turned toward the gate and let myself out. I kept my head down as the sky opened up and rain began to darken the side-walk in front of me.

CHAPTER 3

I stayed up all night downloading music into the iPod I'd received for Christmas and that was still in the box seven months later. The gift was from Sophie Wallen, latent hippie wannabe and professor of historic preservation at the College of Charleston and, inexplicably, my best friend. We'd met when a colleague suggested I consult with Sophie regarding the restoration project of a client's home I was trying to sell in the historic Harleston Village neighborhood. At the time, she wouldn't even speak with me until she'd been allowed to read my tarot cards and forced me to sit in the lotus yoga position on the floor of her office while she meditated and I kept stealing glances at my watch.

Afterward, she took me to Ruth's Bakery and bought me the biggest piece of chocolate torte in the bakery case while she told me that I was borderline obsessive-compulsive, way too repressed as a result of my military upbringing with my father, and apparently I wasn't getting enough sex because I was as uptight as a department store mannequin. But, she'd said, she thought we could work together. We've been close ever since.

Sophie said I needed to relax more and thought that listening to music would help, which is why she bought me a lime green iPod. I'm sure she'd suspect, but not ask, that once I'd taken the time to load music onto it I would spend most of a night playing with different ways to organize the 351 songs on the playlist.

With bleary eyes, I examined the list of songs again, sighing with dismay as I spied several that I had somehow included with the rest of the

ABBA, Tom Petty, Duran Duran, and the Cars: "Our House," "House of the Rising Sun," "It's My House," "Burning Down the House," and even "Up on the Housetop."

Closing down the computer and unplugging the iPod, I stuck it back in its box and threw it in a hall table drawer. I shuffled into the kitchen and squinted at the clock on the coffeemaker for a long time before I could figure out what it said. Six thirty. I'd wait until seven o'clock to call, allowing for Sophie's tendency to sleep late.

At six fifty-nine I hit the speed dial on my phone.

After eight rings, Sophie picked it up. "Mrmphm."

"Hi, Soph. It's Melanie. I need you to come look at a house with me."

"Mrmphm."

"Can you meet me in an hour?"

There was a short pause. "What in the hell are you doing calling me at seven o'clock on a Sunday morning?"

"Sorry. I thought you'd be up by now."

"No, you didn't. I'm going to hang up now and you can call me around noon."

"Wait! Okay, I'm sorry. But this is really important."

There was another pause and I pictured Sophie rolling her eyes. "All right. Tell me what this is about."

"It seems I've inherited a house."

"Okay," she said slowly. "And this warrants you calling me at the crack of dawn on a Sunday morning because . . . ?"

"Well, it's an old house. South of Broad."

I knew I had her attention now. I could hear the rustling of the bedsheets as she sat up.

"What's the address?"

"Fifty-five Tradd."

"The Vanderhorst house?" She was nearly screeching in my ear. "You've inherited the Vanderhorst house?"

"Well, yes. But I wouldn't get so excited about it. If you could see the condition of it inside—"

"I'll meet you at the front gate at eight o'clock."

I smiled as I heard the click on the other end and hung up the phone. Her excitement had me a bit worried, but I was also relieved.

I would be getting a professional and unbiased opinion on the merits of the house so I could make a sound choice in deciding whether to accept it.

∞

"No matter what this house looks like on the inside, even if the roof's caving in, you've got to keep it."

So much for a professional, unbiased opinion. Sophie stood next to me on the sidewalk with her hands on her hips, staring at my albatross. I'd been waiting in my car with the radio turned up until she'd appeared, eleven minutes late.

I eyed her now. She wore brown suede clogs, a long, gauzelike skirt with embroidered iguanas racing along the hem, and a tie-dyed T-shirt tucked into the elastic waist of the skirt. Her long, curly black hair was pulled into a straggly bun at the back of her head and held in place by what looked like two chopsticks—complete with the name of the Chinese restaurant they had come from.

"Your outfit alone is a strong case against tenure, you know."

She ignored me. "This house appears in just about every textbook on architecture that I've ever read. I mean, it's the quintessential classic Charleston single house. Look at that fan window—still has all the original glass. See how the front door is really on the side of the house? It's to catch the river breezes in the summer. And look at the gorgeous piazza—and with Tower-of-the-Wind pediments, no less. It's perfect."

Annoyed, I said, "I do know about old houses, Sophie. I sell them, remember?"

"You know enough bluster to sell them, but you don't actually know anything about them." She pushed on the gate to enter the garden, and it swung open without resistance. I looked at it in surprise and was about to test the hinges when Sophie said, "I thought you said the house was empty."

"It's supposed to be." I followed her gaze to the front window in the room with the growth chart on the wall and felt the skittering of gooseflesh on the back of my neck and caught the unmistakable scent of roses. "Why?"

"I thought I saw a curtain move."

"Probably just the wind blowing through one of the cracks in the walls."

She frowned at me, then turned back to the house. "I know about ten people who would give their left eyeballs to own this place."

"Great. Keep that list handy."

Ignoring me, she climbed the steps to the piazza and I followed her. She studied the leaded-glass window in the door and sidelights, her hands brushing against the window with reverence. "This is probably a Tiffany—not original to the house, of course, but still quite valuable. Do you know how rare it is to find one of his windows stilt intact in the house it was designed for? Truly amazing, especially considering how long it's been here."

I looked at the windows again, trying to see them with her eyes. But where she saw a work of art and painstaking skill, I saw only an old window that would probably cost a small fortune to repair if it ever got broken. I wanted, for a brief moment, to see the beauty of it, but I hadn't been able to see the beauty in anything since I was seven years old.

Sophie ran her hands along one of the support columns, flicking away a flake of loose plaster and peering at what lay beneath. "Yep—brick. It's brick underneath, which is a very good thing. For one thing, it's stronger than just plaster, and for another, termites don't like brick." She nicked her clog against the top step and shook her head. "Which is more than I can say for this porch. It's got to be replaced, and the columns that support the piazza need replastering. That's a really big job."

She wrinkled her nose in a look I was familiar with and I answered her unasked question. "Supposedly, Mr. Vanderhorst had plenty of money—apparently all left for me so I can fix up this . . . this . . ."

"Beautiful house."

"Well, that wasn't exactly what I was going to say, but I suppose that works."

Sophie stepped back onto the first step and looked up at the front facade. "Wow. So you've inherited this great house and now you're rich, too. Not bad for a single day's work."

"Not exactly. All the money will be tied up in a trust. The trustee will have the discretion to give me money for various home-improvement projects and, if he or she is feeling generous, provide me with a salary as well."

Sophie smiled the smile that somehow usually melted men at her feet but right now only served to annoy me. "Mr. Vanderhorst was a really clever man."

"Not too clever if he made me his heir. I don't want anything to do with this. You know how I feel about old houses. You know how I feel about owning any house at all."

"Yeah. And I also know why, which is why I think this could be good for you."

I looked away, my gaze unfortunately falling on the peeling paint on the shutters and then on the white wicker rocker I had sat in when I read Mr. Vanderhorst's letter. Something had happened to me, then. Something that now made me listen to Sophie and my conscience rather than rejecting this whole horrible proposal out of hand. Something to do with what lay inside the heart of a seven-year-old girl before the realities of life closed in around her.

Turning back to my friend, I reached into my purse and pulled out the letter. "Well, since I've probably lost all chances of an unbiased opinion, you might as well go ahead and read this before we go in."

I sat down in the chair and waited for her to read it, keeping my focus straight ahead toward the street and ignoring the sound of the swing once again emanating from the yard.

"Hey—did you read this part?" Sophie moved to sit down in the chair beside me. "Listen to this: 'My mother loved this house almost as much as she loved me. There are others who disagree, of course, because she deserted both of us when I was a young boy. But there's more to that story, though I have failed to discover what it is. Maybe fate put you in my life to bring the truth to the surface so that she might finally find peace after all these years.' "

"Yes, I read it. I'm not really sure what it means, though, except that he was abandoned by his mother."

Sophie wrinkled her nose again. "Just like you were."

I looked away, still unable to completely forget the overwhelming hurt in a seven-year-old's heart.

Sophie looked back down at the letter. "Actually, I seem to remember something about the history of this house. Like I said, I've seen this house in so many books, and there's some story. . . ." She tapped an unmanicured finger on the paper, her forehead wrinkled in concentration.

I watched her, the sound of the swing louder now.

"Do you hear that?" I asked.

"Hear what?"

"The sound of that rope swing against a tree branch?"

She shook her head. "No. I don't." She studied me closely, but I looked away again, my gaze falling on the missing bricks on the front steps.

Sophie was silent again and I began humming "Dancing Queen," one of the songs I had uploaded onto my iPod the night before, to help block out the sound of the swing.

"ABBA, Melanie?"

I ignored her and walked to the opposite end of the piazza, my heels clicking against the cracked marble tiles.

"Yes! Now I remember!" Sophie jumped out of her chair and came to stand next to me. "It's something that happened in the late twenties or thirties, I believe. Something to do with a love triangle and a woman running off with a man who wasn't her husband—but that's all I remember."

"Great. Since you love this stuff so much, I'll let you research the history of the house and let me know."

"Sorry. No can do. This is the beginning of the semester for me and I'm swamped. I'll be happy to lend you some books, though."

"Yippee. Can't wait." I moved to the front door, a sudden realization hitting me. "I don't have a key."

The front door opened suddenly, and a woman as wide as she was tall, holding the small black-and-white dog I had seen before on my previous visit, stood in the doorway. "Why are y'all standing out there in this heat? Y'all come on in where it's cooler."

Like obedient soldiers, we marched into the foyer. I stuck out my hand. "I'm Melanie . . ."

"I know who you are. You're the spitting image of your grandfather when he was your age."

"You knew my grandfather?"

She looked at me with what only could be described as a scowl. "Of course not. How old do you think I am? Before Mr. Nevin passed, he showed me a picture of his daddy and your granddaddy. I think he told me it was taken on his daddy's wedding day."

"Oh, I'd love to see it. May I?"

"Sure, honey. Though I don't think you need to be asking me since you own it now." She laughed with a surprisingly high, trilling sound made all the more unusual by the fact that it came from such a large body.

Sophie gave the woman one of her smiles. "I'm Dr. Wallen from the College of Charleston. And you would be . . . ?"

"Oh, dear me. Where are my manners? I'm Mrs. Houlihan, the housekeeper. And this"—she raised the front paw of the black-and-white dog in a small wave—"is General Lee."

"The housekeeper?" I noticed again the thick layer of dust and impressive collections of cobwebs in the chandeliers. At the same time I noted the gleaming wood floors and the absence of cobwebs in any of the ceiling corners.

As if reading my mind, Mrs. Houlihan said, "Now don't be jumping to conclusions. According to Mr. Nevin's wishes, I kept the kitchen and bathrooms sparkling clean, as well as his bedroom and anything else I could clean where I wouldn't have to touch or move anything. He was worried about damaging some of his antiques, you see. Everything was falling apart, and it wouldn't take much to ruin something. So it was best to just let things be."

I glanced over at Sophie, but she had already marched into the front drawing room.

"These are the original cypress floors and wall paneling. And look at these cornices! And the carvings in the mantel—totally period Adam. There's some water damage, but it's mostly intact." Her footsteps sounded quickly across the floor, and I followed the sound, Mrs. Houlihan and General Lee close behind me. Sophie was standing by the writing desk that had been pulled out from the wall, her hand touching the burled wood of the drawered cabinet like I would handle a seller's agreement. "This is English Hepplewhite, isn't it?" She stood on her toes and peered at the top of the pediment. "A piece like this is worth thirty thousand easy."

I eyed the piece of furniture with interest. Even I knew what an

English Hepplewhite was. And I couldn't help but think of the money I could make selling it.

The little dog whimpered in Mrs. Houlihan's arms. "He needs his walk, poor dear. He's just been grieving something terrible for his master. Barely picked at his food bowl this morning. And he hasn't been out for a walk since Mr. Nevin passed. I'll let him out into the backyard a few times a day but I can't walk him. I just can't take the heat."

She held the dog out to me, and I stared at it in horror. I'd never willingly touched a dog in my life. "What do you want me to do with it?"

"Take him for a walk. He's yours now."

Sophie had crossed the foyer and was staring into the music room. "More water damage in here. You might need a new roof, Mel."

Mrs. Houlihan thrust the animal into my arms and the little beast barked again before licking my nose. "No, no, no. Nobody said anything about inheriting a dog, too."

The housekeeper tucked her chin into her neck, effectively hiding it from view in the folds of flesh. "Well, there ain't nobody else who can take him. My husband is allergic or I would. He's a really sweet thing. You two will get along just fine."

I stared at her with incomprehension while she pulled a leash out of her housecoat pocket and clipped it onto the dog's collar. Not quite knowing what direction to move in, I watched as Sophie crossed the foyer under the keystone arch and climbed the main staircase, her hands brushing the curved mahogany banister. "This is an incredible house—such a perfect example of classic Charleston architecture. I just can't believe this." I followed her as she turned the corner of the stairs and continued upward to the upstairs hallway. I watched as she put her hand on the first doorknob she saw.

Mrs. Houlihan, who had been following behind me, let out a gasp. "No, don't open that. . . ."

But Sophie had already pulled open the door, allowing the sound of a flock of rustling feathers to filter down to where I stood. Instead of closing the door and moving away from it like most normal people would have done, Sophie moved forward to the small set of wooden stairs behind the door and began climbing.

I turned to the housekeeper. "Where is she going?"

Mrs. Houlihan had already started the laborious struggle of moving her girth up the stairs. "That's the attic, and we have a wee hole there where pigeons like to come in and roost. If the door's left open, we're bound to get—"

Before she could finish, a plump gray-and-white pigeon flew out of the open door and past us down the stairs, and began flying erratically around the foyer. I took the steps two at a time but reached the attic door at the same time Sophie ran out, slamming it behind her.

"You won't believe the stuff in there! Luckily most of it is under tarps, because there's a heck of a lot of pigeon poop over everything, but there's all sorts of interesting things. There's actually what looks like a full-sized stuffed buffalo, but also what appears to be more Hepplewhite and Sheraton pieces."

The pigeon swooped over our heads, and we ducked while General Lee barked frantically. Sophie held out what looked like a walking stick. "Look what I found."

I looked down at the smoothly carved cane, noticing the writing on the side. "What does it say?"

Mrs. Houlihan surprised us by clearing her throat. "It says: 'In the morning I walk on four legs, in the evening two legs and at night three. What am I?'" She looked at us expectantly, and when neither Sophie nor I responded, she said. "The answer is 'man.' Clever, isn't it? The Vanderhorsts have always been known for their fondness of riddles." She smiled warmly at the cane. "Mr. Vanderhorst's grandfather gave that to him on the occasion of his graduation from law school. He sure did like it. He used to keep it in one of the guest bedrooms until the ceiling there sprung a leak, so he moved it to the attic. Not that the attic was much better, of course."

Sophie looked at me with what appeared to be awe in her eyes. "Wow. You own that. You own all of this. You are like the luckiest girl in the world."

"Right. I now own a dog and apparently a buffalo and a house with Swiss cheese for a roof, and this translates to me being the luckiest girl in the world how . . . ?"

I felt the oddest compulsion to cry, so I turned my back and began walking down the stairs, a frantically yelping General Lee in my arms and an attack pigeon close on my heels. *Could this get any worse?*

Sophie called out to me. "Who's the trustee, by the way? You didn't mention it."

I stopped, and looked back in confusion. "I didn't ask. I don't know why, but I guess I was still in shock."

Mrs. Houlihan, panting from the exertion of climbing the stairs, said, "I almost forgot. My first phone message for you, and I almost forgot to tell you. My apologies, as this will never happen again, of course. But, well, a gentleman called about an hour ago. He said he was looking for you, seeing as how he was just informed that he was the trustee to the estate and he needed to speak with you. He'd tried calling your home number first but nobody answered."

"Did he give his name?"

She pulled a folded piece of paper out of her pocket. "Yes. A Colonel James Middleton. He didn't leave a number, although I did ask. He said you would know it."

My eyes met Sophie's widened ones. Yes, things really could get worse. Much worse.

Mrs. Houlihan tilted her head. "Middleton. Are you related to the colonel?"

I forced my throat to work. "Yes. He's my father. It would appear that Mr. Vanderhorst had a sense of humor."

"Oh, that he did. But he also had a strong belief in family. That's probably why he made your father trustee. He was always saying how blood was thicker than water."

She was saying more but I couldn't listen. I needed to get away from the house—and the swooping pigeon—as soon as possible. I put the dog down at the base of the stairs and let it pull me where it wanted to go until I found myself out on the sidewalk next to the gate looking into the garden.

The woman was there again, pushing the boy on the swing. They both looked over at me, and the boy lifted his hand to wave. I was relieved to note that the other, more sinister presence I had detected the previous day was absent, and hoped that he had only been a figment of my overactive imagination. General Lee barked an excited greeting as if he recognized somebody, and I looked down at him in surprise. "You see them, too?"

I turned my gaze back to the scene, but the woman, the boy, and the swing were gone now, and the crickets had resumed their chorus. I stared at the overgrown garden for a long minute, somehow seeing bright-colored flowers and vibrant greens where I knew only brown dirt and straggly weeds now grew. It was as if I were seeing what the house had once been. And what it could be again.

Tugging on the dog's leash, I headed down the street, afraid to look back. I didn't want to see the house in all its columned glory, its alabaster paint shining in the Charleston sun, the shadows of the columns like arms reaching out to grab hold of me and hang on.

I started to jog, heedless of my heels or the heat, racing General Lee around the corner until I could no longer see the house on Tradd Street.

CHAPTER 4

I arrived at my office at seven o'clock on Monday morning, hoping I'd find the office empty, since I still needed more time to think. I had come no closer to a decision than I had the day I'd sat in the office of Drayton, Drayton and Drayton, and my little world had started spinning in the wrong direction. I was still stumbling, looking for sure footing and feeling instead as if I were walking up the down escalator.

Sophie was proving to be no help at all. She hadn't said anything as I'd said goodbye to her on Tradd Street except for one last parting shot as she'd jumped into her Volkswagen Beetle. "'God bless you, Melanie. All of my final hopes rest with you,'" she'd quoted from Nevin Vanderhorst's letter before slamming her door and speeding away, the bright yellow flowers in the dashboard vase swaying with indignation.

I put down my bag of doughnuts and my latte from Ruth's Bakery, sat down at my desk, and turned on my computer. I had just started opening the bag when Nancy Flaherty walked in, holding a golf putter in one hand and a small stack of pink message slips in the other.

I looked up in surprise. "Why are you here so early?"

"Well, Mr. Henderson let me leave early Saturday because I had a golf tournament at the club, so I told him I'd make up the time by coming in early this morning." She smiled. "Don't worry—I'll leave you alone. I just wanted to give you these messages. Three of them are from Jack Trenholm." She smiled even broader now.

"Who?"

"Jack Trenholm—the writer. He writes those cold-case true history's mysteries books. They're always on the bestseller lists. And he's an absolute hottie, if he's anything like the picture on the back of his books."

I had no idea whom she was talking about. The only reading I ever had time for was my daily *Post and Courier* and new real estate listings. A little niggling memory intruded into my thoughts. I leaned forward. "When I was little, my mother's best friend was a Mrs. Trenholm, but I imagine that's a common enough name. And I don't remember her having a son. Even so, why would he be calling me?"

"Well, he's probably a few years younger than you, so maybe he was under your radar when you were little. Or he's not connected to your mother's friend at all." Nancy leaned her putter against my desk and began flipping through the messages. "Let's see. He called three times yesterday—on Sunday. Seems like he's *very* interested in speaking with you. I wasn't here. Otherwise I would have grilled the man and would have known not only why he was calling but what kind of underwear he preferred, too."

I reached out for the messages. "Thanks, Nancy. I'll call him this morning."

"Maybe he saw your picture in one of your ads and wants to ask you for a date."

"Right. And maybe golf will one day replace baseball as the national pastime."

She shook her head. "Oh, ye of little faith. You're only thirty-nine, and you've got a knockout figure"—she eyed the bag of doughnuts on my desk—"although God only knows how. If you would just maybe make yourself a little more approachable, you'd have the guys falling all over you."

I began riffling through the remaining pink slips. "I'll keep that in mind, Nancy. Now, please don't let me interrupt your work." I smiled blandly at her.

She ignored the hint. "You're great handling men on a business level, but you're a hopeless case when it comes to dealing with them socially. It's probably the way you were raised, but for some reason you seem to revert to an awkward teenage girl whenever you're around eligible men."

Annoyed now, I glared at her. "Really? And when did you have time to go to psychology school in between golf games?"

As if I hadn't said anything, she continued. "I think you just need to put yourself out there, get a little practice. You might find that you'll actually enjoy a little social life outside of work."

I picked up the phone and started dialing a number, hoping she'd get the hint. I raised my eyebrow at her when she didn't move.

Leaning over my desk and pointing to the pile of messages, she said, "There's also a message in there from that couple from North Charleston. I took that one Saturday afternoon. Seems as if they've reevaluated their finances and are ready to look at those homes on Daniel Island that you discussed with them."

"I can read my own messages, but thank you. I'll make sure I call them back."

"No problem," she said, walking away from my desk and twirling her putter. "Just don't forget to call Jack Trenholm."

I didn't dignify her comment with a response and hung up the phone before turning to my computerized calendar to check out what appointments I had that day. I had three home previews to make in the morning, but my afternoon was blocked to show several houses to a single professor, Chad Arasi, moving from San Francisco to teach art history at the College of Charleston. From our lengthy phone conversations, in which he'd finished just about every sentence with the word "cool," I'd decided to narrow our search to the new trendy condos and refurbished warehouses on East Bay Street. My evening hours, as usual, were completely blank. Maybe I'd have time to rearrange my sock drawer.

I was just picking up the phone to call Chad to confirm our first appointment when Nancy appeared at my desk again and slapped down a thick hardback book. "I Googled him and found out he's single and lives in the French Quarter."

"Who . . . ?" I started to ask but she'd already left. I hung up my phone and picked up the book and read the title: *Remember the Alamo: What Really Happened to Davey Crockett.* Under the title in even bigger print was the name Jack Trenholm. I was pretty sure that I didn't know him, but his last name was certainly familiar. *Trenholm. Trenholm.* I said the name a couple of times just to see what it would recall, but my mind remained blank. I flipped over the book to read the back-cover copy and came eye to eye with a full, glossy black-and-white of the author.

As a single, career-oriented woman approaching forty, I wish I could say that I'm impervious to a pretty face, and try to stick with my straightforward business attitude. But Mr. Trenholm, well, let's just say that I was suddenly in sixth grade again, swooning because they'd assigned Ned Campbell a locker next to mine.

He had one of those gorgeous all-American faces that said, *I can throw a football, bake a cake, bring you roses, and make the bed shake,* and it was just starting to dawn on me that I actually had his phone number and that he had called me first.

I held the book in my hand and stared at the picture for a full minute, remembering what Nancy had said about making myself approachable and thinking about my social life, or lack thereof. Putting the book down, I scattered the pink message slips across my desk until I found his and yanked up the phone before I could talk myself out of it. Before I could dial, Nancy buzzed me on my intercom. "I told you so."

Without answering her, I hung up, pulled out my cell phone, and walked to Mr. Henderson's office, where I could close the door and speak in private.

I took a deep breath and pretended to myself that I was making a business call. Quickly, I dialed the number on the message slip and waited until it had rung nine times before the answering machine picked up. Assuming that a writer must also be an early riser and therefore thinking he might have been in the shower when I called, I hung up without leaving a message and let it ring nine times again, figuring he had plenty of time to get out of the shower by now. This time my efforts were rewarded with a voice on the other end.

"Who the hell is this? And do you have any idea what time it is?"

I froze in horror. My mouth, for the first time in my life, was unable to come up with a single lowering or sarcastic comment. At that point, I should have done what any other self-respecting woman would do and hang up. But Nancy Flaherty was right: I had suddenly reverted to a tongue-tied twelve-year-old girl calling a boy for the first time. For reasons unknown even to me, I chose to disguise my voice so that it sounded something between a Mexican maid and a Russian diplomat. "I'm zorry. Wrong numberrr."

"Wait a minute. Henderson Realty. I know that name. . . ."

Shit. Caller ID. "One moment, pleaze, sir, while I connect you to Meez Middleton."

I held my hand over the receiver for a few moments before putting it next to my face again and pressing a number button to create a beep. "Hello, this is Melanie Middleton. May I speak with Jack Trenholm, please?"

"Speaking." I heard the distinct sound of a toilet being flushed followed by running water.

"I'm with Henderson Realty, and I'm returning your phone call."

The water stopped. "Yes, thanks for getting back to me." He had something in his mouth that was preventing him from speaking clearly.

"I hope I didn't call you too early. You left three messages yesterday, and I thought it might be urgent."

He didn't answer right away as I heard the sound of teeth brushing and then the sound of expectorating and running water again. "Not to worry. I had to get up to answer the phone, anyway."

I felt my face flush. Irritated, I said, "Look, rather than taking the phone into the shower with you, why don't you just call me back when you have a moment?"

My finger was already on the hang-up button when he spoke. "Because then you'll miss the pleasure of picturing me naked."

I was completely mortified because that was exactly what I was doing. "Excuse me? Of all the arrogant—"

"Look, I'm sorry. I'm just grouchy. I had a late night and didn't expect to be up so early this morning. Can we start this conversation over again?"

I took a deep breath, remembering what Nancy had said. I was going to make an effort, even if it killed me. "All right. This is Melanie Middleton and I'm returning your call."

"Thanks for calling me back, Mellie. I would like to schedule a meeting with you to talk about real estate in the area."

In my surprise, I forgot to mention that nobody called me Mellie. "Are you looking to move?"

"I might be. Let's just say I'm investigating the possibilities right now."

"Okay." I found myself sitting on my boss's desk and doodling hearts on his blotter. I quickly stood up. "Tell me what you're looking for."

"Oh, there's too much to talk about over the phone. Why don't we meet—how about dinner tonight?"

You are a professional, Melanie, I reminded myself as I forced my voice to remain calm. "Tonight? Hang on. Let me check my calendar." I pressed the mute button on my phone and stared at the second hand on my watch, waiting an entire fifty-nine seconds until I took him off mute. "Sorry for the wait. I just needed to juggle a few things to clear my schedule. What time works best for you?"

"How about seven o'clock? I'll pick you up if you'll give me your address." He must have sensed my hesitation because he added, "Not to worry—I'm not a psychopath. My parents own Trenholm's Antiques on King if you want to speak with my mother. She'll give me a good reference."

I knew the store well, although I could only afford to window-shop its gorgeous English and French antiques. Besides, he was a famous author. He'd have a lot more to worry about me stalking him than the other way around.

I gave him my address and was about to hang up when he spoke again.

"Oh, and, Mellie?"

"Yes?"

"Work on your accent. That was terrible."

Without another word, I hung up, then stood in the empty office until I was sure the color of my face had returned to normal.

&

I stood in front of my closet mirror, admiring the little black dress that had set me back nearly an entire commission check. But when I turned around and watched the slinky silk fold around my body, I knew that it had been a fair exchange.

The day had been a fairly good one. My art history professor, Chad, had been the ideal client and loved everything I'd showed him and was deciding between two converted warehouse spaces near Rainbow Row at this very moment. When I'd first met him that morning, he'd been wearing sandals, cutoff jean shorts, a Bermuda shirt, and a ponytail. He'd kissed me on both cheeks in greeting, and when he apologized for being a few minutes late because his yoga class had run over, I knew right then that I had to introduce him to Sophie. Finding her soul mate was the least I could do to thank her for taking General Lee until I could figure out what to do with him. I was already in the throes of planning their wedding reception when my doorbell rang.

Clasping my grandmother Middleton's pearls around my neck, I walked to the door, admiring the way my dress swished around my legs. Giving my upswept and elegant hairdo one last pat, I opened the door.

My first impression was that the photo on his book's dust jacket didn't do him justice. He was very tall, about four inches taller than my own five foot eight, and his very bright blue eyes were looking at me with what I assumed was the same wide-eyed expression I was using on him.

He wore a starched white button-down shirt with its sleeves rolled up to his elbows, khaki shorts, and loafers without socks. I also noticed that he was younger than me, followed in quick succession by the thought that he was dressed for a dinner at Cracker Barrel, and I was dressed for a dinner at Anson's.

Before he could say anything, I said, "Wait a minute. I forgot my purse," and slammed the door in his face. *What now?* Feeling slightly deflated by the fact that I had obviously envisioned a much more elegant evening than he had, my first instinct was to open the door and berate him for misleading me. Instead, remembering my mission, I stood in front of the closed door and quickly raked my fingers through my hair, loosening all bobby pins and letting them fly through the air. When I was sure they were all gone, I flipped my head upside down to fluff my hair into a more casual style, grabbed my purse, which was sitting on the hall table, and opened the door. If this is what it took to make myself more approachable, then maybe I could do it.

I smiled calmly and stuck out my hand. "Sorry about that. I'm Melanie Middleton."

His smile mimicked the one on his dust jacket, and I wondered if he'd practiced it to get it so perfect. If I wasn't such a strong-minded individual, I might even have fallen for it.

His handshake was strong and firm and lasted a little too long. "It's nice to meet you, Mellie. Great dress, by the way."

"Oh, thanks," I said, my lowered opinion of him climbing up a few notches. I smiled brightly as he allowed me to lead us out of the building and to the street, where his car was parked. "And by the way, nobody calls me Mellie."

He stopped in front of a shiny black Porsche and opened the passenger door. "But you look like a Mellie."

I slid onto the leather seat and looked up at him in confusion. "But you called me Mellie before you'd seen me—when we spoke on the phone." I wasn't fishing for a compliment—not really—but I wanted to know if he'd called me because he'd seen my picture in one of my ads. Not that the vanity card was in my deck of vices, but it had been an embarrassingly long time since a guy had called me with anything romantic in mind, and I needed a little ego stroking.

He shrugged as he closed the door, then walked over to his side and slid in behind the wheel. "What can I say? I'm a thorough researcher—it's my job. I wanted to find out more about you. All I had to do was go to the library and search in their archives. Since you're from such a well-known family, I knew you had to be all over the papers. My favorite was the second-place award in the baton-twirling competition in second grade. There was a picture with you and your mom, and I know she referred to you as 'Mellie' in the article."

I looked away. "I prefer Melanie," I said faintly.

The engine hummed softly when he turned the key and headed out into the early-evening traffic and across the Cooper River Bridge. We sped down East Bay and then onto a series of small, side streets. As we paused at a stop sign, I looked at a dilapidated single-story frame house, the porch roof sagging like a drooping eyelid. Sitting in a porch chair was an old man in army fatigues looking at me. I registered immediately that he didn't have any legs and that blood from a bullet wound still clung to his forehead. Shaken, I looked away.

"You look beautiful, by the way. Although I'm not sure why you changed your hair." He again smiled that smile that I was sure was intended to make women melt, not that I had any intention of being affected by it.

"Um, thank you." I smoothed my hand over my hair. "I decided last minute that it looked better down."

He nodded, steering the small car down a street filled with abandoned businesses and pawnbrokers. "We're going to Blackbeard's—have you been there?"

Surely not. "No, actually, although the name is familiar—but I'm sure it's not the same place I'm thinking of. Is it new?"

"Not exactly. I think it's been here since before Prohibition. It's not exactly on the tourist path—which is what I like. Best boiled shrimp I've ever had, though."

"Great," I said, not really picturing the messy eating of shrimp the ideal thing to do on a first date. There's nothing as flattering as little shrimp legs stuck between your teeth when you smiled.

Jack pulled into a parking spot in front of an establishment I could only describe as a "dive," and stopped the engine. Unfortunately, I knew the place well although I'd never had to actually step inside. A man and a woman were wrapped in a tight embrace with lips locked; they appeared to be having fully dressed sex against the wall of the building. Loud music and drunken laughter floated over to me, and I looked around, wondering if there was another place nearby I could suggest instead of Blackbeard's. When I turned to Jack to ask, I was surprised to find him leaning toward me with his arm outstretched.

Without a word, he systematically plucked two bobby pins out of my hair and held them out in front of me. "You forgot these."

"Thanks," I said, grasping the pins, my attention shifting again to the bar we'd parked in front of. The name on the sign over the door read *Blackbeard's Bar and Grill.* My images of broiled salmon and turtle soup fled, quickly supplanted by the image of a plastic bib big enough to cover my designer dress so I wouldn't get shrimp peelings all over it.

I looked down the street, not seeing the familiar 1986 navy blue LeSabre I had been praying I wouldn't see. "We're eating here?" I couldn't quite hide the peevishness in my voice.

"Trust me—you'll love the food. And the ambience isn't too bad, either."

"Compared to what?" I asked under my breath as I allowed him to lead me inside.

The interior of the establishment was a definite improvement over the exterior. I don't know if I was expecting dirt and rushes to be covering the floor, but I was surprised to see highly polished wood instead. Several people turned around to shout greetings at Jack, and he returned each one by name. I scanned the crowd, sighing with relief when I didn't recognize anybody.

We were escorted by a fawning girl whose mincing footsteps seemed to be hampered by her voluminous breasts, both of which appeared to be of enormous interest to my date.

She brought us to a clean table in a back corner, where the Southern rock being played by the live band wasn't too loud to talk over. The girl placed two plastic menus on the linoleum table, then kissed Jack on the lips before walking away with our drink orders, her hips swaying in the age-old human mating ritual.

Jack took his eyes off the departing waitress long enough to pull my chair out for me, and I sat, trying to unobtrusively wipe off my seat before sitting down. He pulled his own chair up to the table. "Isn't this great?"

"Oh, definitely," I said as I looked around, wishing I'd brought my antibacterial wipes. The walls were covered with neon beer signs and an assortment of dried alligator heads, one of which seemed to be peering at me with interest. A crowd of men at the bar gave a loud cheer and raised beer bottles in an apparent toast to one of their group who was seated and hidden from view.

I made a point to smile as we made small talk, and I perused the menu, looking for something safe to eat. When the waitress returned to take our order, I selected a blackened chicken sandwich with a side of rice.

Jack looked surprised. "Don't you like shrimp?"

"Yes, I do, but . . ."

He waved his hand at me. "You've got to get them, then." He looked up at the waitress. "A bucket for two, please, with red potatoes and corn bread—extra butter."

I looked at him with irritation but kept my thoughts to myself for now, remembering what Nancy had said about making myself more approachable—although when I saw her again, I'd have to ask her to what depths I should be prepared to sink to before I could claim success.

I sipped on my sweet tea while he drank a Coke, and I was trying to remember if I'd brought my dental floss when he spoke.

"So, how did you know Nevin Vanderhorst?"

"Excuse me?"

"He left his house to you, didn't he? I was just wondering how you knew him."

Charleston might like to think of itself as a big city, but it was really nothing more than a big small town where everybody liked to gossip over the back fence with the rate of exchange faster than e-mail.

"I didn't. I went to visit him to talk about allowing me to list his house when he retired to an assisted-living facility, and the next thing I knew, he'd died and left his house to me."

He nodded slowly, his eyes narrowed. "Well, that's a first for me. I've researched stories where people left their earthly possessions to their cat or dog and even a guinea pig, but never to a complete stranger." He grinned that grin again. "So, when do you move in?"

The already fragile image of my dream date shattered completely, and I leaned back in my chair, trying not to think about my wasted expensive dress or all the blank spaces on my calendar. "You didn't really ask me out to talk about real estate, did you?"

He at least managed to look sheepish. "Well, sort of. Your new house on Tradd is real estate, isn't it?"

"It's not *my* house—I haven't agreed to anything yet." I studied his face and the way his shoulders filled out his shirt so nicely, and already regretted what I was going to say. But the humiliation of my own foolish wishes fueled my hurt pride.

I slid my chair back. "Look, I don't think this is going to work. Call Mr. Vanderhorst's lawyer if you want to know anything about the house. I'll call a taxi."

He grabbed my hand and held on before I could stand. "I'm sorry. I should have been straight with you. But you have something of a tough-girl reputation, you know, and I figured the only way I'd get you to talk with me would be to approach you in a more social setting." He smiled broadly. "Seriously, I really am sorry. And you know, after seeing your picture in your newspaper ads, I didn't think it would be much of a hardship."

My wounded ego refused to take the bait. "I'm not a biscuit, so don't try to butter me up. Good night."

I tried to pull away but he held tight. "Please. We're already here. Let's go ahead and eat and chat a bit. I might even be able to get all the information I need so that you'll never have to see my face again."

The waitress returned with our bucket of shrimp and red potatoes and two plastic bibs. My mouth started to water. "I don't know. . . ."

He must have sensed my hesitation because he tilted the bucket so

I could see the succulent boiled shrimp and smell the Lowcountry spices. I caught his gaze. Surely one evening in his company wouldn't be the worst way to pass the time.

I settled back into my seat. "Well, since you've gone through all this trouble already, I guess we could chat. I have to say, though, that I know next to nothing about the house, except that it's falling apart and I want nothing to do with it. I'm supposed to make a decision by tomorrow as to whether I'll take it. I can't say I'm anywhere near making a decision."

He leaned forward on his elbows. "Fair enough. But let me tell you this much. I've been working with an idea for my next book. In nineteen thirty, there was a lot of intrigue surrounding your house, you know. A devoted wife and mother supposedly ran off with another man, leaving behind her eight-year-old son, and then there're the rumors about her husband's bootlegging business and speculation as to what really happened to his wife. I was hoping that maybe Mr. Vanderhorst told you something about it that might jump start my research." He smiled that smile again and I would be lying if I said I was immune. "I promise I won't make it painful. You might even find that you're having a good time while I'm squeezing you for information."

I eyed a Mississippi mud pie being brought to the table next to us. "All right. But you only have"—I checked my watch—"two hours and nineteen minutes. I'm in bed by nine thirty every night."

"Deal. We'll talk while we eat. Give me your plate." He filled my plate while I fastened the bib around my neck. "Have you ever heard of Joseph Longo?"

"Vaguely. Should I know him?" I eyed the plate of bright-eyed bottom crawlers, smelling the spicy seasonings, and began to peel the shells off the meat. I didn't care what I looked like while doing it since I was no longer officially on a date and, therefore, had no more need to be approachable.

"If you knew anything about the history of your house, you would. He was behind most of the organized crime that took place in the city during Prohibition—prostitution, liquor, gambling—whatever. He was also infatuated with the renowned beauty Louisa Gibbes of Charleston."

"Okay. So what does this have to do with my house?"

He looked at me with amusement. "'My' house, huh?"

I slathered butter on a slab of corn bread. "You know what I meant."

He just nodded and picked up a large shrimp. "Well, Miss Louisa Gibbes was engaged to Robert Vanderhorst, father of the late Nevin Vanderhorst."

I waited for him to drain his beer bottle before continuing.

"According to my research, Joseph didn't stop pursuing the fair Miss Louisa even after she was married although everybody believed her to be very much in love with her husband. Seems like the man couldn't take no for an answer."

"Typical male behavior."

Jack raised an eyebrow but didn't comment. "Anyway, Louisa had a son and seemed very content with her life. At least until her son was around eight years old. Not long after the stock market crash of 'twenty-nine, she disappeared, abandoning her only child. And so did Joseph Longo. Rumors speculated that they had run off together."

Right after the stock market crash, she disappeared, abandoning her only child. Suddenly, I had no appetite. "Did they ever find her?"

Jack cracked open a shrimp shell and held it up to his mouth. "Nope. No trace of her or Mr. Longo. They've been missing for over seventy years and nobody's ever seen or heard from them."

I took a long drink from my sweet tea, trying to swallow the powdery taste of loss and abandonment that always seemed to linger in the back of my throat. I placed my hands flat on the linoleum to still them. "I don't think her son ever believed that she deserted him."

"What makes you say that?"

"Mr. Vanderhorst left me a letter. In it he said that his mother had loved the house as much as she loved him, but that most people didn't believe that since she had abandoned both of them." I closed my eyes for a moment, seeing the bold handwriting on the letter that I'd read so many times now that the paper had become soft. "He said that there was more to that story, and that maybe fate had brought me to him to bring out the truth. So that his mother might finally find peace."

Jack leaned back in his chair, his food forgotten. "Sounds like a ghost story to me. Have you seen or heard anything?"

I looked up at him, startled. "No, of course not. Why would you ask?"

He crossed his arms over his chest and didn't look away. "Well, your mother was pretty famous around here for her . . . I guess you'd call it her sixth sense. She was really popular at parties, from what I've read. I thought maybe that if there's any truth in her abilities, you might have inherited some of them. And that you could save me a lot of research and investigation if you could just ask the source, if you know what I mean."

The tips of my fingers were turning white as I pressed them hard against the table. "I don't think that kind of thing is genetic—assuming you believe in that sort of thing." The waitress came and I told her to take my half-finished plate.

"Did Mr. Vanderhorst say anything else? Anything about any particular valuables or jewelry that might be in the house?"

Surprised, I said, "No, not at all. He bequeathed everything to me, but nobody's mentioned any specific item." I eyed him suspiciously. "Why? Is there something I should be aware of?"

He shrugged. "No—just wondering. Seeing as how he didn't seem to mention leaving you the house, I was curious as to what he actually *did* mention."

Did you see her? In the garden—did you see her? She only appears to people she approves of, you know. Jack was looking at my hands and reached over to take them in his own.

"They're like blocks of ice."

"I'm very cold-natured. My hands and feet are always cold."

He raised an eyebrow. "Do you really want me to respond to that?"

I tried to jerk my hands away, but he didn't let go. "So, what do you think? We could work together. You could give me access to the house, and I'll share any information I find. I'm also an old hat at restoration work. I helped with my condo in the French Quarter, and my parents are an encyclopedia of information on all things old."

"What happened to me not having to set eyes on you again?"

"Did I say that?"

"Yes, you did. That was the main reason why I agreed to stay and have dinner with you tonight."

He pretended to think for a minute. "But don't you think it would be much more fun to be partners and work on this together? I'd get the info I need for my book, and you'll get the answers for Mr. Vanderhorst."

The group of men at the bar was shouting and laughing loudly now at some joke one of them was telling, and I glanced over my shoulder to where the crowd had parted and saw that the man sitting down was wearing an old U.S. Army uniform. A pit of dread began to grow in my stomach.

Jack let go of my hand and looked at his watch. "Forty-five minutes, Mellie. I really don't want to pressure you, but I think we both know what your answer should be."

The laughter from the bar was becoming almost too loud to talk over. When I looked at the group again, I saw that the man in the uniform had tried to stand but had fallen, taking his barstool with him.

I jerked my attention back to Jack and studied this overconfident, almost-arrogant, and way too good-looking man, and I could suddenly see in my mind's eye the bold script on Mr. Vanderhorst's letter.

> *But there's more to that story, though I have failed to discover what it is. Maybe fate put you in my life to bring the truth to the surface so that she might finally find peace after all these years. God bless you, Melanie. All of my final hopes rest with you.*

The sound of breaking glass brought us both to our feet, and I saw that the uniformed man had attempted to stand again but his grasp on the bar had apparently failed, and he had slid to the ground again, taking several of the beer bottles on the bar with him.

I stared at him, at the still-thick head of graying hair and the sharp, fine bones of his face, which alcohol had softened like a putty knife to wet clay, and felt the familiar jolt of embarrassment mixed with resignation cut through me. I headed to the bar, Jack right behind me.

"Do you think you should get involved, Mellie? I think the guy has enough friends to help him out."

I stood over the man, watching as a stain of wet beer darkened the front of his khaki shirt, spreading its shame like a red letter on his chest. "Jack, would you please help him out to your car while I go call Mr. Drayton and tell him I'll sign the papers?"

He looked at me with confusion. "Do you know this man?"

I knelt down. "Jack Trenholm, meet Colonel James Middleton. Dad? This is Jack Trenholm. He's going to bring you home."

My dad looked at us, his bloodshot hazel eyes staring up at me. At least he still had it in him to look ashamed. His words slurred together, bumping into one another like falling dominoes. "Sorry, Melanie. I only meant to have one."

Jack put his hand on my arm. "I'll take care of it. Go make your call." He gave me that trademark grin of his again. "We're partners now, remember?"

I rolled my eyes in mock resignation. "Yeah, great. Just make sure he pukes before he gets into your Porsche."

I turned my back on them and headed out into the sticky air of a late Charleston summer and took great, gasping lungfuls of it while trying to breathe out all the disappointments and hopelessness that I had carried inside of me for thirty-three years. Then I fished my cell phone out of my purse and dialed Mr. Drayton's number.

CHAPTER 5

Three days after my "come to Jesus meeting" at Blackbeard's, I was the owner of an antique pile of rotten lumber, and encumbered by a dog, a housekeeper, and a guilt trip as long as the Cooper River. Later I would come to wonder how my perfect life had changed so quickly, and the only thing I could come up with was that in a moment of weakness I had been taken in by something as simple as a rose-painted piece of china and a handwritten letter on beautiful stationery.

I returned to the house on Tradd Street, dressed to do battle. I even brought along a rake, a trowel, and a handheld gardening implement with pointy prongs, the name of which I couldn't recall. They were lent to me by our receptionist, Nancy Flaherty, when I told her the condition of the garden. She even knew of the Louisa rose, and I felt like Sir Lancelot as she'd handed me the trowel and said solemnly, "The very existence of that rose in this world is in your hands, Melanie."

I rolled my eyes. "And when did you take time away from your golf game to learn horticulture?"

She'd refused to take my bait. "Gardening isn't something you learn, Melanie." She pressed her golf-glove-covered fist to her chest. "It's something that's there. You're either born with it or you're not. And who knows? Maybe you've got it."

"I'm not the nurturing type—you know that. I don't even keep houseplants. Why don't I just pave over the whole garden and be done with it?"

She looked at me as if she thought I was joking. "Just give it a try. You might just find that you love tending a garden."

I headed toward the door, gardening implements in hand. "Right.

And I might even find that I actually love old houses instead of thinking that they're huge holes in the ground that stupid people throw money into."

She held the door open as I headed down the outside steps. "Stranger things have happened."

I was on the sidewalk when Nancy called out to me again. "And you're wrong, you know."

I stopped and looked up at her. "About what?"

"About you not being the nurturing type. Most people would have written your father off long ago."

She didn't wait for an answer as she closed the office door, leaving me standing on the sidewalk, staring at the closed door with a mixture of resentment and admiration. I headed down the street toward my car with a small feeling of hope that maybe I wasn't so desperate in the home-horticulture department.

But as I stood on the other side of the gate at 55 Tradd Street, I knew without a doubt that Nancy had been all wrong, and I thought again of my idea to pave over the garden as a strong contender on my list of options.

I opened the gate and stepped through it, noticing again how easily it swung on its hinges without any protest. I stood for a moment, listening, and was relieved to hear nothing but birds and the occasional drone of a bee before proceeding into the side garden with its impressive collection of weeds and the forlorn fountain.

The smell of roses was overpowering there, but not in a sickening, cloying way. Rather, it was more of a good memory, like that of a beloved grandmother putting you to bed at night. I had no such memory, but I still found an odd comfort from the aroma that permeated this corner of the garden.

I put down the bag Nancy had given me and walked slowly around the fountain again, avoiding the pained look of the lonely cherub, and tramping down the tall weeds with my Keds-clad feet until I stood in the middle of the rose garden. I marveled again at the smell a mere four rosebushes could create before bending down to tug out a weed that had managed to creep up through the freshly laid cedar shavings. I spotted another and bent down to pull it out, too.

Before I knew it, I was hunkered down by the base of the fountain and working my way around it with the single determination to rid it of weeds.

I don't know how long I was bent at my task, but eventually I became aware of the fact that I was no longer alone. I stopped and slowly stood, feeling my back pop from the effort after having been stooped over for so long. The back of my neck tingled with the familiar mixture of heat and cold, and I turned to where I'd seen the swing before with the woman and the little boy.

I knew before I turned around that I wouldn't find them there. There was no sound of rope against tree trunk and even the chirping of the birds had ceased. The aroma of roses had changed from that of fresh flowers to that of dead and decaying petals that had sat in a vase of water too long. I wrinkled my nose as I faced the side of the house, and my eyes were drawn to the second-story windows.

The sun dipped behind a cloud as I stared at the dark shadow that seemed to fill the window. It took on the distinct shape of a man, and I could feel the penetrating stare from where the face would be. The stench in the garden thickened, and I gagged as I staggered away from the rose garden and made my way to the steps leading up to the piazza.

Sun glinted off the Tiffany rose window on the front door as I fished the key out of my pocket with trembling fingers. In my long experience with these things, I knew I had two choices: I could ignore it in the hopes it would go away, or I could confront whatever it was to make them go away faster. With this thought, I thrust the key in the lock and pushed the door open.

The cloying aroma of decay was stronger inside, and I pressed the hem of my shirt up to my nose as I forced myself up the main staircase and found my way to the room on the side of the house where I'd seen the ominous shadow in the window. *I am stronger than you. I am stronger than you,* I whispered quietly to myself, surprised to find the words my mother taught me so readily on my lips.

I stood outside the door and slowly turned the brass doorknob. With a quick shove, the door opened on quiet hinges, softly hitting the wall behind it. I sensed immediately that whatever had been in there was gone. I peeked inside the room, taking in the large half-tester bed, the thick damask draperies, and the heavy chest-on-chest drawers, feeling guilty for snooping. I was halfway into the hall when I realized that I now owned this room and all its contents and that I could not only leave the door wide-open, but that I could go in without feeling as if I were invading somebody else's privacy.

I forced myself to go stand by the side window, and took a deep breath, surprised to smell the roses again. I checked to ensure that the windows in the room were closed and frowned to myself, wondering how the aroma of roses two stories down and through a closed window could be as strong as if I were sticking my nose in one.

With my hands behind my back, I walked around the room, realizing that this must have been Nevin Vanderhorst's. On the side table by the bed and on the chest of drawers opposite, a cluster of silver-framed black-and-white photographs covered the dark wood. I moved closer, studying each one like a botanist would study butterflies under glass, examining the small details that showed the viewer the relationships between the specimens.

With a start, I realized that the woman in many of the photos was the woman I'd seen in the garden. There were several photos of a young Nevin with the same woman, and I realized it had to be Louisa Vanderhorst. She was young and beautiful, with large dark eyes identical to her son's, and wearing the same warm smile. There was her wedding photo with a very tall man and a picture of her holding a newborn baby. The frame closest to the bed, the one picture that Mr. Vanderhorst must have seen last thing at night before he turned off his light and the first thing each morning, was a studio portrait of him as a small boy sitting on his mother's lap. They were facing each other and smiling, their noses almost touching. I picked up the frame to look at it more closely, realizing that the smell of roses had grown stronger.

I squinted and brought the picture closer to my face, wishing I had my glasses to study it better. But I didn't think I needed them to know that this wasn't the picture of a woman who would abandon her son. I closed my eyes, recalling the words from Mr. Vanderhorst's letter that I couldn't seem to forget.

My mother loved this house almost as much as she loved me. There are others who disagree, of course, because she deserted both of us when I was a young boy. But there's more to that story, though I have failed to discover what it is. Maybe fate put you in my life to bring the truth to the surface so that she might finally find peace after all these years.

I put the picture down suddenly, knocking it over. It fell facedown and I didn't pick it up, not wanting to see the picture of mother and child anymore. I knew better than most, after all, how deceptive a mother's smile could be.

Turning on my heel, I ran headfirst into something warm and solid and decidedly male, and screamed.

Strong arms gripped my shoulders. "Mellie—it's only me. Jack."

I stared into his face for a long moment as I waited for my heart to stop racing before jerking away from his grasp. "What in the hell are you doing in here?" I shouted at him even though he was less than a foot away from me. I was more scared than I cared to admit, and my mother had done a good job of teaching me that anger could chase the fright away. "And my name's Melanie," I added, annoyed at his use of the nickname, which added insult to injury even if he was unaware of its effect on me.

"You invited me, remember? You told me to meet you at the house at nine thirty."

I glanced at the brass anniversary clock sitting on top of the chest of drawers. "You're late. It's nine forty-five. And, besides, haven't you ever heard of a doorbell?"

He smiled his special smile and I had to grit my teeth.

"Sorry I'm late. I had to help a friend at the library this morning." He hooked his thumbs into the waist of his jeans, making me wonder what kind of "friend" he'd had to help so early in the morning. He continued. "As for not using the doorbell, I thought that the wide-open door was an invitation to come right in. You know, you really shouldn't do that. Considering the stuff that's in this house, you should always set the alarm whether you're here or not."

"There isn't one. Mr. Vanderhorst told me that he's had some vandalism recently but that he hadn't put in an alarm."

Jack pulled a small notebook out of his back pocket and unclipped a short pencil from the metal rings. "That should be the first thing on our list, then."

I glanced up at the cracked plaster and a large dark spot in a corner of the room that looked suspiciously like mildew. I turned to him, a little irritated at his mention of "our" list. "Really, Jack. I think we have bigger problems than an alarm. Besides, I would think that most vandals would be discouraged from breaking in by the condition of the outside. I know I would be. Unless you think they'll take pity on me and sneak in at night with paint and paintbrushes."

He ignored me, continuing to jot down notes on his pad. "I've a friend in the home-security business. I'll give him a call and set up a meeting, ASAP."

"I really don't think it's neces . . ."

His blue eyes rested on my face, the expression unsettling. "Believe me, it's necessary." He dipped his head to write something else in his notepad but paused briefly, looking back at me as if an afterthought. "You said yourself that Mr. Vanderhorst had experienced some vandalism. Now that you'll be living here by yourself, it would be a good idea to have a little security."

I found his insistence that I get an alarm as soon as possible odd, but the last part of his sentence caught me off guard. "I didn't say that I would be living here. . . ."

His eyes met mine again, but this time with the addition of a raised eyebrow. "You told me that part of Mr. Vanderhorst's will required you to live in the house for a year."

My chest felt like a deflated balloon. I'd somehow forgotten about that little gem. I looked around me again at the mildew and plaster damage. "Assuming the walls don't crumble down around me first, I guess I'm going to have to." I sighed, blowing out the air through full cheeks. "Go ahead and call your friend. Guess I've got to start spending that sack of money somewhere. Might as well be an alarm system. Maybe we'll be able to salvage it after the house crumbles down around our ears."

I turned to leave.

"So, this was Nevin's room."

I faced Jack again and found him studying the framed pictures on the bedside table. He picked up the photo of Louisa and her son, which I had knocked over and left facedown. Jack looked at me with an accusing glance before studying it. "They must have been close."

I recalled Christmas card photos of me as a young girl with both my parents, beaming at the photographer with bright smiles and frigid poses. "I think that would be a hard thing to judge from just a picture."

He didn't saying anything as he put the frame gently on the table and looked around at the furniture. "My parents would have a fit if they could get their hands on some of this stuff for their store. Have you had a chance to go through anything yet?"

I had to remind myself that he had a reason to be so nosy about the house and its previous inhabitants. "No. I had thought to get started this morning but I ended up working for a bit in the garden instead."

"I didn't picture you to be a gardener type."

"I'm not." I shrugged. "Nor have I ever had an interest in owning an old house, much less restoring one. Go figure."

"Melanie? Are you here?" Sophie's voice called up from the foyer. "You left the door open, so I'm letting myself in."

I shot Jack an annoyed look. "If you're so concerned about people breaking in, maybe you should try closing the door behind you."

He looked surprised. "But I did. I made sure of it. I even slid the dead bolt from the inside to make sure it worked."

My eyes met his briefly before I looked away. "The door must not have been latched before you slid the dead bolt," I explained as I exited the room and made my way to the staircase, convinced that Jack didn't believe my explanation any more than I did.

Sophie stood at the bottom of the staircase, examining the Chinese wallpaper that sagged off the wall at the seams, too tired to cling to the house any longer. She wore her ubiquitous Birkenstocks and, defying all logic or fashion sense, striped knee socks and a tie-dyed shirtdress. Her curly hair was piled on top of her head, exposing her slim white neck—the only part of her that could remotely be called vulnerable. I think it was this contrast between hard and soft that men seemed to find so attractive about Sophie. It certainly couldn't have been her sense of style.

She didn't look up as we approached, seemingly mesmerized by the wall. "This stuff is all handpainted and probably imported from China. Just look at that technique! Reminds me of the time I took up painting in the nude art class—wow, that was an experience. You should try it sometime, Melanie. Release some of that pent-up sexual tension you wear like a chastity belt . . ." Her voice trailed away as she looked up and realized I wasn't alone. A knowing smile lit her lips as she watched

Jack come down the stairs behind me. "Well, well," she said with a smirk.

I gave her a look that any normal person would have taken to mean "back off" but which Sophie completely ignored. As Jack approached her, she stuck out her hand. "Dr. Sophie Wallen. Pleased to meet you. . . ."

He took her hand in both of his, and I thought I saw her melt a little as he smiled down at her. "Jack Trenholm. And the pleasure is all mine. I'm very aware of your work with the Historic Preservation Society. Very impressive."

I could have sworn that Sophie blushed, something I'd never seen her do before. "Thank you. And I must admit I'm a huge fan of your work. I absolutely loved *Suicide or Murder: The Death of Napoleon.* When you postulated that it was the arsenic in his wallpaper that had killed him, I was blown away. It was totally conceivable, considering there was no evidence to support suicide or murder." She beamed up at him. "And even your Alamo book, despite what happened on *Nightline,* had a lot of merit. The media shouldn't have trashed you the way they did without looking at all the facts."

"Thank you," he said, his voice tight. Jack finally dropped her hands as a shadow crossed his face. I could tell that Sophie saw it, too, because she beamed back up at him before turning to me and changing the subject. "So, how do you two know each other?"

"New friends," Jack said.

"Practically strangers," I said simultaneously.

Sophie's brows furrowed for a moment before she began nodding knowingly. "Ah. A little anonymous sex in the afternoon."

"No!" I shouted.

"Count me in," Jack said at the same time.

I glowered at both of them. "Mr. Trenholm—Jack—is writing a book about the disappearance of Louisa Vanderhorst, the late Mr. Vanderhorst's mother. I said I would give him access to the house in exchange for a little help with the restoration and the sharing of information."

Sophie wrinkled her nose and I held my breath, waiting for her to impart the next bombshell and leave me with no dignity whatsoever. "Perfect," she said simply. "Like yin and yang." She smiled. "Did Mel happen to mention why she wants to find out what happened to Louisa?"

"She mentioned a letter that Mr. Vanderhorst left her. How he thought she might be the one to answer that question."

She wrinkled her nose again, a habit I was beginning to hate. "Well, that's part of it anyway. Maybe she'll tell you the rest of it once she gets to know you better. Now *that* would make an interesting book."

I glowered at her as Jack raised his eyebrow. "I'll look forward to that." His voice sent little chill bumps down my spine as his words conjured up all sorts of hidden meanings.

I squared my shoulders, determined to be impervious to his cheap charms. "Don't hold your breath." I pretended to think a moment. "Better yet, please do." I turned to Sophie, eyeing the loose-leaf notebook in her hands. Regardless of how flaky she could be at times, she was always the consummate teacher: always prepared.

She blew a loose strand of hair out of her face. "I thought we could sort of start by inventorying everything structural that requires fixing so that we can prioritize what needs to be done first."

As if in agreement, a small chip of paint chose that moment to dislodge itself from the ceiling and float down to earth, settling in Sophie's nest of hair. She eagerly pulled it out from the tangled curls and smiled. "How perfect! Now we won't have to worry about damaging the wall to get a paint chip to match the paint color in here—the house gave me one!"

Her enthusiasm seemed so misplaced that I couldn't do more than grimace back at her. "Yippee," I said, reaching for her notebook. I unclipped the pen that had been stuck to the cover, flipped open to the first page and wrote number one: *Match decrepit paint color from ceiling. See if it can be ordered by the boatload.*

I pressed the notebook to my chest as soon as I became aware of Jack peering over my shoulder.

"Maybe while you two are doing that, I can start in the attic cataloging personal effects and furniture. I brought a Polaroid camera in my car to take pictures for the record. If I get stuck identifying anything, I can get my parents to take a look."

Sophie's eyes widened. "Wait a minute—Trenholm Antiques on King? Is that your parents'?"

"Yep. Sure is. You familiar with it?"

"I can't afford anything in there, but I certainly know it. You can't be an architecture scholar without understanding the furniture and accessories of the period, you know?"

"I've always thought the same thing," Jack said, his "holy cow" grin making me want to throw up. "Great minds think alike, huh?"

Sophie smiled brightly. "Absolutely." She turned back to me. "I thought you wanted to start working in the garden today."

"I have. I got here early and started clearing the weeds in the rose garden. I was thinking that pulling everything up and just laying down Astroturf would be a great low-maintenance solution. . . ." My words trailed off as I noticed a look passing between Jack and Sophie.

"What?" I asked.

Sophie cleared her throat. "You were planning on working outside in the yard and you wore that?"

I looked down at my Lily Pulitzer pink-and-white gingham halter with matching white capris and pale pink Keds. "What's wrong with my outfit?"

Jack's gaze started at the strand of pearls around my neck, then traveled slowly down my body, making me squirm. "Nothing. If you're going to a garden party."

Sophie stepped forward. "Come on, Mel. Don't you have some old T-shirts and cutoff jeans? Restoring an old house and garden is dirty, messy work. You might even chip a nail."

I looked down at my broken thumbnail, snagged that morning on the weeds outside. "I have no intention of lowering my personal standards just to do a little bit of manual work. And it wouldn't hurt you to follow my example, Sophie," I added, looking pointedly at her striped socks tucked into ratty brown Birkenstocks.

She was saved from answering by a knock on the front door. I slid the dead bolt and chain, then unlocked the door handle. "Soph, this isn't Fort Knox. One lock is sufficient."

"But I didn't . . ."

I didn't allow her to answer, knowing what she was going to say. I opened the door, then wished I hadn't. My father, in a cleaned and pressed golf shirt and khaki pants, stood in front of me, his hair still wet as if he'd just stepped out of the shower.

I looked at my watch. "It's a little early for you to be out of bed, isn't it? It's not yet noon."

He looked at me with eyes the same color as mine—hazel eyes my mother once told me made her fall in love with him. "I haven't been drinking."

This wasn't the first time I'd heard him say that. "Yeah, well, it's still early." I stood rigidly in the doorway, blocking his entrance. "What are you doing here?"

Jack spoke from behind me. "I invited him. I figured since he holds the purse strings, he should be with us to inspect the damage so that when we ask for money he'll know what for."

I stared at him for a long moment, angrier than I remembered being for a long time. I didn't really allow myself to get angry; my life was much too controlled to let in extraneous people and events that might shift my world off-kilter. Until the last week, anyway.

"Who the hell are you to invite people to my house without my permission? And why are you so damned anxious to get the ball rolling on this restoration, anyway? I'm sure all the information you'll need for your book is up in the attic and won't take you more than a day or two to find. Unless there's some treasure map hidden in the walls that you're not telling me about, I expect you to keep a backseat and let me deal with everything, okay?"

He hesitated for a moment, and an odd look I couldn't identify crossed his face. But then he smiled and said, "You're right. I'm sorry. You call the shots from here on out. But since your father is already here, we might as well let him inside. It's hot out there."

Reluctantly, I stepped back as Jack extended his hand to my father. "Colonel Middleton, it's a pleasure to see you again."

My dad shook Jack's hand and smiled. "Thanks for the drive home the other night. Don't think I could have managed it on my own."

"Glad I could help. How was your meeting last night?"

Dad slid a furtive glance in my direction. "Fine. Just fine."

Sophie stepped up and gave my father a kiss on the cheek. "How are you, Colonel?"

He seemed to glow under Sophie's gaze, and I rolled my eyes, wondering once again how she did it and if any male, of any age, was immune. "I'm doing real good, darlin'. Real good. A kiss from you can cure a thousand ills."

She reached up and gave him a kiss on his other cheek. "There.

That should be even better, then." She squeezed his hand. "You went to a meeting, huh? That's great news."

I knew then what Julius Caesar must have felt like that last time in the senate. *"Et tu, Brute?"* I said under my breath as Sophie stepped back to allow Jack to close the door. I figured my dad had been to an AA meeting, and I didn't want to speculate as to how Jack knew about it. Nor did I want to give it any credence at all. I had lost count of the number of times my dad had gone to a first meeting and then to a bar instead for the second. Dwelling in disappointment was an exercise I had long since given up.

I crossed my arms over my chest, wondering yet again how my tightly controlled life had managed to become a kite pulled from its string in strong wind. Any moment it could plummet down to earth, and I'd be left to pick up the pieces. Again. I consoled myself with the knowledge that I had already experienced the worst and that from there on out it could only get better.

My dad approached me, his eyes and mouth holding something back, and I started to doubt my surety about the "things only getting better" part.

"Hello, Melanie." He didn't move to touch me and I was glad. He cleared his throat. "Your mother called yesterday. She would like to talk to you."

I stared into his eyes, and felt the kite slowly spiraling down to a crash landing.

CHAPTER 6

I slammed the lid of the suitcase and was in the process of sitting on it while trying to latch it closed when the doorbell of my condo rang. I wouldn't have heard it except for the fact that the tracks on my CD were in the middle of changing from "Waterloo" to "SOS," so there was a lull in the music.

I peered through the eyehole in the door and stepped back quickly, hoping Jack hadn't seen me.

"I heard you, Mellie. You're going to have to let me in now."

"You're too late," I said. "And stop calling me Mellie. My name is Melanie."

"I'm not late. You said to come over this evening to help you move some of your stuff over to the house. So here I am."

"Well, you're too late. It's my bedtime and I'm already in my pajamas. Evening to most people means before nine o'clock. It's officially night now and no longer evening."

"But it's only nine o'clock now."

"That's right. And that's almost my bedtime."

I heard a slight thunk on the other side of the door, and I pictured him hitting his forehead against the doorframe. "I did some research today that I think you'd be interested in hearing about."

I paused, considering.

"We can go get dessert somewhere, and I can tell you all about it."

"Dessert?" I pretended to weigh my options for a moment. "Oh, all right." I quickly scrubbed off my moisturizing mask with the sleeve of my pink terry cloth bathrobe and opened the door. "And on the way back, we can drop off my suitcases."

Jack took in my robe and fluffy bedroom slippers with a mock look of horror. "You didn't need to dress up just for me, you know."

"It's my bedtime, remember?"

He raised his eyebrows. "Oh. Well, in that case, we could just stay in."

I put my hand on my hip. "Can't you have a conversation with a woman that doesn't contain sexual overtones or innuendos? It's comments like that which will prevent you from ever having a serious relationship with a woman, you know."

His smile remained on his face but the light in his eyes dimmed for a moment. "Been there, done that, bought the T-shirt, thank you very much. Have no interest in a repeat performance."

So that's how it is, I thought to myself. *Damaged goods.* As if I needed yet another reason to stay far away from Jack Trenholm.

He looked toward one of the Bose speakers I had mounted in the corner of the living room and narrowed his eyes. "What's that noise?"

"It's ABBA."

"ABBA?"

"Sold more albums than the Beatles. But maybe you haven't heard of them, either."

Jack scratched his chin. "I'm familiar with both. It's just that I don't think I've heard an ABBA song since I was sitting in the backseat of my mother's car while she listened to her eight-tracks."

I walked over to the stereo and flipped it off. "No need wasting good music on unappreciative ears, then." I headed toward my bedroom. "Let me go change. I'll just be a minute."

"Don't change too much," he called after me. "I kinda like you the way you are."

I didn't turn around until I'd reached my room so he couldn't see me smile.

When I returned he'd made himself comfortable on my black leather sofa and had his feet up on the glass coffee table while he thumbed through a recent issue of *Psychology Today.* I dropped my suitcases, then slapped my hand against his shoes. "Off."

"Yes, ma'am," he said, sliding his feet to the floor before standing up. He held up the magazine. "Pretty heavy stuff."

I took the magazine from him and placed it back on the coffee table, aligning its edges with the other three already there. "Sophie bought me a subscription for some reason. I just use them for coffee table decoration."

He shoved his hands into the front pockets of his jeans and looked up at the ceiling as if he were trying to recall something. "Oh, that's right. What did she say about you yesterday? Something like 'your pent-up sexual tension that you wear like a chastity belt?'" He winked. "Don't think this is the right kind of magazine to help you with that."

"Can we go now?" I asked, making a mental note to kill Sophie later.

"After you," he said, holding his arm out to allow me to go first before picking up both of my suitcases.

I headed toward the front door. "Hang on. I have to get my purse and my BlackBerry."

After dropping the heavy suitcases, he stood in the small foyer and glanced in to the kitchen, from where I'd already set up my cereal bowl and spoon for the next morning next to where I'd placed my BlackBerry so I'd be ready to answer messages first thing.

As I was sliding it into my purse, Jack said, "I love what you've done to the place."

We both looked around at the blank white walls, white carpeting, and sparse ultramodern furniture. I wasn't sure if he was being sarcastic or not; it was hard to tell with him. I simply said, "Thanks," and pulled my purse strap over my shoulder. "It's home."

"Guess it will be pretty traumatic leaving this place for the old house, huh? No ghosts here."

I looked at him, suspicious. "What do you mean?"

"Well, you know. Your sixth sense. There're bound to be ghosts in a house as old as the one on Tradd."

I jerked open the door. "Look, I told you before. Regardless of what you read about my mother, I haven't inherited anything from her—sixth sense or otherwise. I don't see dead people, okay? And I'll thank you not to bring it up again."

He held the door for me. "Okay, truce. I won't mention ghosts again. For tonight anyway."

He had unnerved me and I couldn't bite back my next words. "Great. And as long as you keep your word, I won't mention your old girlfriend, either."

Jack raised his eyebrows but didn't say a word as he picked up my bags again, then shut the door behind us.

I picked the restaurant this time. Even though we were only going out for dessert and coffee, I felt the need to eat off of something other than paper plates. We drove into town to Cru Café on Pinckney Street, where I was on a first-name basis with their famed molten chocolate torte. Most of the diners had already left, so there was no trouble finding a small table and ordering just coffee and dessert. I thought Jack would order a beer or scotch, and was surprised when he asked for a decaf coffee instead.

He must have noticed my look of surprise because he said, "Have to keep my wits about me when I'm with you. Don't want you taking advantage of me or anything."

I rolled my eyes, then ordered my cappuccino and chocolate cake. I must have been feeling magnanimous because I asked for two forks although most friends knew that sharing a dessert with me put their extremities in direct peril of being impaled by my fork.

As we sipped our coffees—his black and mine with two packets of sugar—and waited for the cake, I asked, "So, what did you find out today?"

He leaned forward, his coffee cup between long, tanned fingers. "Remember I told you about Joseph Longo? How he had this thing about Louisa and that everybody thinks they disappeared together?"

"Yes. You mentioned that he even pursued her after she was married."

"Right. Although from everything I've discovered so far, his affections weren't returned. By all accounts she loved her husband and son."

"I've heard that before," I said under my breath as I fiddled with the napkin on my lap.

He considered me for a moment before continuing. "I couldn't believe how much stuff was written about Mr. Longo. He was a very connected man here in Charleston in the twenties and thirties. Owned a few businesses—construction mostly but also a couple of restaurants and a beauty salon. His name was all over the newspapers for this and that: openings, ceremonies, ribbon cuttings, that sort of thing."

The waiter appeared at our table and refilled Jack's cup. He continued. "Interesting thing, though, is that he rarely appeared in any of the society pages. Like he wasn't accepted in Old Charleston because of his new money. Or maybe people knew something about his business practices and didn't want to mingle with that sort of person. Not that old-money Charleston didn't know anything about nefarious business practices—it's just that they had the good manners not to go around flaunting them."

Jack put a hand over his mouth to stifle a huge yawn. "Excuse me," he said, sounding sheepish. "I was at the library at the crack of dawn, and I'm exhausted."

"I didn't know the library was open that early."

"It's not."

"Then how . . . ?"

He smiled and then I wished I hadn't asked. "I know somebody who works there," he said. "She owed me a favor."

"A favor, huh?"

"Yeah, a favor. So she let me in early so I could have access to sensitive documents without having to go through all the red tape."

I crossed my arms across my chest and continued to silently appraise him. According to Nancy Flaherty, Jack was constantly seen in the social column of the paper with one gorgeous woman after another. Apparently, he had a lot of friends.

The waiter chose that opportune moment to reappear with my torte and laid the massive piece of cake with a flourish in the middle of the table.

"Wow," said Jack. "That could feed a family of six for a week."

I picked up my fork and grinned. "Or just one very hungry woman." Reluctantly, I offered the extra fork to him.

He shook his head. "No, thanks. Don't think I could afford the calories."

I recalled his flat abs and slim hips. "Really?"

"Okay, not really. I've just learned by experience to never come between a woman and her chocolate."

I took a mouthful and pointed my fork at him. "Smart boy," I said after I swallowed the first heavenly bite and took another.

"You're one of those people who can eat anything you want without gaining a pound, aren't you?"

I nodded. "I've been like this since birth. Don't know how, but I don't second-guess it."

He watched me put another forkful into my mouth. "You know, if I were a woman, I would probably hate you."

"Yeah, well, it's not my fault and I take every advantage of it."

He leaned back in his chair, crossing his arms across his chest. He raised an eyebrow in a gesture I was beginning to recognize as his "I'm about to say something you're not going to like but I'm going to say it anyway" look. I paused in my chewing and waited.

"Did you ever think it's your fidgety-ness that burns all those calories?"

I took a sip of my coffee and swallowed. "My 'fidgety-ness'?"

"Yeah. I don't think I've ever known a more fidgety woman. You're always moving about or shaking something. Like your leg. Can't you just sit still?"

I made a conscious effort to still my leg and took another bite. After swallowing, I wiped my mouth. "Can we get back to business, please? You were talking about Mr. Longo, I recall, before your mind strayed and you started uttering inanities."

Jack took a slow sip from his coffee before grinning back at me. "Inanities, huh? I don't think I've ever heard that word used in a sentence before."

"That wouldn't surprise me." I smiled. "Now, about Joseph Longo?"

"Well, as I mentioned, he was quite the businessman. It was widely believed that he controlled the booze in Charleston during Prohibition, supplying speakeasies and private homes—which is probably the reason why he was never busted. Kinda hard to arrest the guy who's supplying the police chief with his dinner wine."

"So what's this got to do with Louisa's disappearance?"

He leaned forward. "Here's the kicker. All accounts—including the eyewitness report of Joseph's son—say that on the same day Louisa vanished, Joseph was last seen on his way to the Vanderhorst house at Fifty-five Tradd Street."

A biteful of chocolate cake stuck in my throat. I took a sip of my tepid cappuccino. "To get Louisa. So they could go away together." That wasn't the answer I had been looking for.

"It would certainly seem that way, wouldn't it? And it must have certainly looked that way to her husband. He was very vocal in his condemnation of her for deserting him and their child."

I pushed away my half-eaten piece of cake. "But Nevin Vanderhorst was so hopeful . . ." I started, but was unable to continue as I pictured Mr. Vanderhorst showing me his growth chart on the drawing room wall and the initials MBG. "My best guy," I said aloud, unaware that I'd spoken.

"What?"

"Oh, nothing really. Just something Louisa called her son: 'my best guy.'"

"How do you know that?"

"It's written on the wall in the drawing room, by the grandfather clock. It's part of his growth chart." I shook my head. "It doesn't make any sense: the chart, all of the pictures of Nevin and his mother. But the fact remains that Joseph Longo was last seen going to her house and that was the last day anybody saw either one of them. It certainly points to them running away together."

Jack crossed his arms over his chest and leaned back, his expression thoughtful. "It's been my experience that the most obvious answer is rarely the right one." He sat forward, putting his elbows on the table. "Did you ever see a magician take a coin in his closed fist and pass his other hand over it? And then you had to guess what hand it was in? I always picked the one I least expected to hold the coin. I was right about ninety-nine percent of the time. It's just sleight of hand. That's all. A sleight of hand."

"But Louisa disappeared. The husband and child she supposedly loved so much never saw her or heard from her again."

He reached into his back pocket and pulled out a quarter, holding it out in his right hand with both palms up. "Don't always look for the obvious, Mellie." He closed both hands into fists and then moved each hand over the other several times before holding each fist out in front of me. "Which hand is it in?"

I'd been watching him closely and hadn't seen the quarter pass from his right hand. I pointed to it and said, "This one."

Slowly, he opened up his palm and displayed nothing but smooth skin, his fingers long and tapered. *Sensitive fingers,* I thought and shivered. He opened his left fist and the quarter rolled out, spinning quickly until it fell heads up on the table.

Jack smiled. "See? Sleight of hand. There's something else there. Something we're not seeing yet. I guarantee it."

I regarded him openly, wondering if his bravado came from years of always being right or from something else entirely. "How can you be so sure?" I asked, scrutinizing his face as he answered.

"Because a mother who calls her son 'my best guy' and who has dozens of portraits taken of the two of them together just does not disappear off the face of the earth without contacting him again. Trust me. There's something else there. My gut instinct and my experience with this kind of thing tells me that there has to be something else. There're a few more places around town where I plan to dig into the archives, and there's sure to be a bunch of clues in your attic. I'd also like to see that growth chart, Mellie. You never know where a clue might show up."

"I doubt it, but you're welcome to look. I've put you on the work schedule to begin at seven o'clock tomorrow morning, so if you get there a bit early, you'll have time to examine it. Or you could wait until your lunch break."

He stared at me silently for a long moment. "Did you say lunch break?"

"Yes. I figured if you got started promptly at seven o'clock, you'd be ready for a lunch break at noon." I fished in my purse for the spreadsheet printout I had made. "I'll be there at seven tomorrow to meet with a roofing contractor for an estimate on replacing the roof, and then I can help you sort through the attic until I have to leave at eleven to meet with a new client. I have office hours until six o'clock, when I will return to the house and continue where you stopped at five until my bedtime at nine thirty."

"You did a spreadsheet."

My eyes met his, not comprehending his confusion. "Yes. It's easier to divvy up the workload that way and make sure everybody gets his or her lunch break. Sophie said she can also join us after her last class for a couple of hours, so I've got her stripping the corkscrew spindles from three o'clock until five."

"Lunch break."

"Do you have a hearing problem? Or do you just need people to speak slowly?"

He coughed into his fist and it sounded almost like a laugh. "No. Hearing's fine. It's just, well, a spreadsheet?"

I laid the piece of paper down on the table and sat back in my chair. "Look, I thought you said you were willing to help with the restoration in return for complete access to the house. I've even signed a contract for a new alarm system at your urging. So if you're having second thoughts, let me know now so I can make other arrangements."

He held his hand up in front of him, and this time I was sure he was laughing. "No, no, no. Of course I'm ready, willing, and able to help. It's just that you're so . . ." He looked up at the ceiling as if looking for a word that wouldn't offend me. "You're just so, well, organized about it."

Annoyed now, I placed both palms flat on the table on top of the work sheet, which had taken me all afternoon to draw up. I'd originally put in potty breaks but had second thoughts about that, thankfully, judging from Jack's reaction to the whole thing. "Look, I don't know how it operates in the book-writing world, but in the real world, a professional has to be organized about things to be successful. If I have a new client, I spend hours on the phone or face-to-face to find out exactly what he or she wants and needs. Then I spend several days making a dream list of perfect houses that meets every need. I schedule specific appointment times that are convenient to both the client and home owner to view each and every property." I smacked my palm against the table. "And that's why I'm a million-dollar seller and not some tentative wannabe Realtor."

He leaned forward, and I noticed how his eyes matched his shirt. Quietly, he said, "And your specialty is historic homes, but from what I can tell, you prefer to live in a brand-new condo with white walls and hotel furniture. Does that have anything to do with your mother's house?"

I slid my chair back and signaled to the waiter. "I think we're done here." I made a move to stand, but he held me back with a hand on my arm.

"I'm sorry. It's just that it does make me wonder. And I have a feeling it has something to do with your mother because of the way you reacted yesterday when your dad said that she'd called. My guess would be that you haven't called her back."

I started to tell him in one way or another that it was none of his business when I felt the familiar tingling on the back of my neck. I shifted my gaze to the spot behind Jack's shoulder and saw the distinctive shape of a young woman. She was looking at Jack, her eyes sad and pleading, before she turned her head sharply toward me. She had dark circles under her eyes and hallows beneath her cheekbones as if she were ill. But her eyes seemed lit from within, and I had the distinct impression that the light had something to do with Jack.

"What's wrong?" he asked.

The woman's image faded like smoke from an extinguished candle, and I turned my gaze back to Jack. "Is somebody close to you . . . ill?"

He looked at me oddly. "No. Not that I know of. Why?"

"A young woman. Slim. Blond. Any of that ring a bell?"

"That description rings lots of bells, but nobody I know like that is ill." His tone was light, but sounded forced.

A soft sigh drifted across my ear and then she was gone. "It's nothing. Forget I said anything." I stood. "Come on, let's go. It's past my bedtime."

He pulled a few bills out of his wallet and left them on the table before following me out of the restaurant.

We drove the short distance to Tradd Street in silence, listening to Carolina beach music, which always reminded me of summer. Jack slid his car into a spot in front of the house, then went around to the back to take my suitcases out. I held open the gate for him and then opened the door leading to the piazza and stopped. The front door stood wide-open, and when I took a step forward, I felt something like glass crunch underneath my sandal.

My first thought was how expensive that damn Tiffany window would be to replace. And then I remembered that I had not only ensured that the door was closed but that I had dead-bolted it from the outside with my key.

I heard Jack put the suitcases down beside me. Whispering, he asked, "Do you have your cell phone in your purse?"

I nodded.

"I want you to move over to the side of the piazza, where somebody running out of the house can't see you, and then I want you to call the police. I'm going in to see if the sonuvabitch is still inside."

"No!" I grabbed at his arm. "It could be dangerous."

He gave me that grin that even in the dark and standing on broken glass, I had to admit was very effective. "Your concern flatters me, Mellie. But I guess this means you haven't Googled me yet or else you'd know that you don't need to worry on my behalf. I can handle it."

He slipped inside before I could tell him not to call me Mellie and that Googling him hadn't even crossed my mind. Which was a lie because I'd tried, but my computer had frozen, and I hadn't had a chance to try again because I'd had to run off to meet a client. But still.

I moved into the dark shadows on the far side of the piazza and flipped open my phone. I leaned back against the house, smelling the Charleston night full of Confederate jasmine and gardenias, and slowly became aware of the sound of the steady rhythm of a rope swing against the trunk of the old oak. I closed my eyes, trying to block out all sights and sounds, and calmly spoke into the phone.

CHAPTER 7

I blinked my eyes against the glare of the sun off the Cooper River as I crossed the bridge to downtown Charleston. We hadn't finished with the police until after two a.m., and by the time I'd finally fallen asleep, it had been almost time to wake up again. Nothing had been taken from the house, thankfully—or not, I hadn't quite decided—which had baffled not only the police but Jack and me as well. And the broken glass hadn't been the Tiffany window but a broken beer bottle that had been thrown against the closed door. But the strangest part of all was the fact that the door was wide-open with no signs of forced entry, but also with no signs that anyone had actually entered the house. It was almost as if the would-be vandal and/or burglar had been scared away by whoever or whatever had opened the door. I refused to speculate on what that might have been, despite the many sidelong glances I was getting from Jack.

My eyes were gritty and red, and I felt sorry for the clients I had to meet with that day but would try to help matters by asking Ruth for an extra jolt of espresso. That would at least get me through until my eleven o'clock meeting with Chad Arasi, who was so laid-back he probably wouldn't notice if I dozed in midsentence. I still hadn't figured out a way for him to meet Sophie, and I wasn't sure if Sophie deserved to meet him. "Sexual tension I wear around like a chastity belt," indeed! I had a good feeling that Jack Trenholm would use that against me again and again, ad nauseum. So why did that thought make me smile?

I parked my car in the usual spot and headed for Ruth's. The bell over the door chimed as I walked in. "Just a little change to the usual, Ruth."

She leaned her fleshy elbows on the top of the glass case. "Well, amen to that, Miss Melanie. Can I fix you some eggs and sausage? I got 'em fresh for you just this morning."

I smiled. "Thanks, but I need my sugar fix. How about just adding an extra glazed doughnut and giving me a double shot of espresso in my latte? Maybe I'll try your eggs and sausage another time."

Ruth shook her head and clucked her tongue. "One day your bad habits are gonna sneak up on you and bite you in the behind, and you'll wake up lookin' like me."

I eyed her ample bosom, which could do double duty as a shelf, and laughed. "That wouldn't be such a bad thing, you know. At least I'd have a reason for wearing a bra."

She threw back her head and laughed, her white teeth bright in her dark face. "That's for sure, honey. That's for sure."

I reached inside my briefcase and pulled out a thick manila envelope. "I brought your coupons."

She took the envelope from me and peeked inside. "You're too nice to keep doing this for me, Miss Melanie, but I sure appreciate it." She stuck a meaty finger inside and poked around the coupons. "And you always have them so nice and sorted and clipped together."

I pointed to a stack she held in her hand. "And I used Post-its this time to indicate those coupons with expiration dates in the next week so you'll know to use them first."

Ruth stared at me for a long moment with grateful eyes, but I had the strong impression that she was trying very hard not to laugh. "You're too much, Miss Melanie. Too much. I'm truly grateful."

I shrugged, embarrassed by her gratitude. I knew that she lived with sixteen assorted nieces, nephews, and children of her own, and I'd learned long ago that accepting my Sunday coupons was the closest she'd ever come to accepting charity. "There's a "buy one, get one free" for Cheerios I thought you could use with the two babies who are just learning to eat solid foods."

She nodded, then placed the coupons back in the envelope and tucked it under the counter. "Your extra doughnut's on the house." She picked up the tongs and added a doughnut to the bag that had already been waiting on the counter before she turned to the coffee machine. "That sure was a pretty picture of you in Sunday's paper,

Miss Melanie. I didn't know you own one of those big houses down there south of Broad."

"What? I was in the newspaper?"

"Sure was. You didn't see it?"

I was too embarrassed to tell her that I only took out the real estate listings and tossed the rest. "No, I must have missed it. What section was it in?"

"I got it right here in the back. Let me go get it."

I waited as she waddled to the back of the store and came back with the Sunday paper. She slapped it on top of the pastry case and opened it to the people section. On the first page, in a short column on the right-hand side, was my stock photo found on my employer's Web site. Unfortunately, the picture had been taken after a trip to a new hair stylist who had convinced me to go with a short perm. It was a mix between Little Orphan Annie and an eighties rock star, and had been a blessedly brief experience as my hair hadn't tolerated the perm for very long. Getting the photo replaced had been one of those things lingering somewhere in the middle of my to-do list. I made a mental note to move it to a priority position.

My gaze drifted to the short column beneath the photo that contained a brief commentary on my "precipitous windfall" by inheriting the Vanderhorst home from my deceased client. I wondered if anybody else caught the snide undertones that hinted at me being less than ethical in the deal.

"This is horrible," I said, guessing that it had probably been Mr. Henderson who had called the newspaper to brag about my "coup" as he would have termed it. I realized for the first time that he probably expected me to sell the house through the agency at the end of the year, which would generate not only dollars but a lot of prestige.

Ruth pointed to the picture with a plastic-gloved hand. "It's not so bad, Miss Melanie. Besides, it's so small, I don't think anybody would have paid it any mind. I only saw it because I recognized your skinny face in that photo."

The bell rang over the door, and a businessman clutching a leather briefcase walked into the store. I was sure I'd never met him before, but he smiled at me as if we were old friends.

"I'll have one of your sunrise-special bagels with egg and bacon, please," he said to Ruth as he slapped a twenty down on the glass.

I waved to Ruth and began to back out of the door, clutching my bag and my drink. The man turned to me. "Nice picture in the paper."

I paused. "Do I know you?"

"No. But everybody sees the pictures on the front page of the people section." He pointed at my hair. "Like the way you're wearing your hair nowadays."

"Um, thanks," I said as I exited the store, completely mortified.

I walked to my office, wondering if it was my imagination that made me think that people were looking at me differently. Nancy Flaherty met me at the front desk. She wore a hands-free phone set on her head as she stood in front of the reception desk, attempting to hit a golf ball through an upended cup. She looked up and smiled as I entered.

"Good morning, Melanie. You're very popular this morning. I guess on account of that article in the paper yesterday. That was Tom's idea, by the way. Anyway, I've taken five phone calls for you already, and it's not even nine o'clock yet."

I held up the hand with the paper sack, and let her stick the five pink slips between my fingers.

"One of them is from that delicious Jack Trenholm. You have to have him meet you at the office sometime so I can get a good look at him."

"Jack called?" I was already annoyed with him, and it wasn't even noon. I'd been at the house at seven o'clock that morning until about eight thirty, meeting with the roofing guy, and Jack hadn't bothered to show up. I'd tried reaching him on his cell and home phones, but both had quickly gone to voice mail. I wanted to think it was because I'd neglected to give him a copy of the spreadsheet and he'd forgotten when he was supposed to be there, but I'd expressly said he needed to be at the house at seven o'clock to get to work on the attic papers. "What did he want?"

"It's on the message. Something about being late this morning because he was doing more research at the library and couldn't get away."

"Research," I snorted, heading toward my office.

Nancy called after me, "He said something about adjusting the work schedule to make sure he was working the same amount of hours, and I told him you wouldn't mind. Please tell me you didn't draw up one of your anal-retentive spreadsheets and actually show it to him."

I stepped in to my office and turned to shut the door.

"Melanie! Please tell me that you didn't!"

I closed the door in time to miss the golf ball that had been lobbed in my direction.

I put everything down on my desk and began to thumb through the messages. I tried again to reach Jack and got his voice mail. There was a message from Sophie saying she'd be at the house around three o'clock to finish her evaluation—I made a note to adjust the spreadsheet—and a message from my father with only the number four written on it. I suppose that was the number of days he'd been sober so far. I crumpled it up and tossed it in the wastebasket. There was a message from Chad Arasi saying he would be late for our meeting and could we meet closer to the College of Charleston campus. Against my better judgment, I made a note to call him back and tell him to meet me at the house on Tradd Street at three o'clock when I knew Sophie would be there. They would thank me for it someday, I was sure. Maybe they would name their firstborn after me.

The last message made me pause. It was from a man named Marc with no last name. I was pretty sure I didn't know any Marcs. I ate my first doughnut in silence, tapping my nails against the top of my desk as I tried to recall where I might have met him. There was no phone number or message, just a check in the box that read "will call back."

I pressed the button for the front desk and waited for Nancy to pick up.

"Yes, Melanie."

"I was just looking at this message from a guy named Marc. Did he give you a last name?"

"No. And he didn't want to leave a message or give me his phone number. Said he'd call you back when he got a chance."

"Thanks, Nancy." I hung up the phone, then wadded up the message and threw it away, forgetting all about it before it hit the garbage can. Then I flipped on my computer and reached for another doughnut. I had barely taken the first bite when Nancy buzzed my office.

"You've got a visitor."

There was something in her voice I didn't quite like, like a contented kitten who'd had more than her fair share of the cream. "Who is it?"

I definitely heard the smirk this time. "Jack Trenholm. He said you were expecting him."

I sighed. "I wasn't, but go ahead and send him back, please."

"Will do."

I barely had enough time to stash the doughnut bag in a desk drawer before I heard a brief knock on my office door. Nancy opened it and let Jack enter. She wiggled her eyebrows at me from behind his shoulder and flashed her open palms at me to indicate the number ten before closing the door behind him.

"Is she single?" Jack asked, indicating the closed door.

"Married. Very. Two daughters. Any more illuminating comments this morning?"

He held up a golf ball. "She asked me to sign this when I had a chance. I have to say that I've never been asked to autograph a golf ball before. A woman's chest, yes, and even a menu, but a golf ball is a first. I told her I needed a Sharpie and would bring it back to her after I signed it. Remind me if I forget."

I snorted in response.

Jack carried a rolled-up newspaper and was wearing the same outfit he'd been wearing the night before, his previously starched shirt crumpled and looking a little worse for wear.

"Nice shirt," I said, sounding even more self-righteous than I had meant to.

"Nice hair," he said, opening the paper to the people page, where my photo smiled out at both of us, and slid it across my desk toward me. "Thought you'd want an extra copy for your scrapbook."

I met his eyes. "How did you know that I kept a scrapbook?"

He shrugged. "Lucky guess."

I snatched the paper from him and shoved it in the garbage. "Why are you here? Aren't you supposed to be at the house?"

"Didn't Nancy give you my message?"

"Yes, but I assumed that after your 'research' was done, you'd be at the house going through the attic. Remember—the sooner you get the information you need, the sooner we can part company."

He scratched his cheek, which was beginning to show a shadow.

"Yes, well, about that. I'm really more of a night owl and do most of my best work after hours. Mornings, well, we're just not compatible."

I leaned back in my chair, thinking about all the changes I'd need to make to the work schedule. "So why are you here?"

"I promise that I'll be at the house as soon as I grab a little sleep and a shower. But I wanted to let you know what I found out first. I was hoping that maybe what I had to tell you would soften you up a bit so you wouldn't be mad at me for standing you up this morning."

I twirled a pencil between my fingers. "I doubt it, but go ahead." I listened with one ear, my mind mostly occupied with my schedule for the rest of the day.

He sat on the edge of my desk, something that nobody in the office dared to do, not even my boss. I gave him an irritated look, but he either ignored it or didn't see it. "After I got home last night, I couldn't stop thinking about Joseph Longo. He was a main figure in Charleston for so long, and he had three sons who at the time of Joseph's death were involved in the family businesses."

He stopped speaking, looking at me oddly. "Do you have any more doughnuts left?"

"Doughnuts?" I tried to look innocent.

He wiped an imaginary crumb from the corner of his mouth. "You have glazed sugar icing on your cheek. I was hoping you'd have some left because I haven't eaten and I'm starved."

Reluctantly, I pulled out the bottom drawer and handed him the bag with the extra doughnut and handed it to him. "You owe me," I said as I wiped my hand over my mouth.

He took a bite and smiled. "And I look forward to paying you back."

I rolled my eyes. "Go on. Some of us have work to do."

"Anyway, I figured that a guy with three sons would probably have descendants still living here. And maybe somewhere in their houses they'd have letters or something, or family stories handed down over the generations, that might fill in some of the missing pieces. Like where Joseph might have gone after he supposedly left town with Louisa. Maybe he had a house in France or an apartment in New York—who knows? But chances are, if there's anything handed down over the years, I would think that the current generation would have access to it."

I sat up. "Good point. So what did you find out?"

He took a large bite from the doughnut and smiled broadly as he chewed. "Well, there're quite a few Longos still living here in Charleston, although a little under the radar. You don't see them on the society pages of *Charleston* magazine or attending the St. Cecilia Ball. But they have several businesses except now they seem be actual legitimate businesses. Well diversified, too. The eldest grandson, Marc Longo, is the most visible. He's got a bunch of real estate holdings as well as a brick foundry and a new start-up high-tech firm that has something to do with satellites. And get this. He bought the old Vanderhorst plantation, Magnolia Ridge, last year. Rumor has it that they're planning on starting a vineyard there to make their own wine."

"A winery? In South Carolina?"

"Believe it or not, they're not the first. For certain types of grapes, it's a viable industry. Still in its cradle, so it will be interesting to see what happens with it."

I realized that Jack was staring at my crossed leg as it bounced up and down. With a concentrated effort I made it stop, tapping my fingernails against my desk instead. "Do you think they're approachable? Assuming they know anything about their past, they'll know that there was bad blood between the Vanderhorsts and Longos, and once they know that we're trying to clear Louisa's name, they might be reluctant to help out the enemy, so to speak."

He raised his eyebrows. "Very true." He wiped his face with a napkin Ruth had stuck inside the bag, and stood. "Which is why we're going to visit somebody who knows everybody in Charleston—below the radar or not—and can tell us which one among them might be the most approachable."

I looked at my watch, realizing that I didn't have to meet with anybody now until three o'clock. "I do have a little bit of time." I stood and took my purse off the back of my chair. "I hope this isn't one of your ex-girlfriends or something."

Jack held the door open for me. "Hardly. It's my mother."

"Oh," I said, looking up at him. "We're going to go meet your mother?"

He looked down at me and grinned. "You look fine."

I met his gaze, annoyed. "It's not that. You've mentioned your parents before, so it's not like I didn't know. It's just that, well, you don't seem to be the type to have a mother."

He laughed. "Not the type? I'll have to tell her that. You'll like her. Everybody does."

"Probably because they feel sorry for her, since you're an only child."

"Ha! So you *did* Google me. I knew it was only a matter of time."

Luckily, we'd reached the reception area, so I didn't need to lie about how, during a weak moment earlier that morning before the roofing guy arrived, I'd used my laptop to do just that. Instead, I practiced a look of righteous indignation as we faced the receptionist.

Nancy beamed at us. "Hey, Melanie. Are you and Mr. Trenholm out for the rest of the day?"

"I'm hoping," said Jack.

"Of course not," I said simultaneously.

Jack smiled brightly at Nancy. "I'm looking forward to seeing you again. And I'll remember to bring back your signed golf ball. And please call me Jack."

Nancy flushed. "Thank you, Jack. My ladies' nine-holers golf group will be so jealous. Not that I'll use it when we play next, but I'll bring it to show off."

Jack took her hand in both of his. "It was a pleasure meeting you, Nancy."

"And you, too, Jack."

On the point of nausea at this fan fest, I pushed open the front door. "I'll have my cell on if you need to reach me. I'm meeting Mr. Arasi at three o'clock at the Tradd Street house. I'll come back here after that to make some phone calls."

"Got it! Oh, and by the way, I saved that article for you from the paper for your scrapbook. You know, I really like the way you're wearing your hair now much better."

"Gee, thanks, Nancy. I'll keep that in mind the next time I want a perm."

Nancy waved us out and Jack held open the door for me. "Yours or mine?" he asked.

His Porsche was sitting in front of my white Cadillac. "If I said mine, you wouldn't take it quietly, would you?"

"Probably not," he said as he made his way to the passenger side of the Porsche and opened the door for me.

As I approached the door, I stopped, my mouth wide-open with surprise.

"Are you trying to catch flies, or do you have something to tell me?"

I hit the palm of my hand against my forehead. "Marc Longo. You said he's the eldest of Joseph Longo's grandsons. Well, a guy named Marc called me at the office but didn't leave a message or a phone number—just his first name. I threw the message away and forgot all about it. I don't know any Marcs, and I'm just thinking it's kind of weird that we'd be talking about Marc Longo. Maybe it's the same guy. He might need a Realtor."

Jack raised his eyebrow. "That's a possibility."

I sat in the passenger seat and waited for Jack to close my door and come around the car to the driver's side. "If it is the same guy, do you think it's just a coincidence?"

Jack looked at me with an expression similar to the one in the picture on the back of his book jacket, and it became clear to me why he'd been such a hit on the morning talk show circuit—something else I'd found out when I'd Googled him.

"Trust me, Mellie. In my line of work, where old secrets go to great lengths to stay hidden, there's no such thing as coincidences." He started the car and pulled out onto the street.

I started to tell him again that my name wasn't Mellie, that the only person who had ever used that name had forever ruined it for me, but I stopped. I was looking at his profile, where a pulse had begun in his jaw. His brows were furrowed in concentration and I thought that perhaps he was inadvertently allowing me to see the real Jack Trenholm—the Jack Trenholm he hid from the eyes of admiring fans and talk show hosts.

The Jack I saw smoldered with something dark and burning—something that drove him forward fast enough that he didn't have the time to sit and dwell. And I sensed, without a doubt, that whatever it was had something to do with the specter of a woman whose unsettled presence lingered with him. I sensed her now: the sadness, the loss. I felt something else, too; this woman, whoever she was, had a secret.

A secret that she wanted Jack to know. And, unfortunately, she had chosen me to figure out what it was.

I turned my head away to stare out the window and at the old streets of the Holy City and wished, not for the first time, that dead people would just leave me alone.

CHAPTER 8

I kept my gaze focused outside, not even commenting when Jack made a detour north of Market to make a quick bank run. He parked in front of the bank, an edifice that had become synonymous with "toadstool building," on the corner of Gadsden and Calhoun. It was easily a contender for the city's ugliest building and widely disdained by not only the city's preservationists but also by any passerby with good taste.

"Why did you go so far out of your way? Aren't there ATMs closer to your parents' store?" I asked as Jack got back into the car.

He flashed his trademark grin. "Because I happen to know the head teller in this branch, and she always takes the time to make sure I'm a happy customer."

I pressed my lips firmly together so he could tell I wasn't amused. "Couldn't this have waited?"

"Sorry. But I owed my mom some money, and I knew she'd be expecting it the next time she saw me."

Surprised, I asked, "You borrowed money from your mother?"

"Lost a bet," he said as he started the car and pulled out onto Calhoun Street.

I smirked. "You made a bet with your mother and lost? What was it about?"

With a sidelong glance, he said, "I can't tell you."

"You can't tell me? Why on earth not? It's not like you're a bastion of secrecy. Everything anybody wants to know about you is there for everybody to see on the Internet."

He set his jaw. "Yeah, well, there're some things even Google can't reveal."

Annoyed that he wouldn't divulge his secret to me, I crossed my arms. "Like how you can't stand to lose—even if it's to your own mother."

"That, too," he said, grinning. "Among other things."

I looked away, not wanting him to see how his sudden need to be private and secretive somehow excited me. Maybe it was because he already seemed to know so much about me. Or maybe it was something else entirely.

We rode in silence for a few blocks until we reached King Street, and he found a curbside parking space not far from Trenholm's Antiques. I was nervous about meeting Jack's mother, although not for the reasons he assumed. I stood and straightened my white linen pencil skirt and walked with Jack toward the imposing wood and stained-glass doors that lead inside the venerable antiques store.

The smell affected me in the same way as that of old houses—a reminder of decay and rot, huge repair bills and dead people. It also brought back old memories that I had no wish to ever revisit.

Highly polished dark wood furniture crowded the showroom floor without being overwhelming. Small occasional tables held delicate accessories and complemented the dark red walls and bright gilt chandeliers that shimmered from the ceiling. Oil paintings of various men, women, and children stared down their noses at us from walls capped with decorative moldings, as if trying to show Charleston homeowners how the beautiful furniture and wall hangings would look in their own opulent houses. I had never walked down King Street without peering into these shop windows, wanting to go in and touch the old wood almost as much as I wanted to turn away and forget why I hated old houses and furniture in the first place.

A petite blond woman, with her hair pulled back in a French twist and wearing a St. John suit and Chanel shoes, approached us from the rear of the store. I recognized her immediately as Jack's mother from the dark blue of her eyes and the elegant shape of her eyebrows. I wondered if he'd learned the inquisitive lift of one eyebrow from her or if it was just some inherited Trenholm trait.

"Jack, darling. It's about time you decided to drop by and visit with your poor old mother." She took both of his hands and stood on tiptoes to raise her cheek to be kissed. She had smooth, flawless skin and one of those faces that seemed to get more beautiful with age, as if only good experiences had ever happened to her so as not to mar her complexion with lines and folds. Which didn't make any sense if she was indeed Jack's mother. "Did you bring my money?"

He kissed her and then enveloped her with a bear hug that she seemed completely comfortable with and that made me smile. "You get younger ever time I see you, Mother. One day you'll have to show me where you found your fountain of youth. And, yes, I have your money. We'll settle up before I leave."

She smiled and then they both turned identical eyes in my direction. "Mother, I'd like to introduce you to my new friend, Melanie Middleton. And, Melanie, this is my mother, Amelia Trenholm."

She faced me and held out her hand. I shook it, surprised at the firmness of it, considering her skin was as soft as it looked. She continued to hold my hand for a moment longer as she stared in my face, and a sinking feeling crept into the pit of my stomach.

"It's a pleasure meeting you," I said in an attempt to avert disaster.

"We've met before," she said, both of her hands now enclosing mine. "At your grandmother's house on Legare when you were just a little girl. We were good friends, you know, your mother and I." She peered closely into my face.

"I remember," I said, finding it hard to meet her eyes. "I just never made the connection between my mother's friend and Jack's mother, even though you had the same name. I guess it's because I didn't remember you having a son."

She nodded. "Yes, well, you wouldn't. When I'd go to see your mother, I'd leave Jack behind. Ginette, well, except for you, she didn't really enjoy small children."

I know why, I wanted to say but remained silent. I'd happily buried the memory of my mother long ago, and I wasn't about to resurrect her ghost now.

Mrs. Trenholm smiled. "You look like her in the face. You have your father's eyes, but the rest of you is all Prioleau. Do you sing, too?"

"Not a note," I said, dropping my hand, eager to change the subject but somehow sad to let go of the warmth of her hand. It had been a very long time since I was reminded of what I had missed for so long. But it was hard to miss something you'd been telling yourself you never really had.

"Do you at least enjoy opera? Your mother's made quite a name for herself in Europe. I supposed it would be inevitable that you would have an ear for it."

Jack snickered from behind me. "Mother, she listens to ABBA. I think that says it all."

I felt like snapping back at Jack how I listened to other music, too, just never opera, but for some reason I wanted to be on my best behavior in front of his mother.

Mrs. Trenholm hooked her hand in the crook of my elbow and smiled. "All music has its merits. Would you like some coffee, dear? I've just made a fresh pot. We could sit down and have a nice chat while Jack goes in the back to help his father unpack boxes of silver serving pieces and flatware he brought back from an estate auction in France."

Jack frowned down at his mother but didn't argue. "All right, Mother. But don't mention any of my childhood embarrassments, all right?"

"We'd be here all month if I did that, Jack. Now go help your father. And don't hurry back."

Amelia Trenholm gently propelled me toward the back of the store while Jack went through a side door I hadn't noticed before. An oval mahogany dining table had been set with a Limoges coffee service and white linen place mats and napkins. A tall silver coffee urn sat on a matching sideboard with elegant curved legs, and a silver platter holding dainty pastries sat in the middle of the table.

"Please sit, dear, while I pour the coffee. Or do you prefer tea?"

"Coffee's fine, thank you." I stared at the sideboard. "Is that a Thomas Elfe piece?"

She finished pouring coffee into my cup. "Good eye, dear. It's one of very few still in existence, so not everybody understands the price we're asking. But I suppose your knowledge of good furniture should be expected."

My eyes met hers as she placed the delicate china cup and saucer in front of me. "I'm sorry, Melanie. I don't mean to upset you. But your mother and I were once dear friends, and we still occasionally keep in touch, so I suppose it's only natural that I would think of her when speaking to you." She sat down in a Chippendale chair and pulled it up to the head of the table. "I understand why you're a little prickly every time there's a mention of your mother—any normal person would be the same. I also understand the circumstances surrounding her departure from your life. So perhaps I can offer some insight. . . ."

I put my coffee cup down with a small rattle. "Mrs. Trenholm, I really have no interest in talking about my mother or even trying to understand her. I'm a big believer in moving forward, and she is definitely part of my past. So, thanks for the coffee, but I think it's time for me to leave."

She put a firm hand on my arm, her insistence reminding me so much of her son that I almost smiled. "You have your father's temper, don't you? Why don't you sit down and let's start all over? I won't mention your mother, and instead we can sit and chat about Jack. Or about your new house and its furnishings, which I know are marvelous, because I've been in the house before at some function or another. And please call me Amelia."

She removed her hand from my arm and smiled at me, which reminded me of her son, and I relaxed. I settled back down. "I'm sorry. I'm not usually so edgy. I think it's all that's been happening in my life, lately—first with Mr. Vanderhorst's passing and my inheriting his house. It makes me lie awake at night."

Mrs. Trenholm patted my arm and nodded sympathetically. "That's perfectly understandable. I'd probably be the same way if I were in your situation. No offense taken."

"Thanks," I said, and began to add three sugar packets and cream to my coffee. To her credit, she didn't comment, and instead slid the tray of pastries closer to my plate. Knowing I didn't need to impress this woman, I helped myself to two of them.

I took a sip of coffee before speaking. "As soon as I complete my inventory of all the furnishings in the house, I'd like to get your help in determining the value of some of the bigger pieces as well as advising me on any repairs. I'm a bit over my head with it all, I'm afraid. My own condo is more Pier One and Pottery Barn than Chippendale and

Sheraton." I laughed at my own joke and was dismayed by Amelia's grimace.

"Sorry, dear. It's just a bit of a shock, knowing, well, you were raised with the good stuff and you have a houseful of it now, so I just can't imagine . . ."

My smile tightened. "I was raised by my father from the age of seven, so I learned not to have anything too valuable or permanent. It saddles you with too much baggage so that it's harder to move on."

"I see," she said, surprising me by smiling brightly. "Now I know why, besides the obvious, Jack feels such a connection to you. You're both brilliant at denial."

I almost spit out my coffee. Instead, I stuck a pastry in my mouth to prevent my first words from making it past my lips.

I swallowed and took a sip of my coffee. "Mrs. Trenholm—Amelia—if we can't steer the conversation away from my past, then I really am going to have to leave. I'm not in denial. I've just made peace with my past so that I can move forward."

Her eyes were warm as she took a sip from her coffee and nodded as if she agreed, but I wasn't fooled. Still, despite her comments, I felt that I had somehow found an ally.

"All right, Melanie. We'll change the subject. You're a progressive woman. And a successful businesswoman, too, from what I've heard. I'm surprised your path hasn't crossed with mine before now. Or at least crossed with Jack's. He's pretty much on top of all the eligible Charleston single women. He must be losing his touch."

I almost choked on my coffee and then realized that she had no idea that she'd made a double entendre, and I had to fight to keep a straight face. I cleared my throat. "My job keeps me pretty busy, so that's probably why. It doesn't leave me a lot of time for a social life."

She took a sip from her cup, then studied it for a moment. "Jack's been a little off the social circuit lately, too. Not too hard to figure out why, but it's been over a year now, so I was hopeful when he told us about you."

I'd lost count of how many of the small pastries I had eaten, and I pushed my plate away, suddenly feeling queasy. I sat forward. "Um, what do you mean—that he told you about me?"

Amelia waved a manicured hand at me. "Oh, it wasn't like that at all. It was just that he was finally excited about this new book project after the fiasco with his last book, and you and your house were sort of like the answer to a prayer for him."

I had no idea what she was talking about. In my Googling, there had been more links than I'd had time to investigate. In my haste to find out something personal, I'd apparently missed something pretty big. "I'm not sure what you mean. In what way was I an answer to his prayers?"

She looked at me with clear blue eyes. "You don't know the story, do you?"

"I guess not."

She pursed her lips. "Well, Jack's last book, the one about the heroes of the Alamo, was publicly debunked on national television—completely discrediting him and all of his work." She closed her eyes for a moment and shook her head. "Through intensive research, Jack had enough information to completely alter the historical account of what really happened at the Alamo. He'd even found a diary that experts were ninety-nine percent sure was Davey Crockett's that corroborated Jack's story. Unfortunately, Davey Crockett's descendants unearthed a trunk supposedly belonging to their famous ancestor and opened it on a special edition of *Nightline*."

"But how would that discredit Jack and his research?"

Amelia shrugged. "The trunk was full of documents, but none of the handwriting matched that in Jack's diary. Either those documents are a forgery or Jack's diary is—and public opinion was not about to sway in favor of a man whose own ancestor was supposedly the basis for the Rhett Butler character in *Gone With the Wind*."

"What?"

She smiled, looking remarkably like her son. "Yes, George Trenholm is an ancestor of ours. Used to embarrass Jack a lot until he learned how to use it to his advantage." She raised an eyebrow while I tucked that little gem of information away for future use.

"So what happened?" I asked.

"The book sold poorly and his publisher canceled his contract and the media made him a laughingstock. He still has his loyal fans, of course, who will be first in line to buy his next book, but the problem is finding a story big enough that will earn him the another book contract."

I frowned. "I can't imagine that the story of Louisa Vanderhorst and Joseph Longo would interest anybody outside of Charleston, to be honest with you. I hope he's not holding out hope that this story will be the big break he needs."

Amelia looked at me oddly. "Louisa and Joseph? I'm not sure if . . ."

The phone rang and Amelia stopped speaking. After excusing herself, she stood to go answer it. I stood, too, drawn to the beautiful furnishings that surrounded me. I had told Jack that I'd never been here before because I couldn't afford it, but that was only half the truth. The real reason was the same reason I avoided old houses: people didn't like leaving either one behind when it came time to depart this earth.

While sitting and talking with Jack's mother, I had heard whispers coming from the room behind me, and the distinct drop in temperature as something brushed the back of my hair. *I am stronger than you,* I said to myself if only to remind me that the goose bumps on the back of my neck were from the cold chill and not from fear.

I felt more than saw four gentlemen in clothing from the eighteenth century sitting at a game table and a young boy in short pants and suspenders riding astride a rocking horse. I kept my gaze focused, ignoring them in the hopes that they would ignore me, but found myself drawn to a small oval box sitting on a small table by the front window. It was made of burl walnut and had a tasseled brass key sticking out of its lock on the front.

I hesitated before touching it, having learning one too many times that sometimes old, loved items carried with them the memories of their prior owners—owners who were usually eager to talk to me. I placed my hands on it and was relieved to feel nothing but the hard wood under my fingers. Carefully, I turned the key and opened the lid, finding inside a silver canister in the middle flanked on both sides by small wooden compartments.

"It's a Regency-era tea caddy. It's beautiful, isn't it?" Mrs. Trenholm spoke behind me, giving me a start.

"It's lovely," I said, my fingers tracing the intricate leaf-design inlay decorating the top of the box. I had seen antique tea caddies before, of course, but this one intrigued me, making me stroke its smooth wood as if it were an old friend.

"It's odd, Melanie, that of all the objects in this store you would be drawn to this particular item."

I lifted my hand quickly as if it had been burned. "Why is that?"

"It was a gift to me." Her eyes met mine. "From Jack's fiancée."

I couldn't hide my surprise. "Jack's engaged?"

"Not anymore." She shook her head and I smelled her perfume, which reminded me of gardenias and my mother. I wrinkled my nose.

I handed her the box. "Oh, I'm sorry. He didn't mention . . ."

"He wouldn't. He doesn't talk about it at all."

"But why? It happens a lot more than you think. And it's always better to break an engagement than get a divorce."

"That's very true, dear. But the two of them were very much in love. When Emily left him literally standing at the altar, we were all devastated." She took the box from my hands and replaced it on the table, her fingers lingering on the polished wood just as mine had. "I didn't think Jack would ever recover, and I must say that for a long time I hated her for doing that to him."

"Did she offer any kind of explanation or apology?"

Amelia shook her head. "Nothing—well, except for the horrendous scene at the church when she told Jack in front of all the guests that she couldn't go through with it. She had no family, so there was nobody else to soften the blow for Jack. Emily just . . . disappeared from our lives. Which is probably the best thing, considering how small Charleston is. If she'd remained, Jack would have been running into her everywhere."

"So she left town?" I don't know why it meant so much to me to know that I wouldn't be running into Jack's ex-fiancée.

"Upstate New York, of all places. I heard that from her editor at the *Post and Courier.* Emily was a writer, in charge of the people column. They met while Jack was doing research for a book." She looked pointedly at me.

"How nice for them," I said, distracted by an old woman in full mourning dress of the late-nineteenth century sitting in rail-backed rocking chair behind us. Her face was covered by a heavy veil, and as I watched, she stood and began walking toward me, her gait uneven as she leaned heavily on a cane. I took a step back, horrified that she might want to talk to me.

A hand touched my arm and the woman vanished as I stifled a scream.

"It's all right, Melanie. It's only me." Amelia's eyes searched mine. "Your mother saw them, too. That's why she didn't like coming here."

I knew that denying it would be pointless. Instead, I swallowed heavily and looked at my watch. "I think I've intruded on your time long enough and I've got to get back to the office to return a few phone calls. Do you mind if I go get Jack?"

"I'll do it," she said, but didn't move. "It's why your mother wanted you out of your grandmother's house on Legare. She didn't think it was safe for you to be there."

I had a brief flash of memory of me with my mother staring at a wrought iron gate in front of the house my mother had grown up in. *This will all be yours one day, Mellie. All of this wonderful family history will be yours to carry on to the next generation.* I blinked, trying to rid myself of the memory and swallowed hard. "I guess that story works as good as any."

Amelia stared at me for a long moment before moving away. She stopped when I spoke.

"Please don't mention to Jack about . . . well, you know. It's not something I really want spread about as common knowledge."

She tilted her head to the side as she regarded me. "I won't bring it up, but I think he's already aware. Surely you guessed that's the reason he brought you here today?"

I hadn't but I didn't deny it. I remembered my initial conversation with Jack at Blackbeard's when he'd asked me if I'd inherited my mother's sixth sense, and knew she was right. Instead, I said, "It's been a pleasure seeing you again, Amelia. Thanks for the coffee and the pastries."

"You're very welcome, dear. I hope to run into you again soon."

"Me, too," I said, meaning it. "If you don't mind, I'm going to wait outside on the sidewalk and make a few phone calls while you get Jack."

"Sure," she said before turning away and disappearing behind the same door I'd watched Jack go through earlier.

I stood out on the sidewalk and flipped open my phone to begin retuning a few of my calls. I faced the store, concentrating on my own reflection so I wouldn't have to see anybody I didn't want to, but was distracted when Jack and his mother returned to the showroom. I watched as Jack opened up his wallet and handed his mother several bills. They walked over to the far side of the showroom, where a large rolltop desk loomed in the corner. Mrs. Trenholm turned a key and pulled out her purse and then, after counting the bills Jack had given her, placed them in her purse before relocking the desk.

They began talking again, so I made another phone call while I waited, annoyed at the drips of perspiration that were snaking their way down my blouse but finding that preferable to going back inside to the whispering and invisible eyes.

Finally, after giving his mother another huge bear hug, Jack emerged with his trademark grin, causing me to almost forgive him for making me wait in the heat.

"Sorry," he said. "I had to ask my mom about the Longos."

We headed for his car. "I'd almost forgotten. Does she know them?"

We seated ourselves in the Porsche and headed out into the late-midmorning traffic. "Oh, yes. They're apparently big customers at the shop. My mother says they don't know a Hepplewhite from their asses—not in those words, of course—but they figure if they spend the money, they'll get the quality they need for the look they're going for in their house on Montagu Street."

"That's north of Broad." I slipped my sunglasses on, thinking about the difference in prestige and home prices based solely on whether you were a S.O.B or a N.O.B.

"You bet. Probably kills them every time they think about old Joseph not having the good sense to buy south of Broad when he moved here."

"Well, the connection with your parents gives us a little bit of an 'in' with the family, don't you think? And did your mom suggest anybody who might be approachable?"

"She wasn't very complimentary about the family in general, saying there're rumors about gambling and debts and charity pledges that don't happen. But one of the grandsons might be a person willing to at least talk to us. And you'll never guess what his name is."

"Marc Longo." I slid my glasses down to look at Jack.

"You got it. Did I mention that I don't believe in coincidences?"

Just then my cell phone buzzed, alerting me to a text message. I pulled it out of my purse and read from the screen. "It's from Nancy at the office."

Jack raised an eyebrow in true Rhett Butler fashion.

"Guess who just called?" I flipped the phone shut.

"I have an idea, but I'm going to let you tell me."

"Marc Longo," I said.

"Very interesting." Jack pressed his foot down on the accelerator. "As I mentioned before, there is no such thing as a coincidence."

I nodded but remained silent, afraid to acknowledge that he might be right. How else to explain that our mothers had been friends? I thought about telling Jack that Marc Longo could be calling me because he'd been attracted to my photo in the paper. But then I remembered the photo and knew that couldn't be it.

"Let's go find out what he wants, then." Jack hit the accelerator a little harder, and I held on to the side of the door, feeling once more that my life was no longer under my control and still unsure whether that was a good thing or not.

CHAPTER 9

I deliberately arrived at the Tradd Street house earlier than when I knew the others were expected. I had something to do that might be construed as sentimental, and that was one label I had avoided since about the time I was old enough to know what it meant.

I parked my car at the curb, then picked up the small bag on the seat next to me. At the gate I paused, as had become my habit, to see if I could hear the sound of a rope swing. Satisfied that the only noises from the garden were those that should be there, I pushed open the gate and made my way to the front door. After fumbling for my keys and turning the lock, the door swung open, and I was greeted by the high-pitched beep of the new alarm warning me that a door had been opened.

Turning to the number panel behind the door, I typed in the four-digit code, 1221—easily remembered because the digits corresponded to the letters ABBA—and the annoying sound went away. I still wasn't quite convinced that Jack's insistence on getting the alarm as soon as possible was warranted, but since this would be my first night alone in the house, it did give me a measure of reassurance. Of course, experience had also made me realize that all threats weren't necessarily of the living, breathing kind.

I set down my briefcase and purse inside the door, then carried the small bag to the dining room. This room was separated from the opulent drawing room by large mahogany pocket doors that were stuck at a half-open position, warped from water and age. I turned sideways to fit through the opening, then moved to the massive breakfront that dominated the wall between the two floor-to-ceiling windows. The piece of furniture seemed to hold up the rose-patterned wallpaper that drooped from the ceiling like the sagging shoulders of an old man, the roses themselves freckled with mildew and yellowed glue.

Carefully, I put the bag down on the inlaid cherrywood dining table and pulled out the china plate that Mr. Vanderhorst had given to me on my first visit to the house, recalling what he'd said to me when I'd tried to give it back to him. *It will be back amongst the other plates sooner than you'd think.* Had he known then that he was about to die? I had pretty much figured out that he'd picked me as his victim to inherit his albatross as soon as I admitted I could see the woman outside. As for him knowing that his end was near, I'd had enough experience with the unexplainable to take for granted that he had. Of course, none of that made me any more forgiving toward the likable old man, who had saddled me with my worst nightmare.

I tripped on a floorboard, a gash that looked remarkably like the heel of a boot grabbing at my four-inch heel. I juggled the china plate for a minute until bringing it to safety against my chest. "I'm sorry for thinking bad thoughts about your house," I said aloud just in case anybody was listening. I had no intention of falling through a hole in the floor and ending up where nobody could find me.

Gingerly, I tugged on the glass-and-wood door of the breakfront, tugging harder and harder until the dusty china and crystal inside began to chatter in protest. With one final tug, the door opened, and I sneezed at the puff of dust that blew into my face, bringing with it the unmistakable scent of roses. I ignored the sensation of my hair standing on end at the back of my neck as I scanned the shelves, looking for a place before carefully putting the dessert plate in a spot where it seemed to belong. I shut the door with a small snap and stood for a moment looking inside at all of the crystal and china, and remembered something else Mr. Vanderhorst had told me about his mother and the roses—something about how the china had been designed after the roses that had been named after her. The *Louisa* rose, I recalled. And then I remembered that I wasn't the sentimental type and began wondering what it all might be worth. I made a mental note to ask Mrs. Trenholm when she stopped by.

The doorbell rang, and I went to answer the front door, noticing how the scent of roses gradually dissipated. On the porch stood Mrs.

Houlihan, wearing a large floral muumuu and carrying a casserole dish with two oven mitt–covered hands.

"I'm sorry I'm a little late, but I had to wait for the lasagna to come out of the oven."

"Lasagna?" I asked as I opened the door wide so she could come inside.

"Yes, lasagna." She eyed me from top to bottom. "You're nothing but skin and bones, and besides continuing to clean this house for you, I insist that I also try and feed you."

I closed the door but didn't lock it since I knew that Jack, Sophie and Chad would be there shortly. I followed the housekeeper past the music room with the closed and out-of-tune grand piano and back to the kitchen. "But, Mrs. Houlihan, it's not from lack of eat—"

"I don't want any argument from you. You need to eat good, healthy meals, and I intend to provide them for you. Especially because you're going to need all the energy you've got to restore this old house." She indicated the harvest gold–and–avocado green kitchen that hadn't been updated since President Ford was in office.

"Oh, but I have no intention of actually doing the work myself. . . ."

Mrs. Houlihan snorted as she placed the lasagna on a chipped Formica countertop. "That's what they all say. And then they catch the restoration bug, and they're hooked like some of those kids you hear about nowadays on crack cocaine."

"Trust me, Mrs. Houlihan. That won't be me. I don't even like old houses. Never have. I just want to fulfill my obligation and get the house put back together and then move on."

She looked at me with a raised eyebrow that would have made Scarlett O'Hara proud before returning her attention to the lasagna, gently peeling back the foil cover and letting the smell of marinara-and-meat sauce tease my nose. "Well, we'll have to see about that. In the meantime, I'm going to feed you, so please don't argue with me, Miss Melanie."

I felt a little guilty, but I *had* tried to refuse. It wasn't my fault she was bossier than me. "All right. But only because you insist."

"I do insist. And it's the least I can do to thank you for letting me keep my job after poor Mr. Vanderhorst passed."

She leaned forward and sniffed the wonderful aroma creeping out from around the foil cover. I was having warm and fond thoughts about the large woman and was about to offer her a raise when she said, "And since I made extra, I invited your father to join you for dinner. He said he could be here around five thirty."

Following my initial shock, I opened my mouth to tell her that the chance of my father actually dragging himself from a bar to show up somewhere on time was about the same chance I had of actually falling in love with restoring this pile of termite-infested lumber. We were both saved by the doorbell. I felt annoyed as I went to answer it because whoever had rung the bell hadn't walked in like I'd told them to do.

I opened the door to find Sophie standing in front of me holding the little black-and-white dog that I had inherited but had blessedly forgotten about. Sophie wore an oversized red-and-blue-paisley peasant blouse held on to her body by a swinging hemp rope. She had gone all the way out on the limb of bad taste and paired it with black stirrup pants, identical to the ones that I had once worn in the eighties but had been given to Goodwill long before the fashion trend had ended. On her feet were her ubiquitous Birkenstocks and, wrapped around her hair like a headband, was a red-and-white kerchief that remarkably matched her eyes.

She sneezed loudly, startling the small dog and making him leap from her arms and come stand next to me. He looked up at me with soulful eyes that I felt sure were designed to take people off guard. I gave him a suspicious look before turning my attention back to Sophie. "What's wrong? Do you have a cold?"

She shook her head and sneezed again, causing the little dog to press up against my leg. "I think I might be allergic to dogs." Because her nose seemed to be congested, most of her vowels were slurred, and her consonants were dropped entirely so it took me a moment to realize what she was saying.

I looked down at the little dog in horror. There was no way I was going to be forced to become a dog owner on top of everything else. "Maybe you just need to give it a little more time to know for sure."

"Trust me," she said, sounding more like "Tuss me." "I know what an allergic reaction is, and having red eyes that would make Stephen King proud would count."

"Maybe you've just developed a new allergy to your carpet or something," I suggested hopefully.

"Nice try, Melanie, but it's time to face the fact that General Lee is yours," she said as she stepped into the foyer. "He's a sweet little guy, once you get to know him. No trouble at all—unless you happen to be allergic." She sneezed again to punctuate her words.

I eyed the little dog. "I guess I could always take him to a shelter and hope he gets adopted."

"Don't you dare," she said, and I thought I saw the dog's brown eyes widen in horror and indignation. He even took a step away from me.

"I was just kidding," I said to him more than Sophie, shutting the door and turning the handle to test the key in the dead bolt to make sure that it was unlocked. "And why did you ring the doorbell? I told you I would leave the door unlocked."

"It was locked. You must have forgotten."

I looked back at the door as if it could reassure me. "That's odd. I distinctly remember unlocking it. And I didn't have to unlock it to let you in, either."

Before she could respond, the doorbell rang again. General Lee let out a bark to let me know there was someone at the door, just in case I had missed hearing the doorbell. Annoyed, I grabbed the handle to throw open the door and berate the newcomer about ringing the doorbell when I'd left the door unlocked, and found myself jerked back by the locked door.

"What the . . . ?" I asked as I unlocked the door and threw it open to find Jack and Chad chatting like old friends.

Chad's hair was pulled back in a ponytail, and he carried what looked like a yoga mat under his arm. He saw me looking at it and grinned. "Didn't want to leave this on my bike so it could get stolen."

"Good idea," I said as I scanned the curb in front of the house, looking for a Harley or at least something with a motor. Instead, I found what looked suspiciously like a Schwinn, complete with a basket on the front and no hand brakes.

"Nice bike, man," said Jack, catching on to the Left Coast lingo. I shook my head and stepped back, then let the two men enter.

Chad looked up at the ceiling and dropped his mat. "Wow, Melanie, this house is yours? This is like awesome."

I made a mental note to suggest a few speech classes during his winter break.

Chad continued to spin around to take in everything. "This is totally great. It's like taking an architecture class just standing here, you know? A few years back I helped a friend of mine back in San Francisco restore his old house in the Marina District for room and board. Hard work, man, but I've never had so much fun in my life."

"So you know a lot about restoration work?" Even I heard the excitement in my voice.

He shrugged. "I wouldn't say I know a lot, but I do know how to strip paint and plaster a wall. And I'm awesome with an electric floor sander."

I was already adding his name to my mental spreadsheet when I felt Jack poke me in the middle of my back. I grunted and shot him a look.

I turned back to Chad. "Chad, there's somebody I want you to meet."

But when I faced Sophie, she was vigorously shaking her head. I would have liked to think that it was because she was embarrassed about her outfit but knew it was something else entirely. Even I had to admit that with her flaming eyes and running nose, she definitely wasn't looking her best, although with Chad I was pretty sure that none of that would matter.

Chad was already moving toward her. "I thought that was you. Weren't you in my yoga class this morning?"

Sophie sniffed, then nodded, looking miserable. "Yes. That was me."

"Did you enjoy the class? I haven't been teaching that long, so it's like, you know, hard to tell if people are having a good time yet or not."

She nodded again but continued to look miserable, definitely not the reaction I'd imagined. I didn't hear wedding bells at all. Instead I imagined the discordant crash of two hands falling on a keyboard. "It was the best class I've ever been to."

"Glad to hear it." He reached into his back pocket and pulled out a cleaned and pressed white linen handkerchief. Jack and I exchanged looks as Chad handed it to Sophie. Reluctantly, she took it and then dabbed her eyes before blowing her nose in it like a goose signaling its friends in the back of the "v" formation.

Chad squatted down and began scratching a grateful General Lee behind the ears. "Dog allergies, huh? I used to have them as a kid, but since I've been eating organically, I've found that I don't really react as much to stuff that used to make me sneeze."

Because he'd used a sentence with the word "organic" in it, I thought that Sophie would immediately fall on her knees and propose marriage. Instead she managed to look even more miserable.

I stepped forward. "Sophie, I'd like you to meet a client of mine, Chad Arasi. He's new to town and will be teaching art history at the college. Chad, I'd like you to meet my good friend Dr. Sophie Warren. She's a professor of historical preservation at the college. Isn't that great? You're colleagues!" I sounded so much like a cheerleader during the last seconds of the final quarter that I didn't even grunt this time when Jack poked me again in the middle of my back.

Chad stuck out his hand to shake but dropped it when Sophie held hers up and waved the wadded up handkerchief. "Awesome. You're the first colleague I've met. Maybe you can show me around, give me some tips and stuff."

"Yeah. That would be great," she muttered with the same sort of enthusiasm one would give to taking out the garbage. In the rain.

The old grandfather clock in the front drawing room chimed three o'clock, reminding me of my schedule. I clapped my hands together. "Okay, everybody. Since we're all here, let me go over the schedule for the rest of the afternoon. Sophie, I need you to finish the inventory and then give me an idea of what we should start on first. I've already met with one roofing contractor, and I have an appointment to meet with another tomorrow afternoon, so I've got that covered. As far as what to do next, I haven't a clue. I was also hoping you'd give me a list of maybe some of the supplies I need to get."

"Yo—I can help Sophie with that." Chad rubbed his hands together in anticipation.

Sophie's eyes widened. "I thought Melanie was taking you out to see some properties this afternoon."

"Yes, actually, I am." I glanced at my watch. "And if we don't hurry, we'll miss our first appointment."

Chad glanced from me, to Sophie, then up at the sagging wallpaper. "I don't know, Melanie. Looks like Sophie could really use my help today. Besides, I was thinking that the warehouse spaces on East Bay you were going to show me today might not work anyhow. It's a long trip on my bike to the school, you know?"

I sighed, trying not to show my annoyance. After all, I seemed to be getting an extra pair of hands, at least for the rest of the day. "Fine," I said, resigned. "I'll look over any properties in your budget that are near the college and call you tomorrow with a game plan."

Chad sent me two thumbs-up and smiled with his blindingly white teeth. "Sounds like a plan." He turned to smile at Sophie, and she sent him a weary grin. I'd have to sit her down and have a talk. In my mind they should already be married, and I couldn't understand why Sophie wasn't seeing it, too.

The sound of something small but heavy falling onto the wood floor came from the drawing room. General Lee had fallen asleep at Chad's feet, and I could still hear Mrs. Houlihan in the kitchen, and the rest of us were all together still in the foyer. Jack must have reached the same conclusion since he indicated for us to stand behind him as he approached the drawing room. From his vantage point at the threshold, he had a clear view of the entire empty room. He straightened and I followed him as he walked over to the grandfather clock before bending down again to retrieve something from the floor.

It was the old photo of Mr. Vanderhorst and his mother on the piano bench—the same photo that I had most recently seen on the table by the sofa. Across the room. I moved to Jack's side to take the frame from him, and it was then that I noticed the heavy scent of roses. "Do you smell that?" I asked.

Jack's eyebrows furrowed. "Smell what?"

Chad and Sophie followed us into the drawing room as Chad sniffed one of his underarms. "It's not me, whatever it is you're smelling."

I watched as Sophie hid a smile. "Never mind," I said. I looked down at the portrait of mother and son in my hands and felt a cold breath on my cheek. I glanced up quickly, meeting Jack's eyes.

"What is it?" Jack asked quietly, his eyes measuring.

We looked at each other for a long moment before I turned away. "Nothing," I said. I smiled at Sophie and Chad. "Mrs. Houlihan must have put it on top of the clock or something while she was dusting, and forgot about it. The vibrations from the chiming clock probably knocked it loose."

I felt three pairs of eyes staring at me, but not one of them said anything about how tall the clock was or even about how a fall onto hardwood floors didn't break the glass on the frame. I rubbed the glass against my skirt to get the dust off of it and returned it to its place by the sofa.

When I turned around, Sophie was standing on her tiptoes and peering at the face of the clock. "Did you know this is a William Johnstone, Melanie?"

I shook my head. "Who's he?" I didn't know a lot about antique clocks, and I was happy to keep it that way.

Sophie shook her head. "Only about the most prominent clock maker in the country around the time of the Civil War. Not a lot of examples of his work remain locally, which is odd since he was from Charleston. But his rate of production was pretty slow, which could also be the reason why there aren't too many examples left."

Jack peered at the naval scene painted on the face. "I also seem to recall that he was a Confederate cavalry officer. And very good friends with your Mr. Vanderhorst, Mellie."

Sophie pulled on the brass handle of the glass door covering the face of the clock. "This is really weird," she said, straining to see higher.

"What?" I asked, peering over her shoulder.

She pointed to the demilune painting that filled the top quarter of the face. "On all of the Johnstone clocks I've seen or studied, they always have pastoral scenes. It was sort of his trademark. His mother was Dutch, and before the war they always had dairy cows on their plantation on the Ashley. But this—" She shook her head. "The face shows what looks like a battle scene from Charleston Harbor, and the little rotating half-circle inset which shows daylight and nighttime looks like a bunch of signal flags in a row. I wonder if they say anything." She put her heels down and faced us. "The picture makes a full rotation every twenty-four hours, so we could take a picture every three hours to get the whole thing."

I felt three pairs of eyes on me again. "I go to bed at nine thirty. Ten on weekends—tops. Besides, with the condition of the rest of the house, this should be on the very bottom of the priority list."

Jack cleared his throat. "Since I love mysteries, and I'm a night owl, I'll volunteer to sleep on the couch with a camera." He grinned innocently at me. "You won't even know I'm here."

"That's doubtful," I said, frowning but feeling an unmistakable rush of excitement traipse up my spine. I hadn't really been all that thrilled about spending a night alone in the big house by myself, and his presence—anybody's presence, I tried to convince myself—would be welcome. "But go ahead if you want. Just know that I'll be very cranky if my sleep is disrupted."

Jack winked. "And that would be different how . . . ?"

Sophie snorted and Chad coughed into his hand. I sent them both a glaring look.

Sophie began backing out of the room and Chad followed her. "I'd better get busy with this inventory. It could take a while."

Chad sent us a small wave. "Later, dudes," he said before disappearing with Sophie.

I was about to protest being called a "dude" when Jack drew my attention back to the clock. He had pulled aside the curtain next to it, revealing the penciled lines I had discovered on my first visit to the house with Mr. Vanderhorst.

"MBG—this must be the growth chart you were telling me about."

I stood next to him, appreciating the smell of his cologne but trying very hard not to show it. "Yeah. It's sweet, isn't it?"

"What did you say it stood for?"

He stood very close to me in the crowded space, and I focused my gaze on the chart. "My best guy. Mr. Vanderhorst said that's what his mother called him."

I sensed him nodding. "Not the sort of thing a mother would call a son she planned to abandon."

"I thought the same thing." I brushed my hand over a section of the small lettering. "I was thinking about covering this whole part of the wall with clear Plexiglas to preserve it when we repaint the wall."

He didn't say anything, so I turned my head, too late realizing that we were almost nose to nose.

"Careful, Mellie," he said quietly. "People might begin to think that you're getting sentimental."

I felt flustered and breathless all at the same time. I took a quick step back. "I'm not getting sentimental—just practical. Preserving that part of the house's history could make it more valuable."

His eyes continued to bore into mine but he didn't say anything. He didn't have to.

I began to back away. "I've got to get back to the office and make a few phone calls. I'll be back later to help you in the attic."

I was almost out of the room before he said, "Bye, Mellie."

I faced him, glad to have something to be angry about. "I think I've told you, Jack, that I don't like being called 'Mellie.'"

With a self-righteous toss of my hair, I spun around and headed for the front door, pleased to have had the last word. I almost had it closed behind me when I heard Jack call out, "Bye, dude."

I slammed the door, then covered my mouth with my hand so nobody could hear me laugh.

CHAPTER 10

I arrived back at the house around six thirty, dismayed to find my father's car parked at the curb. The only thought that saved me from sinking into a complete funk was the fact that Chad had called me earlier to ask if he could take General Lee home with him until I was ready to take care of the little dog. Feigning uncertainty, which I'm sure didn't fool Chad at all, I'd agreed.

As I fumbled for my keys on the front porch, I spoke to the closed door. "Don't mess with me tonight. I am not in the mood."

The door was reassuringly locked as I pressed my key into the lock and turned it, the warm aromas of lasagna and garlic bread greeting me through the opened door. Still clutching my bags of supplies from the local home-improvement store, purchased with a list from Sophie, I resignedly followed the sound of male voices coming from the drawing room.

I was relieved to find that Mrs. Houlihan had taken the dust covers off of the rest of the furniture, and I could smell polish and vinegar melding with that of the food. Despite the tired ruin of the once resplendent room, it did appear marginally brighter. My father sat on the sofa and was in the middle of a conversation with Jack, who sat perched on a Chippendale chair opposite. I tensed as they both turned to me.

Jack stood and approached me with outstretched arms. "Let me take those." He peeked inside. "Looks like you're going to have a lot of stuff to put on your work sheet."

Ignoring him, I took a seat next to his chair, while he placed the packages on the floor next to the grandfather clock. Two tall glasses of what looked like ice water sat on coasters on the dark wood coffee table that crouched low to the floor on ball and claw feet.

"Hello, Dad. I'm surprised to see you here."

He smiled, the old smile I remembered from when I was a young girl and he was still the perfect father. "Mrs. Houlihan called and I couldn't resist the offer of a home-cooked meal."

I wondered if that was meant to be a dig at me for not cooking for my father at all, much less on a regular basis. But I thought not. He and I had long since progressed from mere digs. "I meant that bars are usually open by now, aren't they? I didn't expect you here for dinner."

He flinched and I looked away, feeling sorry for both of us. But it was hard to find forgiveness for a man who'd taught his ten-year-old daughter how to force an aspirin down the throat of a drunk man so that he'd be able to face going to work the next morning. And I couldn't forget how that same ten-year-old had learned to wake up early and get herself ready for school so that she could make sure her father actually made it to work.

Jack picked up both glasses. "Looks like we could both use a refill. Can I get you anything, Mellie?"

My dad's eyes searched my face for some sort of reaction to the name but I wouldn't give him the satisfaction. "Sweet tea, please. With lemon."

We listened to Jack's footsteps disappearing down the hallway. My dad leaned on his elbows, his hands folded together. I noticed they were shaking but he seemed unable to make it stop. "Your mother called again. She was wondering if I'd given you her message."

My eyes met his. "What did you tell her?"

He shrugged and I noticed his shoulders were softer than I remembered, rounded like an old man's. It was with a little jolt that I realized he would be sixty-five in a couple of years, a senior citizen and not the handsome, young father in the sharp-looking uniform anymore. But he hadn't been that man for a very long time. Sometimes, I even wondered if I'd made him up in my young girl dreams—a fantasy I had devised to soften the edges of my life.

"I told her that you would call her when you were ready. And that I didn't think it would be anytime soon. She said she had something important to tell you."

I looked down at my clasped hands, noticing the whiteness at the tips from clenching them too tightly. I felt the old anger, born of grief and abandonment, tumble through my veins like a storm surge. Meeting my father's eyes, I said, "If she calls you again, please let her know that I got her message."

His eyes widened. "Are you going to call her back?"

"No."

Jack walked back into the room and gave us our drinks. I took mine and gulped it until all that was left was clinking ice, trying to fill that part of me that had remained empty for so many years.

Jack watched me as I placed my glass back on the coaster. I gave him a look I hoped he understood meant to remain silent, then dug in my purse for the receipt for the supplies. I slid it across the coffee table to my father. "Here's the receipt from today's shopping trip, and I'm sure there's going to be a lot more. I had the alarm company send the bill directly to you, so you should be getting that anyday now." I swallowed, trying to find a nonchalant tone to continue. "I am going to suggest opening up a separate checking account for me to write checks on and have access to cash for use on the house. I can supply you with the receipts on a monthly basis for you to verify where the funds are being spent. That way, you won't have to come here at all."

My father coughed and gave Jack a quick glance. "Melanie, about that. I . . . uh . . . that's one of the things I wanted to talk with you about tonight. I'd actually like to be more involved than just doling out the money." He sent me a weak smile. "I'd like to swing a hammer, strip some wallpaper. That sort of thing. It would be good for me. For us."

I swallowed, my mouth suddenly dry, and I wished that I hadn't drunk all of my iced tea. "And what would be the purpose of that?"

"I've been sober for six days now. That's the longest I've ever been sober since I started drinking. I think it's a good start. And maybe"—he looked down at his trembling hands—"and maybe it means we've got a chance to start over."

I put my hands on my temples and rubbed, trying to ward off the headache I knew was approaching. "Dad, I'm glad to know you're trying. Really, I am. And six days is a good start. But I can't . . ." I closed my eyes, pressing harder on my temples. "I just can't pretend that it's a chance for us to start over. I've done it so many times that I just don't think I could take the disappointment one more time."

Jack cleared his throat. "Why don't you give him a probationary period or something? Put him on your schedule. Make him responsible for showing up and getting his jobs done. I'll even be in charge of that if it makes it easier. That way you're sort of removed from the process."

"It won't work. It never does." I grabbed my empty glass and tilted it so that I got a few drops of melted water.

"Give him a chance, Mellie. Everybody deserves another chance."

I eyed Jack's water glass and suddenly it all made sense to me. The reason Jack and my dad had so much to say to each other. The way Jack knew my father had started in AA again. And then I thought of Mr. Vanderhorst, who'd never given up believing his mother loved him, despite all the facts that said otherwise, and whose dying wish was to prove that he was right.

I looked at Jack and then my father. "Fine," I said, standing. "Fine. But Jack's in charge where you're concerned. And the first time that you don't show up when you're supposed to will be the last time."

My dad nodded. "That's fair. And I promise that I won't disappoint you."

I slowly exhaled. "Forgive me if I don't jump up and down with excitement, Dad, but I've heard that before."

I felt a blast of warm outside air as if someone had thrown open a window. The mosquitoes in Charleston in the summertime were legendary, and I was pretty sure that none of the people currently in the house would have been stupid enough to leave a window open. Except for Jack, maybe, because the reasoning and thought-processing center in his brain seemed to be damaged.

I stepped into the foyer and was met by the wide-open front door. I rushed to close it, noticing how the dead bolt was out, but not connected to the doorjamb. Nor was there any damage to the woodwork surrounding the door that might indicate a forced entry.

My dad stooped to examine the bolt. "Looks like you didn't close the door all the way before you bolted it."

Our eyes met, and I saw in his the same denial he had been practicing with me since I was very small and had first seen the old woman in the long dress knitting in a rocking chair in the corner of my bedroom. Never mind that I'd described his grandmother perfectly, he'd insisted—and still would, I was sure—that it was my active imagination.

"That must be it," I said as I closed the door firmly and slid the latch so everyone could hear.

My dad tugged on the doorknob, just to make sure. "Still, Melanie, I don't like the fact that you'll be here all by yourself at night."

Jack stepped forward. "Oh, no need to worry about that at least for tonight, Colonel. I'll be sleeping over."

My father's eyes widened as his eyebrows went up high enough to almost touch his receding hairline. "I beg your pardon?"

"Dad, it's not what you think," I hastened, spearing Jack with what I hoped was a chastising look. "Jack's sleeping on the couch down here tonight to take pictures of the grandfather clock. It has an unusual face that can't be seen all at once without taking it apart. He's going to take photos of it every three hours so that we can get a complete picture."

Jack grinned, and my father's face returned to normal at the same time Mrs. Houlihan arrived to tell us that dinner was ready and waiting for us in the dining room. I followed her, the two men behind me allowing me to hear their conversation.

"Sorry, sir, for the misunderstanding. I never meant to insinuate that your daughter was in any danger from me."

I heard a soft snort. "It wasn't her I was worried about, son."

They both laughed softly until I turned around to glare at them. With a bit of throat clearing and coughing, they continued to follow me into the dining room.

∞

I sat at the Victorian dressing table in Mr. Vanderhorst's old room, feeling the cold marble tabletop with my fingertips. Mrs. Houlihan had boxed up all of Mr. Vanderhorst's personal property to be donated to charity later, but it still didn't feel like anybody else's room except his. It was past ten o'clock but I didn't feel sleepy. Part of that could have been because of the exertion required to turn on the taps and regulate the bathwater temperature in the clawfoot tub in the antiquated bathroom. After tonight, updating the plumbing had climbed to the number-two position on my list—right after the roof—and it couldn't happen soon enough.

My father had left around eight thirty, following a delicious dinner filled with wonderful food and stilted conversation. He and I were experts at dancing around the obvious, so neither one of us spoke unless spoken to, leaving Jack to carry the conversation. Fortunately, this was something he seemed adept at, or else he just enjoyed hearing himself talk. We had dessert in the drawing room, and Mrs. Houlihan used the rose plates, explaining that they had been Mr. Vanderhorst's favorites because they had belonged to his mother.

After my father left, Jack climbed the stairs to the attic—protected now by a tarp over the roof—and said he planned to work there all night, setting an alarm to remind him to take a picture of the clock every three hours. He insisted on sleeping on the couch if he needed to, but I still had Mrs. Houlihan put fresh sheets in a guest bedroom as far away down the hall as I could find.

I pulled down the sheets and set my alarm for six o'clock in the morning, then turned out the light just as the grandfather clock downstairs chimed the half hour. I lay in the four-poster rice bed staring up at the ceiling, dimly lit by the streetlight outside, and listened to the creaks and sighs of the house, reminding me of an elderly person trying to settle down at night. Listening to old houses was usually an activity that I wholeheartedly avoided because it invariably ended with me hearing something I didn't want to, but this house was different. I had no illusions as to what was going on with the front door. But other than the door, the fallen picture, and the occasional scent of roses, I had a feeling that the house—and its inhabitants—was remaining dutifully quiet. It was either that, or they were merely waiting. I closed my eyes and listened to a tree branch brush against a window shutter, and felt that I, too, was waiting. For what, I wasn't sure.

I heard a door shut and then the sound of Jack's footsteps coming from the attic and making their way down the hall to the bathroom. I had begun to drift off to sleep when a loud curse jerked me upright and out of the bed. After tossing on my robe and putting on my fuzzy slippers, I threw open my door and ran to the bathroom, a golden line of light showing from underneath the door.

I knocked loudly. "Jack? Are you all right?"

"Mmhmphmm."

"What?"

"Mmhmphmm."

"If you're not going to speak English, I'm going to open this door and come in."

I heard the door handle turn and then the door opened, allowing me to spot a shirtless Jack with a towel pressed against his face.

I stepped inside, noticing too late how very nice he looked without his shirt. Even if I couldn't see his face. "What's wrong? Did you catch sight of your reflection?"

My words at least got a reluctant folding down of the towel from the top portion of his face. "I was trying to wash the dust off my face and hands without getting my shirt wet. And now it's my turn for a question. Would you please tell me why scalding-hot water comes out of your cold-water tap?"

I eyed the offending sink. "I have no idea and please don't call it mine. I'll call a plumber first thing." I took my time staring at his bare torso since he'd put the towel back over his face. "And I'll get an estimate on what it would take to add a few bathrooms upstairs so that people don't have to share. That would really help the market value." But then I'd miss seeing things like a nice male chest.

"I'm a seventeen, thirty-six."

"Excuse me?" I said, coloring. He'd taken the towel off of his face while I'd been busy staring. I had hoped he hadn't seen me. I didn't think his ego needed the stroking.

"That's my shirt size. It looked like you were measuring me for a new one."

"I wasn't . . . ," I said, backing out of the bathroom and stubbing my heel on the doorframe.

He grinned. "But I'm glad you're awake. There's something I want to show you."

"That's the oldest line in the book," I said, seeing that he was leading me to the guest bedroom.

"Fine," he said, not slowing or looking back. "But I thought you might be interested in seeing Louisa's photo album."

That had my attention. Pulling the belt on my robe tighter, I eagerly followed him into the far bedroom at the end of the hall.

The large leather-bound album sat in the middle of the bed, the cover cracked and peeling as if it had been handled many times. I noticed Jack had placed a sheet beneath it to protect the bedspread from dust, and my estimation of him went up a notch.

"How do you know it's hers?" I asked as I approached the book, being careful not to touch it.

Without saying anything, he reached across me and carefully turned the front cover back. The words were too small for me to read, and I hadn't brought my reading glasses. I squinted, trying to hide this fact from Jack, but, of course, he caught on right away.

"I keep on forgetting that you're older than me, Mellie. Here, let me read them out loud."

I stewed in silence as he began to read: *To Louisa with all my love, given to you on the occasion of the birth of our first child, Nevin Pinckney Vanderhorst. May these pages, once filled, illustrate the love we have for each other and for our son. A love that will never diminish with the passage of time.*

I love you forever,

Robert.

On the first page, facing the dedication, was a sepia-toned wedding photograph of Louisa and Robert, one identical to the framed photo in my bedroom. But this time I looked closer and noticed the roses in her veil and in her bouquet: Louisa roses.

"Wow," I said, my voice cracking and my annoyance with Jack forgotten. "It's dated nineteen twenty-one—nine years before her disappearance. Either this whole thing is a complete lie, or a lot changed in nine years."

He stood next to me, as if waiting to see if I would turn the page, but I didn't. I didn't move. The temperature in the room had dropped, and I wondered if Jack was aware that I could see his breath now when he spoke.

"There're about nine more of these albums—one for each year would be my guess. I left them up in the attic for now. But look what else I found," he said, turning to an oak captain's chest at the foot of the bed.

I turned slowly, feeling the hair on the back of my neck and arms stand on end, alarmed because I didn't smell the roses.

He lifted a small, boxy antique camera, its lightness apparent by the way Jack held it in the palm of his hand. "This is a Brownie—the very first handheld camera. It was invented for the everyday person because it was easy to use and only cost a dollar. You told me that Nevin's mother liked to take photographs of him, so I'm assuming this might have been hers."

I reached my hand up to touch the camera but pulled back.

"Are you all right?" He put the camera back down and shivered. "And something's wrong with your central air-conditioning. It's freezing in here." He reached for the shirt he'd thrown on the bed and began putting it on.

My voice was stiff. "There isn't any."

He stopped buttoning midway up the shirt. "There isn't any what?"

"Central air," I whispered, barely able to speak. I'd felt the other presence, the non-roses presence. And I'd begun to smell rotting earth and decaying flesh, but I couldn't seem to find the energy to raise my hand to my nose. *I am stronger than you. I am stronger than you.*

Jack was looking at me oddly. "There's something wrong here, isn't there? Do you see something?"

I swallowed, forcing bile down my throat as I saw the distinct shadow of a man begin to solidify behind Jack. "I don't feel so good," I bit out through frozen jaws. "Can we go downstairs?"

His expression turned to one of concern as he moved to take my arm. At that moment something punched me in my back, making the air leave my lungs in a loud whoosh and sending me sprawling facedown on the rug in the hallway. I tasted wool and dust and decay, making me gag.

"Are you all right?" Jack knelt by my side, peering into my face. "What happened?"

I tried to sit up and catch my breath at the same time, thankful doing so gave me a little time to think of an answer. Jack pulled me into a sitting position, keeping his arm around my shoulders, which I'm sure I might have appreciated at another time.

"I tripped."

"But you were standing still."

"I'm really clumsy," I said, trying to stand so that I could put more distance between me and the dark shadow that now filled the doorway.

"Hold on," Jack said, pressing down on my shoulders. "We need to see if you're hurt."

"I'm fine," I said, managing to pull away from him.

His next words were drowned out by the explosion of sound from something large, heavy, and glass crashing downstairs.

"Can you stand?" Jack asked, urgently tugging on my hand.

I tested both feet, then nodded.

"Let's go." He held on to my hand as he pulled me toward the stairs, flipping on the foyer chandelier. We peered over the railing into the foyer and saw nothing except the general dilapidation and neglect we'd grown used to.

"What in the hell do you think that was?" he asked.

I shook my head, more afraid than I ever remembered being, and definitely more than I would ever admit. We moved down the stairs, then stood at the bottom, listening.

"Where do you think that came from?" Jack asked.

"I'm not sure but I have a good idea." I led him into the drawing room, my slippered feet crunching on what felt like broken glass. "Flip on the light switch."

All we heard was a buzzing sound and a pop, neither of which was accompanied by light.

Jack quickly switched it off, then followed me as I walked into the center of the room, the light from the foyer glinting off hundreds of crystal shards that had erupted all over the Aubusson rug. My foot hit something large and I stopped, then looked down at what I'd kicked and found the supine body of the shattered chandelier lying prostrate on the floor and strongly resembling an octopus carcass with its broken arms and pendants scattered around it. A gaping hole in the center of the ceiling medallion spewed out electrical wires, and the plaster surrounding it appeared to be contemplating a suicide leap.

Jack stood beside me, looking at the wreckage of what had once been merely a shabby drawing room. "Looks like fixing the plumbing isn't going to be your next priority."

I was about to make a glib comment when the grandfather clock began to chime the midnight hour. Jack crunched over to the end table, where he'd left his camera, and took a picture of the face of the clock, the flash illuminating the room and the slight figure of a woman standing by the growth chart. And then the room was dark again, leaving only the strong scent of roses.

CHAPTER 11

I sat at my desk hunched over approximately a dozen architecture textbooks that Sophie had been kind enough to lend to me. I stared bleary-eyed at yet another example of an Adamesque fireplace mantel, this one complete with pilasters and floral and swag decorations. Or were they called incised wood carvings and stucco relief decorations with floral sprays?

Closing my eyes, I leaned forward until my forehead rested on the detailed illustrations of a Federal-style pediment and a Georgian-style pediment, both of which looked identical to me despite the fact that I had just spent the last forty-five minutes studying them and the other sticky-note-marked pages of Sophie's books. Granted, I knew enough of vague lingo to sell an old house to unsuspecting future owners, but apparently not nearly enough to actually restore one. And somehow my blank stare in response to Sophie's instructions about how to remove layers of paint from the upstairs drawing room mantel (involving really tiny brushes and razors) had made her put on her teacher persona and tell me I had to learn the importance and rarity of what was in the house before I'd be allowed near anything with a brush, much less a razor.

Besides, she explained, I couldn't look like a fool if I ever had to go before the dreaded Board of Architectural Review during the restoration process. Being ignorant could make the difference between a new roof or living with patchwork.

Adding insult to injury, I reached for my latte cup only to find it empty. So was the bag of doughnuts sitting next to it. I sat up and began to dig beneath the pile of books to find my phone and ask Nancy if she'd made the coffee yet. I hadn't seen her when I'd come in, but I knew she was in the building because I'd spotted her hybrid SUV in the parking lot with the "Have You Hugged Your Clubs Today?" bumper sticker.

Before I had the chance to push the button, my phone rang. I picked it up. "Hi, Nancy."

"Good morning, Miss Middleton. You have a visitor."

I frowned into the receiver. "Nancy? Why are you acting like a receptionist is supposed to? It's weird."

"Yes, ma'am. I'll have him wait a few moments while you finish with your client."

"What's going on, Nancy? Is it Jack?"

She waited a few moments while I presumed the visitor made his way to the waiting area. Then I had to press my ear to the receiver to hear her because she was now whispering. "It's him. That Marc guy who keeps calling and who never leaves a return number. He's here and he wants to see you. And his last name's Longo."

I sat up straighter. Going on Jack's hunch that there were no coincidences, he and I had tried to find out more about Marc Longo, and had even spent time in a coffee shop outside where his office supposedly was to get a glimpse of him, but the elusive Mr. Longo apparently didn't want to be found.

"So why are you whispering?"

There was a slight pause. "Wait until you see him. He doesn't seem the type to put up with anything bordering on casual."

"Thanks for the warning. Don't send him back, okay? I'll come up and get him."

I used the small hand mirror in my drawer while I wiped off any stray doughnut crumbs or powdered sugar and applied fresh lipstick before heading up to the waiting area. I'd worn my new aqua silk Elie Tahari suit with knockout Manolo Blahnik pumps and knew I looked good and certainly ready to meet a guy whose appearance was enough to make Nancy Flaherty nervous.

Nancy raised her eyebrows as I rounded the reception desk and headed toward the bank of sofas and tables arranged around the front bay window. Marc Longo was busy typing something into his BlackBerry but looked up and stood as I entered.

He was very tall, with dark hair and eyes; he wore a custom-made suit complete with French cuffs and Gucci loafers. Definitely *GQ* material, and if this had been a social setting, I would have stumbled over my own name during the introduction and tripped over my Manolos. Drooling would probably be added to the equation. But this was business, and I slid my businesswoman persona on like a suit and extended my hand.

"Mr. Longo? I'm Melanie Middleton. What can I do for you?"

His handshake was firm, his skin soft, making me think he was probably the type of guy who got manicures. Not necessarily a bad thing, but I did have a problem with guys who had softer hands than I did.

"Thanks for seeing me without an appointment." He smiled, revealing perfect white teeth set off nicely by his tanned skin. "I'd like to talk with you about real estate. I've heard you're the best."

I blushed under his flattering stare. "I don't know if I'm the best, but I do work very hard for my clients. Why don't we go back to my office so we can talk more?" I turned to Nancy. "Could you please bring us coffee? And hold my calls."

"Yes, Miss Middleton," she said, raising her eyebrow and smirking when she thought Mr. Longo wasn't looking.

I led the way and felt his eyes on my back, making me self-conscious but grateful I'd worn my SPANX. When Sophie gave me grief when she found out I wore them, I'd scoffed at her, reminding her that even skinny girls had visible panty lines.

I sat down at my desk and drew out a blank paper pad and indicated for my visitor to sit at the chair on the other side of my desk. I noticed his interest in my architecture books as he sat. "What can I do for you, Mr. Longo?"

"Please," he said, leaning forward, "call me Marc."

"All right, Marc." I smiled, not sure why he was making me nervous. Maybe it was because his dark eyes never left my face. Or because he was probably the most gorgeous man I'd ever been this close to with the exception of pictures in a magazine. Or maybe it was because of his last name and possible connection to the man who might have been behind Louisa's disappearance. Either way, I was completely unnerved, and I had to keep reminding myself that I was a successful businesswoman. "What can I do for you?"

He sat back in his chair, his gaze never leaving my face. "I'd like to make an investment in residential real estate."

I felt the usual excitement rise at the scent of a hot prospect. I was already tallying up in my head the list of high-end new construction on Daniel Island and Isle of Palms that I would show him. I blinked, realizing I'd misunderstood the last part of his sentence. "Excuse me?"

"I said that I'm especially interested in historical real estate."

"Oh," I said, surprised. From his high-end clothing style and apparent self-confidence, he'd struck me as the sort of person who wanted sleek, new, and modern. Lots of stainless steel and white walls. Like my own condo.

"You sound surprised."

I smiled to hide my embarrassment. "It's just, well, you don't seem the type."

"I see." He rested his elbows on the arms of his chair and steepled his fingers. "In what way?"

I felt my leg bouncing furiously under my desk, and I willed it to stop. "Well, for starters, you're single."

He lifted a dark eyebrow.

I blushed a little, wondering why I'd blurted out that little tidbit and trying to find a way out of the hole I seemed to be digging for myself. "I noticed that you're not wearing a wedding ring."

He smiled a warm and engaging smile. "Not every married man wears one. What else?"

I cringed. Even I knew lots of married men who didn't wear rings. "Well, your clothes made me think that you might lean more to . . . contemporary tastes, I guess. Like a sweeping loft space or a glass-walled house on the water."

His fingers tapped against one another on opposing hands. "But I already have those. I wanted something different."

"But . . ." I stopped, confused now but unable to stop digging.

"But what?" he countered.

"You're obviously a successful man, so you've probably made some good decisions in the past regarding investments. Which, to be honest, just boggles my mind as to why on earth . . ."

"Go on." He seemed amused. Almost as if he knew what I was about to say.

I took a deep breath, unable to stop myself. "Why on earth you'd want to spend quite a lot of money on an historical house that will continue to require more and more funds just toward upkeep. They will take their toll on you physically and mentally, and no matter how much care and money you throw at them, you could still end up with a hole in your roof and a termite infestation."

He narrowed his eyes. "I thought your specialty was selling historic real estate."

"It is," I said, confused. Why would I be trying to dissuade a potential client? I wasn't sure of the answer, but I was sure that it had something to do my recent renovation experiences. And how I couldn't picture Marc Longo entrusted with an old Charleston home. *Did I really just think that?*

I continued, trying to recover my ground. "I'm sorry if you think I'm being a bit rough. It's just that most people who love to look at old houses have very little idea of what it's like to actually live in one. I like to lay it all out on the line at this juncture so that there aren't any surprises later."

He nodded. "I appreciate that—but my brother owns the old family Victorian on Montagu Street, so I'm no stranger to the upkeep required. And your honesty is probably why you have such a good reputation in your business."

I felt myself blushing again and focused on the clean notepad in front of me. "Well, now that we're both on the same page, why don't you tell me what you're looking for in terms of size, location, and price? There's not a lot of inventory right now, but if I have a very specific idea of what you're looking for, I can be on the lookout for when something hits the market—and sometimes before."

He smiled. "That should be easy. I know exactly what I want."

I held my pen poised above the blank page, and smiled brightly. "Go ahead, shoot."

"Fifty-five Tradd Street."

I started writing and had almost finished the address before I stopped. "Wait. Did you say Fifty-five Tradd?"

"Yes. I did."

I stared at him for a moment before putting down my pen. "Mr. Longo. Marc. I'm sure you wouldn't be here unless you were aware that I owned that house."

He smiled and nodded slowly. "Of course. I read the paper just like everybody else. Lovely picture of you, by the way." He glanced at my hair but refrained from commenting. "I must say I was initially intrigued by your story when I read who had owned the house before you. The Vanderhorsts and my family have an old connection."

"I know." I had the satisfaction of seeing the surprise in his face.

"Interesting," he said. "I was under the impression that you'd only been inside the house once before you inherited it."

"True. But I did have a nice conversation with Mr. Vanderhorst about the house's past history, including the disappearance of his mother."

"Ah, yes. Poor Mr. Vanderhorst." He crossed an elegant foot across his knee and leaned back.

"Poor Mr. Vanderhorst? Why do you say that?"

Marc shrugged. "From what my father told me, Mr. Vanderhorst never quite believed that his mother could possibly have been attracted to someone like my grandfather."

"And you have evidence to the contrary?" I felt the doughnuts I'd eaten for breakfast flipping over in a single lump. I wanted him to say no. I pictured Mr. Vanderhorst again, looking at the growth chart by the old clock, and realized that I would rather never know the truth of what had happened to Louisa than know for sure that she'd run off with Marc's grandfather.

Marc shrugged again. "It doesn't matter now, does it? What's past is past. I'd rather focus on the present, and that would consist of purchasing your beautiful historical house on Tradd. I found it almost serendipitous that the house with a family connection might actually be available to purchase at the same time I decided to invest in the market."

I thought of the ancient plumbing, warped wood floors, and falling plaster, and my leg started shaking up and down again, the prospect of not having to deal with any of it making me giddy. I pressed my palm against my knee, stilling it, hoping Marc hadn't noticed. And then I remembered the terms of the will and how I couldn't sell so much as a doorknob until a year had passed.

I frowned. "I'm sorry, Marc, to have wasted your time, but the house isn't for sale. Not because I don't want to sell it—believe me—but because I can't. The terms are very specific. I'm to use funds to restore it, but I can't sell it or its contents for a year. So, unless you want me to help you find another house, I'm afraid you'll have to come back in a year."

He thought for a moment, concentrating on his hands. "But if you don't want the house, they can't make you take it, right?"

"Legally, sure. I could walk away and abandon the property and let the law figure out who owns it. But that could take years." *And,* I wanted to add, *if I did that, I might never find out what happened to Mr. Vanderhorst's mother.* The sentimental thought surprised me. For me, the old houses in the historic district had always been about the money. It had never been about anything as sentimental as continuing a legacy or finding an answer for an old man.

Marc returned to steepling his fingers. "I see. Well, then, I guess you need to start showing me other houses."

I studied him carefully. "Marc, before we go any further, I really have to ask—why me? I know of your reputation in real estate development. Surely you have Realtors on staff who know your needs better than I would."

He didn't blink. "Sure. But they don't know Charleston or its historic districts and homes like you do. You're known in the industry as an expert, and if I've learned anything in my years in the business world, it's to always go to the best when you need something done."

I felt myself warming to his praise. "Well, thank you. I'm sure you won't be disappointed with what I can offer you." I sat up, pleased to hear that I hadn't lost a prospect after all. "Now, I'm sure we can find something with as much history as the Vanderhorst house—but hopefully with less work involved." I pulled my pad closer and poised my pen above it again. "All right. For starters, why don't you tell me the square footage you're interested in and how many bedrooms and baths?"

Glancing at his watch, he said, "Actually, I have another appointment I need to get to. Why don't we continue this discussion later?" He smiled. "Perhaps over dinner tomorrow night?"

I realized my mouth was open and made a point to close it. I was pretty sure he was asking me for a date, but he was sitting in front of my desk, so I couldn't pretend to consult my empty evening schedule. "I . . . ah . . . yes, I'm available tomorrow evening."

He stood and reached over to shake my hand, covering mine with both of his. "I'll pick you up at seven o'clock then. Do you like Magnolia's?"

I smiled, relieved he hadn't said Blackbeard's. "It's one of my favorites. I'll see you at seven, then. You know the address."

"I'll see myself out. It was a pleasure meeting you, Melanie. I'll look forward to seeing you again later."

I watched him leave, already thinking about what I would wear. And as I sat back down, I thought about all the turmoil the house had brought into my life, but how it had also managed to bring about the first two dates I'd had in almost as many years.

∞

The house was empty by the time I returned home at around nine o'clock in the evening. Mrs. Houlihan had left dinner on the stove for me on a foil-wrapped rose china plate, and I noticed drop cloths taped into place beneath the curving staircase. Paper face masks, like the kind dentists wore, and sandpaper lay stacked on the bottom step. Apparently somebody was paying attention to my spreadsheet, because I could see that the first spindle had been stripped to its original wood. I glanced up the banister and counted. That left about 106 more to do. By hand. I sigh, tired at the thought of all the work. And that was only the inside.

My footsteps echoed as I stepped into the foyer and considered the exterior work that Sophie had told me would need to be taken care of. Apparently, I wasn't allowed to do anything to the outside of the house—including replacing the roof—until I'd received the go-ahead from the infamous Charleston Board of Architectural Review. Lucky for me, Sophie said she'd handle the three-part application process while I simply sat and stewed about my leaking roof and pictured a nice convenience store or gas station on the lot where the house now stood. So maybe it was a good idea that Sophie dealt with the BAR instead of me.

What remained of the chandelier was propped against the wall in the foyer, the painstaking task of picking up shattered crystal having lasted most of the previous night. Yet still, when I walked across the scuffed marble floor, I felt my feet crunching on minuscule particles like little reminders of last night's catastrophe and of the specter of a woman who had disappeared almost at the same moment as she appeared.

I ate my dinner cold, not able to find the energy to actually reheat it in the oven. Apparently, Mr. Vanderhorst hadn't discovered the joys of microwaving, and his kitchen and his appliances had become stranded somewhere in the 1970s, finding kindred spirits with the heating and air systems as well as the plumbing.

I made sure the front door was locked, then set the alarm before dragging myself upstairs. I fought with the taps on the tub to avoid scalding myself and managed to take a warm bath and brush my teeth without injury.

By ten o'clock I was in bed with the lights out, listening to the silence around me and feeling very much as if I weren't alone. I tossed and turned, listening as the clock struck every quarter hour, reminding me that I needed to ask Jack what he'd discovered from his pictures. When the clock struck eleven, I sat up abruptly, a pressing thought on the edge of my consciousness and carrying with it the distinct impression that the thought hadn't come from me. *The photo album.* I sat on the edge of the bed and strained my ears, trying to hear the voice I was sure had spoken the first time. I recalled that when I was a child, before I'd learned to ignore such things, if I were paying very close attention, I could hear the murmur of very low voices all the time as if someone had left a radio on in a distant room. But tonight all I heard was silence, and the pressing thought inside my skull. *The photo album.*

I put on my robe and slippers and headed toward the guest bedroom, turning on every light as I went. Regardless of how many times I saw them, it was always easier to see dead people when the lights were on.

I pushed the door open slowly, sliding my hand around the doorframe to flip on the light before actually stepping inside. The old ceiling fixture popped, then spluttered out, as if telling me that the room preferred it dark. A triangle of light from the hallway acted like a spotlight for the bed, highlighting the dark arms of the canopy and, in the middle of the lumpy mattress, Louisa's photo album.

Tentatively, I stepped inside, breathing in deeply, and relieved I smelled neither the noxious odor of decay nor of roses. However, as I stepped nearer the bed, I picked up the peculiar odor of fresh-cut grass, and from far away, I thought I could hear a baby crying, and I wished for the first time in a long time that my mother was near. It was an odd thought, considering, but back when I was small, she had always been the buffer between me and things that I couldn't understand.

I looked at my pale fingers, splayed above the closed album, and recalled how my mother had always worn gloves. It had become part of her elegant persona, but I had always known the truth: they were a filter to defuse the strength of whatever she might encounter by inadvertently touching an object or someone's hand. Now, even in cold weather, I couldn't bear the thought of wearing gloves.

With a deep breath, I picked up the album, my senses suddenly overloaded with emotions and smells that had nothing to do with me, or the guest bedroom at the end of the hall or even this moment in time. I flipped the album open to the first page with the wedding photograph of Louisa and Robert, and tears flooded my eyes. These were Louisa's memories, contained in this book as precisely as a black-and-white photo, and as I sank down on the floor with the album in my lap, I thought I could feel the press of corset stays against my back and see a man with a large straw hat pushing a manual mower in the back garden. Even as I shuddered to a sitting position on the floor, leaning against the bed, I could feel the hardness of a fountain pen in my hand, the thick paper of the album sliding beneath my palm as I wrote words onto the now-blank album page.

June 5, 1921—Our wedding day—Robert Nevin Vanderhorst and Louisa Chisholm Gibbes. Even though this album was given to me more than a year since the day of my wedding on the occasion of our son's birth, I wanted to start this story of our lives with the picture that really is the beginning of our lives together. For both of us, it was the happiest day of our lives thus far. I never imagined being in love could be like this, being so satiated that the thought of food or drink is superfluous. We said our vows at St. Michael's, and the ceremony was followed by a garden reception at Robert's house on Tradd Street—now my home, of course. He surprised me by transplanting one of the bushes of my Louisa roses from my parents' house to his, and it was truly a homecoming to me. He knows my every wish and desire before I even express it, and it will be my goal to do the same for him. We are of one accord, Robert and I, and I see us living happily ever after in this beautiful house until we are old and gray. Even with those things beyond our control which might conspire to mar our happiness, I know we will persevere.

I saw hands that weren't mine turning the page to a photograph of the house taken from the side. The rose garden was there, the blooms heavy and ripe like fruit, the sepia-toned drops of blood on the photograph. But the fountain was missing, presumably not built yet, and I heard the voice again telling me to notice the garden, to see the roses. To stick my hands in the rich earth. I stared closely, smelling the roses along with the fresh-mown grass and moist dirt, and saw the place where the fountain now stood, the grass brown beneath the shade of the giant oak tree. *Look,* I heard the voice again, and I pulled back to see the whole picture of the house that still looked old ninety years before. But there was no sagging porches or missing roof tiles, and no weeds littered the garden. Sprays of forsythia and fat gardenia blossoms clung to the shrubs at the side of the house. But it was Louisa's roses that stood out in the black-and-white photo as I imagined they had in living color when they were still new to the house. *Look,* I heard again.

I felt the pen in the hand that wasn't mine as it began to write the caption under the photo of the house.

55 Tradd Street—Our home. I choose this photograph as the second one in my album because this is where our lives together began. I love this house as if it has always been mine. Robert tells me the stories of the Vanderhorst women who have lived in this house for generations and how I inherited their legacy when I married him. It is a legacy I hold to my heart, and as a newlywed I looked forward to putting my stamp on this house so the next generations will remember me. When I moved in, Robert's mother had been gone nearly ten years, and I'm afraid the house had the air of a bachelor's home. Even the gardens, while well-maintained, show the lack of a woman's touch. I decided right after our marriage that I would begin my transformation in the garden. Because a garden is the heart of a house, where love is the seed and the dark earth like a mother who nurtures her saplings until they bloom, and then waits for them with furrowed arms to return. It is the story told again and again from my garden: from dust we begin, and to dust we will return again. Perhaps that is why the garden is my favorite place of all in my new house—perhaps because when I sink my hands in the moist earth, I feel that I'm already home.

I let go of the album and raised my empty hands to my face, smelling dirt and becoming gradually aware of the room around me, of the four-poster bed and the Hepplewhite writing desk on the far wall. And of the sound of footsteps in the foyer below. Quietly, I slipped the album off my lap, and stood, my head spinning as if I'd just been awakened from a sound sleep. Seeing on the dressing table what looked like a Staffordshire figurine that might be used for a weapon, I grabbed it and quietly made my way to the door before opening it.

And then I remembered that I had set the alarm and figured that whoever or whatever the footsteps belonged to, they probably wouldn't be fended off by a small china statue. Still, I crept silently into the brightly lit upstairs hallway and peered over the railing into the foyer below. "Who's there?" I shouted, my voice sounding a lot more confident then I felt. "I have a weapon and I've already called nine-one-one." I wondered if I should run back to my room to pick up the phone but found I didn't want to turn my back on whatever was lurking downstairs. I looked at the figurine closely and saw he was a young shepherd complete with baby lamb and stuck it under the lapel of my robe so that it might resemble an actual weapon.

I heard the footsteps again, sounding as if they might be coming from the downstairs drawing room, and stopped, the thought running through my head that this intruder might actually be real. *But I remembered setting the alarm.* I leaned over the banister and peered through the darkened foyer to where I could see the front door and the system's panel next to it. The green READY button glowed in the dark, indicating that the system was off.

I straightened quickly, feeling as if my heart had migrated up to my head, where I could hear it thrumming wildly.

"Hello?" I said again. "I have a weapon and I'm not afraid to use it. Show yourself now and nobody will get hurt." It didn't cross my mind to consider if the intruder would actually call my bluff and appear. I must have rationalized that I could hold him off with my figurine-loaded bathrobe until I could call the police.

A dark figure darted out from the drawing room and across the foyer in front of me, causing me to reel back in surprise and drop the figurine at the same time I heard the front door slam. I leapt down the final four steps, the smashed china crunching under my slippers, and raced to the front door. I reached for the doorknob, my fingers barely brushing the brass knob before something hard and unyielding blocked my progress, the force of my impeded forward motion knocking me backward onto the floor.

The air left my lungs with a surprised whoosh, and I lay on the floor, trying to catch my breath, while frantically searching around the dim foyer for whatever it was that had knocked me off my feet. It was then that I noticed the rancid smell, so potent and fetid that I began to retch as I struggled to sit up. My heels searched for purchase on the slick marble floor but I couldn't move. It was if I were being held down by two very strong, yet completely invisible hands.

I am stronger than you, I am stronger than you, I repeated in my head, searching for the strength it was supposed to bring. I kicked and twisted, the taste of bile and terror choking me. "Let me go!" I screamed, feeling as helpless and alone as I had that morning when I was six years old and woke up to find my mother gone. The anger the memory evoked made me struggle anew, the salty taste of tears harsh on the back of my throat. "Let me go!" I half screamed and half sobbed, arching my back in my impotent fury.

And then the invisible arms that had been holding me simply let go, allowing me to lurch forward as I pressed against something that wasn't there anymore. I shivered, feeling the iciness of the room for the first time, and watching my breath blowing out puffs of fear and relief as I sat on the floor. The fetid smell dissipated, erased by the pungent aroma of roses.

From where I sat, I could see the alarm panel, the green READY light still glowing brightly. I knew I had set the alarm, remembered doing so with intricate detail. So why was it disarmed? I hadn't heard a warning beep signaling that somebody had entered the house, so it would have had to be disarmed from the inside. A shudder coursed through my body as I remembered the dark form that had run in front of me and then out the door. The intruder had been flesh and blood, someone who could have hurt me or worse, but had chosen not to. And then I remembered the hands holding me down, as if making sure I couldn't run after the intruder. Like they were both after the same thing.

Still trembling I stood, holding on to the wall for support until I could trust my legs. Then I dead-bolted the door and reset the alarm before carefully making my way to the drawing room, where I picked up the phone. I flipped on a table lamp and looked around to see if anything was missing, my eyes telling me in a glance that nothing was out of place: the Canton porcelain bowls on the mantel, the silver tea service, the oil paintings on the walls of long-dead Vanderhorsts were all where they were supposed to be.

I took a step forward, and my foot caught on something, pitching me forward. Looking down, I realized that the rug had been flipped up on the corner as if somebody had been trying to find something hidden underneath.

Out of the corner of my eye, I saw something flit across the room, landing with a soft thud on the rug in front of me. It was a frame, the one containing the photograph of Louisa and her young son, and it lay at my feet where it fell, the faces staring up at me. I picked it up and nearly dropped it again when the doorbell rang.

Clutching the phone, I crept to the front door, ready to dial 911. I peered through the sidelights, recognizing a familiar form.

The doorbell rang again. "It's me, Mellie—Jack. If you're going to call me in the middle of the night, I expect you to be ready to open the door when I get here."

I was so relieved to see him that I didn't waste any time asking him what in the hell he was talking about. I threw back the dead bolt and disarmed the alarm before pulling open the door and launching myself at him.

"Wow, Mellie—it's good to see you, too. But could you wait until I got my clothes off first?"

I dug my face into the crook of his neck, enjoying the scent, and pounded him on the back with one of my fists.

"You're shaking." His voice was full of concern as he lifted me and carried me over the threshold, kicking the door shut behind him. "What happened? You look like you've seen a ghost."

I held my hysterical laughter in check, afraid that if I started I wouldn't be able to stop. An odd sense of déjà vu fell over me, recalling another scene like this but not with Jack. It had something to do with my mother, but I quickly shoved the memory to the recesses of my brain, where the rest of the past I didn't want to revisit lived.

Jack pushed the hair out of my face, cupping my jaw in his hands. "I was worried. Your number kept flashing on my caller ID, but you wouldn't stay on the line long enough to talk to me. It was a little unnerving. But I was awake anyway, so I figured I'd come by to see if you were okay."

I looked into his face, wondering if he might be joking. "I never called you. Not once. From here or my cell phone."

I watched the look of confusion pass over his features at the same time the old clock began to chime midnight and the smell of fresh roses permeated the air around us. I lifted my hands to touch his and that was when we both noticed the dark earth clinging to my skin.

CHAPTER 12

Jack and I sat at the end of the long communal counter at Gaulart & Maliclet on Broad, locally known as Fast & French, drinking coffee and having breakfast. I was on my third chocolate-filled croissant when Sophie walked in wearing a hideous combination of Pippi Longstocking striped tights paired with an Indian sari. Her aged and bulging messenger bag was slung across her midriff, cementing the homeless refugee look. It never ceased to amaze me that somebody that smart could be so completely clueless about fashion.

"You two look like hell. Like you haven't slept," she said as she slid into the booth next to me. Then she froze, her gaze shifting from me to Jack and then back again. "Oh," she said, with a surprised grin.

I shoved her in the arm. "We didn't get any sleep last night, but it's not because of what you're thinking. It's because the police were at the house again until four a.m. We had another break-in."

Jack drained his cup and banged it down on the table. "Yeah. Pretty brazen guy. Broke in while Mellie was in the house, presumably asleep."

Sophie's eyes widened in alarm. "Oh, my gosh. Please tell me that he didn't break the glass in the door or the sidelights."

"Thanks for your concern," I said. "I'm fine."

Jack leaned forward to speak but paused as the waitress refilled our coffee cups and took Sophie's order. "The weird thing is that Mellie remembers setting the alarm before she went to bed. But when she first heard the intruder and went downstairs to investigate, the system had been disarmed. From the inside."

Sophie furrowed her eyebrows. "That's weird. Are you sure you set the alarm?"

I nodded. "Positive."

"So how was the system disarmed from the inside if you were the only one there?" she asked and I could tell from her tone that she already had a pretty good idea.

I shot her a warning glance—something that wasn't lost on Jack.

"It must be a problem with the system," I said. "I'm having the alarm company come out to look at it today."

Jack looked at Sophie, pointedly ignoring me. "That wasn't the only inexplicable thing that happened last night, either. Somehow Mellie stuck her hands into dirt and has no idea how that happened."

Sophie regarded me closely, but I focused on draining the rest of my cold coffee from the bottom of my mug. "I picked up something to use as a weapon, and it must have had some dirt on it."

There was complete silence as the waitress brought Sophie's green tea and cereal with yogurt to the counter. Sophie waited until she was gone before speaking again. "Right," she said, splaying her fingers onto the tabletop as if to indicate she was changing the conversation. "Was anything taken?"

"Not that I could tell. I did a pretty thorough inventory this morning and didn't find anything missing." I decided not to tell her about the shattered Staffordshire shepherd boy. She'd probably make me scrape the shards out of the trash and try to glue them back together.

Jack said, "I'm assuming that the intruder would have known about Mr. Vanderhorst's passing and thought the house was vacant, considering the condition it's in. As it is, the only thing we could tell that was disturbed was the rug in the drawing room. Two of the corners had been flipped up, like they were looking for something hidden beneath the floor."

Sophie sipped her tea thoughtfully. "Well, if there's anything there, it'll be easy to find. I thought we would start on that room anyway, and the first order of business is to remove all the furnishings and the rug so we can get to work on the ceiling and plasterwork. If there's anything hidden under the floor, we'll find it." She dug into her messenger bag and pulled out a folder. "Oh, and before I forget, I've got the papers for the Board of Architectural Review. I'm submitting it, but as owner, you'll need to sign them. I'm going to send one of my students to come take pictures of the exterior areas we want to work on—the roof, the columns out front, the piazzas, and the windows. The BAR's going to need five copies of those."

"The windows?" I asked. "What's wrong with them besides being old and drafty? I thought it was a requirement for all historic houses to have old and drafty windows."

Sophie refused to take the bait. "At some point, somebody replaced the original windows with four-over-four window sashes. Replacing them with nine-over-nine windows would make them more authentic to the period the house was built. Would make the house less drafty, too."

"That's going to be a lot of money, Soph. I think we should talk with my dad first, to make sure there's enough."

Jack and Sophie glanced at each other as Sophie replied. "Actually, I have." She held up her hand before I could ask her why she'd be talking to my dad without me. "You gave me carte blanche on this project remember? In exchange for my expertise, you put me in charge and are allowing my students to use the restoration as an extended classroom."

I slid my empty plate away in agitation. "Yes, but—"

Jack interrupted. "And you told me that you didn't want to have to deal with your father at all. So Soph and I went to see him together." They exchanged a quick glance again.

"Was he sober?"

Jack's lips thinned. "Completely. It's been over a week now, you know, and he's been attending his meetings. He's been spending his time creating a spreadsheet for the restoration budget. Tracks expenses on each area with estimated costs furnished by Soph here. It's pretty sophisticated." He smiled, softening his tone. "I guess that's where you get your anal retentive . . . um . . . I mean, organizational bug from."

My eyes met his. "Or maybe . . ." I stopped, not sure what I was going to say.

Sophie leaned forward and put her hand on my arm. "Melanie had a pretty shitty childhood, Jack. She's so anal because being organized was the only way she could take some control over her life."

I looked up at the ceiling, trying to hide my embarrassment. "Thanks, Dr. Freud. I guess you and Nancy Flaherty got your psychiatry degrees from the same school."

Sophie leaned back with a smile. "Yep. The school of Melanie Middleton. You're the perfect case study." She finished her tea and placed her cup back on the counter. "So, what are you going to do now? Move back into your condo?"

"I wish. But I can't. The conditions of the will stipulate that I have to live in the house for a year before I sell it. The lawyers are keeping track, and it's been exactly two nights. Just 363 more to go."

"But alone, Melanie. That makes me a little worried."

Jack thrummed his fingers on the table. "Don't worry, Soph. I've already told her that I'm moving into the guest room. She shouldn't be in that big house by herself."

I groaned aloud. "Jack, we've had this conversation already, and I told you no. I don't need you or anybody else in the house with me. The alarm guy will fix the alarm, and that'll be that."

They both stared at me silently.

"You could have been seriously hurt, Melanie." Sophie's warm brown eyes radiated concern.

"But I wasn't. I handled the situation just fine."

"Right. Until the next time when the guy is smart enough to bring a gun." Jack's hand had closed into a fist, and I remembered what I'd discovered on the Internet about his time in the military. I wouldn't mention it unless he did—just in case he accused me of Googling him again—but it did make me think twice about turning him down. Still, the thought of sleeping under the same roof with him, albeit in separate bedrooms, sounded like a completely bad idea.

I felt my foot shaking in agitation under the table as I searched for any reason I could come up with. "But what would Mrs. Houlihan think?"

Sophie snorted. "You're what, thirty-nine?"

I glared at her but she ignored me. She knew how I hated advertising my age, especially in front of somebody I suspected might be a year or two younger than me. She poked Jack on the arm with her fork. "And you're how old?"

"Thirty-five," he said, grinning at me.

She sat back. "Well, then, I'd say that you both classify as adults and therefore can make your own sleeping arrangements with impunity."

I pulled my wallet from my purse and placed a ten on the counter. "Great argument, Sophie. You almost have me convinced."

Jack leaned back on his stool and smiled, a look of smug confidence on his face. "Don't worry, Soph. I'm not taking no for an answer. Whether Mellie wants to admit it, we would all feel better with me in the house at night. Besides, I need to finish taking pictures of the clock."

I smiled patiently. "Look, I think everybody is losing sight of the fact that it's my house, which means I should be the one consulted about everything—including who's going to be sleeping there."

Sophie didn't bother smiling back. "Melanie, we're your friends. We're here to save you from making mistakes. Do I need to remind you about your picture in the paper? Please recall that I told you before you had your hair done that a perm would be a bad idea."

I looked away, too embarrassed to admit she was right.

"Besides, this project is way too big for you, and we want to help. And we won't forget that you're in charge. Will we, Jack?" She turned to face Jack, who shook his head somberly.

I threw my hands up. "Fine, fine, fine. Whatever. Just try to give me my space, and if I find the toilet seat left up just once, you're out of there."

Jack winked and extended his hand. "You drive a hard bargain, ma'am, but I think I can live with that."

I narrowed my eyes as we shook hands. "Me, too," I said. "And I hope I don't live to regret this." I looked at my watch. "I've got to run to the office now." I stood and faced Jack again. "Speaking about needing my space, I'd appreciate it if you would clear out before seven. I have a date tonight, and I don't think it would look great if you were there when he showed up."

"A date?" Sophie and Jack spoke simultaneously but with matching tones of surprise.

"Yes, a date," I said, annoyed. "Don't expect me to start wearing stockings that bag around my ankles and spritz myself with moth spray just because I own an old house now. I'm entitled to a social life, you know."

"Absolutely," said Sophie. "I'm just . . . surprised. You haven't mentioned anybody, so it's a bit sudden."

"And speaking of dates," I said, desperate to change the subject, "what was that going on between you and Chad? I figured you two would be picking out china together by now."

Her face blanched a little. "I have no idea why you'd be thinking that. I can't imagine that we'd have anything in common."

Jack tried to keep a straight face. "Sophie, I haven't known you that long, but I have to say that you and Mr. Arasi do seem to be a good match. I mean, he rides a bike and teaches yoga. I also heard him say the word 'organic.' Need I say more?"

Sophie looked up at the ceiling and took a deep breath, then blew it out slowly through puffed-out cheeks. "Okay. You want to know why? It's not that we don't have anything in common." She paused for a moment, looking at each of us. "That first time I saw him in yoga class, he told us that he's a Capricorn." When neither of us said anything, she elaborated. "And I'm a Gemini." She looked at each of us again, as if she didn't need to explain further.

Jack took the bait. "Okay. So what's the problem?"

Sophie looked like the mayor of Pisa who'd just been told by the architect of his tower that it was supposed to lean. " 'What's the problem'?" She slapped her hand on her forehead. "Those are only the two most incompatible signs of the zodiac. Getting together with him would be the greatest disaster of my life."

I could tell that Jack was trying to keep a straight face. "The greatest disaster?"

Sophie had the good sense to look sheepish. "Well, maybe not the greatest. That would be the time my grandmother took me shopping at Lilly Pulitzer. But still, it would be horrible. We'd end up hating each other. Or worse."

I wasn't going to speculate on what "worse" could mean. I was too busy wondering how such a talented, educated woman could not only be the world's worst dresser, but also believe in all of that zodiac crap. Then again, who was I to question her? I was the one who saw dead people.

Besides, I had more practical concerns to worry about. "Would it be okay with you if Chad helps out with the restoration work? He's volunteered and it would be very hard to tell him no."

Sophie looked miserable. "I guess I can't stop you, but please try not to schedule us at the same time, okay?" I nodded and she narrowed her eyes. "And, by the way, your change of subject has not made me forget about your date tonight. So spill the beans—who is it?"

I took a deep breath of resignation. "Oh, that. Yes, well, it's actually a client. He came in to see me yesterday about real estate and ended up asking me to dinner."

"Anybody we would know?" asked Jack with studied nonchalance.

"No, I'm pretty sure you wouldn't."

Sophie's eyes widened. "Is this the guy who's been calling your office and not leaving a number or last name?"

I sent her a warning look but it was too late. Jack looked at me. "Marc Longo? You're going to dinner with Marc Longo?"

I sat back down, figuring this might take a while. "Yes, as a matter of fact, I am. He seems like a really nice guy. Dresses well, too." I looked pointedly at Jack's jeans and ubiquitous oxford cloth shirt with rolled-up sleeves.

His eyes were serious. "Mellie, remember how I told you that there are no coincidences? Don't you find it odd that this Marc Longo, a direct descendant of Joseph Longo, has suddenly appeared on your doorstep, asking you for a date?"

Bristling, I sat up straight. "It wasn't like that. He wants me to show him some houses. That's all. And we ran out of time in our meeting, so he invited me to continue our conversation over dinner. It was all very innocent."

"So, he didn't mention the Tradd Street house at all." Jack crossed his arms over his chest.

I contemplated lying just to wipe the smugness off his face, but figured he'd find out eventually. "Actually, he did. He was interested in buying it until I told him that it wouldn't be available for another year. He had seen the article in the paper and remembered the connection between his family and the Vanderhorsts, and thought maybe that house would make a great first residential real estate investment."

"I bet he did. So whose idea was it to look for more houses after you told him yours wasn't available?"

"His," I said. "But what does it matter? I'm sure that whatever happened to Louisa and Joseph isn't on the top of Marc's list of important things to find out. And I'm sorry if you think that a guy has to have ulterior motives to ask me out on a date."

I could feel Sophie next to me straining to keep her mouth shut. Jack surprised me by leaning forward and taking my hands in his. He used what I could only describe as his bedroom voice when he spoke. "I could never think that, Melanie."

My eyes flew to his at his use of my full name. Irritated by the way my hands and arms were tingling, I yanked them back and cleared my throat. "Well, it doesn't sound that way to me."

He frowned, as if weighing what his next words should be. Finally, he said, "I'm just asking that you be cautious. From what I've learned, Marc Longo isn't somebody you should be messing with."

"I'm not 'messing' with him. I'm just having a business dinner with him."

"Where? Magnolia's?"

I frowned at his accuracy. "Certainly not Blackbeard's. He has better taste than that."

He surprised me by laughing. "Yeah, well, at least I wasn't as obvious as Magnolia's. The guy must be desperate to get on your good side if he's taking you there for a first date, and I'd like to find out why. Maybe you should wear a wire."

I stood abruptly. "I think I've heard enough. I'm leaving."

Sophie swiveled in her seat and waved her hand at me. "Don't forget to sign up for my haunted Halloween walking tour. The sign-ups went online this morning."

I closed my eyes, remembering the disaster of the previous year's fund-raiser. "You won't need me, Soph. You'll have no problem filling your tour without packing the audience with your friends."

Her eyes sparkled. "Yes, well, but you always add that special touch."

I sent her a warning glance.

Jack's gaze moved from my face to Sophie's. "Am I invited, too? Sounds right up my alley. You have no idea how much I like a good ghost story." This last comment was directed at me.

"Do what you want," I said to him as I turned to walk away. "But Sophie moves fast, and you might trip over your ego trying to catch up."

I waved and left quickly before Jack could respond and before I was forced to explain my need to have a dinner date with a good-looking, successful man, regardless of his motives. I was supposed to be a confident, self-made, successful woman, not the kind of person who rarely had a date and usually tripped over her own tongue when speaking to a member of the opposite sex on a topic that didn't involve mortgages or real estate appraisals. I felt like the plain girl being asked to the prom by the captain of the football team, and I wasn't about to let Jack Trenholm spoil my fun.

∞

When I was about four years old, I got a phone call from my grandmother Middleton. I picked up the phone in the hallway when it rang, knowing before it rang that it was for me, and she began speaking as soon as I brought the receiver to my ear. She told me how much she loved me and how special I was, and how I should never worry about what other people might think. I must have fallen asleep listening to her, because the next thing I remembered was my daddy picking me off the floor and carrying me to my room.

I told him that I was talking to Grandma on the phone, and he got very angry with me. I didn't know it then, but my grandma had been dead for less than forty-eight hours, and my daddy had been wondering how to tell me when he found me on the floor with the phone cradled next to me. I suppose that was when I first began to understand that I was different, that not everybody saw people who weren't really there, and that it made other children avoid me on the playground. By the time I was six, the only person I ever told was my mother. And then she was gone, and there was nobody else but me.

I slid the black dress over my head, then fastened my grandmother Middleton's pearls around my neck, just as I had done for my "date" with Jack. But this time, I knew where we were going, and my black dress, pearls, and French chignon would not be out of place.

The doorbell rang just as I was adjusting the straps on my shoes, and I listened as Mrs. Houlihan's heavy tread slowly made its way to the front door. I waited a few moments to hear her greeting, and when nothing happened I cracked the door a little bit to listen. Mrs. Houlihan's grunts filled the downstairs foyer, so I gave up on making my date wait ten minutes and ventured out of my room, peering over the banister as I walked down the stairs.

Mrs. Houlihan was gripping the door handle with both hands and had one knee on the doorframe as she grunted and pulled on the door to open it.

"What's wrong with the door?" I asked as I approached.

Her forehead glistened with sweat. "I don't know, Miss Melanie. But the door's stuck. I've checked to make sure it's unlocked but I just can't open it."

An impatient jab on the doorbell sounded again. "Just a minute," I called out. I motioned Mrs. Houlihan aside, and after double-checking that everything was unlocked, I turned the handle and pulled. The smooth brass doorknob twisted in my hand but it might as well have been attached to a wall.

"Can I help you with that, ladies?"

I turned with a start and found Jack approaching us in bare feet. His shirt was untucked, and his hair looked like he'd just woken up. "Where did you come from?"

He grinned. "I was taking a nap in my room. Had a late night last night, and I intend to take another stab at the attic tonight, so I figured I should grab some sleep while I could."

I was angry that he'd ignored my request to stay away from the house tonight when my date arrived, but too eager to get the door opened to say anything. "The door won't open—can you give it a shot?"

Mrs. Houlihan and I stepped back as Jack grasped the door handle and turned it, the door opening smoothly toward him. Mrs. Houlihan and I stood speechless, staring at each other and then at the irate Marc Longo on the other side of the door.

Jack held out his hand. "Hi, there. I'm Jack Trenholm. And you must be Matt."

Marc hesitated just for a moment before taking Jack's hand. "Actually, it's Marc. And I'm here to see Melanie. . . ." He looked behind Jack's shoulder.

I pushed Jack aside. "Hi, Marc. I'm so sorry—we were having trouble opening the door, and Jack was nice enough to help us out."

"Jack?" Marc looked pointedly at me.

"Trenholm," Jack supplied again, speaking slowly as if he were speaking with somebody of limited intelligence. "I live here."

"No, he doesn't." I fluttered my hands, flustered. "Actually, he does. But only temporarily."

Jack began tucking in his shirt and doing a bad job of trying to look apologetic. "Sorry. I just got out of bed." He winked at Marc, and I had the strong desire to go find the mate of the Staffordshire statuette I'd broken the night before and once more make them a matching set with the help of Jack's hard head.

"He's just helping out with cataloging everything in the house. He keeps odd hours, so I offered him the use of the guest bedroom." I emphasized the last two words so that everybody was on the same page regarding my relationship and sleeping arrangements with Jack.

Jack put his arm around Mrs. Houlihan. "Well, there's that and there's also the fact that the best chef in Charleston, the lovely Mrs. Houlihan, allows me to eat in her kitchen."

Mrs. Houlihan blushed, then excused herself to go back to the kitchen to place a foil-wrapped plate for Jack on the stove before packing up and heading home to her husband.

Marc was studying Jack as if trying to place him. "Wait a minute—I thought your name sounded familiar. Aren't you that guy who wrote the book about the Alamo? There was a lot of publicity surrounding it, as I recall, although I don't remember what it was all about."

I glanced at Marc, not sure if he was being serious or condescending, and then realizing that it didn't matter. Jack was a big boy and certainly didn't need my help. Besides, having been the spider under Jack's magnifying glass, it was fun watching the role reversal.

Jack's smile didn't dim, but I saw his shoulders tense. "Yes, well, that was an unfortunate situation, especially since I had a band of experts on my side supporting the book who nobody wanted to listen to." He shrugged. "But I have every faith that the truth will come out eventually, and the book will sell a million copies because of all the free publicity." He bared his teeth in an effort to widen his smile. "But at least that's freed up my time so I can focus on a new project. Mellie here is allowing me to use her gorgeous house to research a new book I'm working on."

"Oh, really? What's it about?" Marc was studying Jack intently, and I was surprised to see that he wasn't feigning interest.

Jack didn't break eye contact as the two men sized each other up, standing closer as if they were in a boxing ring, and excluding me completely. I wondered if this was how the female lion felt during mating season—unwanted and superfluous until the battle was won and it was time to get down to business. Although comparing myself to a lion in heat was as humiliating as it was accurate.

"A previous owner, Louisa Vanderhorst, vanished from this house in nineteen thirty and was never seen or heard from again. On the same day an unwanted suitor—a Joseph Longo—also vanished. Could he be any relation to you?"

Marc crossed his arms over his chest, exposing the large gold Rolex watch he wore on his right wrist. "Yes, as a matter of fact, Joseph Longo was my grandfather."

Jack raised his eyebrows. "Oh, isn't that interesting? Maybe we should share notes sometime. Who knows? Maybe we can come up with an answer after all these years."

Marc assessed Jack, his expression making it clear that he found him lacking. "Who knows, indeed? We should definitely compare notes. I'll call you." He paused for a moment and then added almost as an afterthought, "And maybe during your research in this house you might dig up even more mysteries from the past."

Something I couldn't identify flitted over Jack's face. "What kinds of mysteries?"

Marc smiled so that his calculating expression now matched Jack's. "Oh, I don't know. It's an old house. I believe Melanie told me it was built in eighteen forty-eight. That's a lot of years, a lot of history. There's bound to be a skeleton or two in the closets."

"There sure is," Jack said slowly, and I was once again struck by the thought that he was holding something back.

"Well," said Marc, glancing at his watch, "our reservations are at seven thirty, and I don't want to be late."

"No, we wouldn't want that, would we, Mellie?" Jack moved to stand next to me and casually draped his arm over my shoulders. I wondered how the female lion would react to this twist on the circling-lion scenario.

I slid out from Jack's embrace and reached for my evening bag and silk shawl, which I had left on the hall table. If I had forgotten them upstairs, I would have left them there rather than abandon the two men alone together in the foyer even for the three minutes it would have taken for me to retrieve the two items.

Marc took the shawl from me and spread it over my shoulders, turning his back to Jack in a clearly dismissive gesture. "I don't think I had a chance to mention how very beautiful you look this evening, Melanie."

I blushed, feeling self-conscious in the direct gaze of two very different but extremely attractive men. "Thank you," I said and should have stopped there. "I got the dress on sale at RTW on King Street." I bit my lip thinking of the many times Sophie had suggested we role-play before my dates to make sure I didn't say anything stupid, which I normally did whenever I was embarrassed or flustered. I made a mental note to take her up on her offer, assuming I ever had another date.

Marc opened the door and offered his arm to me before leading me outside. "Maybe when I bring you home, you'll have time to show me around this gorgeous house of yours. Because of the family connection, I've always wanted to see what it looked like on the inside."

I opened my mouth to reply but was cut off by Jack calling from the doorway, "Good to meet you, Matt." He tapped his watch. "I'll wait up—so don't be too late."

I didn't look back but felt Marc's arm muscles tense under my hand as he led me through the side entrance and out onto the front walk. As he closed the door behind us, something made me turn toward the old oak tree. The woman was standing next to the still swing, the small boy sitting poised on the wooden slatted seat, clutching the ropes. They were both looking at me, but neither one was smiling.

I jerked my attention back to Marc and allowed him to lead me to his car parked on the curb, feeling the two sets of eyes on me like points of light in a darkened room until I had disappeared from their sight.

CHAPTER 13

I closed the door with a heavy sigh and leaned against it, savoring the food, conversation, and male attention I'd been experiencing for the last three and a half hours. I shut my eyes, still smelling the wine, the crab cakes, and the scent of Marc's cologne in the cocooned leather interior of his car.

It had been the perfect evening, but I'd been overrelieved when Marc had declined to come inside for a drink and a nighttime tour of the house and instead accepted my offered rain check. I didn't think either one of us had the energy to face Jack again.

After pulling away from the closed door, I set the alarm, then turned off the lights that had been left on for me before wearily climbing the stairs. It was long past my bedtime, and I was beginning to feel it. The sound of television voices and the dim blue glow of light in the hallway brought me to the upstairs drawing room.

I stood in the doorway for a moment, taking in the scene. The drawing room, with its elaborate moldings and Adam fireplace mantel, was an eclectic mix of eighteenth-century antiques and nineteen fifties kitsch. This must have been the room Mr. Vanderhorst used the most as many of the antiques had been sequestered to a corner to make room for a television and its orange metal stand, as well as an overstuffed recliner and an upholstered couch, whose floral design made me place it somewhere circa nineteen fifty-five.

Being a man with limited exposure to Charleston women excused Mr. Vanderhorst from the unspoken Charleston rule concerning priceless family heirloom furniture: those that have it, use it. The best way to mark a newcomer to the city (anybody whose family wasn't living here by the Revolution) was his avoidance of using the Chippendale sofa to watch television and eat their frozen dinners.

A rerun of *Walker, Texas Ranger* ran across the TV screen, the voices mixed with soft snoring coming from the couch. Jack's arm was thrown over his head, and he was smiling in his sleep, altering his handsome face into that of a little boy and doing something entirely weird to my blood flow.

Quietly, I moved toward the television and switched it off, then turned to pull a knitted afghan off the recliner to cover Jack in case he got cold. I stood over Jack with the blanket clasped in my hands when I became aware of the drop in temperature and another presence in the room hovering somewhere behind Jack's head. With dread, I watched as the figure of the young woman slowly materialized in front of me and became not a solid person, but instead more like a reflection in a pool. I could see all of her features clearly, but I could also see what was behind her, and I had the oddest thought that if I stared really hard at her, I could see myself.

She cupped her hand, then touched the back of her folded fingers against Jack's temple. I watched his smile broaden as he brought his hand up to his face as if to grasp the hand that was now stroking his skin.

A tiny droplet of water landed on Jack's cheek, and for a moment I thought the roof was leaking, until I realized the woman was crying.

I wanted to leave the room, to deny what I was seeing, but I knew I couldn't. My mother had told me that I was allowed to walk away, but that wouldn't mean that I would forget. The woman's hand now cupped Jack's cheek and I watched as Jack moved his hand and placed it over hers, holding it close to him. Overwhelming grief surged through me, and I wanted to double over with the pain of it, but I couldn't. I was mesmerized by what this woman was showing me, and I began to hear her voice.

I never stopped loving him. I never stopped. The words weren't spoken aloud; they never were. I heard them in my head, echoing and hollow like a copper penny shaken in a metal cup. *Tell him I love him still.*

I shivered, watching as my breath curled around me. The woman had begun to fade, and I reached my hand out to her but felt only empty air. I turned my palm up and caught a tear, the wetness stinging my hand until it simply vanished.

I stood there for a long time with the afghan in my hand, my unasked question frozen on my tongue. *Who are you?*

Jack stirred, rubbing his hands over his face before opening his eyes, his gaze slowly focusing on me. "Nice dress," he said, sitting up and looking adorably rumpled, "although I could swear I've seen it before."

I dropped the afghan on the floor, not wanting to be caught doing something nice for him. I grimaced, having trouble finding my voice. "Good job waiting up."

He slid his feet to the floor and frowned as he stared at his hands. He swept them together as if trying to dry them. "I had the weirdest dream. . . ." He trailed off before looking back at me and finding his killer grin again. "So, did he kiss you good night?"

"Who?"

Jack simply raised an eyebrow.

"That's none of your business."

Jack sat back. "Ah, so he didn't. But don't worry. You'll find someone else."

I folded my arms across my chest. "He's coming by Sunday to tour the house and take me out to brunch."

"I see," he said. His eyes narrowed, and I thought he was about to say something more. Instead, he stood. "Well, now that you're home, I'm going back up to the attic. Good night."

I followed him out into the hallway and was on my way to my bedroom when Jack spoke again. "I think I've found all of Louisa's albums if you'd like to bring them downstairs to get a better look at them. I could help you carry them, so it should only take a couple of trips."

I hesitated for a moment. "Sure. Just let me get changed first."

He saluted, then headed up the attic stairs. I ran into my room and slipped on my pajamas, slippers, and robe, then scurried down to the kitchen to find Mrs. Houlihan's yellow rubber dish gloves and put them on.

I stood at the top of the attic steps and peered into the gloom lit only by a single bulb with a pull chain.

"Be still my heart," said Jack, looking at me. "I must have missed that page in the Victoria's Secret catalog. And I must say that the rubber gloves add a special touch to the entire ensemble."

"My hands are cold."

He looked at me for a long moment. "Mellie, It's seventy-six degrees outside, and this is an unair-conditioned space. It is not cold."

I avoided his gaze as I picked my way into the cluttered attic. "I have poor circulation in my hands and feet." I picked up the cane Sophie had found on our first visit to the house and read the inscribed riddle out loud. " 'I walk on four legs in the morning, two in the evening and three at night. What am I?'" I looked at Jack expectantly.

"Man," he answered without pausing to think.

"Couldn't you at least pretend to be stumped?" I replaced the cane against the wall. "Mrs. Houlihan said that the Vanderhorsts were known for their love of riddles."

"Really?"

I looked at Jack, curious at the tone of his voice, but he'd already gone back to examining a box of what appeared to be old shoes. I looked around me at the stacks of books, papers, trunks, old clothing, and furniture. The blue tarp covering the hole in the roof chatted in the breeze, reminding me of why there seemed to be pigeon crap over most of everything, including the huge buffalo that dominated one side of the sizable attic. The smells of mildew, dust, and humid outside air were nearly too thick to breathe.

Jack followed my gaze. "I think we should get all of this stuff out of here as soon as possible, before there's any further damage. We'll have to do it before they repair the roof anyway, so we might as well do it now."

I nodded. "We can sort of triage the stuff we find and then have your parents come over to tell us what kind of furniture we have."

Jack moved toward an open trunk near the door. "I think the only reason why the photo albums and camera were in such good condition is because they were in the trunk. No pigeon crap."

I peered inside the trunk and saw seven more albums identical to the one I'd already started looking through. Even with gloves, I was hesitant to reach in and touch them. The out-of-body experience I'd had the previous day wasn't something I was eager to repeat. Unfortunately, I knew that I didn't have a choice.

"Check this out," Jack called from the opposite end of the attic. He'd opened a tall armoire, exposing yards of lace, silk, and feathers. "It's like a twenties costume store in here."

Happy to leave the scrapbooks behind for now, I went over to investigate. Hatboxes were crammed on a shelf above the dresses, and satin shoes with buckles and heels crowded the space below. I touched a faded peach silk dress with my gloved hands, its hem blackened with mildew. "I bet these were Louisa's," I said softly.

"I think you're right," said Jack as he pulled back the neck of the dress to find a hand-sewn label: *Made expressively for Louisa Gibbes Vanderhorst.* He pulled open a small drawer inside the armoire. "And look inside here. All of her lace handkerchiefs with her monogram and silk stockings." He reached inside and held up a handful of brittle dried rose petals. "Looks like somebody stuck these in here to keep the clothes fresh." He put them back inside the drawer and wrinkled his nose as the smell of rotting clothes and mildew wafted out at us. "Sort of like insuring your boat after the storm." He stared into the dark armoire. "You know, if I were Mr. Vanderhorst and my wife had run off with another man, I would have burned all of her things. Or at least given them away. I don't think I would have saved everything like a kind of memorial for her."

"Maybe he thought she was coming back."

Jack looked at me, his eyes sad, and I wondered if he was thinking of the woman he'd once planned to marry. "I don't think so. He had the entire armoire moved up here, out of his sight. Like he knew she was gone for good, but he couldn't stand to get rid of everything that reminded him of her." He shook his head. "No, he knew she wasn't coming back. But he never stopped missing her."

I remembered the ghost I'd seen with Jack and recalled what she'd said. *I never stopped loving him. I never stopped.* And then, right before she vanished, *Tell him I love him still.* I wondered briefly if I had it all wrong, if the woman was really Louisa and she hadn't been talking about Jack at all. But she didn't appear to resemble the photographs I'd seen of Louisa, and she was definitely different from the woman I saw in the garden, and when I'd seen her with Jack, I'd felt that love and grief had been directed at him. I'd felt the tears she'd shed for him and so had Jack, although he didn't know it.

I studied Jack's face in the dim light of the single bulb, seeing his chiseled features and sad eyes, and listened as the house breathed around us, as I reconciled myself to the fact that I needed to find not one missing woman, but two. I told myself it wasn't to right old wrongs, or grant an old man's dying request; it had everything to do with getting the dead people to leave me alone. But even I had limits to lying to myself.

"Do you still miss her?" I asked.

He looked at me sharply. "Miss who?"

"Emily."

He didn't look away. "How do you know about Emily?"

"Your mother."

He was silent for a moment. "What did she tell you?"

"That she literally left you at the altar. That she moved to New York, and you've never heard from her again." I chewed on my bottom lip, unsure of my next words. Finally, I said, "Your mother told me that Emily was a journalist with the *Post and Courier* and that you met when you were doing research for a book." I felt myself blushing and hoped he couldn't notice in the dim light.

Jack turned away, facing a tall stack of books that looked like they'd been pulled from other parts of the attic and piled there, since they appeared amazingly dust-free.

"My mother is a wonderful woman, but she really needs to learn when it's okay to share information and when it's not. Did she tell you any embarrassing stories about when I was a toddler and liked to run around in a cowboy hat, holster, boots, and nothing else?"

I stared at the back of his neck, where his dark hair curled, making me think of what an adorable little boy he must have once been, and reminding me of how he looked asleep when his defenses were down and he was unaware that anyone was watching. "So, do you?" I persisted.

He didn't turn around, nor did he ask me what I was talking about. Finally, he said, "Yeah, I suppose I do. I kept a box with her ring and hairbrush in it, so I guess I must. But I don't think that she's ever coming back."

Softly, I said, "I don't think she is either."

I had walked toward him and the stack of books, and I didn't think he'd heard me, because when he spun around, he seemed startled to find me so close. His eyes were wide as he stared into mine. He put his hands on my upper arms and put his face close to mine. "What makes you say that? Do you know something?" His hands squeezed a little tighter. "Did you see anything?"

I looked away. "It's just a feeling." I swallowed. "After speaking with your mother, I realized that Emily was probably gone for good."

He dropped his hands. "I think you're right. It's just hard to believe that the person you think you're going to spend the rest of your life with can disappear from your life."

"So you don't know what happened to her?"

He shook his head. "Not a word. Not even her boss at the paper knows exactly where she went or why."

I wanted to tell him then what I'd seen, and deliver the message I'd been given. But when a person escapes being brutalized on the playground by denying what she really sees and hears, it's not easy to believe that adults will have a different attitude. And besides, I told myself, I had no evidence that the woman I'd seen was Emily.

Jack moved away as if eager to change the conversation, and I got a good view of the books that had been stacked in front of him. I picked up the book on top and looked at it, reading the title out loud. *"Ciphers of the Civil War."* I picked up the next one. "*The Adventure of the Dancing Men*. Sherlock Homes." I turned to Jack. "Where did you find these?"

He didn't answer right away. "I found them here and there in the attic. Some are moldy but a lot are in good condition. I guess a previous owner was really interested in ciphers." He moved closer to me and took the two books from my hands. "It's kind of an interest of mine, too, and I was hoping you'd let me read them while I was here."

"By ciphers, do you mean secret codes?"

"Pretty much. In some of my previous books, especially those that involved espionage, I learned a lot about codes and code breaking. It's a guy thing, I guess."

"Well, you're welcome to read them. But if you bring them downstairs, make sure you don't flake off any mold onto the furniture."

"Yes, ma'am," he said as he placed the books back onto the stack.

I continue to rummage, lifting dusty sheets to see what lay underneath and finding not only exquisite antique furniture but also everything from moth-eaten Civil War uniforms to piles of old magazines and brittle newspapers from the last hundred and fifty years. A heavy oak plantation desk sat partially hidden behind the buffalo, and I had to squeeze myself between them to examine the desk more closely. I pulled open the large center drawer, surprised at how easily it opened, almost as if someone had already been there before me. I reached in and took out a stack of papers.

Jack spoke from behind me. "The style of furniture is so different from what's in this house that I'm thinking it might have come from the Vanderhorsts' plantation."

I nodded, my eyes scanning the documents as I riffled through them. "Do you recall the name of the plantation?"

"Magnolia Ridge."

My eyes met his. "I think you're right. Most of these papers are just shopping lists for supply trips into town and receipts for bolts of cloth and salt. But this"—I took out a sheet from the middle of the stack—"looks like the deed to the property."

Jack stepped forward, tripping over a deer head in his haste, and stood next to me. "Can I see that?"

I handed him the sheet of paper and he held it so that the single bulb shone on it. I peered over his shoulder, noting the date printed at the top: November 1, 1929. "Wasn't that the year of the stock market crash?"

Jack nodded, his eyes scanning the small printing and squinting at the signatures on the bottom of the page.

"What is it?" I asked.

"It's a property deed to the Magnolia Ridge plantation. It would appear from this document that Robert Vanderhorst deeded the property to his wife, Louisa."

I squinted my eyes at the signatures on the bottom, wondering why one of them looked familiar, but Jack stuck it back in the pile, and my thoughts were distracted by his last words. "Why would he have done that? They were married, and I'm not sure what the laws were back then, but I would bet that what was hers was now his."

"That's about it. But sometimes a man would deed property to his wife or relative in order to escape paying taxes. Or—" He stopped, as if hesitant to give anything away.

"Or what?" I persisted.

"Or to avoid having it confiscated by the government. Like for illegal activity."

"Illegal activity? The Vanderhorsts?"

Jack grinned. "Oh, grasshopper, you have much to learn. Feel free to call me master as I enlighten you."

I rolled my eyes. "It's late. Could you just tell me so I can go to bed?"

He stared patiently at me. "Mellie, what big social upheaval was going on in the late twenties and early thirties?"

I thought for a long moment. After I had reached the age of six, history ceased to be relevant to me, and I'd barely got by in my history classes in school as I learned enough to pass an exam and then happily forgot everything. "Well, girls started showing their ankles and dancing the Charleston. And you have to give me credit for knowing about the stock market crash." I smiled up at him, proud to have dug that one out of the recesses of my memory.

"Does the Eighteenth Amendment or the Volstead Act ring any bells?"

"Happily, no." I grinned.

"I'm talking about Prohibition. I've actually been out to Magnolia Ridge—before Mr. Longo purchased it—and I saw the remains of several stills. Apparently, Nevin Vanderhorst's father was a bootlegger. Not that Charleston Country ever really went dry, but there was a lot of money to be made supplying the surrounding counties and states."

"Sorry if I don't get excited about this history lesson. But I saw no need to know my history when I was in school, and I see even less reason now. It's all about dead people anyway."

Jack raised an eyebrow as he turned his head to peruse the document again. "I guess you would know."

I sucked in my breath. "Excuse me?"

Without looking at me, he said, "You dislike old houses because they seem to be owned by people mired in the past, and you'd rather see the real estate used for something more useful like a parking lot—unless you can sell an old house to some poor sod who doesn't know what he's in for and make a lot of money. So it doesn't surprise me that you equate history with dead people, as something no longer relevant. And I'm sure none of it has anything to do with the fact that you were supposed to inherit your mother's family home on Legare but instead she sold it to strangers after your parents separated."

My shock and embarrassment quickly turned to anger. "Did my father tell you that little gem?"

"He didn't have to. My mother told me after we stopped by for our visit." He slid the document back into the drawer and closed it. "I guess that makes us even, then," he said quietly.

"I guess so," I replied, feeling tired all of a sudden. "I'm going to take a couple of these albums on my way down. We don't need to get them all tonight, but if you could bring a couple down and leave them outside my door when you're done up here, I'd appreciate it."

"Sure," he said as I gathered up two albums into my arms.

Straightening, I said, "By the way, have you had a chance to get your photos of the clock face printed yet?"

For a moment I thought from his expression that he wasn't sure what I was talking about. "Oh, right. No. I haven't had a chance. My camera's not digital, so I have to actually take the film in to be processed. I'll let you know when I'm done." He rubbed his hands together. "So, what's on the schedule for tomorrow?"

"I've got to go into the office tomorrow morning for a few appointments, but I should be back by noon. I've printed copies of the work sheet for everybody and e-mailed them—yours I put on your bed so you won't need to be confused when you wake up in the morning and wonder what you should be doing."

"I'm usually confused when I wake up in the morning, but I'm sure your work sheet will anchor me. Thank you." He smiled brightly at me. "You know, this restoration stuff could be a whole lot of fun."

I snorted. "Right. As fun as a root canal." I switched the albums to my other arm. "I'll see you tomorrow then."

"Looking forward to it," he said, a grin in his voice.

I grunted in response, afraid that if I said anything, he would hear in my voice that maybe I was, too.

"By the way, you're adorable when you blush."

"I wasn't blushing," I stammered.

"Yes, you were. When you were talking about Emily and how she and I had met while I was doing research for a book. You blushed. Or maybe it was a hot flash."

I jostled the albums in my arms and scowled at him. "I'm not that old."

"Then it must have been a blush," he said, and I could hear the laughter in his voice.

I forced back a smile. "Good night, Jack."

I headed toward the stairs, and before I'd reached the top step, he said, "Good night, Melanie."

A sharp retort asking him to stop calling me by my nickname was already on my tongue, and I had to cough to cover it up. Instead, I headed down the steps and called back over my shoulder when I'd reached the bottom, "Good night, dude."

I heard him laughing as I made my way back to my bedroom.

ꕤ

I put the stack of albums on the dresser next to the first album I'd already brought from the guest room. I took off the gloves, my robe, and slippers and crawled into bed, no longer tired, but I figured I had to at least try to sleep. The sound of footsteps and boxes being dragged drifted into the room from the attic—at least I hoped that was where the noises were coming from. With a heavy sigh, I turned on my side and caught sight of the stack of albums highlighted in a crease of light from the shut draperies.

I stared for a long time before finally sitting up and flipping on my bedside light. With a deep breath I walked over to the dresser and picked up the first album without thinking, feeling the tickle of anticipation race up my arms as I held it.

This time I smelled the heavy scent of oiled leather and the unmistakable odor of fuel exhaust. I wiped at my face, expecting to feel silk chiffon draping across my cheeks, but touched only my skin. Slowly sinking to the floor, I opened the album, the scents of horse and hay added now, and I sneezed.

The album opened to a photo of Robert and Louisa sitting in a Model T. A tall gold trophy cup was perched on the seat between them, and they were looking at each other, smiling. Across Louisa's face was a sheer silk scarf to protect her from road dust in the absence of a windshield, and both occupants wore goggles sitting atop their heads. A group of laughing people surrounded the car, and behind them, an alley of oaks leading to the columned portico of a Greek Revival mansion. *Magnolia Ridge,* I thought to myself, knowing what it was even though I'd never seen it before. Two Arabian horses stood at a fence lining the drive, looking toward the camera. *How do I know they're Arabian horses?*

A lone man stood apart from the crowd, only the headlight of another car visible behind his left hip. He was noticeable because he was the only person not smiling in the entire photograph. And because he looked exactly like Marc Longo.

It became difficult to take a deep breath, as if I were wearing a corset, and once again I felt in my hand a fountain pen that wasn't mine as I began to read the caption.

August 5, 1921

On a whim, my darling Robert made a wager that his car was the fastest in Charleston. I thought it a silly wager since his car was made in Detroit with the exact same materials as all the other ones, but I suppose you can't tell that to a man who's obsessed with his new toy. [The hand that held the pen stiffened as it wrote the next line.] Joseph Longo was the sole opponent, and the reason Robert gave me for the wager was simply that Mr. Longo was purported to say that he never lost at anything. Never one to suffer a braggart or a liar, Robert readily agreed to the wager. But even though we won, I can't help but think that Mr. Longo isn't finished with trying to prove himself right.

Something drifted to the ground next to my foot, startling me. It hadn't come from the photo album or from anywhere else that I could determine. It had apparently drifted out of midair. It was a rectangular cream-colored card a little larger than a business card, and when I picked it off the rug, I could see there was writing on one side.

At the top was Louisa's monogram, LCG, her maiden name. In elegant cursive, she'd written the date *April 2, 1918* and below that:

Dear Mr. Longo,

I regret to inform you that my family and I will be unable to attend your Fort Sumter remembrance ball on the 12th as I have a previous engagement.

Cordially yours,
Miss Louisa Gibbes

I tucked the card into the photo album and closed it thoughtfully, recalling what Louisa had written about Joseph Longo: *I can't help but think that Mr. Longo isn't finished with trying to prove himself right.* Was this proof, then, that he had pursued her before she was married and hadn't given up even after she married Robert? Was their disappearance on the same day, then, also proof that he had succeeded in finally winning her?

I pushed the album off my lap and crawled into bed again, checking the four corners of the room before flipping off my bedside lamp. I lay awake for a long time, listening to the quarterly chime of the grandfather clock downstairs, and smelling again the unmistakable scent of roses. And when the clock chimed two o'clock, it finally occurred to me why the signature at the bottom of the deed for Magnolia Ridge seemed so familiar. It was Augustus P. Middleton's signature, lawyer, Charlestonian, best friend of Robert Vanderhorst and, most important, my grandfather.

I turned over and closed my eyes, sleepily reminding myself to tell Jack in the morning, then finally drifting to sleep before the clock struck again.

CHAPTER 14

I sat on my accustomed bench at White Point Gardens with a fast food hamburger in one hand and a set of closing papers in my other watching as children clambered over the scattered assortment of cannons. The Battery had always been my favorite Charleston spot, despite its reputation for being steeped in history and the throngs of tourists that congregate throughout the year in this place where the Ashley and Cooper rivers meet and where Fort Sumter can be seen far out in the harbor.

"Fast food can kill you, you know."

I looked up at the familiar voice, shading the sun from my eyes with my hand. My dad, fresh-shaven and clear-eyed, wore a navy blue golf shirt and khaki pants with loafers and I couldn't help but grin. "Is Jack dressing you these days, Dad?"

He grinned back. "Well, he did take me shopping and gave me a few recommendations, is all. Why? Don't you like the new look?"

He turned for me with his hands held out from his sides like a model, as I admired the crisp pleat of his pants and the layered cut of his clean hair and felt an unreasonable stab of jealousy that he'd gone shopping with Jack instead of with me. I guess he'd known that Jack would pick up the phone when he called to ask, whereas I didn't come with that kind of guarantee.

"Looking good, Dad," I said, meaning it. "What's the big occasion?"

He sat down on the bench next to me, his eyes somber as he regarded me closely. "It's been three weeks now. Not a single drink." He patted his pocket, and I saw his hands still shook a little. "Been chewing lots of gum, though. Jack said it helped him, so I thought I'd give it a try."

I nodded, then looked down at my paperwork, my eyes blurring. I didn't want to feel the rush of excitement and hope. The crash hurt so much more when you allowed yourself to fly.

He touched my arm, then quickly pulled his hand away. "I know you can't get excited for me. I don't blame you for that. But I wanted you to know."

I nodded again, not wanting to give voice to my hope. Instead, I turned to him and asked, "How did you find me?"

"Your receptionist, Nancy. She wasn't going to tell me where you were at first even after I told her I was your father."

"What made her crack?"

"Well, she was standing there jostling golf tees in her pocket, so I figured she had to like golf."

"Yeah, you could say that. 'Obsessed' works, too."

He grinned and his eyes sparkled, something I hadn't seen in a very long time. "So I told her I had a friend who knew a friend who knew Tiger Woods's publicist and that I would try to get her an autograph."

"And she folded."

"Like a house of cards," he said, grinning. He tapped his fingers on his leg as his grin faded. "Although I don't think she would have given me what I was asking for if she didn't think it was in your best interests. She just needed me to think that I didn't have a chance and see what I would do. Kind of to prove myself, you know?"

"And it's a good thing you passed. She keeps a nine iron behind her desk in case any visitors get unruly."

"After meeting her, I can believe it."

I took my last bite of hamburger and offered him a french fry. After swallowing, I asked, "So what did you need to see me about that you couldn't take care of with a phone call?"

He looked at me with his old eyes—the eyes he'd once had when there were three of us in our family, eyes that were clear and sparkled with a hidden joke. "I didn't think you'd answer your phone. And I was pretty sure you wouldn't run away from me in a public setting."

I rolled my eyes but didn't say anything because he was right.

He continued. "Nancy said you come here on most nice days to eat your lunch. It surprised me."

I crumpled up my empty hamburger wrapper. "Why? A lot of people eat lunch on the Battery."

He looked at me, a question in his eyes. "Because your mother used to take you here all the time. She loved telling you about the history of the place, and at one time you could name the families in every house on East Battery." He leaned back, his thick hands, with gray hairs sprouting from the backs of them, on his thighs. "You used to laugh and laugh at the story about the fake Revolutionary War nine-pounder at the end of the path from Church Street. You'd tell the story to anybody who would listen and then practically fall over with laughter."

I looked down at my papers, remembering the story but not my mother's involvement in it. And I wondered, briefly, how over the years I had managed to chisel my mother out of my personal history.

I felt half of my mouth tilt up as I recalled the story of how the city government had removed an antique British cannon from Longitude Lane to be placed on the Battery, not anticipating the uproar by the residents at its removal. To placate them, a fake cannon was made—complete with pitting and an inscription to make it look authentic—and then "purchased" and offered to the irate residents of Longitude Lane. Being Charlestonians, they rejected it as not having been the original, and the fake cannon was donated to the city, placed on the opposite end of the Battery from the real cannon, its secret safe until someone tried to steal the real cannon. The authentic one was removed, leaving only the little impostor to fool all the tourists and those residents of Charleston too new to know the difference.

"I'd forgotten about that," I said, turning toward my father with a full grin. "Only in Charleston, you know?"

He smiled back. "Yeah. That's for sure."

We sat there smiling at each other until I realized what I was doing and looked away. "I need to get back to the office and make a few phone calls before I head back to the house."

I stood suddenly, dropping my pen. He leaned down to get it and handed it to me as he stood, too. "I guess I'll see you at the house, then."

I nodded. "Yes, I guess you will."

He looked at me for a moment before saying, "You always call it 'the house.' Never 'my house.' "

"Well, it's hardly mine, is it?" I asked, annoyed that he could be so perceptive. He'd been that way when I was a little girl, always knowing without me telling him if I were sad or lonely or just needed somebody to talk to. But that was a very long time ago when I used to need somebody to tell me how I was feeling.

I brushed crumbs off of my skirt. "You never told me what you came here to tell me."

"Right." He looked a little sheepish. "Well, I wanted to know why you hadn't put me on the work sheet for the week."

I sat back down, stunned that it would be important enough to him to make him track me down to ask me why. "I guess because I figured you could help Jack wherever he needed help."

He sat down again, too, and I watched as a muscle jerked in my father's cheek. "I'm sure you've already noticed, but Jack's a grown man. He doesn't need me to be dogging his steps and getting in the way. I need my own projects. Jack can make sure I show up and do a good job, but he doesn't need to supervise me twenty-four-seven."

"Oh," I said, no other words coming readily to my tongue. "I'm sorry. I didn't mean it that way. I just thought . . ." I swallowed, trying to recall exactly what it was I had been thinking. I certainly needed the help, and surely I was old enough that I didn't have to punish a father who had ceased to be a factor in my life many years before. For an answer, I shrugged.

He slapped his palms against his thighs. "Great. I'm glad we're in agreement on this matter. I can be there at eight o'clock tomorrow morning. You can just leave my revised schedule on one of the porch rockers, and I'll get it."

"Fine," I said, trying to think back to the last time my father had voluntarily awoken before noon. And then I remembered something else: a memory of my father with a shovel in the backyard of another house, making holes for hydrangea bushes. It didn't matter that we didn't live there long enough to see them bloom. It mattered that I remembered and that he'd been sober and happy when he'd thought to plant bushes in front of our rental unit. "How about the garden? There are some rare rosebushes in the back behind the fountain. The rest of the yard is pretty much a weed fest. I'm afraid that if I pull weeds, I wouldn't recognize the difference between what should stay and what should go."

His smile brightened, and I thought, *He remembers, too,* and I looked away so he couldn't see my smile.

"I'd like that," he said gruffly. "I haven't had a garden in a very long time."

"Good, it's settled then." I straightened the papers on my lap and stood.

"Oh, one more thing." He reached into his back pocket, pulled out a piece of paper, and handed it to me.

I opened it and read a name and phone number. "What's this?"

"Sophie mentioned that there's some wood rot on the mantelpiece in the upstairs drawing room, as well as on some of the cornices above the doors downstairs. One of my buddies owns an antiques salvage yard, and if he knows what you're looking for, he can get it for you. He swears that he doesn't do any of the demolitions, that he's just there to give remnants from demolished houses a second life, but it would still be better if you didn't mention it to Sophie. She gets real emotional when you talk about tearing down old houses."

"That she does," I said as I tucked the piece of paper into my purse. "For such a smart person, she can be pretty stupid when it comes to old houses."

"Careful, Melanie. I hear it's contagious."

I snorted. "Don't worry. I'm immune."

He stared at me for a moment. "Sure, you are." He shoved his hands in his pockets. "I'd like to spend this afternoon researching Charleston gardens and yours in particular to give me an idea of what it should look like. If it's all right with you, I'll just see you tomorrow at the house."

"Fine," I said, still wary. "See you tomorrow."

I watched as he walked away, disappearing into the clusters of tourists and school groups. Then I turned around and began to make my way back to the office, avoiding the little cannon that wasn't what it seemed, and the memory of the mother who had once held my hand and told me stories that I remembered still.

∞

There were so many vehicles parked outside the house that I had to park my car two blocks away, meaning I was sweating and annoyed by the time I reached the house. As I opened the door to the piazza, I was horrified to see Marc Longo sitting on one of the porch rockers, his fingers tapping frantically into his BlackBerry. He smiled, then slid it into his jacket pocket as he stood.

Thankfully ignoring my perspiring face and limp hair, he said, "You're looking beautiful today as always, Melanie." He took my hands and kissed me on both cheeks. I couldn't keep myself from being grateful that Jack hadn't been around to witness his actions, because I'm sure I wouldn't stop hearing about them for weeks.

"What a nice surprise," I said. "But did I forget an appointment?"

"Not at all." He sent me a reproachful look. "I'm hoping that we're good enough friends now that I wouldn't need an appointment to see you again."

"No, of course not—it's just, well, I know how busy you are, and I wasn't expecting to see you so soon."

He took my hands in his again. "I know, but I couldn't stop thinking about you since our dinner. Very distracting, you know."

I blushed under the intensity of his gaze and tried to come up with a suave response that didn't involve stammering or more blushing. I remained silent.

He continued. "I also wanted to find out if you already had plans for this weekend. I have a house on Isle of Palms right on the beach, and I was wondering if you'd like to join me for a little end-of-the-week rest and relaxation."

I opened my mouth to respond, wanting to say yes and no at the same time, and confusing myself in the process. Here was an exceptionally handsome and successful man asking me to spend the weekend at his beach house, but there was also the fact that I had known him for less than a week. Despite my being thirty-nine in real time, my dating age was closer to thirteen.

After watching my mouth move for several moments, Marc said, "Don't worry. There are eight bedrooms and you'd have one all to yourself. I just wanted to spend more time with you without . . . distractions." He jerked his head in the direction of the house, where hammering had begun somewhere inside.

"That's so nice of you to offer," I finally managed. "I just don't know if I can get away with all the work that's going on in the house. . . ."

The piazza door opened and Chad breezed in, wearing a Hawaiian shirt and cutoff jeans and carrying his yoga mat under one arm and General Lee, now sporting a red bandanna, under the other. "Hey, Melanie. What's up?"

He leaned the yoga mat against the front of the house, then stuck his hand out toward Marc. "Chad Arasi," he said, introducing himself. "Are you one of the roofer dudes who's supposed to come today? Sophie told me to be on the lookout for you in case you got here before she did."

"Hi, Chad," I said, feeling Marc stiffen beside me. "Mr. Longo is another client of mine. And a friend," I hastily added. "I haven't seen the roofing people yet, but I'll go talk to them when they get here."

I turned to Marc. "Dr. Arasi is a professor of art history at the college. He's had some renovation experience and has kindly donated his time to help."

Marc took the offered hand but pulled it back quickly when General Lee began a low growl, baring small fangs that looked about as fierce as marshmallows.

Chad pulled General Lee back. "Whoa, little doggie. That's no way to be nice." Looking back at Marc, he said, "Sorry about that. Don't know what came over the little guy. He's usually just chillin'."

Marc smiled but it did nothing to alter General Lee's opinion of him. The little dog continued to growl and bare his teeth until the front door opened and Jack stuck his head out. The dog leapt from Chad's arms and ran to Jack, who quickly scooped General Lee up and began scratching him behind the ears like somebody who'd owned dogs all of his life.

Jack stuck a hand out to Marc. "Well, hey, there, Matt. Glad you could stop by again so soon. Hope you brought a change of clothes, because this kind of work can get messy."

Marc shook Jack's hand halfheartedly. "It's Marc, actually, and I was just stopping by to say hello to Melanie and to issue an invitation for this weekend. I don't think she's answered me yet, however."

Jack looked at me, his eyes penetrating. "Well, except for working on the house, I know I'm free. What about you, Mellie?"

I wish he'd been standing closer because I would have kicked him. I smiled, hoping he could read the real message in my eyes. "I believe the invitation was just for me, Jack. But I wasn't sure what was going on this weekend at the house. I haven't done the work schedules that far in advance."

Jack held up a palm. "Say no more. I understand. I'm sure the four of us and the assorted hangers-on can manage without Mellie for a weekend. Just bring your phone in case of emergencies. You never know what can go wrong with one of these old houses."

"Four of you?" Marc raised an eyebrow.

Jack nodded. "Yep. There's Chad here and myself, Mellie's friend Sophie and Mellie's dad. We'll all be working here this weekend."

"Well, then," Marc said, "looks like you've got it covered. And I'm sure you'd agree that Melanie here could use a little bit of rest and relaxation. She's had a difficult month."

Jack's smile didn't dim. "And I guess you would know best."

We had all managed to walk into the foyer at some point in the awkward conversation. Chad passed us and was now staring into the drawing room with his hands on his hips, surveying the broken chandelier lying on the floor and the hole in the ceiling. "Man, that must have hurt."

The three of us moved to stand behind Chad in the doorway. "Luckily, no one was in here when it happened," I said.

Marc kneeled in front of the chandelier and was inspecting it closely. "Looks like it's Italian. I wonder if it's even repairable." He picked up a loose teardrop pendant. "Of course, you could always sell if for salvage. Old-house owners are always looking for the odd crystal pendant missing from their grandmother's chandelier."

"Actually, it's nineteenth-century Baccarat and worth a fortune." Sophie had come in without me hearing her and was standing next to Chad in an identical position with her hands on her hips. She was frowning at Marc as she spoke. "I have an expert coming in tomorrow to take it to be repaired. Luckily, it fell on the rug and not the hard floor, so it's not as irreparable as one would think. It will be expensive to repair, but compared to its value, it's nothing."

Marc stood, brushing off his pants knees as he did. "That's amazing. You'd think it was made of diamonds or something." He watched me closely as he spoke, making me wonder if I had missed something.

"It definitely wasn't," said Sophie, leaning down to pick up a crushed piece of crystal that had been half hidden under the rug. "The poor Aubusson would have a huge hole in the middle if that were the case." She held up the crushed crystal in her open palm. "Diamonds are a lot more lethal to old rugs than crystal." She smiled before dropping the pendant into her pocket.

"Oh, my goodness! What happened in here?" We all turned around to find Mrs. Trenholm standing behind us in the doorway, taking in the damage. Her eyes finally settled on Jack. "Please tell me that you had nothing to do with this."

Jack reached her side and kissed her on both cheeks in greeting. "No, Mother. It just fell out of the old plaster. But thank you for thinking me capable of ripping a chandelier out of a fourteen-foot-high ceiling."

Mrs. Trenholm shook her head sadly. "I knew you as a toddler, remember." She approached the chandelier. "Definitely Baccarat. Mid-nineteenth century would be my guess. And certainly worth repairing."

"That's what I thought, too," said Sophie as she offered her hand and then introduced herself.

I greeted Jack's mother and then introduced the remaining people in the room, ending with Marc.

"Oh, yes. Mr. Longo. I believe we spoke several times on the phone last spring regarding the Gibbes Museum's AIDS benefit." She raised an elegant eyebrow, and I thought I could see Marc squirm under her scrutiny.

"Yes. I do remember. It's a pleasure to finally meet you in person, Mrs. Trenholm."

"Likewise," she said with a polite smile.

I introduced Amelia to Sophie and Chad, then turned my attention to her. "Thanks for coming by. Please excuse the mess." I indicated the tarps covering the marble floor in the entranceway and the short scaffolding Chad had been erecting in the foyer to begin the arduous process of peeling off fifty-year-old wallpaper without damaging the 150-year-old handpainted wallpaper underneath. With much frowning and agitated sighs, Sophie had finally agreed to show Chad how to do it, figuring it would keep him away from her for a good long while. Chad's eagerness had bordered on pathetic.

"It's not a mess, dear. Just a work in progress. And I'm sorry to intrude. Jack called me this morning and wanted me to take a look at some of the things he found in the attic."

I faced Jack. "Did you finish going through everything already?"

"I couldn't sleep after you left last night." He paused—the innuendo intentional, I was sure. "So I decided to finish sorting through the attic. I brought most of the boxes and smaller items and stored them in the two extra bedrooms on my side of the house. The bigger stuff—like your buffalo—I left up there. When Mom's done, Chad here can help me move the more valuable furniture to other spots in the house—at least until we get the roof repaired."

"I'm working on it," said Sophie. "I've got our paperwork into the BAR, and I'm waiting to hear from them. Hopefully we'll just be rubber-stamped. In the meantime, I've got some guys coming over today to patch some of those holes over the attic."

Marc crossed his arms and frowned. "Ah, yes. The BAR. Aren't they the ones referred to as the second cousin who comes for a visit and stays too long?" Marc looked around for corroboration.

His words echoed my sentiments exactly, but hearing them said out loud embarrassed me, made me feel like an impostor, reminded me that there had been a time when I'd once thought that the oak-lined streets of the historic district were the most beautiful streets in the world.

Marc clasped his hands together at the deafening silence. "Well, then, would this be a good time for a tour?"

"Sure," I said, avoiding Jack's glance. "Let's head up to the attic first to show Mrs. Trenholm some of the treasures Jack's uncovered, if you'd like to get started there."

"Sounds like a plan," he said, heading eagerly toward the staircase. The rest of us followed, including General Lee, who seemed to be adopting the annoying habit of gluing himself to my side whenever we were in the same room together.

As we walked up the stairs, Mrs. Trenholm paused halfway, admiring the view into the foyer. "You truly are lucky, Melanie. I know many people who would just kill to get their hands on this furniture, much less the house! Speaking of which, I have connections with several museums, two of whom have expressed an interest in housing some of your collections while you're in a state of renovation. I was thinking mostly of some of the museum-quality pieces Jack suspects you might have in your attic, but now that I see the extent of the work being done in the house, you might consider lending a few of the other pieces that are in the way." She looked around her again with narrowed eyes. "How long are you anticipating the restoration will take?"

"I'm giving it a year, tops. And then I'll be able to sell it."

I watched as Amelia's eyes met Jack's over my head. "A year, hmm? I'm thinking you've never worked much with contractors, have you?"

I crossed my arms over my chest, feeling defensive. "Not really. Which is one of the reasons I always prefer to live in new construction."

"I see," she said, and those two words seemed to mean a lot more than I could translate at the moment.

We continued on our way up the stairs. "I'd love for you to take that grandfather clock in the downstairs drawing room. It chimes every fifteen minutes all through the day and night, and it is driving me crazy. Sophie wants to get started on the ceiling and walls in there, but it's going to be hard to work around it."

Mrs. Trenholm stopped at the top of the stairs and looked at me. "Oh, no, Melanie. You shouldn't move that clock. It's bad luck—or haven't you heard?" She put her finger to her chin, a small line forming between her brows. "There's some sort of story, made up years ago, I'm sure, about that clock. It's been here since about the time of the War Between the States, and has never been moved. The story says that it's cursed or some such nonsense and that anybody who tries to move it meets with some horrible fate—but I have a feeling that whoever started that story was probably somebody's husband who didn't want to break his back because his wife wanted to rearrange the furniture again." She winked. "You know how men can be."

Jack grunted, but everybody else remained silent as we made our way to the attic. We crowded around the space inside the door as Jack went ahead to flip on the single bulb.

"Oh, my goodness," exclaimed Mrs. Trenholm as she studied her surroundings. "It's like finding treasure." She walked over to a low chest with a bowed front and elaborate brass fixtures. Kneeling in front of it, she slid open a drawer and peered inside. "French, seventeenth century at the latest. Very well made." She stood and patted the top of it the way a mother would before sending her child off on his first day of kindergarten. "It needs refinishing but other than that it's in good shape." She faced me. "Melanie, you really need to get it out of this humid attic. I'll have my museum friend contact you tomorrow."

"Thank you," I said, adding that to my never-ending and growing to-do list.

General Lee ran past me toward the buffalo and began barking. Chad laughed. "Look at that. He thinks he's found a friend."

Sophie stepped forward, her attempt at sending Chad a withering glance failing miserably. "No, actually. He seems to be barking at the desk next to Mr. Buffalo."

She sneezed as Chad joined her and picked up the dog. "What's wrong, big guy? Something spooked you?"

General Lee responded with a resounding yap and twisted in Chad's arms to face the desk again.

Jack and I joined them near the desk as Sophie stepped forward and opened the desk drawer. "Look—there's a stack of papers in here."

Jack reached in and lifted them out. "I know. Mellie and I found them last night. When I get a chance I'll go through them, although at first glance I don't think there's anything of real significance here." He moved to stick them back in the drawer when I remembered what I'd thought about the night before as I'd gone to sleep. I put my hand on his wrist. "Wait a minute. I want to look at that deed again."

For a moment I had the extraordinary thought that he was going to refuse. "Sure," he said, riffling through the documents until he pulled out the right one and handed it to me.

I scanned the document, my eyes settling at the bottom, confirming what I'd thought before. "I know the person who witnessed this." I looked up, meeting Jack's eyes, and it became apparent to me that he already knew. "My grandfather—Augustus Middleton."

General Lee let out a bark as Sophie and Chad gathered around us to get a closer look at the deed. Sophie took the paper from me and squinted at the small print. "I guess it makes sense since your grandfather was not only a friend but also a lawyer. But why would Mr. Vanderhorst deed the property to his wife?"

Chad reached down to pick up General Lee, who was jumping up as if to get a better look. "It sure is a mystery," he said, looking around. "But I bet if we put our four heads together we could figure it out."

Mrs. Trenholm made a strangled sound in her throat, and then coughed. "Jack, what was that silly cartoon with the dog and his four friends that you used to watch every Saturday morning? They would solve mysteries and drive a van." I watched as a grin spread across Mrs. Trenholm's face.

Jack's brow furrowed. "You mean *Scooby-Doo*?"

Sophie snorted. "With Shaggy, Fred, Velma, and Daphne?"

"Yes! That's it." Amelia put her hand over her mouth to stifle a laugh.

"Ruh-roh!" said Chad, obviously getting the joke that so far eluded me.

When Jack and Sophie began laughing, too, my annoyance turned into peevishness. "I guess some of us had better things to do than sit in front of a television set on Saturday mornings," I said, remembering how I'd used that time to sit by my father's bed with a bucket so that when he threw up after his Friday night binges, I wouldn't have to clean up.

Marc cleared his throat. "The resemblance is a bit uncanny. But wouldn't you need a ghost, too?"

That quickly sobered everyone up, and I wondered if they were all remembering the flying picture frame in the drawing room. I avoided Jack's eyes as I turned back to the deed. "Didn't I hear somewhere lately that Magnolia Ridge had been purchased recently?"

Marc coughed again. "I own it, actually. Sort of my first foray into historical real estate investment. Magnolia Ridge plantation had been abandoned and then owned by the state for years and was about to go up for auction. I guess you can say I was in the right place at the right time."

"What a coincidence," Jack said with a tight smile.

"Yes, wasn't it?" Marc smiled, then turned back to me. "I'm sorry to be leaving so soon, but I've got another appointment. I'll ask for my tour another time, Melanie, when you're not so busy. And I'll pick you up at five o'clock on Friday, all right? All you'll need is a toothbrush and a bathing suit."

All eyes turned to me, and I felt my cheeks burn, feeling guilty that I could be considering time off when everybody else had been working long days with only a minor stipend—my father's idea—and good food provided by Mrs. Houlihan as payment. Except for Chad's motivations involving Sophie, I wouldn't entertain the possibility that people would restore an old house for fun. I looked down at my chipped fingernails, courtesy of scraping decades of paint layers from the corkscrew spindles on the central staircase, and remembered that I'd missed yet another appointment with my hair colorist because I'd been waiting on the electrician again.

"If it makes you feel any better, I promise you that it won't all be leisure," Marc added. "We can finish our discussion about historic real estate in Charleston and maybe come up with a list of houses to see in the next week."

The talk of doing work did assuage my conscience somewhat, and when I spied my neglected fingernails again, my mind was made up. Defiantly, I raised my chin. "Yes, that would be great. I'll be ready."

His look of surprise was quickly hidden behind a smile. "Great. I'll see you then." He kissed me briefly on the cheek, his warm breath teasing my nerves and making me blush. I was grateful for the dim lighting.

"I'll see you out," I said, following Marc to the door.

"Me, too," said Jack as he followed us both to the stairs. I didn't bother sending him a scathing look, knowing that it wouldn't make any difference.

Marc paused halfway down the stairs. "This is such a beautiful home. I'll admit to being a bit disappointed that it's not for sale. Then again, look at all this work. I'm not sure if I were in your position I'd be willing to see it through."

We reached the front door. "Believe me," I said, "I have second thoughts every day about my sanity in deciding to stay here."

Marc smiled, his eyes warm. "There's nothing wrong with your sanity, Melanie. You made a promise to an old man, which shows you have a warm and generous heart. That's a very good thing, you know."

I thought he was about to kiss me, and I wasn't opposed to the idea, when Jack spoke up from behind us. "That's our Mellie. Heart of gold." He stepped around us and pulled open the door. "Thanks for stopping by, Matt. We'll see you later."

A flash of loathing appeared in Marc's eyes and then just as quickly was gone. Marc looked at me again, his brown eyes penetrating. "I'll see you Friday."

"Looking forward to it," I said as I watched him head down the piazza, wondering if he really would have kissed me if Jack hadn't been there.

I closed the door, then turned around, almost jumping in surprise to find Jack standing so close. He wasn't smiling.

"Remember what I said about coincidences, Mellie? They don't exist. Regardless of what he wants you to think, it is not a coincidence that Marc Longo not only owns Magnolia Ridge, but also showed up on your doorstep asking to buy this house."

Irritated, I pushed away from him and headed back to the stairs. "I told you, he's a businessman. It would only make sense that he'd want to invest in real estate in his hometown."

Jack followed me, his heels digging into the floor with each step. "But why you? Why this house? Don't you think there's something else here?"

I stood on the third step and turned around to face him. "Like what? That he found out his grandfather and Louisa really did have an affair? Why would that make him want to buy up all the real estate that had anything to do with her? Marc Longo is simply not the kind of man who would get sentimental over an old love story or a past scandal. He's a businessman, remember? He's looking for ways to make money."

I was shaking now, angry beyond reason as I turned back around and began running up the stairs. Jack tugged on my arm, jerking me back and bringing me to a halt. "He is using you to get to something. I-I'm not sure what, but it has something to do with this house. I'm guessing he looked for whatever it is at Magnolia Ridge, and when he didn't find it, he assumed it's here in this house."

I jerked my arm away but Jack didn't back down. He continued. "I've been asking around town and found out that Marc Longo is deeply in debt and needs some cash flow. My own mother will tell you how he stiffed the AIDS charity they were talking about earlier. He's never paid up. He's got creditors crawling out of the woodwork." He leaned toward me. "He wants something, Mellie. And he's not the kind of guy who takes no for an answer."

My chest tightened, the familiar feeling of disappointment filling the space, and I twirled around and began running up the stairs. "Is it too much for you to believe that an attractive and intelligent man could possibly be interested in just me?" I swallowed, embarrassed to hear the tears in my voice. *Was I really that desperate?* I paused on the top step, trying to catch my breath. "Okay. So what if his motives aren't so honorable? At this point in my life, I don't care. He's attractive and attentive, and he likes taking me out. We're both having fun and not planning a wedding, for crying out loud." I took a shuddering breath, trying not to sound as desperate as I felt. "Look, I'm a big girl, and I can take care of myself. Did you ever stop to think that maybe I just want to have a little fun with a good-looking guy? Is that so wrong?"

His voice was soft behind me. "Would it be too difficult for you to believe that I care about you and don't want you hurt?"

I was too angry and upset to believe anything he said, and I wanted to hurt him as much as he had hurt me. I turned back to face him as I grasped the banister. "Why did your fiancée leave you, Jack?"

His face remained impassive but I saw the light dim in his eyes and knew I'd reached my target. At first I thought he wasn't going to answer. Then quietly, he said, "She told me that she didn't love me. That she had never really loved me."

Any satisfaction I would have felt evaporated quickly at the hurt and loss that filled his eyes. "Jack, I . . ." I had a split second to register the familiar putrid smell around me before the words were knocked out of my mouth by the distinct feeling of two ice-cold hands punching me in the back, sending me toppling forward straight into Jack. He managed to break my fall with one arm while holding on to the banister with the other.

"You've got to stop throwing yourself at me, Mellie," he began before I felt another shove aimed at the middle of my back, sending us both sprawling down the stairs toward the marble floor. Jack pressed his arms around me, twisting himself so that he landed on the hardwood stairs, taking the brunt of the fall. Our momentum carried us down the stairs at a growing speed, and I sensed Jack trying to turn us around so that we wouldn't land headfirst.

Then, just as suddenly as the push from behind, we stopped abruptly on the last step. Jack's face was less then an inch from mine, so close that I could see the beads of perspiration gathering on his forehead. "What the . . . ?" I felt the rapid rise and fall of his chest as we lay pressed together where we'd landed. He didn't try to move me off of him, his arms still wrapped around me. In a different situation, I might even have enjoyed it. "Are you all right?"

Too stunned to speak, I nodded, taking a mental inventory of all my limbs. I already felt the bruising in the two places the unseen hands had made contact with my back.

"How did that happen, Mellie? You were standing still, and then all of a sudden you were flying at me, as if you'd been pushed."

My teeth began to chatter, and he tightened his arms around me. "I'm—I'm just clumsy. I trip easily."

He stared at me for a long moment, his breath warm on my cheek. Neither one of us attempted to move.

Jack continued. "And I could have sworn that somebody—or something—just broke our fall. It felt like we landed on a pillow."

I clamped my teeth down to prevent them from chattering before I spoke again. "I can't imagine what that could have been," I said, our noses touching along with just about everything else along our fronts.

"Really?" he asked, raising an eyebrow.

"Really," I said.

"So there's nothing else going on here that I should know about. Nothing that's putting you—or me—in danger."

I shook my head, beginning to smell the scent of roses again. My chattering stopped.

"You're not aware of any . . . spirits who might be trying to get your attention for one reason or another, assuming you believe in that kind of thing."

Again, I shook my head. "No, of course not."

The sound of something solid hitting the floor in the adjacent drawing room startled both of us, but neither one of us moved. We'd both heard that sound before, after all.

Jack had pulled back slightly and was staring at my lips in a way that made my skin feel tight around my bones. "Well, if it's all the same to you," he said in a quiet voice, "I'm going to continue to stick around to protect you from yourself, all right?"

I nodded, not able to find the breath required to speak.

"Yo, dudes. Sorry to interrupt, but I think the little guy needs to go pee."

Jack and I scrambled to standing positions, then stood on opposite sides of the stairs to watch nonchalantly as Chad carried the dog downstairs, his Birkenstocks quiet on the treads, which is probably why we hadn't heard him coming from the attic.

Chad's gaze drifted from me to Jack and then back again as a slow smile spread across his face. As he walked to the front door, he called over his shoulder, "I'll knock first before I come back in."

As soon as I heard the front door shut, I walked to the drawing room, Jack close behind me. In front of the grandfather clock, lying on its back with the faces of the two people staring up at us, was the framed photograph of Nevin Vanderhorst and his mother.

Jack picked it up and looked at me. "So there's nothing out of the ordinary that's going on in this house."

"Not at all," I said, not meeting his eyes as I plucked the frame out of his hands and replaced it on the side table, where it had been last time I saw it less than an hour before.

Remembering that I was still angry at him, I left the room without another word and headed up the stairs, feeling his gaze on my back the entire way.

CHAPTER 15

The weeks passed quickly, the days filled with sawdust, the smell of fresh plaster and the tread of feet. I was on a first-name basis with an electrician, a plumber, a roofer, an arborist (on account of the oak tree outside developing a fungus my father couldn't identify), a feng shui decorator (Chad's recommendation), an exterminator (thanks to the colonies of termites calling the foundation their home), and a massage therapist (to deal with the various muscle pains and frequent headaches these relationships caused). My manicurist and hairstylist had begun calling and leaving worried messages, assuming I had been in a horrible accident or had died since in the past these two scenarios would have been the only excuses I'd allow for me to miss an appointment.

We had managed to roll up the Aubusson rug in the drawing room—and found nothing of interest underneath in the floorboard, despite a thorough examination—and sent it away for repairs. We found a temporary home for most of the furniture in the room (except for the grandfather clock) at a newly restored home in the Ansonborough district that was being opened as a house museum. Sophie brought in a colleague and expert in the grad department of historical restoration at the University of Pennsylvania to come look at the ceiling from where the chandelier had taken its suicidal leap. This was the same guy who had been behind the restoration of the grand hall ceiling at Drayton Hall and had won some award for an article he'd written about it.

Even I was impressed as I watched him and one of Sophie's grad students take plaster casts of the existing medallion to be used in replacing those pieces that had been destroyed utilizing the same techniques and materials that had been used to make the original. I watched as they drilled a series of small holes along existing cracks, into which they injected some sort of epoxy filler with huge syringes to prevent further damage and prohibit chunks of ceiling plaster from falling on unsuspecting room occupants.

Leaning more toward conservation than preservation, Sophie had wanted to leave the ceiling as it was after the repair work was done—without hiding the cracks or painting over the repair job. But since I was a Realtor, my goal was to sell the house for as much money as I possibly could. And most people didn't want to see cracks in their ceilings, no matter how authentic it looked.

It wasn't as if I didn't allow compromises, though, as long as they made sense. I'd allowed Sophie to consult with experts and use real plaster instead of Sheetrock in most of the restoration. But I also stood firm when it came to gutting the kitchen and bathrooms, and adding a bathroom to the existing master suite. She'd looked at me as if I were a Hun destroying a village of widows and orphans—or, as she put it, not respecting the original builder's vision of the house. I shouldered her disapproval as the first wall was knocked down between my bedroom and the next to expand the space and make room for plumbing, but even I felt a little tremor of loss as the dust from the plaster exploded into the room, little puffs of dust raining down like ghosts.

To appease Sophie, I followed her instructions on the meticulous and painstakingly correct procedures for stripping wallpaper and paint, which involved impossibly tiny razors and awkward knives, regardless of how time-consuming they were. I was kneeling in front of the drawing room's fireplace, digging a putty knife into what seemed like twelve layers of paint in an attempt to uncover what looked to be a giant breadfruit tree, when Jack entered the room, his own putty knife held aloft.

"Sophie said you might need some help."

"I'm beginning to think that an ax might be more effective than this stupid putty knife. I've worked on the same spot for over an hour, and I've managed to remove all the layers of paint from an area the size of a golf ball."

We stood together, examining the old fireplace. Even I had to admit that the detailing was truly a work of art and not something that I had ever seen in contemporary homes, regardless of their cost. Elaborate fluted columns capped with Corinthian capitols and rosettes flanked each side of the fireplace and supported the surround, on which foxes and hounds dashed around a series of breadfruit trees. My admiration would have been greater if I wasn't the one in charge of removing thick layers of paint from between the leaves on the trees, which at that moment seemed less defined than their artist had originally intended.

Jack stood beside me and regarded my handiwork. "Good job, Mellie. At this rate we'll be done with this mantel next December sometime. At least you'll be getting lots of practice. How many fireplaces are in this house, anyway—three?"

"Six," I said, feeling slightly nauseous.

Jack stepped forward to stand on the opposite side of the fireplace from me, and raised his knife. Alarmed, I held up my hand, imaging Sophie's horror if a piece of tree trunk or hound head got lopped off. "Do you know how to use that?"

He raised his eyebrow in that wicked look of his that always managed to surprise my blood flow. "I'm pretty handy with my tools."

I paused in my work and sent him a withering look.

"Get your head out of the gutter, Mellie. I meant that I currently live in an eighteen fifties rice warehouse converted to condos that I restored all by myself, so I'm familiar with scraping paint from old mantels."

I returned my focus to my work, feeling myself blush up to my hairline. "I knew what you meant, Jack. You're just immature enough to think otherwise."

He chuckled softly, making me laugh, too, but I kept myself focused on the hideous green paint.

We worked in companionable silence for a long while, the only interruptions our gruntings as we encountered a particularly stubborn chunk of paint and the sound of Sophie's instructions to Chad downstairs regarding hand sanding the balustrade.

We were working on the flat surface of the mantel, supposedly the easiest part, and were standing fairly close to each other as we worked on opposite sides. After our close encounter at the bottom of the stairs, I had become hypersensitive to his presence, sort of like me being an infrared camera and him being the heat source. I scraped my fingers several more times with my knife thanks to Jack, and I kept reminding myself that the pain in my thumb was all his fault.

"Any more phone calls?" Jack paused next to me but I didn't look up.

I thought about lying for a moment, but decided I'd already done enough of that. "Yes, actually, there have been. About two or three a night now. Last night, I finally decided to unplug the phone when I went to sleep."

"What if there's an emergency?"

I enjoyed hearing the concern in his voice. I felt mollified, somewhat, since feeling his presence in my house at night kept the fear from pressing in around me. There were things in the dark—things I didn't want to see. And knowing Jack was around helped me keep them at bay. Not that I would ever tell him, of course.

"I keep my cell phone on the table next to me in case I need to reach someone in the middle of the night. I keep it on vibrate just in case they decide to call me on that number."

"Still no idea who it could be?"

I shook my head. "No, which is weird since nowadays I thought any number could be traced. Maybe if I got the police involved they could, but it's probably just some kid, and I don't want to ruin his life over something like a prank call."

This was only half true. Since the phone calls had begun the week before, it had been nothing more than an annoyance and an interruption to my sleep. The male person on the other line would disguise his voice and ask for me by name and then breathe heavily until I hung up. The caller ID on my phone simply said "not a known number." I'd neglected to tell Jack about the last phone call I received—just after I pulled the cord out of the wall.

I had just drifted off to sleep when the phone rang. In my half-asleep mode, I forgot that the phone was no longer connected to the wall; otherwise I probably wouldn't have answered it. The third time it rang, I picked it up, ready to unload a few expletives that had never crossed my lips before. But the breathing this time was different, lighter. Like a woman's. And when I heard the voice, I collapsed back on my pillow, my limbs suddenly boneless. "Hello, Peanut," came the crackling voice on the other end of the phone, "I've missed you."

Only one person had ever called me "Peanut," and she'd been dead for almost thirty-four years. "Grandma?" I whispered, my hands frozen as they grasped the receiver.

"You need to stop by, Peanut. Come sit in my garden and have a sweet tea like you used to. It's going to be yours one day, you know. So you might as well come by and sit for a spell to see how well it fits."

The receiver banged against my ear as the hand clutching it began to shake. "Grandma?" I said again through suddenly parched lips.

"You need to call your mama, Peanut." The line had gone all staticy, making it hard to hear. When I heard her voice again, I pressed my ear to the receiver, her voice sounding far away. "She misses you so." The voice faded away and the line went clear, leaving nothing but dead air.

I threw the phone into the corner of the room, then huddled under my covers until dawn started to creep through the blinds.

Jack lifted his forearm and rubbed it against his hair to dislodge a large paint flake. "If it's all right with you, I'll keep a phone in my room, so if the prankster calls again, he'll know that you're not alone. That might be all we need to discourage him."

"Thanks," I said, hoping Jack wouldn't get any phone calls from my grandmother, too. Even I didn't think I'd be able to explain that.

We turned back to scraping, and I slid a glance over to Jack, wondering why he was so silent. I saw his jaw ticking in rhythm with his scraping and knew he was struggling hard to remain quiet. Finally, he said, "Has he kissed you yet?"

"Who? General Lee? I don't let him close enough."

Jack smirked. "I guess that means no, then."

"How do you know he hasn't kissed me?"

He faced me and I met his gaze. "I do now, don't I?"

Too flustered to answer, I dug my knife into another latex layer, picturing Jack as I filleted the paint.

"Don't you think that's a bit odd, Mellie? You've spent a weekend at his beach house, gone with him to dinners or the theater or some event about three times a week, and then hung out here with him just about every other evening. Either he's gay, or there's something else."

I dropped my knife and looked at him. "Why would that make him gay?"

Jack turned to face me, and his eyes seemed darker than usual. "Because if a guy has spent that much time with you and still hasn't even kissed you, there must be another explanation."

I opened my mouth to defend myself, then ended up only stammering as I realized what Jack was really saying. I clamped my lips together and focused on picking up the jewelry knife Sophie had given me to pry old paint out of the intricate carvings of bread tree leaves.

Jack kept looking at me. Softly, he said, "So I'm guessing there's something else."

I couldn't decide whether I should be flattered or angry, so I kept quiet.

"Have you showed him many houses?"

"A few. Nothing that suited him, though," I said, remembering Marc's brief interest in the properties we'd seen.

"Just let me know if he ever decides to buy. I'd bet money that he doesn't."

"We'll see about that," I said, lifting my chin.

"Yeah, I guess we will," said Jack, stabbing his putty knife into the mantel.

We were quiet for a while before I remembered what I'd been meaning to ask. "How's your book coming along?"

"Slowly. Very slowly, thank you. I've been doing lots of research on the Vanderhorst family, which is very interesting if not very illuminating. Real Charleston blue bloods—they've been here since it was still called Charles Towne. Sent their men to fight in every war since the Revolution. But nothing new that we didn't already know about the disappearance of Louisa Vanderhorst in nineteen thirty. Although I did find proof that Robert Vanderhorst and your grandfather were great friends and attended law school together. I believe Gus was Robert's best man at his wedding."

"I know—Mrs. Houlihan showed me the photograph. It's in a frame in the upstairs drawing room if you want to see it. Not that it means anything, of course, except I have Grandfather Gus to thank for the predicament I'm in. If he'd been a stranger to Mr. Vanderhorst, this never would have happened."

Jack raised an eyebrow but didn't say anything.

I plucked a flake of paint out of my hair, where it had landed. "Did you find anything interesting in the pile of papers in the desk in the attic?"

"Still going through them. I did find out that the state ended up owning Magnolia Ridge because of failure to pay the taxes on the property. The interesting part is that Mr. Vanderhorst was still a wealthy man, even through the Depression—which is an interesting fact on its own—but he chose not to pay the taxes. Like he just didn't care about it anymore after his wife died."

"Like he probably didn't care about this place anymore, either, judging by the condition of the kitchen and plumbing. I don't think they've changed since the twenties."

Jack snorted. "Judging by the ice-cold shower I took this morning, I'd have to say you're right. Speaking of showers, you left your bra hanging on the curtain rod. I left it there but tried not to get any water on it."

I chewed the inside of my cheek to hide my embarrassment. At least he wasn't making any jokes about how small it was. "Thanks for letting me know."

"You're welcome," he said, and I could hear the smile in his voice. "I thought it was a slingshot at first until I saw the two little cups."

"That's enough, Jack."

"Yes, ma'am," he said, making a studious effort to concentrate on the job of chipping away old paint.

We worked for another hour or so, our conversation meandering everywhere from current events to the ridiculous so that I was almost enjoying myself until I realized that together we had collectively removed the paint from an area totaling that of a dinner plate. Jack plunked his putty knife down, and wiped his forehead with his hand. The new and functioning central air wasn't being installed until the following week, so we had fans lined up on the floor, but they did nothing except move the sweat around your skin. "I have an idea. I'll be right back."

He returned about five minutes later, holding a heat gun. "I got it from your dad. He's been taking some classes at the Home Depot, and they told him this would help with some of the projects here. Sophie took one look at it and told him to put it away, so you'll have to promise me that Sophie won't find out about this. She would rather we lose all ten digits on our hands than stoop to using modern methods, but I figure it's your house, right?"

Without a second thought, I dropped my knife. "Close the door and lock it."

Jack shut the door quietly, turning the key in the lock until it clicked. "If she knocks, we can pretend we've been wrestling naked."

I put my hands on my hips. "In that case, I think I'd rather she know that we cheated."

He grinned and walked over to the mantel. "And look—here's an outlet right next to the fireplace. Surely this was meant to be." He plugged the heat gun in and turned it on, listening to the satisfying whir of the little motor. "What would you do without me?" he asked.

"Pour a can of kerosene around the house and light a match."

"It's a good thing I'm here, then."

"Whatever," I said as I watched the thick latex paint peel and curl under the heat gun. "I'm still going to need to manually scrape out the paint from around those danged leaves."

"Yep. But that's where the fun comes in."

I rolled my eyes, but only halfheartedly. I would never admit this to him, but seeing art carved by hand by an artist more than one hundred years ago come to life again with the removal of all those layers of paint had been almost gratifying. Not as gratifying as selling this house for a huge amount of money would be but still gratifying.

I halfheartedly returned to the more intricate parts of the design with the jeweler's knife, while Jack had the mentally daunting task of swiping the heat gun over the painted surfaces and watching the paint curl and peel. He focused on the spot where the fireplace was attached to the wall and where the thick paint had built up so that there was no separation between the two surfaces. He was squatting near the bottom and brushing off the peeled paint with a clean paint brush when he flicked the heat gun off. "What's this?" he asked.

I squatted down next to him and peered into the now exposed crack between the wall and the mantel and saw what appeared to be a rectangular scrap of fabric. "Hang on," I said as I crossed the room to where an old radio with long antennas sat on the floor, unplugged to make room for the fans, and brought it back to the fireplace. Using one of the antennas, I stuck it in the small crack and dragged the scrap toward the edge, where Jack used a fingernail to pry it from its prison.

"It looks like a cross-stitch sampler," he said. Flattening it on his knee, we saw that it was very old linen, yellowed and brittle but surprisingly intact considering its age, the silk thread faded yet the colors still identifiable. In the middle was stitched an incredibly accurate representation of the house we were now standing in, and surrounding it were intricately worked lawn scenes with animals, trees, potted plants, and a great assortment of sampler motifs as if the stitcher had decided to include every motif that she had learned.

The words *Emily Vanderhorst, age 13 years, 1849* were delicately worked with pale yellow thread into the bottom of the sampler and encircled in an undulating vine, with little bees buzzing around beehives flanking the verse above the name. I read the verse out loud: " 'Do not resort to ghosts and spirits, nor make yourselves unclean by seeking them out. I am the Lord your God. Leviticus 19:31.' "

I met Jack's eyes over the sampler. With a raised eyebrow, he said, "I thought they were supposed to put generic Bible quotes on their samplers."

I nodded, my eyes drawn back to the stitch work, almost as if I would miss something if I looked away. "They usually do. How odd that this one is so . . . so different."

I could feel Jack looking at me. "It's almost like she's writing it as punishment, isn't it? Like a teacher making a student write 'I will not talk in class' one hundred times on the blackboard. Like poor Emily here was made to stitch this Bible quote so she'd remember it."

My voice stuck in my throat.

"It makes me think that maybe Emily said something about seeing a ghost and her parents got angry." Jack paused. "You know they say that some houses are like beacons to those spirits who haven't passed on."

I thought of Louisa and her scent of roses, and the menacing figure with the putrid smell I'd seen in the window and felt on my back. I also recalled the fleeting glimpse of an old gentleman in a Confederate uniform, the boy in the swing, and a teenage girl who walked gracefully across the upstairs hallway, disappearing into a doorway that didn't exist anymore. And the woman who sought after Jack and all the voices I could hear whispering to me if I stopped and paid attention. I read somewhere once that renovations disturbed old spirits, making them come out of hiding to see what was going on or to voice their displeasure. Or just maybe these spirits had been here all along, waiting for someone like me to come and look.

"Really?" I answered, my voice not sounding like my own.

"And some people are, too. Beacons, I mean."

"Is that so?" I asked, keeping my eyes focused on the scrap of yellowed linen. "I've never heard that before." I swallowed. "You know, Jack, I think you're reading too much into it. Maybe Emily was just . . . different." Gently, I picked up the fabric scrap. "I wonder what it was doing behind the mantel. Maybe her mother had propped it up there to display, and then it accidentally fell behind it and was forgotten."

"Or maybe," Jack added, "her mother accidentally on purpose lost it."

I finally looked at him. "What do you mean?"

"When I was a little boy, I had a favorite book that I made my mother read to me at bedtime at least sixteen times each night. It had lots of different characters, so when she read it, she had to make up all those voices. It must have been exhausting for her." He looked down at the sampler for a moment, smiling to himself. "Anyway, one day the book just vanished. She helped me look and look for that book, but we never did find it. It was only a couple of years ago that she finally confessed to me that she hid it in the bottom of her cedar chest, where I would never find it, because she thought she might go mad if she ever had to read it again. She only saved it so that I could give it to my own child so that I might also be forced to read it ad nauseum."

I laughed. "Yeah, I can see your mother doing that." I stared down at the fabric, sober suddenly. "Maybe Emily's mother thought Emily had been punished enough, so she got rid of it." Standing, I held the sampler up to the light, illuminating the intricate stitches.

"It's like holding a piece of history in your hands, isn't it?" asked Jack.

I stilled, hearing the voice of an old man saying almost the exact same words—words that I remembered even now despite the fact that when I'd first heard them they'd held no meaning for me. *This house is more than brick, mortar and lumber. It's a connection to the past and those who have gone before us. It's memories and belonging. It's a home that on the inside has seen the birth of children and the death of the old folks and the changing of the world from the outside. It's a piece of history you can hold in your hands.*

I lowered my arms, feeling as if I had seen another ghost. Averting my eyes, I said, "I'll go show it to Sophie and ask her about finding somebody to frame it. Then I can hang it in the foyer—those old-house buyers always love that kitschy nostalgic stuff in their houses."

I was halfway to the door when somebody knocked. I stopped. "Who is it?"

"It's just your dad."

I exchanged a look of relief with Jack, then unlocked the door. My dad stood on the other side, holding up another heat gun. I smiled when I saw it and nearly pulled my dad into the room, locking the door behind him.

"I figured you could use two. How many fireplaces do you have in this house? Three?"

"Six," I said, taking the heat gun from him. "This will certainly come in handy. Thank you."

He eyed the locked door behind him. "Am I outside my bounds asking why the door is locked?"

The question was directed at me, but Jack answered. "No, sir. Can't say we'll be honest in our answer, but you can certainly ask."

My dad nodded his head. "Uh-huh. You're hiding from Sophie, aren't you? Not that I blame you. She's already spoken to me several times about using nonorganic fertilizers in the garden. She doesn't want anything used that wasn't available at the time the house was built."

"Which leaves you with water and horse manure, basically," said Jack.

"Yep, that would be correct."

The two of them laughed as I studied my dad, his face and arms bronzed from working outside in the garden, his gaze steady. I held myself very still, not wanting to go backward or forward, but stay there where we were. It was all I had really ever wanted since I was a child, and now that I saw it, I was afraid to move on. Afraid it wouldn't last. I turned away. "I've got to show this to Sophie. I'll see you later."

"Actually, Melanie, let me come out with you. I want to show you something I found in the garden."

"What—like an unidentified shrub? You're asking the wrong person."

He sent me a lopsided grin. "Yeah, I know. I never did quite get around to teaching you about gardening, did I?"

"No, Dad, you didn't." I saw the hesitation in his eyes and stopped. *A truce, then,* I thought. *For now.*

"It's actually the fountain. I cleared away all the weeds from the base, and I found something interesting carved into it. Nothing like any of the architectural elements I've been studying in my night class at the college." He glanced up at me and shrugged. "Just something Sophie suggested I do to help with the restoration. Anyway, I wanted you to look at, see if it means anything to you." He glanced behind me to Jack. "I'd like you to take a look, too."

"I'm right behind you," Jack said as he hid the heat guns beneath a chair, then followed us out.

The garden had undergone a complete transformation. Shrubs and beds that had not been part of the original design had been removed, and brick pavers replaced with old bricks to create winding paths throughout. Bright patches of noisette roses and camellias crept along the edge of the house and peered out from new beds filled with lush greens and freshly tilled earth.

I felt guilty because I'd not spent the time in the garden to see what my father had been working on so hard. It had never occurred to me that he could have accomplished anything so beautiful. So vibrant. "It's wonderful, Dad. It's right out of a gardening magazine."

He tucked in his chin, like a bashful child. "I'm glad you like it, Melanie. I've had a lot of fun with it. But look over here—this is what I wanted you to see."

I felt a movement at the far side of the garden and slid my gaze to the old oak tree. The woman was there again and the boy sat next to her, the swing still. They both looked at me expectantly.

"Are you all right?" Jack had stopped on the path next to me.

"Yes, I'm fine," I said, jerking my gaze away. "Just admiring the tree, that's all."

He nodded and waited for me to move down the path before following me. I sucked in a breath when we caught up to my father, amazed that this could be the same garden I'd seen on my first visit. No water came from the fountain still—and wouldn't until we could figure out all the plumbing issues in the house—but the cherub had been sandblasted clean and now was a smooth ivory, covered only in sunlight and shadow. The Louisa rosebushes hung heavy with giant scarlet blooms, dotting the border behind the fountain like drops of blood on a white handkerchief.

My dad knelt down in front of the fountain and pulled back a covering of spider grass. With the other hand he pointed to a slightly raised panel in the stone that encircled the entire base of the fountain. Carved into the middle of the panel was the Roman numeral *XLIII.* Moving around the base, he pointed out two different numerals, *XXIV* and *XLI*, each one spread out from the others.

Jack stared at the last number for a minute. "That's *forty-three, twenty-four,* and *forty-one.* Does that mean anything to anybody?"

"I have no idea," my dad said. "But maybe as we continue with the restoration, it'll come to us."

Jack began walking around the fountain, pushing back the grass as he walked and studying the numbers until he'd completed the circle. He turned to me. "Was the fountain original to the house?"

"No. Sophie had to do the research for the BAR application and found out that the fountain wasn't put in until nineteen thirty-one." Our eyes met, and I knew we were both thinking the same thing—that it was put in a year after Louisa's disappearance.

"Guess I've got some researching to do," said Jack. "Let's order takeout and go through those papers I found in the attic. Maybe one of them can point us in the right direction."

With some satisfaction, I said, "I can't. I'm going to dinner with Marc."

Jack nodded, his lips thin. "Maybe he'll finally kiss you."

My dad brushed his hands together and coughed. "Look, I've got to go back to that organic nursery and get more fertilizer. Let me know if you find anything."

"Will do," said Jack. I said goodbye and watched as my dad crossed one of the brick walkways and left the garden.

"So, you have another date with Marc Longo tonight."

"Yes, just dinner. I'm bringing a few listings with me to show him to see if he'd like me to make an appointment."

"And he can't do this during normal working hours."

Jack's tone and mood confused me. If I were vain, I'd assume he was jealous. But his irrational dislike of Marc, coupled with his conviction that Marc was out for something else, was just confusing, if not just a little bit more than insulting. I straightened my shoulders. "He's a very busy man. Evenings are more low-key for him."

"I'm sure they are," said Jack. "As are weekends on the Isle of Palms."

"Exactly," I said, my voice lacking conviction. I had half hoped that more than just business would have occurred, but Marc had been the consummate gentleman, considerate of all my comforts and needs and, unfortunately, my privacy. I'd like to think that he was genuinely concerned about my need for rest and relaxation, and that he considered me a lady, but still. And I was attracted to him. He was dark and mysterious and had a wry sense of humor. But whenever I looked up into his brown eyes, I found myself wanting to see bright blue ones instead.

"I'll be here when you get back, going through those papers, if you want to stop in. I'll let you know if the phone rings and nobody's there."

"Thanks," I said. "Have fun."

He raised his hand in farewell, then shoved his hands into his pockets and walked away. I caught a movement from the corner of my eye and turned slightly to see the woman and child by the tree again. I turned to face them directly, and they disappeared, the swing still as if they had never been there at all.

CHAPTER 16

I juggled General Lee's leash in one hand and a tall glass of ice-cold Coke in the other while trying to unlock the dead bolts on the front door. It was almost dusk, and I still hadn't dressed for my dinner with Marc, but Chad had asked if I'd take the dog for his walk while he accompanied Sophie to their yoga class. I hadn't the heart to tell him that his insistent courtship of Sophie was a lost cause although they'd taken to calling each other Velma and Shaggy—which I didn't understand—so maybe all wasn't lost. I still had visions of throwing rice at their wedding, so I gave in. Besides, since technically the dog belonged to me, I didn't feel it right to refuse, so there I was, struggling with the door, while General Lee waited patiently with a bored look on his face. I'm sure if he'd had a nail file, he'd have been busy giving himself a manicure while he waited for me to figure it out.

"Can I help you with that, Miz Middleton?"

I turned to see my plumber, Rich Kobylt, coming down the stairs loaded down with all of his gear, apparently leaving for the day. Rich was working in the house so much that I was ready to offer him a room free of charge. "Thank you," I said gratefully.

He slid the dead bolts and held the door open for me while General Lee and I passed through onto the piazza. I gave him my key and waited for him to lock the door. "Thanks again," I said. "I guess I'll see you tomorrow morning."

Rich didn't move to pick up his things, for which I was partially grateful, considering his girth and the looseness of his pants in the rear.

"Miz Middleton, can I ask you something?"

I had a flash of worry that he was about to tell me that I was stuck with the plumbing the way it was or that he was quitting before he'd finished my master bath. "Sure," I said.

He scratched his rounded cheek covered with dark, three-day-old bristles. "Um, are you the only one living in this house?"

"Yes," I said, his question taking me by surprise. "Well, except for Mr. Trenholm, who sleeps in the guest room. Temporarily," I added hastily.

"Yeah, I know that." He scratched his cheek again as if unsure how to proceed. "I guess what I meant was if maybe your sister or friend was visiting or something."

I stilled. "No. Why do you ask?"

He laughed weakly. "You're going to think this is weird, and I hope I'm not jeopardizing my job or anything, but every time I walk past that drawing room, I always see a lady standing next to the big clock out of the corner of my eye. But when I turn to look right at her, she's gone."

"What does she look like?" I asked, my voice calm.

"I've never seen her long enough to get a good look at her face, but her clothes are old-fashioned. Like the kind they wore in that gangster movie *Bonnie and Clyde.*"

I felt a bubble of nervous laughter approach my lips but held it back. *Louisa,* I thought, and then I almost told Rich that it was a good thing that he saw her, remembering what Mr. Vanderhorst had said to me. *She only appears to those she approves of.* At the very least I supposed Louisa was telling me that she liked my choice of a plumber. "Anything else you remember?"

He nodded. "The smell of roses. It was so strong that I thought my grandmother was standing there. She's dead now, but I still remember that rose perfume she used to wear." He sent me a level look. "Miz Middleton, I don't mean to scare you, but I think your house might be haunted."

I had another insane urge to burst out laughing. Instead, I managed to keep a straight face. "Do you really think so?"

"Yes, ma'am. Not that I think you need to be frightened of her or anything, because she seemed like a nice enough lady, but I thought you should know. Although . . ." He stopped, his eyes skittering away.

"Although what?"

"Again, Miz Middleton, I don't want to scare you, and I don't really like to talk about this to other people too much, but I have what they call a gift about these things. You know, like a second sight. So I see things most people don't."

I nodded sympathetically. "Believe me, I understand."

"I knew you would, Miz Middleton. When you were so nice and understanding about being without water for three days, I figured you'd be nice and understanding about this, too." He smiled hesitantly. "So, anyway, that lady's not the only . . . um . . . spirit I've seen. There's something in the upstairs hallway, around those stairs that go up to the attic. It's a man and he's not so nice, and I don't think he wants any of us here—and especially not up in that attic." His eyebrows knitted as he gave me a serious look. "You need to be careful around him. Although . . ."

"What, Rich? You can tell me."

"Well"—he scratched the back of his neck—"I just got the strangest impression that the lady downstairs was keeping the bad man upstairs. Like, as long as she was around, he wouldn't mess with me."

I swallowed heavily, remembering my own encounters with both ghosts and realizing he was right.

Rich continued. "And I was thinking you should hire one of those psychic people who like to talk to ghosts to come find out what he wants. Then maybe he'll go away."

"That's a good idea, Rich. I'll look into it. And I promise your secret is safe with me."

"I appreciate it, ma'am." He picked up his gear while I looked up at the flaking paint on the piazza ceiling and followed him to the door. Almost as an afterthought, he said, "I'm still having trouble getting the water out to that fountain. I've checked all the pipes, and everything's intact with no leaks or blockages, but I just can't figure it out. I'm thinking we're going to have to get some earth-moving equipment and dig a bigger hole out in your backyard."

I thought of all of my dad's hard work, of the beauty he'd created in the once desolate garden and I paused. "Why don't we wait on that, Rich? There's still so much to be done on the inside, why don't we concentrate on that, and then see if we really need any water in the fountain at all?"

He held the door open for General Lee and me, and we passed through it, followed by Rich. "If you want, Miz Middleton. It's your house after all. But I think a fountain without water in it makes as much sense as a light beer. Like, what's the point, you know?"

I grinned. "I get what you're saying, Rich. And I know you're a perfectionist with your work." Which was one of the reasons why I didn't completely lose it on the third day we'd been without water. "But let's hold off on the fountain for now. We'll come back to it later—promise."

We'd moved out onto the sidewalk and stood in front of his pickup truck parked at the curb. "Sounds good." He set his toolbox down by his feet. "I'll see you tomorrow, then. I'm still not happy with the insulation around the pipes in your new bathroom so I wanted to tinker with it a little tomorrow before we get the drywall people in. I'll be here around six thirty, if that's all right."

I gave an inward groan. Honestly, I should just give the man a key and assign him a bedroom. "That's fine, Rich. I'll see you then."

We said our goodbyes, and I turned with General Lee before I had to witness Rich bending over to retrieve his toolbox.

Since the little dog seemed to know where he was going, I allowed him to lead me. Every once in a while, he'd tilt his head up at me to make sure I was following and then go back to prancing down the sidewalk, his plumed tail swishing over his back like a feathered fan.

Not that I would readily admit this to anyone, especially not to Jack, but in my months of living south of Broad, I'd started to grudgingly appreciate the beauty and charm of this Charleston neighborhood, and could almost understand the hordes of tourists who flocked here with their cameras. There was something otherworldly that lingered here in the walled gardens, whose fragrant blooms escaped through decorative wrought iron gates to entice passersby to stop and notice. Or perhaps it was the old houses themselves, having withstood revolution, pestilence, fire, civil war, and civil unrest, and still remained stoic and serene in their classic beauty—true Southern ladies. I was a born and bred Charlestonian, and I would have had to have been completely oblivious if I couldn't admit to even a tiny bit of pride that this was my city, that the area around Tradd Street was my neighborhood, and that I could almost understand—if not fully embrace—all the crazy eccentricities of my preservation-minded neighbors. I could even appreciate the vanity of a city whose building's earthquake rods had decorative lion-head caps on them in a typical Charleston nod of adding beauty to functionality.

Occasionally I would even have the mutinous thought that the homeowners here really did believe they were merely caretakers of these properties, protecting our collective history and preserving them for future generations. I wasn't completely convinced, nor did I want to be. Because I knew better than most that no matter how much you invested in your house and called it yours, you could never own its ghosts.

It wasn't until General Lee turned the corner onto Legare Street that I realized where we were heading. I tried to pull him back, to explore another block, but he dug in his furry paws and couldn't be dissuaded. Reluctantly I followed him, then watched with amazement as he stopped in front of the gate at number thirty-three. I didn't bother tugging on his leash this time. Instead, I stood at the gate next to him and recalled the nighttime phone call from my grandmother about coming to visit her in her garden, and my gaze traveled through the Confederate jasmine vines twisting through wrought iron rails to the small boxwood garden with the stone benches. *Come sit in my garden and have a sweet tea like you used to. It's going to be yours one day, you know. So you might as well come by and sit for a spell to see how well it fits.*

I turned to the General Lee, who was looking at me expectantly. "Did Grandma call you, too?"

He tilted his head, his ears hitching up a notch in a look I'm pretty sure was supposed to mean that he was pretending he didn't understand what I was saying.

I faced the square Georgian brick house with the two-tiered portico on the face, feeling the same way I'd felt when I'd first seen pictures of the *Titanic* on the bottom of the ocean floor—all the beauty and grandeur that had once held so much promise now lost. Except I'd never been told that my grandmother's house was unsinkable; I was just told that one day it would be mine.

I had lived there for a time after my parents separated. I had visited it often, sometimes staying there for months while my parents traveled to faraway places where my father was stationed or where my mother would give concerts. I missed my parents, but my grandmother was the sort of woman who made sure that I'd miss her more when it was time to leave.

She didn't mind if I was loud, or if I slid down the polished mahogany banister, or put on my socks to pretend I was ice-skating in the ballroom. She let me set up my easel in the first-floor drawing room to paint the stained-glass window a Victorian ancestor had added to the house long before the BAR was there to tell him that he couldn't. The window depicted some epic story that neither my grandmother nor I could ever determine, but the way the sun made the vibrant colors bleed into the room during the late afternoon created a stage for my own imagination.

My grandmother told me stories about ancestors who had walked the hallways before me, and the famous visitors—including the Marquis de Lafayette—who had slept in one of its eight bedrooms. My favorite story was of an elderly ancestor during the Revolution who, when the British captured the house and fortified it, gave the order to set it on fire, even providing the arrows with which the act was accomplished, when the Americans arrived to attack the Redcoats. Luckily for future Prioleaus, the British surrendered before the house could be burned to the ground. The first time I'd heard the story, I'd sighed with relief and tears that my beautiful house on Legare had been saved for me.

The garden was my playhouse, and my grandmother a willing participant as we playacted scenes from old family history as well as scenes of what I would be doing when the house became mine. But that was before my mother left my father and came to live in the house. Before I started seeing in the house people who no longer lived there, people who would tug on my sheets at night to try to tell me something only I could hear. Before the nightmares began and I had trouble knowing when the bad dreams ended and reality returned.

The last thing I remember clearly from my time in that house was my mother coming to tell me that my grandmother had died. I was sitting on the garden bench having lemonade with my grandmother so it was a bit of a surprise to me to know that she was dead.

The nightmares came back worse after that, and then, within a month, my mother had left, and I was on a plane with my father flying to Japan. It wasn't for a few more years that my father told me my grandmother's house had been sold to an oil millionaire from Texas looking for a second home. I didn't cry then about losing my house, and I still haven't. And I did such a good job of pretending that I didn't care that eventually even I began to believe it.

I finished the last of my Coke as a quick honk of a car horn sounded from behind us. A new white Cadillac sedan pulled up to the curb, and I recognized Amelia Trenholm behind the wheel.

"What a coincidence," she said as her window slid down. "I was just on my way to see you." Two slender feet encased in Ferragamo pumps appeared on the curb first, and then Amelia pulled herself out of the car. "I just love your sweet dog."

General Lee allowed himself to be scratched behind the ears, helpfully tilting his head to make sure Amelia could easily reach both.

"He's not really mine, you know. Do you want him?"

Amelia straightened, gazing at me softly as General Lee looked up at me with an expression I could only describe as emotionally wounded. "I would love to have him. But I think you might need him more than I do."

I jiggled the remaining ice in my glass, and tilted my head before remembering that General Lee did the same thing when pretending not to understand. "You think so?"

"You've never owned a dog before, have you?

I shook my head.

She smiled. "Well, then, you'll understand soon enough." With a pat on my arm, she walked up to the wrought iron fence, wrinkling her nose. "I can't say that I approve of all the changes those newcomers made to your grandmother's garden."

Confused, I peered into the garden again, finding that none of what I'd just seen was still there. The brick pathways were gone, as were the stone benches and jasmine. In its place were giant cement and glass cubes, stone pillars that I assumed were supposed to resemble the human form, and cacti of every size and shape. I closed my eyes, then opened them again, hoping to make the scene go away.

"It's hideous," I said.

"Not as strong as the word I was thinking of, but it'll do." Smiling, she faced me. "What brings you here?"

"Taking General Lee for a walk. He insisted we come here."

Amelia nodded as if she didn't find it strange at all. "I thought it might have something to do with the house going on the market again."

"What?"

"Oh. I guess you hadn't heard, then. It's not officially on the market yet, of course, but I heard through the grapevine that the owners were considering moving back to Texas full-time. I thought you might have heard."

"No. I haven't."

Amelia's delicate eyebrows furrowed. "You should call your mother. Let her know. Your father said she'd been trying to reach you, anyway. This would be a good excuse to call her back."

I studied the spot where my grandmother's prized camellias had once been and where a mirrored glass blob now stood. "I don't want to speak to her. Besides, if she really wanted to talk to me, she would call me directly."

Amelia was silent for a moment. "I would expect that she wants you to call her so that she knows you're speaking with her because you want to instead of only because you picked up the phone to answer it." She paused. "I wish you would talk to her. It's been a long time, Melanie. I think it's time."

I shook my head, trying to release the old bruises of loss and abandonment that were never far from the surface of my skin. One little tap and I felt them both again as if it were only yesterday when I was calling my mother's name out into an empty house.

"She loves you, you know. She never stopped."

I sent her a sidelong glance, wondering where I'd heard those words before. And then I remembered. *I never stopped loving him. I never stopped. Tell him I love him still.*

"Do you happen to have a photograph of Jack's fiancée?"

Amelia raised an eyebrow in response to my sudden change of topic. "I actually do. I have a photograph of Emily and Jack at their engagement party that I carry in my purse." She shrugged delicately. "I keep it with me because it's the last time I remember seeing Jack completely happy."

"Can I see it?"

"Of course," she said before going back to her car and retrieving her purse from the front seat. She flipped open the top flap and then unzipped an inside compartment. She pulled out a wallet-sized photograph and handed it to me.

I felt the air leave my lips in a small puff as I stared at the photo. I wasn't really surprised, of course. Emily was just as I'd seen her leaning over Jack as he slept, weeping tears that only I could see. But Jack, well, that was the surprise. His eyes were warm and candid, not marred by sarcasm or cynicism. He had his arm around Emily, and he was looking at her as if she held all the answers for him, and I began to understand all that he had lost. All that he had stopped looking for the moment she left him.

"She's beautiful," I said, handing back the photo.

"Yes, she was. Jack always said that her beauty didn't matter to him, that Emily was the other half of his soul. When she left him, it broke something inside of him. I'm not sure if he'll ever be able to open his heart again."

"She really loved him, you know. She still does," I blurted before I could stop myself.

Amelia went rigid. "How do you know this?"

I bit my lip, wishing that I hadn't said anything. Instead of answering her, I asked, "Where did you say that she went?"

"Up north—to upstate New York."

"New York?" I asked, a thought forming in the back of my head.

She nodded. "I believe that's where her boss told me Emily moved. Why? What do you know?"

"Nothing, really. Just a thought. Let me make a few phone calls and see what I can find out. If I find out anything, I'll let you know."

Her clear blue eyes studied me. "Emily's dead, isn't she? You've seen her, haven't you? Just like your mother used to see people who have passed on."

I looked back up at the house that I had once thought would be mine, and had a sudden flash of memory of a crowd of people hovering over my bed and then my mother reaching out for me, pulling me away from them. I thought I could still hear my screams.

I looked back at Amelia Trenholm, at her understanding and calm eyes, and quietly said, "Yes. Yes, I have."

She nodded, then put her hand on my arm. "Don't worry, Melanie. I won't tell Jack. But please, please find out what happened to Emily. I don't think Jack will really ever recover unless he knows that it had nothing to do with him."

I nodded, then looked back up at the house, where I thought I saw movement from an upstairs attic window. Out of habit, I looked away, pretending I hadn't seen anything.

"Before I forget," said Amelia. "The reason I flagged you down today was because I was on my way to your house to give you the name of that master carpenter I was telling you about. He's wonderful, and for all the wood-trim and furniture refurbishing you're going to need, he's the right man for the work. Truly a craftsman." She handed me a business card. "Here's his card. He's in much demand, but tell him that you're a friend of mine."

"Thanks," I said.

She squeezed my hand, then surprised me by leaning forward and kissing me on the cheek. "No, Melanie. Thank *you*."

General Lee and I walked over to her car and watched as she got in. She stuck her head out the window. "One more thing. The grandfather clock in your drawing room? The Johnstone? I'm very familiar with his work, and I'm quite convinced that the clock face is a lot more recent than the rest of the clock. I wouldn't know with any certainty unless I took it apart, but I'm pretty positive that the face is relatively new."

"Thanks, Amelia. Sophie thought the same thing. When I have a chance, I'll have somebody look at it."

"No rush—the clock runs fine. Just in terms of assigning it a value for your records, we'd need to know for sure."

She waved to us, then pulled her car away. Thoughtfully fingering the business card in my pocket, I turned around and headed back to the house on Tradd Street.

∞

Mrs. Houlihan met us at the front door, her chin wobbling with agitation.

"What's wrong?" I asked as I climbed the steps to the piazza.

"I thought everyone was out of the house, but I heard a thump and then some footsteps coming from your room. I thought I'd come out here and wait for you. Maybe you'd know if one of the workmen was still here."

I handed her the dog. "Either that or there's still a lot of settling going on after all the construction work being done on the bathroom. I'll go check it out."

I headed for the stairs with a straight back, trying to exude as much confidence as I wished I felt. When I reached the top of the stairs, I stopped and listened. Hearing nothing, I slowly approached my door and turned the knob.

The room was empty, as I had suspected, but not undisturbed. The telephone, still unplugged from the wall, sat upside down in the middle of the floor, and Louisa's albums lay scattered over the bed and floor like the discarded wardrobe choices of a fickle teenager. I'd been avoiding looking at the albums, since they seemed to drain all of the energy from me and hadn't offered anything more about Louisa other than the fact that she had loved her husband and son. But it seemed that Louisa had done a good job of making sure I couldn't avoid them anymore.

I called down the stairs. "It's all right to come inside, Mrs. Houlihan. A stack of books fell over in my room—that's all."

Annoyed, I reached for the album that lay facedown in the middle of the bed to move it out of the way, realizing my mistake as soon as the shock bolted through my body. Pausing as if to listen to the first hesitant drops of rain, I could hear the soft mewling of a baby, and my own breasts felt heavy as if they were filled with mother's milk. I sank onto the bed, where the album had been, and looked down at the open pages.

The left-hand side of the album contained a photo of Louisa holding baby Nevin in a christening gown, the long lace shimmering and milky as it spilled over Louisa's arms. Half hidden by the baby's head was what appeared to be a necklace with a large stone dangling from Louisa's elegant neck. But it wasn't the photo I was becoming immersed in; it was the feelings emanating from the photo—something warm and whole and maternal that made me want to wrap myself in it, bury my face in it like a mother's lap. I could almost feel my mother's hand on my head just as I cupped the downy head of the baby in my arms. Again, the hard coldness of a pen pressed against the fingers of my right hand, a curious feeling because I had been left-handed since birth, and I watched as the pen scratched against the page.

November 5, 1922

Our son Nevin was christened today at St. Michael's. The old church was filled with flowers and friends, reminding me of my wedding day. But this was even more special: the culmination of our love for each other in the form of a beloved child. We are so blessed. Robert, the proud father, presented me with the most stunning diamond necklace I have ever seen. I scolded him for his extravagance, but he says it's appropriate for the occasion. The diamond is flawless, he explained, just like our love for each other and for our beautiful boy. I wore it for the photo in the newspaper and afterward wished that I hadn't. The day after the photo appeared in the paper, someone attempted to break into the house. Robert moved the necklace to the safe at our bank, and I'm not sure if I will wear it again.

The opposite page held no photo, but stuffed in between the two pages were folded letters, the papers now fragile and yellow with age. Or at least they should have been, but as I opened them, the paper felt crisp and supple under my fingers, the ink bright and clear. The letters were well wishes from friends to the happy couple on the occasion of their firstborn's christening. The last names were familiar to me: Gibbes, Prioleau, Pinckney, Drayton. The same names had probably appeared on the guest list to my own christening.

A smaller note had remained wedged in the spine, and I pulled it out. It was made of ivory card stock, the sort of stationery a lawyer would have or perhaps a businessman with a lack of imagination. I pulled back at this last thought, quite convinced that it hadn't been my own. I spread it open, noticing the creases from where it looked like the note had once been folded into a tiny square either to throw away or to tuck somewhere out of sight. The embossed monogram at the top had been done in bold capital letters and read *JML. Joseph Longo?*

Folded inside the note was a newspaper clipping, the edges ragged as if it had been ripped rather than carefully cut from the newspaper. The clipping fluttered out of the note, landing upside down on the album. Flipping it over with a hand that no longer looked like my own, I saw the photograph of Louisa with Nevin, the necklace a bright spot in the reproduced black-and-white newspaper photo.

I flipped the note over, looking for some sort of writing, but found nothing. Just the yellowed face on brittle and yellowed newspaper print staring up at me. The album slid from my lap, and I found myself breathing heavily. I placed the note and clipping back in the book to show Jack later, then carefully avoided touching any of the other albums as I made my way to my new bathroom to begin getting dressed for my date.

ꝏ

Marc and I went to Anson's, where we sat in the front of the restaurant, facing Anson Street, and watched the horse-drawn carriages trotting outside. I'd enjoyed more than my fair share of a bottle of wine, in addition to their famous shrimp and grits, barbecued lamb, and decadent chocolate torte. Marc had watched me with unconcealed amusement as I'd eaten every last crumb of my dessert, even turning down my offer of a bite because he was too full. I was grateful that I'd been to the restaurant before and knew what to order beforehand, since I couldn't read the menu without my glasses and I refused to put them on in front of him. It was one thing to admit to myself that my eyes weren't what they used to be, but even at thirty-nine, I still clung to whatever vanity I still possessed.

We talked about the houses I'd shown him so far or, rather, why the houses weren't a good fit for him, then quickly moved on to other subjects, both of us avoiding talking about our families. Curious, and feeling emboldened by the wine, I leaned across the table. "Have you or any member of your family tried to figure out what happened to your grandfather?"

His eyes didn't register more than a flicker of interest. "Years ago my father hired a private investigator. Never turned up anything. It's a cold trail by now."

"So he didn't leave behind any correspondence—no letters or journals?"

Marc took a thoughtful sip of his after-dinner cognac. "I don't believe so. My father was the one who handled the estate, and he never said anything to me. I guess it's just one of those mysteries that will remain unsolved." He smiled and leaned forward, his fingers touching mine. "Besides, I'm a progressive man—I'm all about the future. To be honest, I don't seem to have much time or patience for the past."

I looked into his warm brown eyes and took another sip of wine, trying to wet my suddenly dry mouth. "That's very admirable," I said, feeling his fingertips. "But surely you must have felt some curiosity."

"Maybe when I was a kid. But now that I'm grown and I've made my own life, what's come before seems to have less and less significance to my life."

I couldn't see the flaw in his reasoning, and probably would have to admit that at some point in my life, I'd felt the same way. But if I agreed with him, it would seem like some sort of betrayal to Mr. Vanderhorst, so I said nothing.

Still, whether it was the food, the wine, the ambience, or the company, I found myself relaxing and simply enjoying myself for the first time in a long while. It was against my nature to relax, but Marc's company lent itself to quiet, comfortable conversation, the lulls more for peaceful reflection rather than for uncomfortable silences.

I found my mind drifting back to earlier in the day, when I was standing on Legare Street, looking at my grandmother's house, and recalling the picture of Jack that Amelia had showed me. I hadn't been able to identify what I had felt when I'd seen it until now, and it made me take another sip of my wine and settle deeper into my chair. It hadn't been jealousy—how could I be jealous of a dead woman? It had been more like disenchantment—a held-in breath full of hope that had suddenly slipped from my mouth unnoticed.

Maybe it was this unexpected feeling, or the bright stars in a clear Charleston sky, that caused me to ask Marc to leave the car in the lot and take me for a walk in the early-fall evening. Marc surprised me by placing his jacket around my shoulders and taking my hand. I smiled up at him, relaxing into his warmth and enjoying the male scent of his clothing.

We paused outside the gates of St. Philip's cemetery, gazing into the dark shadows at white obelisks punctuating the night. Marc's face was very close to mine as we peered through the gate, and I smelled his cologne as he spoke next to my ear. "Lots of famous people are buried here, you know. John C. Calhoun. Edward Rutledge—signer of the Declaration of Independence. DuBose Heyward." He narrowed his eyes pensively. "I've always found it odd that people who have given so much to the world end up just the same as us ordinary people. Dust in the ground." He smiled, softening his words. "I've always wanted to ask one of them if there's a class system in heaven, too, where the great architects and poets and inventors and all those who've given so much to the world are maybe put in a special place, higher than the rest of us."

I tried to read his eyes, but they were hidden in shadows. "I think they would tell us that God loves us all equally. And that you should feel lucky to have made it to heaven in the first place."

He laughed and put his hand on the small of my back and I liked it there. "You sound like my mother. Always reminding my brothers and me that our earthly successes aren't what's important. I'm sure every mother says that, though."

"I wouldn't know," I said quietly. We began to walk toward Meeting Street and the Circular Church, pausing outside the churchyard. I saw a woman in a long white gown flitting between dimly lit tombstones. She stopped when she saw me, but I looked away, hoping she'd leave me alone. Cemeteries were normally places I avoided, but if I concentrated really hard on something else, I could ignore the activity that seemed to spring up in my wake like water behind a speedboat.

Marc hooked one hand on the gate and faced me. "Did you know that this is the city's oldest burying ground? It's designed in the Richardsonian Romanesque style, which you can tell by the shape of the windows with the curved tops. It's my favorite building because it's so different from anything else in the city."

I laughed at his meticulous historical spiel. "Let me guess. You used to give tours of the city when you were younger."

He smiled broadly, his teeth white in the shadow of his face. "No. I simply love Charleston. Anybody who just sees me as a real estate developer would certainly disagree, but I don't think I could do what I do without appreciating this city for what it is."

I stopped, then turned to face him. "Which is what?"

He was silent for a moment. "A beautiful, old city full of rich history and character and architecturally significant buildings—but whose inhabitants are sometimes blind to the ideas of progress." He drew a deep breath, then took my hand as we continued walking down Meeting past the Palladian-style Gibbes Museum of Art. "As much as I respect the desire of the city's preservationists to protect what is part of our heritage, I can't help but lose patience with their passion for saving crumbling bits of ruin regardless of their condition or worth simply because they're old."

I nodded, completely in harmony with what he was saying. But I thought again of my mother's house and the history it held within its walls, and my own house on Tradd Street. *My house?* Despite my prickly relationship with it, the thought of it being razed for condos or a parking lot made the chocolate torte in my stomach turn. And not just because I had put so much of my own sweat equity in it; it had more to do with the old cross-stitch found behind the fireplace and the growth chart sketched on the wall in the drawing room. I remembered Nevin Vanderhorst and his belief that his house was like the child he had never had, and I thought for the first time that maybe the old man might have been telling the truth. Not that I really wanted to get up close and personal with small children or an old house, but the sentiment did make the space around my heart a little tighter.

We turned onto Archdale Street, and I noticed that our arms were swinging between us as if we were teenagers. We stopped at the corner of Archdale and Market, and Marc placed his hands on my shoulders and turned me so that I was facing east, over to Market Hall, giving me a view I'd never paused long enough to appreciate. The lights of the Holy City blazed from old streetlamps and building windows, illuminating church steeples and ancient facades like halos.

"It's beautiful, isn't it?" ask Marc, his low voice in my ear.

I nodded, too entranced by the view to speak.

"When the Saks Fifth Avenue building was constructed, it was built out to the street to provide a solid street wall to frame the vista of Market Street. It's what the city's preservationists now call an example of good urban design, but at the time it was built, they called it a lot of less flattering names." He took a deep breath and its warmth brushed my neck, making me shiver.

I turned to face him. "So why do you want to own an old house? You're a real estate developer living in an old city that prefers its antiques to anything resembling modern. It doesn't make sense."

He didn't speak at first, and I thought that maybe he wasn't sure what the answer was. Or perhaps he simply didn't want to tell me. "Maybe as a person grows older, he finds the need to get back to his roots, to his family. To his ancestors. Maybe that's the appeal of this city that you and I have been missing."

I opened my mouth to agree, then closed it. Because that would be a lie. I had been born knowing it. It was just that childhood wounds were permanent and the people we grew into couldn't be expected to forget them. Instead, I simply answered, "Maybe."

The wine or the night or his warmth made me sway forward, and he cupped my face in his hands, his eyes unreadable. My blood swished a little faster, and I closed my eyes, surprised to find Jack's face there behind my lids instead of Marc's. Confused, my eyes fluttered open, and I saw that Marc hadn't moved any closer.

"You're a very special woman, Melanie. You're smart, successful, funny." His cheek twitched. "And you have the appetite of a longshoreman but the body of a goddess." He paused, his voice serious again. "You deserve only the best."

So why aren't you kissing me? I swayed closer to him.

I heard him sigh, a sound between resignation and desire, and then his lips were on mine. He tasted of wine and night air, and I thought of how warm and comfortable I felt in his arms. I didn't stop to think that it was comfort I felt more than passion, but simply that it felt good and it had been a very long time since I'd been held like that.

When he pulled back, I smiled. "Well, I guess that proves it then."

"Proves what?"

"That you're not gay."

He coughed. "What?"

I shrugged. "It's just that we've been out so many times, and I thought you were enjoying our time together as much as I was. But you never even tried to kiss me."

His face was serious, almost somber. "I'm not the kind of man who dabbles with women or who enjoys mixing business with pleasure. You've just been, well, an unexpected surprise."

Before I could respond, he pulled me toward him again and kissed me so thoroughly and long that I almost expected the dawn sky to show behind the city's steeples. I kept my eyes open a little so I wouldn't keep seeing Jack's face.

When Marc pulled back, he said, "I should probably take you home now."

My fingers and toes tingled from his kiss, and I felt a stab of disappointment. Unbidden, I remembered Amelia's voice as she'd showed me the picture of Jack and Emily. *Emily was the other half of his soul. When she left, it broke something inside of him. I'm not sure if he'll ever be able to open his heart again.*

I shook my head. "Don't," I said.

He raised his eyebrows in a question, and I didn't hesitate to answer.

"I have a roommate," I said, afraid to break the spell by saying Jack's name out loud. "I'm assuming you don't."

Marc hesitated for before offering his hand to me. "Come on, then. It's getting cold."

I hesitated just for a moment before taking his hand. We walked quickly back to the car, his arm around my shoulder and my face pressed against him, my eyes closed tightly as I tried hard not to remember the photo Amelia had showed me or the bright blue of Jack's eyes.

CHAPTER 17

It was nearly seven o'clock the following morning before I made it back to the house on Tradd Street. Marc was apparently an early riser, too, and had awakened me to French toast in bed. He was quiet and introspective, watching me closely with hooded eyes, and I wondered if it was regret I saw in them before he quickly looked away. His quiet watchfulness would have made me self-conscious if I had thought that any recriminations were directed at me.

His attentiveness dispelled any doubt as he leaned over and kissed me, licking syrup off my lips. "What would you like to do today?"

I had to think for a minute before I remembered it was Saturday. "I'm scheduled to begin scraping the paint from the door cornices in the front hallway with Jack."

"With Jack?"

"Yes. In return for access to anything he can find regarding Louisa's disappearance, he's promised to help with the restoration. He's had some experience restoring his own home so I've put him to work."

A corner of his mouth quirked upward. "And you have a schedule for this?"

I washed down a bite full of French toast with coffee and waved a dismissive hand. "Long story. But I have a houseful of people working on the house today, and it would be conspicuous—if not downright embarrassing—if I didn't show."

"Because your name's on the schedule." He didn't hide the amusement in his voice.

"Exactly." I leaned forward to kiss him, pleased that he'd wanted to spend the day with me. "How about tomorrow? Maybe dinner and a movie?"

He winced a little. "Can't. I have to go out of town for a few days. But I'll call you when I get back, all right?" He kissed my nose as I took another bite of my breakfast.

I chewed slowly, disappointed but also a little relieved. I needed time to sort out my thoughts before I saw Marc again. Most of all, I needed to figure out why I kept seeing Jack's face every time Marc kissed me. It was stupid, really. Jack wasn't my type at all. He was way too self-assured, too cocky, too mocking. And emotionally unavailable. The biggest mistake I could ever make would be to let Jack know that I was attracted to him on any level. Even if that level was base and stupid and had nothing to do with real affection. I figured if I kept telling myself that, I would eventually come to believe it. I'd had years of practice at deceiving myself, after all.

When Marc pulled onto Tradd Street, I cringed when I saw not only the plumber's truck, but also my dad's car parked at the curb. I assumed Jack's Porsche was in its usual place, safely ensconced in the detached garage at the back of the property. It was a single-car garage, remodeled from the former carriage house, and it had been my one concession to Jack to allow him to use it for his precious car.

Marc opened the car door for me and moved as if to escort me to my front door. I shook my head. "I think it's better if I go in alone. My dad's here."

"I understand," said Marc, kissing me lightly on the lips. "No matter how old a woman is, she's always her daddy's little girl."

I nodded, not willing to tell him that I had never considered myself "Daddy's little girl" but that my hesitation stemmed more from the little bit of ick factor involved with walking into a house and facing Jack after having spent the night with another man.

Marc waited until I'd reached the front gate before opening his car door. "I'll call you in a few days."

I waved and watched as he drove down the street. Mentally girding my loins, I hunted through my clutch bag until I found my keys, and opened the front door of the house.

"Where in the hell have you been? We were about to call the police."

This was from Jack and not from my father, who stood behind Jack with an equally disapproving look on his face. Rich the plumber stood by the stairs with a wrench in his hand, also managing to look less than pleased with me.

"I was out with Marc—you knew that, Jack." I glared at him, more angry at him for invading my head than for berating me for staying out all night.

"That's exactly why I was worried. Why weren't you answering your phone?"

Trying to hide my embarrassment with belligerence, I stuck out my chin. "It didn't fit in my purse, so I turned it off and left it in my room."

Jack took a step toward me, his face a mottled dark red. "You left your phone at home because it didn't fit in your little purse? That is the stupidest thing I've ever heard. Did it never occur to you that we might be worried when we couldn't reach you?"

"We wouldn't have been so worried if you'd had your phone, Miz Middleton."

The three of us turned to face the plumber, who had placed both fists on his hips in an accusatory stance. He looked from me to Jack, then to my dad before turning his gaze back to me. None of us said a word. He dropped his hands from his hips. "Um, I'll just get to work on that hall bath, Miz Middleton. Just let me know if you need me."

"Thank you, Rich." I waited until he had disappeared at the top of the stairs before facing Jack again. "Just because you're living under the same roof as me does not give you the right to run my life. Now, let it go because you're starting to piss me off."

My dad laid a restraining hand on Jack's arm. "We were worried sick, Melanie. We're just relieved that you're okay. But you should have called."

I turned on him, not willing to concede that he was right. My embarrassment was acute, as was my annoyance that I was nearing forty and he and I had never had this conversation before. "Isn't it a little bit late for you to be playing the concerned father?"

He flinched, showing that I'd hit my target. I raised my hand in a sign of a truce. "Look, I'm sorry. But I'm tired and I feel as if I've just been attacked in my own home. I appreciate your concern, but I'm thirty-nine years old. I don't need anybody watching out for me." I paused for a moment. "And it's not like I slept with him or anything." I didn't stop to think why I'd felt the need to lie, only that I did it more for Jack's opinion than my dad's. I watched as a glance passed between Jack and my father. Alarmed, I looked from one to the other. "What's wrong?"

They looked at each other again as if to decide who'd drawn the shortest straw and had to be the one to tell me the news.

Jack took a step toward me. "Come into the drawing room. I think you should sit down."

I brushed his hand off. "For what? For you to tell me that Marc is up to something again? No, thanks. I've already heard it. So, if it's all right with you, I'd like to go upstairs and change before getting to work."

I made a move toward the stairs when my dad called me back. "No, Melanie. I think you need to hear what Jack has to say first."

Slowly, I faced my father, recognizing the military voice he had perfected over years of giving orders. It was a voice I'd once admired and tried to emulate but one I hadn't heard in a very long time. I was torn between admiration and reluctance, and in the end I followed Jack into the drawing room, if only because I'd recognized the voice of the father I used to know.

I sat on one of the folding chairs that had been brought into the emptied drawing room as a place to sit while the walls were being re-plastered and painted. I crossed my arms across my chest. "Hurry up with whatever you have to tell me. You and I are scheduled to start painting at eight o'clock."

My dad remained standing by the grandfather clock while Jack pulled up a chair in front of me. I avoided looking directly at him, afraid that I'd see again that face in his mother's photograph. If I'd been honest with myself, I would say that it had affected me a lot more than I cared to admit. And might even have been the reason I had kissed Marc while standing on the corner of Archdale and Market.

"This isn't going to be easy, and I wish you didn't have to hear it from me, but you've got to know."

"Know what?" My crossed leg bounced furiously and I recrossed my legs to still it.

Jack glanced up at my father before returning to study his hands. "As you know, I've been doing a lot of research on the Vanderhorst family. Nothing new there—I've already told you that all accounts point to a happy family." He glanced up at me with a bare hint of his deadly smile, then sat back to look me in the face, his smile gone. "As you also know, I've been investigating the Longo family, to see where the two families might have intersected. So far, I've found nothing—although I'm convinced there's something there. I think it might have something to do with the fact that neither family really seemed to suffer any financial setbacks after the stock market crash of nineteen twenty-nine."

"This is all fascinating, Jack, but what has any of that got to do with me?"

"I'm getting to that." He stood and began walking around the drawing room, touching the mantel and walls, then pausing to absently pat the Plexiglas that had been installed over Nevin's growth chart before facing me again. "While investigating Longo's business dealings, I got ahold of more current documents reflecting the current Longo family's financial affairs."

I slammed both feet on the ground. "That's none of your business, Jack. And I'm pretty sure you shouldn't be privy to that information to begin with."

He held up his hand to stop me from saying anything more. "I didn't do anything illegal, if that's what you're insinuating. I'm essentially a reporter, remember? I know what questions to ask and I know who to ask—it's as simple as that. And that's how I found out about your Marc Longo."

I stood abruptly, the chair scraping the floor as I pushed it with the back of my legs. "Oh, I see. This is about Marc—not about Louisa or Joseph or the house." I turned and started to walk away. "I don't have time for this. I've got walls to paint."

"Marc's in debt up to his eyeballs. His winery is sucking money faster than water down the drain. And he's got some pretty impressive gambling debts. As a matter of fact, he's scheduled to play in a high-stakes poker game in Las Vegas tomorrow. Did he mention that he had to go away on business?"

I stopped, keeping my back to him.

Jack continued. "He's in dire need of a hefty cash infusion. I think that's where you come in."

Slowly, I turned. "Do you mean this house?" I indicated the tarps and the half-finished restoration work that seemed to have erupted onto every wall in the house like a bad case of chicken pox. "In case you haven't noticed, except for the new roof—which cost more than some new houses—this house is in worse shape than when I inherited it. Anybody looking for easy cash would not look here."

I made to leave again but my father stopped me. "There's more, Melanie. And you need to hear it."

Jack was motioning toward my vacated chair. "I really think you should be sitting down before I tell you this."

"I prefer to stand, thank you. And please hurry. Sophie and Chad will be here soon."

He took a deep breath. "Fine. Suit yourself. I'm not sure where to begin, so I guess I'll start at the beginning. In eighteen sixty-two, the sultan of Brunei, Abdul Momin, gave to the Confederacy six ten-carat flawless diamonds to support the Southern cause."

Jack paused, his blue eyes piercing, and I had to remind myself that I had spent the night with another man—the same man Jack was in the process of trying to discredit. I met his gaze without flinching.

He continued. "No records exist to confirm the transaction and there are only two eyewitness reports, handed down over several generations, of the diamonds actually being in this country and stored in the Confederate capital of Richmond with the fabled Confederate gold."

I glanced impatiently at the clock that had just struck the quarter hour. "Look, I'm sure you find this history fascinating, but I don't and I have no idea why you think I need a history lesson right now. So why don't you just pretend I'm here and continue talking while I go upstairs?"

I was almost out of the room when he spoke again. "I think the diamonds are in this house and I think Marc Longo thinks so, too."

I marched back in, noticing that my father was watching me closely. "What? What are you talking about? I've never heard of secret diamonds, and they sure as hell aren't here—we would have found them by now. And if this is your way of getting me to stop seeing Marc, forget it. Maybe if you told me he was the king of England you'd have a better chance of me believing you."

Jack stalked across the room toward me. "Dammit, Mellie—would you just listen for five minutes? There is enough of a paper trail that shows that when President Jefferson Davis escaped from Richmond with the Confederate treasury, the diamonds were with him. They made it as far south as Washington, Georgia, before Jefferson ordered the treasure be divided and sent separate ways."

"So what?" I answered but even I could hear the uncertainty in my voice.

Jack continued, looking steadily at me as if to gauge my reaction. "A large portion of the gold was hidden in the false bottom of a wagon and given to a trusted cavalry officer, who would take the gold to his hometown, Charleston. The cavalry officer, John Nevin Vanderhorst, arrived in Charleston without the gold or the wagon, saying he'd been attacked by thieves who had stolen the wagon. Nothing was ever mentioned about the rumored diamonds, and Vanderhorst was killed in battle shortly afterward."

Jack passed his hands through his hair, and when he looked at me, his face was ragged and I was glad, because I had begun to feel that the worst part of what he wanted to tell me was yet to come.

"I really think you need to sit down for this, Mellie."

My dad approached and moved the chair closer to me, his presence jarring because I'd forgotten he was there. His absence from my life was expected, and his being there was oddly comforting until I realized that he was somehow privy to what Jack was about to say.

"No," I said combatively. I had stopped crying at the age of seven and wasn't about to start now. I figured being belligerent, stubborn, and combative just might help me mask the tears I felt vying for my attention somewhere in the back of my throat.

Jack slid his chair closer to where I stood. "Then you'll have to forgive me for sitting in a lady's presence, but I need to."

I didn't say anything else, so he continued. "The legend holds that Vanderhorst hid the diamonds either at his plantation, Magnolia Ridge, or in his Charleston town house. Despite numerous searches for the rumored diamonds, one hundred forty-two years later, they have never been found, and most historians refuse to recognize their very existence."

The silence in the room was punctuated by the ticking of the large clock, as if reminding us of its presence. I kept my voice calm, surprising myself. "But you know differently."

"Yes, I do."

I stared at him expectantly.

He coughed. "I discovered I had a gift with breaking codes when I was in the military. It became kind of a hobby for me to hunt for ciphers and see if I could solve them. I accompanied my parents to an estate auction in Washington, Georgia, and while I was there, I visited the museum where the trunk that supposedly held a portion of the Confederate gold was kept. And right there, carved around the bottom of the trunk so that it looked like part of the design, and in front of anybody actually paying attention, was an old Atbash substitution cipher. It was supposedly used by the Knights Templar and replaces the first letter of the Hebrew alphabet for the last and so on. Not very difficult if you know what you're looking at. Otherwise, it looks like a fancy border used to decorate a trunk. Which is why I think it had gone undetected for all of these years."

"And what did the cipher say?" My voice cracked and I coughed to hide it.

He watched me closely as he answered. "I don't remember it verbatim, but translated loosely it said something like 'A fortune in gold for our hero's souls; their widows shed tears of glittering ice.' "

" 'Glittering ice,' " I repeated, my voice mocking. "No such thing as coincidences, right?"

He simply returned my gaze, his expression flat.

"And you think that's enough evidence to prove that the diamonds were real and part of the treasury?"

"I'm positive. After I saw the trunk, I took a trip to the University of Texas at Austin, where they have a large collection of Davis's papers. I found a letter he wrote to General Lee before Davis fled from Richmond, stating how he had the means to support Confederate widows regardless of the outcome of the war. I was pretty sure what he was implying, and that I had discovered the validation needed to prove that the diamonds existed." He paused and shoved his hands in his pockets, reminding me of the photo on the back cover of his last book, and I had a fleeting thought that the pose wasn't meant to be arrogant or self-assured; it was simply the man I thought I had come to know hiding behind the author. If I hadn't hated him so much at that moment, I might have found it endearing.

Jack continued. "And that's when I decided what my next book would be about."

I unclenched my jaw. "Because you needed something really big to resurrect your career. To make up for the fiasco of your previous book. The book that made you an object of public ridicule and caused your publisher to not renew your contract."

Jack's jaw shifted. "Yeah. Something like that."

"And Colonel Vanderhorst's town house. Where was it?"

He leaned over in his chair, his forearms resting on his knees, and when he looked up, he looked as miserable as I felt. "Here. At Fifty-five Tradd Street."

I nodded, then kept nodding like a dashboard bobblehead, not seeing anything or thinking any coherent thoughts. The idea of Marc possibly deceiving me registered like a leaf falling on a lake in comparison to the feeling that was now taking over—a feeling that reminded me of walking into my mother's closet and finding all of her clothes gone.

"So when we first met and you told me about the book you were working on, it had nothing to do with Louisa and Joseph Longo. That was just a convenient story for you to gain access to my house."

He nodded, his face completely serious for the first time since I'd met him. "Yes, although at the time I was pretty sure that the two mysteries surrounding your house might be related. I still do. I think the disappearance of Louisa and Joseph is connected to the diamonds somehow."

"So you've been lying to me since the day we met." My voice shook, and I hoped he thought it was from anger instead of those damned tears in my throat that wouldn't leave me alone.

He stood and began walking toward me, but my father stopped him with a hand on his shoulder. "I'm sorry. I didn't mean for it to get this far. What I'd heard of your reputation . . . well, I wasn't sure you'd give me carte blanche to scour your new house for a bunch of priceless diamonds. I figured a more personal connection to Mr. Vanderhorst would soften you up, make it easier for me. I planned on just getting the information I needed and then leaving. Even if I discovered the diamonds, I would have given them to you. I just needed them as proof that I'd found them."

I turned away, not able to look at him anymore. "When I showed you Mr. Vanderhorst's letter, you must have jumped up and down at how easy I had made it for you." I stopped for a moment, chewing on my lip and listening to the gentle tick of the clock. "I would have given you access, anyway, you know. If you'd told me why solving this mystery was so important to you, I would have understood. You didn't have to lie at all."

"I know that now, Mellie. But I didn't know you then. And this was so all important to my career that I acted like an asshole and didn't stop to think how it might affect you. I figured I'd be in and out so fast that you wouldn't even care."

I threw back my head and laughed, except it wasn't a real laugh. It sounded more like a hurt bird or a disappointed child. A thought niggled at the back of my brain, and I turned to face him. "That bet you had with your mother—the one you lost. That was about this, wasn't it?"

He nodded, and if I'd had any emotion left at all, I suppose I would have admired his honesty. "She told me to be straight with you right from the start, but I didn't listen. I promised her that I would tell you right away—just as soon as I figured out how receptive you'd be." He stopped, as if unsure how to continue.

"So what was the bet?"

"That I'd wait so long to tell you the truth that eventually I couldn't."

My crossed arms were pressed so tightly against me that they were starting to tingle from loss of circulation. "But why not? After you got to know me, why not tell me?"

A light flickered in his eyes for a moment and then was gone. "Because I ended up liking you too much to let you know that I'd lied to you. Because I was afraid that you would hate me and throw me out on my ear. And because I knew that losing your friendship would be worse than losing my book contract."

I bit down hard on my lip, concentrating on the pain so I couldn't think about the implications of what he'd just said. With a fortifying breath, I said, "Well, guess what. You were right. I do hate you right now." I faced my father. "So you knew all along? I'm the only one who's been kept in the dark?"

"No, Melanie. Jack just told me—out of concern for you because of this Marc Longo fellow. I even tried to persuade Jack to let me tell you that I was the one who found out about the diamonds. But he wanted you to know the truth."

"And Sophie and Chad?" I asked.

"Nobody else," Jack said quietly. "Except for Marc Longo." He took a step toward me, then stopped. "Mellie, I'm sorry. I know that sounds inadequate, but it's true. But regardless of how much you might hate me right now, you need to listen to me about Marc. He's desperate and could be dangerous. I don't think you should be alone with him. Remember the vandalism and the break-in when you were here? Even the phone calls. I wouldn't be surprised if he were responsible. He's desperate, Mellie. And desperate men have been known to do desperate things."

I ignored him, my mind busy replaying the events of the last few months since Jack had come into my life. "So your insistence about the alarm system wasn't about your concern for me at all, was it? It was about these mythical diamonds that may or may not exist. And your idea to move in here was to protect them—not me."

His jaw clenched. "You're wrong, but I don't expect that you would believe me now."

"No, I wouldn't."

My father stepped forward. "Melanie, there's more. And this is probably a rotten time to tell you, but it's all related and might help you figure out what to do next."

My reputation as a hard-ass in the real estate business, while not duplicated in my personal life, was well earned. I blocked out any emotion that didn't involve getting my own way or sealing the deal and faced my father with a hopefully calm demeanor. "What?"

"I've spent the last two days crunching numbers, using Sophie's predictions of expected costs for the work that still needs to be done."

I felt my calm demeanor slip slightly. "And?"

He swallowed but didn't break eye contact. "It . . . uh . . . well, it looks like we're going to run out of money before all of the work is completed."

"How is that possible?" My voice wavered slightly, but I didn't shout.

"Simple, really. The roof replacement took up more than twice what the budget allowed because we originally thought we'd only have to replace part of it and patch others, and the foundation repair, while essential to the rest of the restoration, was completely unexpected. And Sophie's methods"—he shrugged—"well, there's no doubt she knows what she's doing and everything is first-class, but the money is flying out faster than either one of us expected."

The French toast and coffee I'd consumed for breakfast threatened to come back up. "So what are you saying, exactly?"

"That we need those diamonds. If they're found on this property, they will belong to you. So if anybody finds them, it will need to be us."

I waved my hands in front of me, as if I could erase everything that had been said. The lies, the diamonds, the shortage of money—all these thoughts ricocheted around my head like a ball in a pinball machine. I was either going to throw up or cry, either option as equally humiliating as the other. "I can't deal with this now, Dad. I just can't. When Chad and Sophie get here, tell them that they're getting a day off. We'll sit down and talk with Sophie later but not now. I'll let you know." I turned around for the last time, pausing again in the doorway with my back to them. "Jack, I want you packed and out of here within the hour. And I don't ever want to see you again."

"Mellie, stop. Please listen. You could be in danger. Your house has already been broken into twice, remember? Please. It's not about the book anymore. Or my career. It's you I'm concerned about now."

I didn't stop to listen to any more. I made it to the bottom step before I paused. "Just leave. Please. I don't want to hear anything else you have to say." I made it up one step before I paused once more. "And stop calling me Mellie," I called out before running up the stairs, careful to hold in my stupid tears until I'd made it to the safety of my bedroom.

∞

I nearly tripped over one of Louisa's albums as I entered the room, barely catching my balance by grabbing on to the armoire. The album lay neatly on the floor, faceup and open. Ignoring it, I slid down the door until I'd reached the floor, using the heels of my hands to stanch my tears. Eventually I stopped and even managed to open my eyes. Something empty and pulsing inside my chest interrupted my breathing as I sat staring at the open album.

Both pages were filled with amateur photographs of a growing Nevin. In one, I recognized the piazza, where Nevin sat on a rocking chair, his index finger pointed at the invisible photographer, his face creased with laughter. It was slightly blurred, as if the subject had failed at sitting still for the picture, but the spirit of the child had been captured perfectly.

I remembered the Brownie camera that Jack had found in the attic and how Louisa had written that it had been a gift to her from her husband. Even if I hadn't known that, I would have assumed from the look on little Nevin's face that it was his mother behind the camera.

I closed my eyes, not wanting to see the face of the boy I had failed. Regardless of whether the diamonds existed—and even if they did, I was pretty positive that if they were in the house, we would have found them by now—I was no further along in my search for finding out what happened to Louisa than I had been when I'd first sat in the drawing room with Mr. Vanderhorst and ate pralines from the rose china. Without Jack I wasn't sure I'd be able to dig up anything else; I simply didn't know where to look. I felt numb, as if my nerve endings had been scattered into the wind like a dandelion, leaving a bare stem of simple weariness.

Opening my eyes, I stared again at the pictures, at the happy boy who had grown up to be a lonely man wondering why his mother had abandoned him. And who had entrusted me with his house and his dream of finding the truth.

I curled my legs up to my chest and rested my forehead on my knees. There was one thing I could do that I hadn't done yet—something I hadn't done since my grandmother had died and I'd realized that my imaginary friends weren't real but something else entirely.

I took a deep breath through my nose and held it, then slowly exhaled from my mouth, trying to exorcise Jack with the outgoing air. With another deep breath, I looked at the pictures again of the smiling little boy and then around the empty room. "Louisa? Are you here?"

The clock chimed downstairs and then all was silent again. I remained where I was, listening.

"Louisa?" I asked again. I rubbed the heels of my hands into my eyes. "Please let me help you." I kept my hands pressed into my eyes, so all I saw were red spots against my eyelids. "Why would you leave your son when you loved him so much?"

I shivered, and when I opened my eyes, I could see my breath. The dry rustle of paper brought my attention to the album, where the pages were flipping slowly as if blown by an invisible wind. They settled on a double layout of pictures of Louisa's garden, focusing on her roses and a pergola that had since been replaced by the fountain. I sniffed, smelling the roses as if I were sitting in the middle of them on a hot summer day. The pages rustled again, fluttering like moths around a lamp, and a yellowed newspaper clipping caught the current of moving air, twirling twice before landing on the floor at my feet.

The article was dated December 30, 1930, and the small headline read, *Two Prominent Gentlemen End Their Longtime Association.* My eyes scanned down to read the entire article.

> A spokesperson for the esteemed legal practice of Vanderhorst and Middleton reported today that the firm is being dissolved. Assurances are being given that existing clients will continue to be handled in the manner in which they are accustomed, albeit by the lawyer of their choosing. Clients have been notified and can reach the firm at the current address until the first of February.
>
> No reason was cited as to the dissolution of the firm, but many speculate it could be related to the recent disappearance of Mr. Vanderhorst's wife, Louisa Gibbes Vanderhorst. Her whereabouts are unknown as of present, as is her reason for abandoning her husband and eight-year-old son, Nevin.

I stared at the article for a long time before sticking it back into the album. I slowly shut the cover and slid the album to the floor before dropping my head in my hands. Very quietly, I spoke to a woman who had long ago left this house but now seemed reluctant to leave it again. "I know all of this, Louisa. I know about your roses, and how my grandfather and your husband were friends and partners and had a falling-out." I grabbed two fistfuls of my hair in frustration and tugged. "What I don't know is why you left and where you went and why you've come back."

Slowly, I struggled to my feet and stood, smelling now the tangy scent of old roses left too long in a vase. Wrinkling my nose, I reached under my bed and pulled out my suitcase and began packing up as many of my belongings as I could. I wouldn't stay another night in this house, where everywhere I looked I saw my failures. I wasn't used to failing: I'd been the top seller at my agency for the last five years, and a person didn't get to that level by failing. My success was the one thing that kept me from looking backward and seeing a gawky girl whose own mother couldn't find enough in her to love.

I wasn't sure how my desertion would affect the codicils of the will, but I figured I had a little time before I'd have to contact the lawyers. Before that, they wouldn't have to know. My father, who had the most dealings with the lawyers, wouldn't tell them without asking me first. Regardless of all of his other failings, disloyalty had never been one of them.

As I was zipping up my bulging suitcase, I spotted the yellow rubber gloves on the dresser. I hadn't left them there, and wondered who had. My cheek creased in an unwanted smile as I remembered the first time Jack had seen me wearing them.

My eyes then settled on the photo albums holding all the pictures of an amateur photographer who had once taken pictures of her beloved family, her garden, and her house, and then gone away one day and didn't come back. I felt a rush of anger at someone who would go away and never once contact the little boy she left behind—the little boy who never stopped waiting for her to come back. What sort of mother did such a thing to a child?

My anger was irrational, and I'm sure on some level I realized it. But the dark feelings seemed to be leeching from the walls of the old house, feeding my anger like rain on parched soil. The anger made it easier to pack my suitcase, easier to leave this house with its warped floors, hand-carved mantels, and hidden secrets, which looked as if they would remain hidden. With more force than was necessary, I threw the yellow gloves into my suitcase, slammed the lid down, then jerked on the zipper until it was closed.

I'd already heard Jack's departure and then my dad speaking with Chad and Sophie before watching my dad's car leave, so I knew that when I opened my bedroom door I would be greeted only by silence and the incessant ticking of the grandfather clock.

Struggling with the heavy suitcase, I made it down the stairs and out the front door. I closed the door behind me for the last time, making sure the dead bolts were secure before dropping my keys into the bottom of my purse. Letting myself out the front gate, I crossed the street to where my car was parked at the curb and threw my suitcase in the trunk. As I fumbled with my car keys, gooseflesh erupted on the back of my neck. I turned back to the house, staring at the upstairs window of the bedroom I had just left, bringing back the feeling of anger that had dissipated when I left the house. There, outlined in the warped handblown window glass, was the dark shadow of a man.

My keys dug into my palm as I clenched my hand into a fist, my skin raw with fear. I backed up against my car, my hands fumbling for the door latch, because I didn't have the courage to turn my back on the dark entity in the window. I had an odd feeling that to do so might prove fatal.

I slid into the driver's seat, managing to stick my key into the ignition after the third try. My tires squealed as I peeled away, my hands still shaking as they gripped the steering wheel. I paused in the middle of the street, realizing that I'd forgotten to write a note for Mrs. Houlihan. And that the sweet aroma of roses had not appeared to dispel my fear. It was almost as if by abandoning her house, Louisa had abandoned me.

A thickness grew in my throat as I moved slowly down the street, glancing back in my rearview mirror as the house on Tradd Street grew smaller and smaller until I couldn't see it at all.

CHAPTER 18

For the first time in my life, I called in sick to work. I thought I'd called early enough so that I wouldn't have to speak with anybody and could just leave a message on the machine, so when Nancy picked up on the second ring with a bright and cheerful greeting, I was speechless for a moment.

"Hello?" she repeated. "Is anybody there?"

"Sorry, Nancy. It's me—Melanie."

"Oh. Are you here? I didn't see your car, and Ruth said she hadn't seen you this morning when I stopped in for coffee."

"Um, no. I'm still at home. In bed, actually." I wondered for a moment if I should fake a cough and then decided against it. "I'm sick, so I won't be coming in today. I was hoping you could cancel all of my appointments."

There was a long pause. "Hang on. I've got to take these golf ball earrings off because it's too hard to hold the receiver to my ear, and I can't find my headset." The phone clattered on her desk, and I waited for a moment before her voice came back. "I'm sorry. I thought you just said that you were calling in sick."

"Yes, that's right. And I was hoping you could cancel all of my appointments."

"Are you with a man?" She was whispering now.

"No, of course not. I just . . . don't feel good."

"It's Jack, isn't it?"

"No, Nancy. It's not a man. I'm a little under the weather, that's all."

"Well, you've never called in sick before, and as far as I can recall, you've never had a date, either, so I thought that somehow they might be related."

"Nancy?"

"Yes, Melanie?"

"Would you mind keeping those thoughts to yourself?"

"Sorry. You know I'm only here to help you. Besides, I knew it wasn't Jack."

"You did? How?"

"Because he already called here this morning to speak with me."

I frowned into my phone. "With you? What about?"

"You. He wanted to know if you were okay, and when I told him I hadn't seen you yet this morning, he said that I might not. He told me that you'd received some bad news and would need a little TLC today. That's why I went by Ruth's—your bag of favorite doughnuts is sitting on your desk."

My cheek reluctantly creased into a half smile at Jack's thoughtfulness until I recalled that he was responsible for the crappy way I was feeling. "Thanks, Nancy. I appreciate it. But you can go ahead and eat them. I won't be coming in today."

"Hang on. That's my other line. But don't go away."

Music piped in while I waited, my eyes skirting the once comforting walls of my condo—the white, empty walls without cornices or wide baseboards, the large main room devoid of a fireplace or anything that might be even loosely called ornamental. The focal point of the room was the flat-screen television I had bought myself for Christmas the previous year. I watched little on it except for old black-and-white romantic movies on AMC and the Weather Channel. The hardwood floors were prefabricated without any signs of wear and tear, their pristine condition evidence that feet from nearly two hundred years of people hadn't walked across them, leaving heel marks and scratches as a sign of history's passing.

The recessed lights on the ceiling left no room for elaborate chandeliers and spotlighted only stark white walls instead of oil paintings of Charleston Harbor and of people who'd once had breakfast at a mahogany dining room table and slept in the same bed as I had.

The chrome-and-glass furniture, which I had hand selected with excruciating thought, now seemed cold and out of place. Everything seemed new and pristine, as if the person living here had no past. It all felt wrong somehow, as if I were a temporary visitor and my real home was elsewhere.

I mentally shook myself, then forced my brain to remember the backbreaking, grueling work my body had been made to endure over the past four months. My nails were nonexistent, my hair a disaster, and I knew more about stripping paint from an assortment of surfaces than any thirty-nine-year-old single woman had any business knowing. If I focused on those things long enough, I might start thinking that a condo with as much personality as a hotel room could actually be a place to call home.

My caller ID clicked in, and when I checked to see the small screen in the receiver, I saw it was my dad. I stared at the number for a long time and listened to two more clicks before they finally stopped and the number disappeared from my screen.

"Melanie? Are you still there?" Nancy's voice piped through the receiver.

"Yes, I'm here. I don't have anything else to add—just please cancel my appointments."

"I'm going to cancel them for the rest of the week, too. You've been working too hard and need some good old-fashioned R and R. I'm looking at your schedule now, and if I move a few things around and push a few appointments into next week, you should be fine. I'll tell Mr. Henderson that you have the flu or something." I could hear Nancy tapping her pencil against her desk, undoubtedly impatient to get back to practicing her chip shot.

"But . . ."

She cut me off. "But nothing. And don't accuse me of trying to mother you. This was all Jack's idea. Wait—there's my other line again and I've got to take it. Enjoy your week off."

I held the phone in my hand, listening to the dial tone, wondering if I should be angry or relieved. I really didn't think I wanted to have anything to do with houses right now, regardless of whether they were old or new. But to know that it was Jack's idea irked me enough to make me want to stomp into the office. Or worse—into the house on Tradd Street with a bucket of paint.

Then I remembered the diamonds and Jack's lies and my father telling me that we didn't have the money to finish the restoration, and my anger melted into something that seemed a lot like disappointment. So, instead, I crawled back into bed, threw the covers over my head, and went back to sleep.

I spent the next three days in bed, mostly sleeping. I only crept out from under the covers to pay the pizza delivery boy or retrieve my iPod, and then I returned to my cocoon, where I could wallow in my own misery. I purged my address book on my BlackBerry, reorganized my CD collection by title instead of by artist's last name, then created a work sheet that cross-referenced them. I even sorted out my makeup drawer by season, grouping eye shadows with lipsticks. But for some reason, my reorganization didn't give me the same sense of satisfaction it had always given me in the past.

The phone rang incessantly, an unending circle of Sophie, Jack, my dad, and Marc. Even Amelia Trenholm called once, and my hand hovered over the receiver for a long while until the phone stopped ringing. I wasn't angry with her; she'd tried to get Jack to tell me the truth from the beginning. And even I recognized that it was Jack's truth to tell, not hers. Still, I didn't want to think about anything hurtful, and speaking with her would remind me of all the work we'd done on the house on Tradd and all the work that still needed to be done. And how the first man who'd showed me any interest in more than a year had only been interested in that damn house.

Eventually, they all decided to call Nancy, assuming correctly that she was my gatekeeper, and were all informed that I was under the weather and didn't want to be disturbed. Jack was the only one who continued calling, but only once a day. He never left a message. It was almost as if he was making sure I knew he was there, and I found an odd comfort in that. Just not enough to actually pick up the phone and speak to him.

On my first day back to work, I felt no more rested or clearheaded than I had the day I'd told Jack I never wanted to see him again. I left explicit instructions with Nancy that I didn't want to see anybody until I'd had at least half a day to clean off my desk, so I was surprised when she buzzed me in my office to let me know that Marc was in the reception area waiting for me and that he wouldn't take no for an answer.

I met him at Nancy's desk, my tongue feeling thick and swollen either because it wasn't used to talking or because I didn't know what to say.

He stepped forward and took my hands before kissing my cheek. "I've missed you. I hope you're feeling better."

I stared into his dark eyes, trying to see any subterfuge, but all I saw was genuine concern.

"A little," I said.

"Good. I was afraid . . ." He looked up at Nancy, then lowered his voice before speaking again. "I was afraid that you were avoiding me."

I looked down at his Gucci loafers in case he could read the truth in my eyes. Dropping my hands from his, I said, "Let's go outside for a moment so we can talk."

He nodded, then followed me outside.

We walked down Broad Street toward the Old Exchange Building, which was said to be the most haunted building in Charleston because of its years of use as the provost dungeon. I wasn't going to publicly dispute this fact on account of me being reluctant to provide evidence contrary to popular belief, but I'd seen more lost souls wandering the gardens and halls of my grandmother's house on Legare than I'd seen lurking under the barrel vaulted ceilings in the old prison.

We stopped in front of an empty iron-and-wooden bench and sat down. I smiled to myself as Marc held up his hand for me to wait while he wiped my seat with his pocket square. Then he sat down next to me and reached for my hands. After realizing that mine were already safely tucked beneath me, he placed his own on his thighs.

"So what's this all about, Melanie? I thought we . . . were enjoying getting to know each other."

My eyes met his, and I blushed a little, remembering how good a time we'd actually had getting to know each other. Being a businesswoman had taught me to cut to the chase, and I decided to do it now before I completely lost my nerve. "When you said you had to go out of town, did you mean Las Vegas for a high-stakes poker game?"

If he was startled or disappointed, he recovered quickly. "Yes, I was." He breathed a heavy sigh. "My younger brother, Anthony, has a gambling problem. Whenever I hear that he's headed to some big game, I sign up for it, too, to keep an eye on him. To make sure that he doesn't gamble more than he can afford to lose." He shrugged slightly. "I didn't mention this to you because we try to keep our family problems private." His eyes narrowed as he regarded me. "Is that what your silence is about? That you disapprove of gambling?"

I shook my head. "No. It's more that I disapprove of lying, and misrepresenting yourself to get what you want."

He turned his body so that he was completely facing me now. "What are you talking about?"

I looked for any shift in his gaze or any admission of guilt but saw none. "Are you familiar with the legend of the Confederate gold?"

He seemed confused. "Sure, isn't everybody? Jefferson Davis took the gold with him when he retreated from Richmond at the end of the Civil War. It mysteriously disappeared at some point, and nobody knows what happened to it. But what has that got to do with you and me?"

I refused to bend, having already traveled this far. "Have you ever heard that part of the treasury might be hidden in my house on Tradd?"

"Gold? Hidden in your house? With all the reconstruction going on, don't you think it would have been found by now?"

I shook my head again. "Not gold—diamonds." I watched his face to see if any of this was registering with him, but his expression seemed to be that of genuine confusion. I continued. "The sultan of Brunei purportedly gave six valuable diamonds to the Confederates, and they were part of the missing treasury. An ancestor of Mr. Vanderhorst was the last person who had contact with them, but he died in the war. No one has seen or heard of them since."

A small smile touched Marc's lips. "Just like Louisa and Joseph."

"What would make you say that?"

He shrugged. "It's just that historical events with perfectly logical explanations tend to become legends as the years progress. It's much more romantic to assume something magical or mystical than to admit that a housewife got bored with her marriage and ran off with another man, or that a respected Charleston gentlemen embezzled a failing government for an infusion of cash to make sure his family survived the hard times he knew were coming." Marc shrugged again, the smile back on his face. "It's called life. Not mystery."

"So you've never heard of the sultan's diamonds?" I persisted.

Marc managed to extract one of my hands wedged between my legs and the bench. "Look, Melanie. Your friend Jack is probably the one who has filled your head with these ideas. By nature of his occupation, he has an overactive imagination and thinks zebras when what he's really hearing is horses. His career depends on taking normal events in history and making them exciting enough to write a book about. Good for him—we all need an escape from reality now and again. But we can't lose sight of the fact that it's all based on conjecture gleamed from flimsy research at best."

I didn't respond, still waiting to see if he would answer my question.

With another sigh, he said, "Like with every legend involving Charleston, I've probably heard them all at one time or another, so it's completely possible that I heard the one about the diamonds, too. What you're getting at, I assume, is whether or not I believe in it enough to pursue you so that I might gain access to your house."

I looked down at his well-manicured hand holding mine, remembering how nice his hands had felt on other parts of me. I had to force myself to meet his eyes again. "Did you?"

He closed his eyes for a moment, genuinely hurt. "The other night—did that seem fake? Did it seem as if I were forcing myself to make love to you?" He let go of my hand and stood. "And do I seem to be such an incompetent businessman that I couldn't find an alternative to acquire your house—if I truly thought it hid a fortune—than dating you?"

I had to admit to myself that everything he said made perfect sense. Even what he'd said about Jack had a ring of truth to it—made even more plausible by the fact that I was ready to believe the worst about Jack if only to get me to stop thinking about him.

I stood, too, and placed my hands on his shoulders. "I'm sorry, Marc. It's just that . . ." I paused, not yet ready to confide everything. Raising my gaze from the charcoal-colored wool of his lapel, I met his eyes and saw only concern and warmth. "It's just that . . . well, things aren't going well with the restoration, and I just needed to know that I wasn't going to be surprised with more bad news."

He stroked my cheek, sending nice warm flutters down my arms. "What's wrong, Melanie?"

"The restoration is costing us a lot more money than we originally budgeted, and I'm not sure if we're going to be able to afford to complete it."

He raised an eyebrow. "But you don't even particularly like the house. Didn't you once refer to it as the 'goiter on the neck of your life'?" He gave me a soft smile, but his gaze remained intense.

"Yeah, I probably did. But I've invested so much time and energy into it that I can't stand to think that all the work might have to be abandoned."

"And then what would happen?"

"I'm not sure. I need to talk to my dad. As trustee, he'll have to figure it out. I'm assuming, though, that if I move out permanently and abandon it, ownership will revert to somebody else for failure to pay the property taxes. Regardless, I'd end up with nothing." *A house is a piece of history you can hold in your hands.* No matter how hard I tried, I still couldn't get Mr. Vanderhorst's words out of my head.

"Which isn't such a bad thing since you never really wanted it in the first place."

"True," I said, and wondered if he could hear the hollowness in my voice, too.

"Unless you find those elusive diamonds hidden inside. Then all of your problems would be over."

I jerked my gaze up to meet his and saw that he was smiling. "Yeah, something like that," I said, smiling back. I shook my head. "I feel so stupid."

He placed his hands over mine. "You're not stupid. You're incredibly intelligent—but perhaps easily misled by people you trust. And I forgive you for jumping to conclusions. I understand that this whole renovation project has left you a little more stressed than you're used to. So," he said, leaning forward and kissing me on my forehead, "why don't we plan a destressing weekend at my beach house again? I promise you won't have to think about any of it for two whole days. You don't even have to get dressed if you don't want to."

I let myself blush this time and felt no reservations raising my lips to his. "I'm not positive about that last part, but I'm definitely up for the destressing weekend."

Marc's BlackBerry in his coat pocket beeped, and he moved back to answer it. When he was done, he said, "I've got to go now. I'll pick you up on Friday at four o'clock, if that works for you."

I gave him the address of my condo in Mt. Pleasant, then kissed him goodbye. As I watched him walk away, I noticed for the first time the occupant of a nearby bench. The man, dressed in the full Confederate uniform of a cavalry officer, was watching me calmly, and I thought for a moment that he might be a Civil War reenactor—of which the city had plenty—until I realized that I could see the slats of the bench through his torso. Before I could turn away to show him that I wasn't interested, he vanished, leaving only a small breeze that rustled a few fallen leaves on the sidewalk to show that he'd been there at all.

∞

Three days later, I was at Victoria's Secret picking out coordinating lingerie for my weekend trip when my cell phone rang. I almost didn't pick up after seeing that it was Sophie. I hadn't seen her since that disastrous last night at the house on Tradd, although I'd had a conference call with her and my dad to discuss a temporary halt to the renovations. She hadn't really said anything at the time, and I wondered if she was somehow angry with me. As if everything was somehow all my fault.

I flipped open my phone while comparing the silk of one nightgown to another. "Hey, Soph."

"Hi, Mewanie."

"Soph? Is that you? You sound like you've got a cold."

"Just a dog awergy." She sniffled.

"I thought Chad had General Lee."

There was only silence and the sound of sniffling coming over the receiver. Then the sound of low voices and the soft yap of a dog.

"Is Chad over there now, Sophie? What about you being a Gemini and him being a cruciform?"

"That's Capricorn, Melanie. And he's only here because he bought me the complete DVD set of *Scooby-Doo*, and I invited him over to watch it with me. He had to bring the dog because General Lee gets lonely when left alone too long and begins to howl. Chad said that neighbors have started to complain. Right now, his landlord allows dogs in his rental, but Chad thinks if he's not careful, he might change his mind."

I picked the turquoise silk nightgown off the rack and draped it over my arm. I had a sinking feeling I knew what was coming next. "Do you need me to come get him?"

"No. I just took an antihistamine, so I should be okay. I was calling you to remind you of my haunted walking tour this Saturday night—Halloween. You bought a ticket, remember?"

It took me a while to insert consonants and translate nasal vowels to understand what she was saying. I froze. "What? It's this Saturday?"

"It's always the third Saturday in October, Melanie—you know that. I was calling to see if you wanted to meet me for drinks beforehand."

I stared at the gorgeous turquoise silk nightgown draped across my arms. "Um, well, I, uh, I've made other plans."

There was a dead silence on the other end—not counting the labored breathing through a clogged nose—and I started to get nervous. The last time I'd backed out of Sophie's haunted walking tour, she had added my name to the mailing list of every used-clothing boutique in the state of South Carolina, in addition to putting me on the short list as a potential speaker for the national vegan conference.

"You pomised you'd be there." Her accusation was followed by more sniffles.

"I'm sorry, Soph. I forgot. And I've made plans to go away for the weekend."

"With Marc Longo?" Even with all of Sophie's congestion, her reproachment came through quite clearly.

"Yes, as a matter of fact. With Marc."

"After all that Jack told you?"

As much as I wished Jack would disappear from my life, it was abundantly clear that my friend had no such desire. "Jack told you about the supposed diamonds?"

"He did, Melanie. And a little more about Marc Longo. I think you're being incredibly stupid if you don't listen to him."

"I did. I listened as Jack told me himself that he's been lying to me since the moment we first spoke on the telephone."

"And how do you know that Marc isn't?"

I sighed, trying not to remember how many times I'd asked myself the same question. "Because I asked him. And he told me no." That wasn't exactly true, but basically that was what Marc's response had boiled down to. Not to mention the look in his eyes, which was definitely nothing but sincere.

"Right." I listened as she pulled the receiver away from her and then blew her nose. "And you believed him but not Jack. That's very interesting psychology, Melanie. Maybe we should schedule another meditation session so that we can analyze this further."

I grabbed a handful of silk panties from the bin by the register and tossed them on the counter next to the nightgown. "I don't need to be analyzed. I just need to be left alone and allowed to make my own decisions."

"Like deciding to blow off your best friend. The one who came to your aid regardless of her own workload when you told her you needed a little help with an old house you'd inherited."

Ouch. She was playing the guilt card now—something she didn't do often but at least, in this case, was fully justified. I held up my hand to the salesgirl, who was starting to fold the nightgown in soft pink tissue paper. *Wait,* I mouthed to her. Talking into my phone again, I said, "Is this going to be one of those times where you sign me up for a nude-beach vacation or to model at one of your friends' all-plastic fashion shows if I don't show up?"

"Possibly." There was no hint of a smile in Sophie's voice.

I sighed heavily. "Fine. What time do I need to be there?"

She gave me the details, and I hung up. I thanked the salesgirl and told her that I had changed my mind. I then gave one last lingering look at the turquoise silk nightgown before heading out the door. My only hope was that this year Sophie would heed my advice about dressing more conservatively. On her yearly Halloween walks, she pretended to be a psychic who could channel dead spirits, and I took it as a personal affront when she'd dress as a witch or something with fangs. Seeing as how she'd coerced me into giving up a weekend away to attend her faux haunted walk, the least she could do would be to dress like a real psychic and follow my fashion example.

∞

The large group of people clustered like grapes around the gates of St. Philip's cemetery stared openmouthed at the black-robed hooded creature carrying a scythe and wearing a tour guide license around her neck. When the figure took a step forward, and I saw the striped stockings and Birkenstocks, I knew it was Sophie.

She'd taken me to dinner first and given me a ride into town, but she'd dropped me off on King Street to do some shopping while she got ready, so I hadn't had a chance to see her costume yet. Before letting her drive away, I reiterated what I'd said about dressing appropriately, but I was still worried. And with good reason, apparently.

At least she wasn't dressed as a witch or sporting fangs, but I thought the scythe was taking it a little too far.

Other groups stood nearby, but Sophie had commandeered the best spot closest to the grave of Sue Howard Hardy and the site of the city's most talked-about ghost sighting. Supposedly Mrs. Hardy spent a lot of time bent over her child's grave, grieving for a stillborn baby delivered more than one hundred years ago. I knew differently, of course, having spoken with the grieving woman once while out walking with my mother when I was a little girl. My mother had pulled me away from the arm reaching through the gate before the pale white fingers could grasp my coat sleeve. It wasn't until later that night, after my mother had tucked me into bed, that I realized my mother could see her, too.

Sophie acknowledged me with a lifting of her scythe, and I rolled my eyes while keeping my distance from the gates in case anything within wanted to get my attention. I looked around at a few of the other tour groups, feeling justified when I noticed that most of the guides were not in costume. Sophie had tried to explain that dressing up attracted more people to her group, which meant she raised more money for the college, but I wasn't completely convinced. I told her that telling accurate stories would probably be more of an incentive to attending her tour instead of one of her competitor's, but she'd remained doubtful.

Sophie began to speak. "It was here at this spot in nineteen eighty-seven that an amateur photographer took the picture that has made this cemetery the focus of many paranormal investigations. Unbeknownst to the photographer, a former resident of Charleston, Mrs. Sue Howard Hardy, dead of heartbreak over a century before, sat keening over the grave of her stillborn baby. He was very surprised to find the image when he developed his film." Sophie's voice, while still more nasal than usual, took on a tremulous tone, and I almost laughed out loud.

"It almost sounds like she knows what's she's talking about, doesn't it?"

I turned around to defend my friend, then froze. I jerked away when I saw Jack, bumping into a large lady in a Salty Dog T-shirt behind me. "Jack—what are you doing here?"

"Same as you. Supporting the College of Charleston, as well as learning something new about my city."

I looked up into his sparkling blue eyes and had to admit to myself that he looked good. Not good enough for me to ever forgive him or allow him anywhere near me, but still good enough to admire from afar. Very afar. "Good for you, Jack. But while you're listening, please try not to stand anywhere near me. I don't want to see you again, remember?"

I started to make my way to the outside edge of the crowd, but Jack put a hand on my arm. "You haven't returned any of my calls."

"And you're surprised by that?" I tried to tug my arm away, but he held fast. I could tell that the woman in the T-shirt was paying more attention to us now than to Sophie, so I stopped struggling.

"No," he said, lowering his voice. "But I am surprised that you're not giving me a chance to redeem myself." He dropped my arm, then leaned toward me, his face almost touching mine. "I thought we were friends."

"I thought we were, too," I said, stepping back. "And there's nothing you can do to redeem yourself in my eyes, so just go away and leave me alone."

I turned around and began to make my way through the crowd gathering around Sophie, who was now waxing poetic about the spectral spirits that roamed the streets of Charleston at night, completely unaware of the pirate with the noose pulled tight around his neck hanging from the tree behind her inside the cemetery's fence.

Jack followed doggedly behind me. "I can find the diamonds for you. Think about what that would mean. At the very least you'd be able to finish the restoration on your house."

I stopped at the edge of the crowd and faced him. "It's not my house. It never was—not really. And all it's meant to me has been an endless round of frustration. So I'm through. Through with the house and through with you. Just please leave me alone." I turned around to face Sophie, showing my back to Jack and pretending to concentrate on what Sophie was saying.

He kept his voice low, the perfect pitch to hear him over the sound of Sophie speaking. "What about Louisa and Nevin? You're going to abandon them along with the house? Because I think you know as well as I do that Louisa loved her son. That something horrible would have had to happen to her to make her leave him. And that for some reason a smear campaign was set up in the media to make it look like she ran off with Joseph Longo. But you and I both know that's not true, don't we? Remember that photograph in the frame that keeps getting thrown across the room? It's Louisa and Nevin doing that—and don't you dare try to deny it. You and I both know there's something not normal in that house. And that Louisa and Nevin want the truth to be known." Jack tugged on my arm until I faced him. "They need you to help them tell the truth."

"What do you know about the truth?" I yelled, noticing all the heads turning in my direction at the same time I realized that Sophie had just asked the crowd if anybody had ever had a supernatural experience.

Sophie lifted her cowled head and looked in my direction. "The young lady in the back. Did you have an experience you would like to share?"

I looked at her in horror, seeing the pirate again who was now swinging in the night wind. I could hear the creak of rope against tree bark, reminding me of a child on an old wooden swing. "Um, no." I coughed. "Not really."

"Are you sure?" Sophie was frowning hard at me, shifting her eyes like a signal that I was supposed to recognize.

"I'm sure." I watched as several pirates appeared and began to cut down their buddy from the tree, using long, glinting swords.

Sophie persisted. "Because it seemed like you had something to say earlier."

I gave an inward groan. "Fine. All right. I once got a phone call from my grandmother."

The big lady in the T-shirt scowled. "That's not a paranormal experience."

I turned to her and looked into her eyes. "My grandmother had been dead for over twenty years."

The lady stepped back as I heard several snickers in the audience as well as a few remarks like "It was probably a prank call." I looked at Sophie and shrugged.

The crowd turned en masse and followed Sophie down Church Street, to the corner where it intersected Queen Street and stopped in front of the venerable and supposedly haunted Dock Street Theater, currently undergoing a massive renovation. I felt Jack walking silently beside me, but I didn't turn to acknowledge him.

As soon as the crowd had settled around Sophie, she began to speak. "A woman in a dark red dress slowly floats through the halls and along the outside balcony of this building's second floor, and has been seen by night managers, as well as theatergoers."

Something brushed against me, and I jerked toward Jack to tell him again to leave me alone. But Jack was staring straight ahead, listening attentively to Sophie, and completely unaware of the woman who stood behind him resting her head on his back. With a translucent finger, she smoothed an errant wave of black hair off of his ear. Jack reached up as if to shoo away an annoying bug, then stopped with his hand suspended in midair and instead let his hand cup the space where the woman's hand had been. Then, almost as if he were unaware of what he was doing, he tilted his head as a lover might do to hear the quiet whisper of his beloved.

I heard her voice inside my head, although her lips didn't move. And though her eyes were closed, I knew her words were meant for me. *Tell him. Tell him I love him. Tell him that my love for him gave me no choice but to leave. Tell him what you know.* Her eyes opened then, but behind the lids was only empty space. And then she was gone.

I felt a soft tug on my sweater, and I looked down to see a chubby boy around eight years old.

"I saw her, too."

"Who?" I asked nervously.

He looked at me with eyes that were older than he was. "You know." He leaned forward and whispered, "I'm not supposed to talk about it, but I figured if you saw it, too, then I'll know that I'm not really crazy."

My heart broke a little bit as I remembered me at his age being chased on the playground all because I said that Mary Lou Watkins had spent the night with me at my house when everybody knew she'd been killed in a car crash. "You're not crazy," I said to the boy. "And if you're lucky, you might grow out of it."

"You didn't." He looked at me accusingly.

"No, I didn't. But a lot of kids do."

"I hope I don't," he said, then gave me a small smile before rejoining his mother.

"Who was that?" Jack asked, turning around.

I shrugged. "Just a boy. He thought he'd lost his mother."

Jack frowned, learning forward to look closely into my face. "You look like you've just seen a ghost."

With my nerves still raw from the encounter, I barked out a laugh, causing the group to turn around and look at me again. Sophie turned toward me, and I had a fleeting thought that if she asked me to tell another true experience I would throw up.

"I've got to go. Tell Sophie she did a great job, and I'll call her tomorrow." I didn't stop to think how I'd get a ride home.

"I'll come, too. We've got to resolve this thing between us, Melanie. We can't just leave everything as it stands."

"Yes, we can," I said, surprised to find my hands and voice still shaking. I began to walk off down Church Street toward Broad, thinking I'd call Nancy for a ride.

I heard his cell phone ring, and he stopped but I kept going. I had almost reached the next block when I heard him call my name again.

"Melanie, please wait."

I stopped in the middle of the street, my hands on my hips. I thought about telling him about Emily then, to hurt him as much as he'd hurt me. But then I remembered the way he'd tilted his head and the way she had touched his hair, and I knew that I couldn't. He had to know. I just needed to figure out how I could tell him without destroying us both.

"What, Jack? What part of no are you not getting?"

When he reached me, he didn't stop but grabbed my arm and kept walking. "That was your dad."

"Is he all right?" I felt an edge of worry nudge my conscience. I never worried about my father anymore. I'd filled that quota years ago.

"After you told him that you grandfather's name was on the deed to Magnolia Ridge, he decided to go through your grandfather's effects to see if he could find out anything more about your grandfather Gus and his connection to the Vanderhorsts."

"And did he?" I asked, breathless because we were almost running.

"He found a locked humidor that had belonged to Gus. He broke the lock and said that we need to come see what he found inside."

I tried to dig in my heels to make him stop, but that only succeeded in dragging me for a few steps until I could start running again. "Stop it, Jack! No more, remember? There's no more mystery to solve."

He didn't reply but continued to drag me down Church Street, capturing the attention of two people dressed up as salt and pepper shakers walking together on the opposite side of the street.

"Jack, stop. I don't care. None of this matters anymore. Not to mention the facts that I'm pissed at you and my father because I told you to get out of my house and that I never wanted to see you again. And now I find that the two of you have continued to work on this supposed mystery behind my back."

We'd reached his car where he dropped my arm and glared at me. "Let's pretend for one minute that it's not about you or me anymore, all right? That maybe this whole project meant a lot more to your father than either one of us could have guessed. And that without it to focus on, he's a little . . . lost."

My anger dissipated quickly, replaced by the heavy weight of dread. "What are you trying to tell me, Jack? Is my dad drinking again?"

Jack opened the passenger door of his car. "That would depend on how fast we get there, I suppose."

"Get where?"

"To Blackbeard's. He's sitting at a table now with a glass of gin in front of him."

I slid into my seat without another word, wishing that I didn't feel so disappointed and wondering why, after everything I had grown up knowing, I'd still managed to find a small sliver of hope.

CHAPTER 19

The drive to East Bay was short but seemed to take place in slow motion. I kept dialing my father's cell phone, hanging up each time it went to voice mail. My emotions bounced among anger at Jack, worry over my father, and a little nudge of hope that maybe he really had discovered something about Louisa and Nevin.

We parked in the same place we had when we'd been there for our date, then raced into the restaurant. Several waitresses turned and gave Jack a greeting, which he apparently didn't see or didn't care to acknowledge as his eyes swept the patrons in the bar area. We spotted my father at the same time, sitting at a wooden table in the far corner under a Ford Motor Company neon sign. The middle of the table was occupied by a burl walnut humidor, and next to my father's right hand sat a full glass of gin, straight up, the way he liked it. I knew that because he'd taught me how to measure two shots for him when he was too drunk to hold the bottle steady. Being a military man, he always had to have it measured precisely, regardless of the fact that drinking from the bottle would have been equally as effective.

Jack pulled two chairs from another table, and we sat down. My father didn't once look up at us, preferring instead to stare at the clear promise of oblivion offered by the glass of gin.

"Daddy?" I said, not realizing until after I'd said it that I'd reverted back to the old name I'd called him when I was little. "Are you all right?"

He acted as if he hadn't heard me. "It's amazing, isn't it, how something so small can take all your troubles away while at the same time making them so much worse?"

I traded a worried glance with Jack. "You shouldn't be here, Jim," Jack said.

My dad didn't move his head, but his eyes looked up at Jack. "You think I don't know that?"

"How much have you had?" I was proud that my voice was steady, as if I were making a real estate offer on behalf of my clients.

He turned his eyes to me and I saw that they were clear. "Not a drop. Yet."

I sat back but without any relief. He'd turned his fixed gaze on the glass again.

Jack also sat back, feigning a relaxed attitude while both of us watched my dad and the glass like a cat would watch a mouse hole. We didn't say anything else, as if we both realized that my dad needed to talk first, regardless of how long that might take. A waitress appeared—an older woman who apparently didn't know Jack but was still taken with his charms as she made sure to lean down enough to show off her ample cleavage. We each ordered Cokes, then returned to silence as we waited for my dad to speak.

We were halfway through our Cokes before he spoke again. Without looking at either one of us, he said, "What is it with mothers leaving their children? Can there be anything more devastating to a child?"

I felt every muscle and bone go rigid in my body, feeling like a riverbed that had suddenly been sucked dry of water. We didn't talk about my mother's absence. Never. After she'd left, I'd have a screaming fit if anybody mentioned her name. And as I grew older, it began to seem as if she'd never been there at all, and my father and I were content to pretend it was true.

"Daddy, I don't want to talk about that now. This is about you, all right? Jack and I are here to help you."

"But that's it, don't you see? My drinking, and your mother's disappearance, and you—it's all related. There can't be one without the other." He laughed softly. "There I was, in the spare room where I keep all the junk I've accumulated over the years, holding that box and seeing what was inside of it, when it just hit me."

"What, Daddy? What are you talking about?"

He rubbed his eyes with his hands, still avoiding looking at me. "I don't think I can kick this thing if we can't go back to that one thing that changed our lives."

"Daddy, I don't . . ." Jack's hand over mine made me stop.

"I need to tell you a few things, Melanie. Things that won't be easy to hear, but things you need to hear, nevertheless. I can't help but think that once I get all of it out of me, this compulsion to destroy myself with gin might not be as strong."

"And you figured this out by looking inside this box?" I heard the dismissive tone in my voice and cringed, but neither Jack nor my dad said anything. It was almost as if we were all in agreement that I was due a bit of skepticism and recrimination.

"Yep. I did. We've got two stories of missing mothers. And I can't help but think that if we figure out one, we can figure out the other."

Jack squeezed my arm and I looked between him and my father, feeling like a Catholic in the confessional, and not at all sure if my penance would be easier to bear than the weight of my sins. I couldn't speak, but simply nodded, then checked for the nearest exit just in case I had the urge to run away as fast as I could.

"When you and your mother first moved in with your grandmother, it was because of me. We were . . . arguing. It was stupid, really, because it was about your imaginary friends. I didn't think it was healthy but your mother seemed to be encouraging it. But it wasn't really about you at all, you see? Ginette was growing away from me. Her career was starting to take off, and she was getting all sorts of publicity. I wasn't comfortable with that at all, and I made her suffer for it by picking fights and telling her that she wasn't a good mother." He shifted uncomfortably in his seat. "I blamed her for socially isolating you by encouraging your reliance on these imaginary friends that existed only in your head."

He stopped to swallow hard, and I glanced at the back door that I'd spied before, gauging how long it would take for Jack to catch up to me if I ran.

"But she was a good mother, you know. She loved you more than anything. More than her career. More than me. And I was okay with that because I loved you, too. You were a sweet child, Melanie." He turned to Jack. "As hard as you might find that to believe, she really was."

I sent my dad a reproachful look. "Sorry, Melanie, but I just want to make sure Jack is on the same page with us." He continued. "But that night, when we were arguing . . ." He shook his head. "I'd been drinking. I'd always been a social drinker, never really had any trouble keeping in control. But that night I'd read an article about your mother in the paper, about how Charleston couldn't contain such a talent anymore and that it was time for her to spread her wings and show the world what she could do. There was a picture of her. With her manager. I knew there was nothing to it, but the gin got to talking so that by the time she came home there was nothing she could do or say that would make me think otherwise."

He touched the glass for the first time, and began spinning it in a circle on the table. Neither Jack nor I took our eyes off of his fingers as the glass made its etching sound on the wood. "I loved her, you see. Maybe too much. But I didn't want to share her with the rest of the world when all I ever wanted her to be was mine."

He stilled the glass, both palms pressing against its sides. "We fought and said some ugly words to each other. And then . . ." His chin dropped down to his chest. "Damn. I don't . . ." He looked back up at us and his eyes were wet. I'd never seen him like this before. It was honest, and pure and undiluted by alcohol, and I wanted to crawl up in his lap and lay my head on his shoulder as I'd done when I was a little girl.

He took a deep breath. "I told her to leave. To go away. That we didn't need her anyway." He shrugged. "So she did. But she took you with her, and that was the biggest heartbreak of all."

Jack tapped my arm and handed me a paper napkin. I touched my cheek, unaware that I'd been crying and embarrassed to have been caught.

"And then, just when I thought we were working things out, she . . . left. Just left. Leaving you with me." He let go of the glass and leaned his forehead against the heels of his hands and was silent for a long moment. "What I'm trying to say is that her leaving was about her and me—not about you. And that you shouldn't blame her for what she did. I told her that we were better off without her and maybe something happened that made her believe it. I don't know. I never gave her the chance to explain."

"You never talked to her? You just let her go?" For the first time in my life, my loyalty was divided evenly between my parents.

He returned his focus to the glass of gin. "She tried to talk to me, to call me. I wouldn't see her, and I wouldn't take her calls. I was too angry, too hurt. She'd made up her mind, and it didn't matter what I wanted. And I'd started drinking more. Not enough that anybody would notice but enough that I couldn't feel the pain anymore."

"But why didn't she call me? Why didn't she come to see me?"

My dad's eyes met Jack's before turning to me. "She did."

"What?" I stared back at him, incredulous. "Then why did I never see her again or speak with her?" My words slowed like a child's ball that had reached the bottom of the hill, as I realized I'd known the answer before I asked it.

I stood abruptly, ready to leave, but neither one of them made a move to stop me. It was almost as if we all realized that maybe I had finally grown up, and it was time to face the truth.

"I told her you didn't want to see her because it upset you too much. And when she called, I told her the same thing. After a while, it became the truth—remember? Remember how you'd scream if anybody mentioned her name? So then it seemed to me that I wasn't lying anymore. Not that it mattered because I was too busy medicating myself with gin to see how much you must have been hurting."

Stiffly, I sat down again. "How long did she keep trying?"

My dad looked down at his hands, unable to meet my eyes. "Until you went to college. I guess she figured you were adult enough then to call her yourself."

Somehow, Jack had managed to move his chair close enough so that he could put his arm around me. I was too numb to even try to pull away, much less to remember why I wanted to. I indelicately blew my nose into the napkin and then crumpled it into one of my balled fists. "She . . . she tried to reach me. To see me. And you wouldn't let her."

His shoulders slumped as his hands slipped to the edge of the table. "We acted like children, and not like the parents you needed. We wanted to hurt each other—not you. But it seems like that's what ended up happening." Leaning forward, he took both of my frozen hands in his, the skin callused from his months of digging holes and laying bricks. "Never—not ever—did either one of us stop loving you. We never did."

I didn't pull away, but sat feeling my father's work-roughened hands, imagining each brick and each plant he'd placed in my garden as a sort of penance for a sin committed long ago. I wasn't ready to forgive him; I wasn't sure if that was what he was even asking. But maybe, under all of my hurt and loss, I owed him my understanding.

"She still left me. Does it really matter why?"

He shook his head. "She told me she was doing it for you. And that's the last time I allowed her to try and explain anything to me."

I shook my head. "Why are you telling me all this now?"

Slowly, he let go of my hands and slid the humidor closer to him, which at the same time shoved the gin glass out of his direct line of vision. "Because it occurred to me—this whole house thing, and the disappearing mother and the son who never forgot her—I think it all ended up in your lap for a reason. Losing a mother is a horrible thing—not ever knowing the truth is worse still." He rested his hands on top of the polished wood box. "Maybe, in finding out the truth about Louisa Vanderhorst, you might find some understanding of your own past."

I sat back in my chair, feeling the hard wood against my back. I pressed into it, concentrated on feeling the hardness that grounded me to the chair. Because without that, I felt that I might float away, leave that person I had always known as Melanie Middleton, abandoned child, because I no longer thought that I knew her.

"So you don't believe Louisa ran away," I said, staring at the humidor.

He shook his head. "And neither do you. There's too much evidence to the contrary from what Jack has told me." He turned the box around so that I could see the front and the splintered wood where he'd broken the lock. "But we'll never find out unless you allow us to keep looking."

Jack pressed a glass of ice water into my hands. I hadn't been aware of him asking for one, and I think I thanked him for it. I pressed the icy-cold glass against my cheek before taking a long drink. "And what if I find out that Louisa did just leave with Joseph?"

"Then we'll know the truth. But I think, if we dig deep enough, we'll find out that things aren't always what they seem. That maybe people act in ways contrary to what they are because they don't think they have any other choice."

I reached toward the box and pulled it to my side of the table, touching the smooth wood under my outstretched palms, feeling as if I were being presented with a gift—a gift not just for me but for my father as well. Thirty-three years was a long time to be paying penance. "I'll consider it. But first, you need to promise me three things."

He raised an eyebrow.

"I need you to promise that you won't come back here. And that if you feel the urge to drink, I want you to call me first and then Jack."

"Deal," he said. "And what's the third?"

Locking eyes with my dad, I said, "That you won't make me work with Jack on this."

He smiled his old smile and I relaxed a bit. "Only if you want to. But he's the one with all the research connections and the know-how. I think it would be foolish to exclude him."

I refocused my gaze on Jack and was silent for a long moment. "I'll let you work on this with us only if you promise to stay away from me as much as possible."

He had the audacity to not even look offended. Instead, he gave me his back-of-the-book-cover smile and saluted. "Yes, ma'am. You're the captain, and I'm the sailor, and I will take orders from you without meeting your eyes."

"Whatever," I muttered before turning back to the box, tapping my fingers against it.

"Go ahead and open it, Melanie," my dad said gently. "I'm not sure what any of it means, but maybe the three of us can put our heads together and figure it out." His eyes met mine and he added, "For Nevin. And Louisa."

Without allowing myself to think, I lifted the hinged lid, the aroma of old cigars and something else wafting out of it. I sneezed twice, then peered inside the box. Scattered throughout were dried rose petals, detached from the stem most likely from movement of the box. Nestled amid the petals was a canister of old 120 roll film and beneath it an ivory envelope, still sealed. After hesitating briefly, I reached in and pulled it out, breathing in deeply when I saw the underlined name on the front, written in the bold handwriting of a male. *Nevin,* it read. And then, in the bottom right hand corner, was the date *January 15, 1931.*

I glanced up at my dad, not even sure how to formulate my question.

"I'm thinking that maybe Nevin's father gave this to my father for safekeeping."

"In case anything happened to him, perhaps?" Jack pulled his chair closer. "But I thought they had a falling-out shortly after Louisa disappeared in 1930. This is dated a year later."

I nodded. "They did. They even dissolved their law practice. So why would my grandfather have this in his possession when he died?"

We all looked at each other. Finally, Jack said, "Open the letter, Melanie. Maybe that will answer our questions."

I looked at my dad for confirmation, and he nodded. "All right," I said. "I suppose when Mr. Vanderhorst left me his house, he was bound to expect that I'd have access to his personal effects." With a deep breath, I slid my finger under the flap and began to tear. The letter was folded in half, the ink now browned with age. I cleared my throat, my eyes sliding from my dad's face to Jack's, then read out loud.

> *My precious son,*
>
> *You are too young to read this now or even to understand all that is contained in this box. That is why I'm giving it to my friend, Augustus Middleton, in case something should happen to me before you are old enough to know the truth of things.*
>
> *Be vigilant in all that you do, and be secure in the knowledge always that you were greatly loved by both of your parents and all who knew you. Remember what your mother used to call you, and never have any doubt.* Cerca Trova.
>
> *Your Loving Father,*
> *Robert Nevin Vanderhorst*

"How cryptic," I murmured, feeling the soft ivory vellum between my fingers.

"'Cerca Trova'?" my father asked.

Jack frowned for a moment. "Seek and ye shall find. And that's weird because I know I've seen that recently. It'll come to me."

I read the letter again to myself. "But why didn't Robert get the box after Gus died?"

"They died within hours of each other, probably without realizing the other was gone," said Jack. "I found that in my research."

My dad took the letter from me and read it to himself. "I've never even gone through his things. My father died when I was pretty young, and I was raised by an aunt. I've had his stuff in storage ever since I was first sent to basic training camp. I never thought . . ."

I touched his arm. "It's not your fault, Daddy. Nobody could ever have suspected that Grandpa Gus was hiding anything like this. At least you kept it and didn't throw it all away."

Jack was examining the rose stem. "Something tells me that this is a Louisa rose."

I took it from him, feeling the frailness of the dead flower as if the stale air of the old box was being transferred to me like the air from an ancient tomb. "I'll ask Sophie if she knows anybody at the college who could identify this for us."

My dad reached in and took out the roll of film. "What about this? Is it even possible that the images might still be developed?"

"My dad is good friends with Lloyd Sconiers," Jack said. "He buys and sells old cameras and equipment in his store in North Charleston. He's a bit of an oddity but really knows his stuff. I could take these to him and see what he says. Might even be able to develop them himself."

"Great," I said, trying to keep my growing excitement in check. "First thing, I'm going to go see Sophie and bring the rose. What time does Mr. Sconiers open his shop?"

Jack twisted his mouth as if he were trying hard not to smile. "Probably ten o'clock. Would you like to make out a work sheet for us?"

I sent him a withering glance, then slid back my chair. As I slipped my purse onto my shoulder, my father surprised me by putting his arms around me and giving me a hug. I stiffened at first, remembering the old hugs that were meant more to disguise the fact that he couldn't stand unassisted.

"Thank you," he said quietly into my ear.

I pulled back, looking into his face. "For what?"

"For not giving up. Even when you pretended to get on with your life, you always made sure that your cell phone number was programmed into mine. I didn't deserve it. And for coming tonight and letting me be a part of all this. It's given me something to look forward to." He scratched the back of his head. "And it's given me a chance to see the person you've become in spite of me. I'm proud of you." My father coughed in embarrassment, then stepped back. "Yes, well, I guess we should all go home now. We've got to be up and at 'em tomorrow."

I started, a brief sensation of déjà vu settling over me. "Who's Adam?" I asked, smiling softly.

His eyes softened. "You remembered."

"Yeah. Hard to forget something I said every morning." I laughed out loud, remembering my genuine confusion as a child as to why my dad wanted me to get "up and Adam." Even after he'd explained it to me, I stubbornly persisted on asking who Adam was.

"It wasn't all bad, was it, growing up with me?"

I reached for him and hugged him tightly, noticing how he didn't seem so tall or strong anymore. Then I buried my face in the soft wool of his jacket so he couldn't see my tears. "No, Daddy," I said, my voice muffled. "Not all of it."

He patted my back clumsily until Jack interjected, "Okay, okay, you two. You're going to make me cry and ruin my reputation."

We broke apart, still feeling strained and awkward in each other's company, but no longer like the polite strangers we'd been for so long.

We put everything inside the box again, and Jack handed it to me to carry. Then the three of us walked outside onto the sidewalk, and I shivered, feeling the chill of the autumn night yet warmed somehow, too. I turned to my dad. "Will you be all right to go home by yourself?"

"Thank you. I'm all right now."

Impulsively, I leaned forward and kissed him on his cheek. "I'm glad."

He touched his cheek, a boyish grin on his face, which made it obvious to me what it was that must have once attracted my mother.

Jack and I walked him to his car, and he paused for a moment. "There's one more thing, Melanie."

"What?"

"You really need to move back into the house. Not only to keep everything legit, but because I also think there must be more clues in that house that we haven't found yet. And we'll have a much better chance of finding them if you're there."

I stared at him, wondering if there was any hidden meaning behind his request. But his eyes were level and clear, and I had a flash of memory of his reaction when I told him I'd been speaking on the phone to my grandmother, and I knew he'd only meant what he'd said.

"He's right, Melanie. The bathrooms are working, and so is the kitchen, so it won't be too horrible living there." Jack elbowed me gently in the arm. "You can't really call it roughing it if you're in a house on Tradd Street, you know?"

I rolled my eyes but couldn't help smiling. "Yeah. Probably not." I sobered quickly, feeling only sadness instead of the anger at Jack or my practiced ambivalence for the house. The sadness surprised me, and I wondered if in some small way it was because Mr. Vanderhorst's dream of restoring the house to its former grandeur would most likely not happen as long as I owned the house. I had less than a year to go—seven months and three weeks to be exact—and then I could sell it to someone who thought that restoring an old house might be fun. But instead of getting excited about the idea of selling the house and retuning to my condo, I felt only the persistent bruise of regret.

My dad said goodbye; then we watched him drive off before going back to Jack's Porsche. Starting his engine, he turned to me. "So, I guess you wouldn't want to go somewhere for a drink with me. Or dessert?"

"Absolutely not. Just because we're working on this little mystery together does not make us friends or coworkers or whatever else you want to call it."

"Sort of like barely civil strangers."

"Exactly."

"Who've been working side by side for about four months, sharing countless meals, meeting each other's parents, and almost kissed twice."

"Once," I corrected before clamping my hand over my mouth. "I think," I added between my fingers.

"Right," he said, his dimple showing in the light from the streetlamp. "Barely civil strangers."

We didn't speak for the entire ride across the river to Mt. Pleasant. When he slid into a space in front of my building, he turned to me, his eyes serious. "I can't tell you how very sorry I am. About lying to you. That's not the sort of person I am at all—not that I expect you to believe it. It's just . . ." He ran his hands through his hair, making pointy ends stick up behind his ears. "I don't know. I guess Emily's departure made me too cynical. Made me not want to trust anyone. But that's no excuse, and I know that. I just wanted you to know how sorry I am. Sorry that I disappointed you. Sorry that I was such a jerk."

I hesitated, just for a moment, my hand on the door handle. *Tell him. Tell him I love him. Tell him that my love for him gave me no choice but to leave. Tell him what you know.* I opened my mouth to tell him what I'd learned, not because I forgave him but because he needed to forgive himself. "Jack, there's something . . ."

His cell phone rang and he looked down at the number. "It's my friend at the library." He gave me an apologetic smile. "Would you like me to walk you up?"

"No, thanks. I'll just see you tomorrow. Don't want to keep you from your library friend." I smirked.

"Was there something you were about to say?"

I shook my head. "Nothing that can't wait. Good night."

"Good night," he said, the phone already up to his ear. I exited the car, walking quickly as if trying to escape the accusing stare of a woman I couldn't see but could feel nearby. I listened as Jack's car sped away, then let myself in at my front door, closing it softly behind me.

CHAPTER 20

I lay in bed looking up at the plain white ceiling illuminated by the bright white streetlight from outside, feeling completely and totally wide-awake. I was in the middle of doing an estimate in my head of what it would cost to add a ceiling medallion and cornices when a niggling thought interrupted my ruminations. I sat up, startled at the urgency of the thought and half aware that the thought hadn't come from me. It was almost as if someone had whispered it from behind me, sort of like subliminal advertising. *Look at the christening photograph in the album.*

I quickly slid from bed and crossed the room in the dim light, only to remember that I was in my condo with the plain ceilings and that I had left all of Louisa's albums at the house on Tradd Street. Standing in the middle of my room, I closed my eyes, picturing the photo of Louisa with Nevin in his christening gown, trying to remember the details. Mother and child had been radiant, and both dressed in white, the intricate lace of Nevin's gown trailing over Louisa's arms, hiding her hands. Her dark hair had been pulled on top of her head, and she wore no earrings.

My eyes flew open. She wasn't wearing earrings, *but she wore a necklace.* I reached the phone by the side of my bed in one quick step and picked up the receiver, only to hang it up immediately when I saw the bright readout on my alarm clock that said it was three fifteen in the morning. Not one to analyze my feelings, I didn't stop to think why my first thought had been to call Jack and not my father or Marc.

I sat on the edge of my bed, all thoughts of finding sleep now completely gone. I figured I could either stay awake all night, tossing and turning, or I could throw on some sweats and head out to Tradd Street now. It was my house, after all, and I was allowed to come and go as I pleased.

Without thinking any further, I tossed on my clothes, brushed my teeth, then made my bed before heading out to my car. Traffic was light, and I found myself pulling onto Tradd Street not even twenty minutes later. Someone had left the outside lights on, as well as a light in a downstairs window so the house didn't seem as dark and foreboding as I remembered from the last time I'd seen it. Almost as if I were expected.

I scanned the upper windows, willing my heartbeat to slow when I neither saw nor sensed anything staring back at me. I glanced at the light in the lower window, realizing that it came from the first-floor drawing room and that all the furniture and lamps and been taken out over a month ago. *Thanks, Louisa,* I said to myself, feeling comforted by her presence and fortified enough to go inside the empty house.

I unlatched the garden gate and headed up the steps of the piazza, smelling fresh paint and noticing that the missing bricks in the steps had been replaced. I unlocked the front door, satisfied to hear the warning beeps from the alarm before punching in my code 1-2-2-1.

The sleeping house sat still and quiet, the only sound that of the ticking grandfather clock, like a heartbeat. I stepped into the foyer and flipped on the light, noticing that the scaffolding and drop cloths had all been removed. For a moment I thought it was because the work had been abandoned. And then I saw that the wallpaper no longer drooped and the corkscrew spindles all gleamed with fresh paint. Curious, I stepped toward the drawing room and saw the large chandelier hanging from its old spot on the ornate ceiling, its cleaned crystals sparkling and reflecting the gaslight from outside. As I had expected, there was no sign of a light in the room that would have shone from the window.

I spun around the room, smelling the fresh paint and seeing the gleam of the newly waxed and polished hardwood floors, remembering that Chad had once told me he was an expert with an electric floor sander. Apparently, the restoration work had continued in my absence, with Sophie, Jack, and Chad using whatever resources they could find. I was touched but saddened at the same time, oddly wishing that I had been a part of it.

I turned to go upstairs, and my foot kicked something soft, sending it skidding across the freshly polished floors. It was a stuffed dog, dark brown with black spots, and it had pointy, triangular ears and a long, thick tail. Its tail appeared gnawed, and I wondered if somebody had bought General Lee a toy. A red button on one of its paws read *Press Me*, so I did and was rewarded with the dog saying, "Ruh-Roh." It was life had continued in this house without me, with my friends working on the house and even buying toys for my dog. All without my knowledge or participation. As if everybody had been invited to a birthday party but me.

Feeling foolish, I placed the dog on the bottom step and climbed the stairs to my room. I hesitated only for a moment before I turned the knob and let myself in, reassured by the warm temperature of the room that I was alone. I spotted the stacked albums on the dresser, where I'd left them, the last one I'd looked at—the one with the christening photo—on top. Realizing too late that I'd forgotten my gloves, I reached for the album, feeling the resulting tingle of anticipation race up my arms. I made it to the bed and sat down, opening the album on my lap.

I smelled summer grass and Carolina jasmine, and thought I could feel the soft give of earth underneath my feet as I leaned forward to push the wooden swing. Soft bubbles of childish laughter filled the room along with the summer air, and I felt myself smiling although my face didn't move. A tall, dark-haired man faced me, holding the Brownie camera. I felt the rope through my kid leather gloves as I gently stopped the swing so we could gaze together into the camera. The man told us to smile and we did, capturing the beautiful perfection of the summer day.

I looked down and saw the scrapbook again, the long-fingered hand I'd grown used to seeing gripping a fountain pen as it scrawled across the page.

August 31, 1929

My darling Robert is becoming as much of a camera buff as I am and can hardly resist taking photographs of me and our darling Nevin. I don't mind, as I can't imagine ever having enough pictures of our son. However, I do believe we have plenty enough of me, but Robert insists and I humor him. He is so good to us, and is very insistent that the troubled business affairs of most of our friends and neighbors and the high rate of bank closures will not affect us. I do worry, as I feel these difficult times have forced Robert into business associations he would not have considered in the past, but I trust that he will help us all weather this storm. He is a Vanderhorst, after all, as am I now, and this is merely a trifling matter compared to what our ancestors have had to face, and what sacrifices they were forced to make to save our beautiful home here on Tradd Street.

I slid the scrapbook off of my lap and onto the bed, feeling the relief as I slipped back into my own body again. I then used a corner of the sheet to flip through pages filled with photographs of Louisa and Nevin, and still more of the house and garden and even a few of Robert himself, until I stopped on the christening photograph. It might have been my imagination, but it seemed as if Louisa's expression was less serene this time. It was almost as if she were looking at me from behind the camera, an earnestness behind her eyes that made me look closer.

I squinted as I pressed myself forward, studying the necklace with the huge stone around her neck. *Jack was right.* I looked again, just to make sure, but now that I knew what I was looking for, it was fairly obvious that the jewel hanging around Louisa's neck was a very large brilliant-cut diamond.

I reached for my phone to call Jack, assuming it must be at least dawn now, remembering as I did so that the plumber had needed the phone in another part of the house. My purse, with my cell phone inside, had been left on the hall table, where I'd dropped it when I'd entered the house.

Damn, I said to myself as I got to my feet and glanced at the clock. The soft white glow of the numbers read four thirteen. It didn't matter. I needed to call Jack, and I wasn't about to hold this in for two more hours. I blinked my eyes, wondering if it was exhaustion that was fogging my vision. I breathed out, a large puff of white air clouding the space in front of me, and I shivered in the sudden cold.

Warily, I started for the door, walking past the dressing table with the large mirror above it. A movement near the mirror made me spin around to face it as my breath left my lungs in a strong whoosh, sending out a cloud of white frost. *I am stronger than you. I am stronger than you.*

A dark figure of a man peered out at me from the mirror. He stood behind me, and if I could have moved, I would have been able to reach behind me and touch him. His features weren't clear, his eyes hidden by the shadow of a hat's brim. Evil radiated from him like reflected light in a dark well, and I held my breath, not wanting to show my fear.

His reflection began to shimmer as if I'd been staring into a pond and somebody had dropped a stone, warping the image into something more grotesque. I opened my mouth to shout, coughing instead as I inhaled the thick, pungent aroma of smoke. The overhead light fixture flickered once, then twice, then dimmed gradually as if somebody was slowly covering up the bulbs with a black cloth And then they went out completely.

I launched myself at the door, having the forethought to feel the handle first to test for heat before throwing it open. Thin wisps of smoke drifted through the upstairs hallway like clouds from the night sky, the acrid taste of it thick in my nose and mouth. I coughed before bringing the bottom of my sweatshirt over my mouth in an attempt to breathe easier.

I peered over the banister into the foyer below, seeing that the darker, heavier smoke was coming from the back, in the direction of the kitchen. Running down the stairs I became aware of the dreadful silence in the house except for the faint crackling and popping of burning laminate and wood coming from the kitchen and the incessant ticking of the grandfather clock in the front room. The smoke alarms, wired directly to the fire station, were completely silent.

Choking and gasping for air, I stumbled to the front door, unwilling to give in to panic and taking the time to methodically unlock the dead bolts. After ensuring that I'd done them all, I turned the handle and pulled. Nothing happened. Moving faster now, I checked all of the dead bolts again, making sure they were all unlatched and pulled again. The door stuck, as unmovable as if somebody was holding it closed from the other side.

Spots formed in front of me, and I clenched my eyes shut to get the spots to go away, jerking them open again as soon as I realized how very much they wanted to stay closed. I tugged on the door again, slipping down the door to my knees. I gasped again, my lungs desperate now for oxygen, and succeeded only in hyperventilating. The spots danced in front of my eyes again, like a hypnotist's pendulum, begging me to go to sleep.

Wake up, Melanie. Help is on the way. I forced my eyes open, wondering if I'd really heard the woman's voice or if the smoke was getting to my brain. Using the doorknob I struggled to a stand, feeling small hands on my back as if to prop me up. Groggily, I turned to look behind me, then froze as I saw only a dark figure of a man hovering behind the smoke in the drawing room, red pinpricks of light where his eyes should be.

I tugged on the door harder, but I was crying, feeling the helplessness of panic taking hold of me. Exhausted, I let go of the doorknob and slid down the door again, too sleepy to try anymore. I knew that if I could just go to sleep, everything would be all right.

I was vaguely aware of the sound of sirens in the distance gradually growing louder. My head, feeling heavier than I thought possible, dropped down to my chest, and I simply let go of the house and the smoke, and even the incessant woman's voice calling my name over and over, telling me to wake up.

Something hard hit my hip as a chilled breeze brushed my face. I moaned and tried to remember where my hip might be so I could rub it.

"Melanie? Melanie? Are you here?"

A hard and solid object that could have been a shoe jabbed my ribs and then warm fingers were touching my face. It felt nice, and I tried to turn my cheek into the seeking fingers, pretending that they were Jack's but knowing that they couldn't be. He wouldn't be touching me like that. Unless he thought I was Emily. I groaned and tried to roll over, away from him.

Then strong arms were lifting me up. I fought against my rescuer, wanting the warm cocoon of sleep and the sense of carefree peace it had brought to me. The sirens were louder now, and I tried to move my hands over my ears to drown out the noise so I could go back to sleep, but my hands had become leaded weights, and my arms rubber tubes that weren't connected to my body at all.

Cold, prickly grass tickled my skin as I was laid in the garden, and

I thought to myself that this would be a lovely place for them to bury me—here amongst the roses and camellias, where the sweet sent of the Confederate jasmine would remind me each year that spring had arrived.

"Melanie, can you hear me? Melanie, wake up. It's me—it's Jack."

Jack. I wanted to open my eyes to see him again, to see his beautiful blue eyes with their wicked sparkle that I thought was a lot brighter since we first met. I felt Emily close by, and Louisa and the small hands of a child touching my hands as if trying to hold me down on the grass so I couldn't float away into the night sky.

Open your eyes, Melanie. It was my grandmother Prioleau's voice, and I wanted so badly to see her again that I did open my eyes. But I wasn't lying down looking up, I was floating above, looking down at me and Jack, and standing around us was a crowd of people I didn't recognize—except for the gentleman in front, a Confederate cavalry officer who stood respectfully with his hat held over his heart.

My grandmother was kneeling by my head, her hand on my forehead, but she was looking up at me and shaking her head. *It's not your time, sweetheart. You need to come back to my garden and have tea with your mother again. Open your eyes, Melanie. Open them.*

I saw Louisa, too, recognizing her by the dress she wore and the diamond necklace around her neck. She was kneeling in front of the fountain, pushing the grass back as if to expose something around the base, and I saw the Roman numerals that Jack and I had spotted before.

I watched as Jack bent over me, and I felt his warm lips over mine. And then he blew into my mouth, his breath into my body, and it felt like the incoming tide on parched sand, feeding the parts of me that had been shriveled for so long. I closed my eyes, disappearing into the warmth of Jack's breath, feeling like the sun dripping into the night's ocean.

And then I opened my eyes, and it was just Jack and me in Louisa's rose garden, and his face was close to mine, the taste of his lips still lingering on mine.

"Thank God," he said, resting his forehead on mine, his breaths short and quick.

I filled my lungs with air, as if to make sure that I still could, and coughed trying to get the burn of smoke out of them. Then I focused on Jack's face and smiled up at him. "That didn't count as a second kiss, you know." My voice sounded odd, like the words had been rubbed with sandpaper.

And then Jack smiled back at me, his eyes warm and bright, and I knew that everything was going to be all right.

ꝏ

They made me stay in the hospital overnight to treat me for smoke inhalation and for observation. My dad, Jack, Sophie, and surprisingly, Chad, stayed in the waiting room all night, and crowded around me first thing in the morning as soon as my oxygen mask had been removed. I knew it was against hospital policy to have so many visitors at once, and I assumed Jack had charmed the nurses into allowing it, but was surprised when Jack gave all the credit to my dad, who must have treated the medical staff as if they were new recruits.

Chad and Sophie stayed only a short while to say hello and make sure I was all right before Chad left to go feed General Lee and take him out. I watched with amusement as Sophie left with him, muttering some lame excuse about wanting to borrow Chad's yoga mat. But first she kissed me on my forehead, her hemp necklace tickling my nose, and promised that she'd read my tarot cards for me just as soon as I was released. Obviously, we had missed something big, and she wasn't about to let it happen again.

I pulled on her hand. "And one more thing. Remember my grandfather's box that I told you my father found? It contained a shriveled rose in it. We're thinking it might be a Louisa rose, but we were hoping you knew somebody at the college who might be able to identify it. I left it in my car at the house because I was going to bring it to you this morning."

She patted my hand. "Don't worry about a thing. I still have the car key you gave me when you went on vacation three years ago. I'll go get it and find out what I can."

Sophie and Chad left, and then Jack pulled up a chair close to the head of the bed. "So, Melanie, what happened last night?"

I'd already told my story to the police and even I was surprised by how short and simple it had become. My voice still felt raw and raspy as I spoke. "I was upstairs in my bedroom and smelled smoke. I went downstairs and couldn't open the door—I guess the smoke made me confused, and I must not have unlocked all of the dead bolts. I passed out on the floor in front of the door until you came and took me out of the house."

My dad squeezed my hand. "You are one lucky girl. You probably don't remember, but you somehow managed to call the fire department and Jack before you passed out."

I looked at Jack. "I didn't call anybody. I didn't have a phone in my room, and I'd left my purse and cell phone downstairs."

I watched as my dad and Jack exchanged glances before Jack spoke again. "The fire chief told me that the call came from inside the house and that it was a woman—a woman who didn't identify herself."

My dad cupped my hand between his. "Maybe you forgot. Maybe you called first from another room before you came downstairs. It's not surprising that your memory is a little foggy. Smoke inhalation is a serious thing."

I turned my attention to Jack. "But who called you? Did you recognize my voice?"

A muscle ticked in Jack's jaw. "Actually, nobody said anything. Whoever it was kept calling and calling, hanging up when I answered, and then calling again. But it was your cell phone number. I know because I have it programmed into my phone, and your name popped up every time."

"See, Melanie? You must have made the phone calls before you passed out." My dad patted my hand but I could tell that he wasn't completely convinced.

"Is the house okay? Was there extensive damage?" Even I was surprised by my question. It hadn't been that long ago that the house burning down to the ground would have solved all of my problems.

Jack shook his head. "Not really. The fire chief says that the fire originated in the kitchen, probably faulty wiring, and they got there fast enough to contain it. The kitchen is pretty much destroyed—not such a bad thing since it needed to be gutted anyway—and not too much smoke damage in the rest of the house because most of the rugs, furniture, and window hangings had already been removed. He thinks you'll be able to go back in a couple of days—after airing it out—but Mrs. Houlihan is going to have to find another kitchen."

I frowned. "Did he have any idea why the smoke alarms didn't work?"

"No. And he checked them and verified that they were all wired correctly and all had working batteries. I've called the alarm company to check it out tomorrow. But it's a bit of a mystery right now."

"The good news," my dad said, straightening, "is that we'll be able to make an insurance claim for the kitchen damage. I guess Mrs. Houlihan can create her dream kitchen, after all. Just to warn you, though—she's partial to granite and stainless steel."

I looked back at Jack, who was frowning down at me. "What were you doing at the house, Melanie? When I dropped you off at your condo, I assumed you were going to bed."

"I thought I was, too. But then I remembered something I'd seen in one of Louisa's scrapbooks. A photograph of her and Nevin. I was lying in my bed, and all of a sudden I remembered the picture."

I looked from Jack to my dad before continuing. "In it, Louisa is wearing a necklace that Robert gave her. And it looks like there's a large diamond hanging from it."

My father looked alarmed. "Were the albums damaged in the fire?"

I shook my head. "I left them up in the bedroom, so they should be fine. We can go look at them later."

Jack leaned toward me. "You know what this means, don't you? That at the very least her husband knew about the diamonds, and not only knew about them but had access to them, too."

I remembered something else I'd seen in the album before and hadn't considered significant enough to tell Jack. Until now. "Jack, do you have any idea what Joseph Longo's middle name was?"

"As a matter of fact, I do. It's a family name they use in each generation." He smirked a little. "It's Marc."

JML. "Chances are, then, that Joseph Longo was aware that the Vanderhorsts knew where the diamonds were. He sent Louisa a newspaper copy of the photo. Nothing was written on it—it was just folded up in his monogrammed stationery."

"JML." Jack's eyes met mine, and I dared him to say anything about Marc being aware of this but thankfully he remained silent on the subject. He put his elbows on his knees, then steepled his fingers. "Well, now. This is getting interesting."

My dad stood and began pacing, his back straight, as if he were doing a military review. "Let's go over what we know. The legend of the diamonds might actually not be a legend because we have quasi-proof—in the form of a necklace Louisa Vanderhorst was photographed wearing—of their existence. Apparently Joseph Longo—or whoever sent the newspaper clipping—realized this, too, and wanted to let the Vanderhorsts know that he was on to them. We know Longo was heavily involved in bootlegging at the time, and Jack has also found that Magnolia Ridge had more than one still and Vanderhorst might have been either a business rival or an associate of Mr. Longo's. We know that the Vanderhorsts didn't suffer financially during the Depression—either because of the diamonds, or because of his illegal business enterprises. Or maybe both. Either way, I can't imagine that Mr. Longo would be happy to let Vanderhorst not only have the famed Confederate diamonds, but also a stake in what he probably considered his private enterprise."

"And don't forget Louisa," I said. "I think Joseph's losing her to Robert Vanderhorst would have been far more personal than anything to do with money."

My father nodded. "Assuming he really lost her at all. Maybe she married Robert just to find out about the diamonds for Joseph, then ran off with Joseph and took the diamonds with her."

"No," I said. "I guess it's possible, but I know that's not the truth."

They both looked at me as if waiting for an explanation, but I remained silent. I couldn't explain to them how I felt transported into Louisa's body every time I touched one of her albums, feeling the overwhelming love she had for her son, her husband, and their house, any more than I could explain to them that the previous night I had left my body and spoken with my grandmother again.

Jack looked at his watch. "Let's all ponder everything for a while, and we can discuss it later." He turned to me. "They're going to be releasing you in about half an hour. If you'd like, I'll stick around and take you back to your condo."

I could tell there was something else he needed to talk about—something he wasn't sure I wanted my dad to hear. "Yes," I said. "Thanks. I appreciate it. But what about going to see Mr. Sconiers this morning?"

My dad stood, obviously taking the hint. "I'll go see him myself.

I've got the roll of film, so hopefully I'll have some answers by tonight." He leaned down and kissed me, and I was touched by the moisture in his eyes. "I'm glad you're all right, sweetpea. You had me scared there for a while." He kissed me again. "I called your mother to let her know you're all right. She would have been worried when she saw it on the news."

I was softened by the use of my childhood name. "That's fine, Daddy," I said, squeezing his hand.

He said his goodbyes, then left, and then the doctor came in so that I could be released, and within an hour I was sitting in Jack's Porsche, an odd silence between us.

Jack's voice was strained and oddly solicitous. "You'll probably just want to go to sleep for the rest of the day when I get you home."

Considering that my lungs thought they'd swallowed a smoke bomb, I felt pretty good. "Actually, I want to go back to Tradd Street. I need to . . . I want to . . ." I stopped when I realized what I was about to say. *I want to make sure that the house is all right.* And it had nothing to do with the possibility of the hidden diamonds. It had more to do with the fact that the house and all of its contents, and all of its history, were mine. Not that I owned it—I don't think anyone truly ever owns an old house, but I was its caretaker and I wanted to make sure that I hadn't failed it in that capacity.

"I understand," Jack said, and I smiled out the window so he couldn't see, and I knew that he did understand.

He parked at the curb behind my car, still where I'd left it the day before. Yellow tape fluttered around the back of the house, where the kitchen was, and my father's garden appeared trampled and unsettled but still somehow beautiful in its wildness. The rosebushes, a few blooms still tenaciously dangling from their stems despite the lateness of the season, sat clustered together behind the dry fountain, like children on a playground, waiting for someone to throw them a ball.

My eyes traveled to the upper story, to the front window where I'd seen the figure of the man. Then I felt my breath escaping when I saw that he wasn't there.

Jack turned off the ignition but didn't move to exit the car. "I need to . . . I need to tell you something . . . strange. Something that happened last night."

I turned to him, my face deliberately blank.

"I know you didn't make those phone calls. A fireman gave me your purse and your cell phone was inside, turned off. I don't think that during the fire you would have had the forethought to not only turn it off but also to put it neatly in your purse."

I remained quiet, waiting for whatever he was going to say next.

He focused on his hands gripping the steering wheel. "And when I came to the door and I tried to open it, it felt like somebody was holding it closed from the other side. It gave a little and then snapped shut, so I know it wasn't locked. And when I looked through the sidelights next to the door, I saw . . . I saw a woman staring at me. I heard her telling me to hurry although she was inside and I was outside and couldn't have really heard anything. When I tried again the door opened easily, and I found you and brought you outside."

Jack faced me, his skin a little pale. "I got the distinct impression last night that there were two people in the house with you—somebody who was trying to hurt you and a woman who was trying to protect you. It was almost as if once the woman asserted her presence, the other one fled."

I chewed on my lower lip, waiting for the inevitable question.

"So tell me, Melanie"—he took a deep breath and then looked steadily into my eyes—"is your house haunted?"

"Wouldn't it be a lot easier to just believe that you imagined all that and everything had a logical explanation?"

"Yeah, that would be easier. But it wouldn't be the truth, would it?"

"I don't—"

"Melanie, what are you afraid of? That I'll laugh at you? I won't, you know. Wouldn't even occur to me. I actually think it's a pretty amazing gift." He paused for a moment. When I didn't say anything, he asked again, "Your house is haunted, isn't it?"

Slowly, I nodded. Without meeting his eyes, I said, "There're three more prominent ghosts in the house—a woman and a little boy, and a man who is wholly evil. I'm pretty sure the woman and the boy are Louisa and Nevin, but I don't know who the man is. I keep thinking that maybe he's Robert Vanderhorst, but I'm pretty sure it's not. Robert was taller, and Louisa loved him. She wouldn't have loved somebody evil."

Jack raised an eyebrow. "And you know all this because you see dead people."

I looked away, toward the house, noticing as if for the first time its graceful lines and symmetrical perfection, and I felt a small stab of what I could only call pride. *It's a piece of history you can hold in your hands.* I sighed, knowing I would tell Jack the truth. He wouldn't laugh at me because he thought what I had was an amazing gift, and the thought made me smile. "Yes, Jack. I do. I always have. Ever since I was a little girl."

He just nodded and stared out of the windshield for a long moment. "Do you think you could just ask Louisa about the diamonds?"

I laughed, but with my smoke-roughened voice, it sounded more like a bark. He looked at me with a worried frown. "It just doesn't work that way, Jack. Honestly, I wish it did. Because I could just ask these people why they keep following me around and be done with it already."

"Must get annoying." He gave me a crooked grin.

"Yeah, sometimes." My own grin softly faded. "Mostly I can ignore them. But not when I'm living in a house with them." I looked down at my hands, recalling something my mother had once told me. "It's a blessing. And a curse. I can't help all of them, because with each one I listen to, each one I help, it takes a little something from me." I looked into his eyes and saw only interest, not the ridicule or disbelief that I'd grown used to.

"Do they ever scare you?"

I remembered the weeks following my grandmother's death when my mother and I lived in the house on Legare, and dark shadow people began appearing as suddenly as a November storm. I had thought at the time that they were relegated to my nighttime dreams, until my mother woke me in the middle of the night and took me out to my grandmother's garden and told me that she saw them, too. And that they weren't there to ask for my help; they were there to make me one of them. That was when she'd told me that I was stronger than them, and that if I repeated it often enough, I would begin to believe it.

"Yes," I said. "Sometimes they do."

"Like that guy in there."

I nodded, then looked away toward the house again and knew I couldn't put it off any longer. "Emily loved you, Jack. She never stopped." I listened at his sharp intake of breath but couldn't bring myself to look at him.

"You've . . . seen her?"

"A few times, always around you. That's how I figured out at first that it wasn't Louisa. She . . . she wanted me to tell you that she only left because she loved you. And that she loves you still."

I watched as he swallowed and turned away. "Did she tell you why?"

"No. I found that out on my own. When your mother told me that Emily had moved north to New York, I had a suspicion. So I made a few phone calls."

He faced me, his eyes meeting mine, and his face looked like the ones you see on TV of survivors interviewed following some unforeseeable calamity.

"Mount Sinai is in New York." I stopped for a moment to let that sink in, but his face remained impassive. "I found out from her boss at the paper that Emily had a cousin who lived near Rochester, and that's where Emily went after she left Charleston." I was quiet for a moment. "Her cousin told me that Emily had lymphoma, Jack. By the time her doctors here discovered it, it had already spread inside of her. She went to Mount Sinai to see if she could participate in a few clinical trials or investigational treatments." I reached for his hand and felt how cold it was. "There was nothing they could do for her. I'm pretty sure after her original diagnosis she knew she wasn't going to make it, which is why she left you so badly. She didn't want you to suffer, so she tried to make you hate her." I fought back my own sob as I thought of my mother and how I'd never been able to get over losing her. "Hate's a lot easier to get over than love."

He kept his gaze focused on the windshield, a vacant stare seeing something I couldn't. "I did my own research and found out about the cousin in Rochester. That was about the week after she left when I was still so angry. And then I realized that I didn't want to know where she was. She didn't want me anymore, so it didn't make any difference whether she was here in Charleston or someplace else. There was only so much humiliation I could take. It just didn't occur to me that she could be . . ." He squeezed the steering wheel so tightly that it made his knuckles turn white, and then he let his hands drop to his sides. "Do you know where she's buried?"

I shook my head. "I don't. But I could find out if you like."

"Maybe later." Jack sat absolutely still, as if by moving he would shatter into tiny pieces. I knew that feeling, so I did the only thing I could—knew it because it was the one thing I missed the most after my mother left. I reached for him and held him in my arms as his body shook with unshed tears. I couldn't take the pain away, but maybe in the sharing of it, I could at least help him begin to heal.

CHAPTER 21

I left Jack in the car, unsure what he would do next but knowing he wanted to be alone. He'd brought my purse to me at the hospital, so I dug to the bottom for my house keys, then stood in front of the door for a full five minutes before finding the courage to unlock it and step inside.

The acrid smell from the electrical fire hung heavy in the air, soot and dust covering the flat surfaces like an explosion of ash. Footprints had beaten paths through the grit on the floor, calling to mind the footprints of history that had marched across this same floor, and the thought made me smile. It wasn't that long ago that I would have only seen the dirt and the expense involved in hiring extra people to help Mrs. Houlihan in the cleanup. I frowned, realizing that I still needed to do that, but that the money would most likely have to come from my own pocket for now.

I stood in the middle of the foyer and looked up the graceful stairway to the large chandelier hanging above the two stories. "I'm glad you're all right," I said quietly to the house, feeling something thick and heavy in the pit of my stomach as it dawned on me how very close I'd come to losing all of it.

"Me, too," said Jack from behind, and I whirled to face him. "I'm glad you're all right," he repeated.

The color had returned to his face and a little of the sparkle in his eyes, too. I smiled tentatively at him. "I haven't had a chance to thank you for last night."

"I get that a lot," he said, the old familiar grin splitting his face.

I punched him gently on his shoulder. "For saving my life," I said. "Thank you."

"I'm glad I could help." His face sobered as he narrowed his gaze, making me want to step back from the intensity of his eyes. "But I need to thank you, too. In a way, you've saved my life, too." He paused, his eyes seeming to darken as he peered at me. "I've always listened to family members of missing people talk about how not knowing is almost worse than knowing the truth, and I never believed them. I do now." He rubbed his hands over his face, bristling the hair around his forehead, giving him a look of vulnerability that I'd never seen before on him. It warmed me, seeing this softness in him, but I realized I could never let him know.

Jack continued. "It's sort of . . . freeing in a way. Like I've finally been given the go-ahead to grieve and to move on." He looked at me oddly. "It was strange, hearing you tell me something I must have already known. Like my mind had accepted it long ago, and I'd already gone through the five steps of grieving—but I needed to hear it from somebody else before I could give myself permission to move on with my life."

"Good," I said, smiling up at him. "I'm glad I could help."

He stepped a little closer. With a low voice, he said, "The whole time I was sitting in my car, with all of this going through my mind, I couldn't help but think about how your eyes turn from hazel to green when you're annoyed—which happens a lot. Or excited—which doesn't happen enough."

A slow, steady curl of heat unfurled in my stomach, washing into the rest of my bloodstream like a wave heading onshore. Without even realizing what I was doing, I closed my eyes and tilted my head back, waiting to taste his lips again and wondering if it could even be better than when he was giving me mouth-to-mouth.

A loud cracking noise followed by the sound of wood slapping against wood brought my eyes full open in time to see Jack's eyes up close and in a similar state of surprise.

"What the . . . ?" Jack grabbed my hand and pulled me toward the drawing room, where the noise had come from. There, lying in front of the tarp-covered grandfather clock, was the perfectly dust-free picture of Louisa and Nevin. The same framed photograph that I had stored with the other accessories from the room in one of the bedrooms upstairs.

I bent to pick it up. "It's Louisa, I'm sure." I paused, sniffing the air. "Do you smell the roses? That means she's nearby. She's been trying to tell me something for a while now, but I just can't seem to figure it out. Something to do with her and Nevin—I just don't know what."

"Or maybe," said Jack, beginning to roll off the dusty tarp covering the clock, "it has something to do with the grandfather clock since that's what it keeps hitting." He strained to get the cloth over the top of the clock, dropping it in a blue puddle at our feet.

"What do you mean?" I asked.

"Do you remember those photographs I've been taking of the clock? I finally picked them up at the developers."

I felt a little tinge of excitement, and wondered if my eyes were turning green. "Your mother was pretty sure that the face wasn't original to the clock, so it's possible somebody in the Vanderhorst family had it changed. But why?"

"Exactly what I thought, so I was a little surprised when the photographs turned up nothing. The little demilune inset showed only a series of signal flags, apparently in a random order which couldn't be made into a message no matter what combination I tried. Anyway, my mother said that all of the other Johnstone clocks had dairy scenes, but this one was replaced with a maritime theme—showing the firing on Fort Sumter." He grinned at me. "That was where the first shots were fired in the Civil War."

I crossed my arms over my chest. "I know that."

"Well, you once told me that you were blissfully ignorant of history, so I wanted to make sure."

I rolled my eyes. "I'm from Charleston. I'm required to know about Fort Sumter—all native Charlestonians have to, or they throw you out of town."

Jack snorted. "Yeah, something like that. Anyway, at first I thought this had probably been done just to commemorate a part of history this house and its inhabitants had witnessed. But when I examined the face more closely," he said as he twisted the small brass knob and pulled open the glass door over the clock's face, "I realized that a large number of lines that are worked into the painting are three-dimensional, raised up from behind just enough that they can be detected by feel but not by sight."

Tucking the frame securely between my arm and my side, I moved to stand next to him, and ran my index finger over the mast of a large ship where he indicated, and felt the telltale ridge. "You're right. But what would be the purpose of doing that?"

"I bought some art paper and a wax stick, removed the hour and minute hands, and rubbed the wax over the ridges.

"Like a tombstone rubbing," I said.

"Exactly."

"So what did you find?" I was getting impatient. "Did it tell you where the diamonds are? Or what happened to Louisa?"

He gave an exaggerated sigh. "You remember how I asked you if you could just ask the ghosts your questions and let them answer? And you said something like it's not that easy? Well, it's the same thing here. If it were easy, we wouldn't be trying to figure this out now because somebody else would have figured it out a long time ago."

"Good point," I said, slightly mollified. "But what did it say?"

"Gibberish, actually." He pulled out a piece of paper from his back pocket. "I copied it here."

I unfolded the page and saw a string of thirty-two letters from the English alphabet, without spaces and without any discernible order: *IFANKRNGMFEFIVEEMNROQNPDKNIASRKE*. I looked up at Jack. "Is that supposed to mean something?"

"It's a substitution cipher—a basically simple one, as long as you know the key word that makes the code work. Every spare moment I've been trying different words to see if any of them work, but nothing seems to fit."

"So that's what all those cipher books were about in the attic—and why you wanted to borrow them."

"Pretty much." He had the decency to look sheepish. "If I'd discovered anything, I would have told you, you know. Even if I'd known you would be pissed off at me for the rest of my life."

I looked at him with as much hurt and recrimination as I could muster but didn't say anything.

"Anyway, the books are all from the last century, which makes me think it was Robert Vanderhorst who changed the clock face."

"Which means that whatever is revealed by the clock could be about either Louisa or the diamonds."

"Or both," said Jack, carefully closing the clock face again. "And there's one more thing." He turned the old key in the wood casing of the clock and pulled the heavy hinged door open. "I found a secret compartment inside here."

"And you didn't think to show this to me earlier?"

"I didn't see the need. It's empty." He knelt in front of the opening that revealed the clock's inner workings while I peered behind him. Reaching to the far left side, he pressed a button that was flush with the inside cabinet, and made of wood. It had been invisible to the bare eye and most likely could be found only by touch. A small door popped open, and Jack moved back, allowing me to see better.

I stuck my hand in and felt around the inside of the small compartment, knocking on the bottom and sides. The top was open, a dark tunnel going up inside the clock. "I guess you've already figured out that there's no space between the walls of the compartment and the outside of the clock."

"Yep. And I've stuck a flashlight in the hole at the top, and it looks like it goes straight up to the pediment. I'm thinking that if this was ever used to hide the diamonds, they're long gone now."

I stood up and shut the hidden compartment, then closed the glass door, turning the key slowly until it latched. "There's something else—something I remember from last night when you were giving me CPR in the garden."

He raised an eyebrow but I didn't take the bait. "I saw her . . . Louisa. She was kneeling by the fountain, pushing back the grass, as if to show me those Roman numerals. Since the fountain didn't exist when Louisa lived here, I'm assuming Robert had it built. And that the numerals meant something to him."

"I think you're right. I've been playing with the numbers, and so has your dad." He sent me another apologetic look. We've been trying to discover if they correspond with any birthdates, ages, dates in history, or anything significant to the Vanderhorst family. And nothing. We've found absolutely nothing." He ran his hands through his hair, something I began to suspect he did a lot of when trying to work through a problem. I imagined he did it a lot while he was working, like a writerly habit, and I found it just a little bit attractive. He turned to me. "I'd like to see the picture of Louisa and the diamond while we're here. I might be able to tell from the size and shape whether it's what we're looking for."

"Assuming they're still around to be found. But, sure—the albums are upstairs. I'll show you before we leave. And I'd also like to see what you have as far as the clock cipher is concerned. I'm actually pretty good at puzzles."

"Have at it," said Jack. "I'd be more than happy to show you my wax rubbings."

I made a move to elbow him, forgetting that I still held the framed photograph pressed between my elbow and my side, where I'd tucked it to touch the clock face. The frame fell to the floor, the backing separating from the picture and glass. As I bent to retrieve it, I noticed lying under the glass a torn piece of paper that had evidently been stuck between the photograph and the backing of the frame.

"What is it?" asked Jack as I picked it up and straightened.

"I'm not sure. It looks like part of an envelope." The side with part of the flap still intact was blank but when I turned it over, a name and partial return address was scrawled on it: *Susannah Barnsley,* and then the words, *Orchard Lane.* I held it up for Jack to see. "Neither name rings a bell for me."

"Me, neither." He flipped it over several times, apparently deep in thought. "I'll bring this to my friend at the library to see what she can figure out. Who knows: Maybe this Susannah might still be living." He frowned. "But now I'm left to wonder if it wasn't the clock at all that Louisa was trying to draw our attention to."

"It's not always apparent what a spirit is trying to say. And sometimes they're not trying to say anything at all and just want attention."

"Great. So that piece of envelope could just be something to make the picture fit better in the frame and mean nothing."

"Or this Susannah Barnsley, whoever she is, and assuming she's still among the living, could know where the diamonds are. Or where Louisa is."

"Or maybe we're both just crazy for believing that dead people can make contact with the living."

I raised an eyebrow.

"Or not," said Jack with his trademark grin. "Why don't you take me upstairs and show me the picture of the diamond? Then I'll head out to the library while you get some rest. Hopefully, by the time I get back, we'll have heard from your dad and Sophie."

"Sounds like a plan," I said as I headed toward the stairs while Jack followed behind me. I stopped and turned around to face him. "Why are you calling me by my full name?"

His eyes widened innocently. "Because you told me to."

"Oh. I did, didn't I?" I chewed on my bottom lip for a moment as we continued to watch each other closely. Finally, I turned around and headed toward the stairs. "Well, you can stop it now. It sounds . . . odd coming from you."

I heard the smile in his voice. "Yes, ma'am."

We walked up a few steps, then Jack spoke again. "By the way, that was almost kiss number two, just in case you're still counting."

"I'm not," I said as I made my way up the stairs, feeling Jack's eyes on me the entire way to the top.

I was exhausted by the time Jack left after having seen the picture and verifying that the diamond Louisa wore was most probably one of the fabled diamonds. The near-sleepless night caught up to me as I opened up all the windows upstairs to create a cross breeze, and then, instead of driving back to my condo, I curled up on the sofa—feeling somewhat safer in the light of day—in the upstairs drawing room and fell into a dreamless sleep.

I'm not sure how long I slept, only that when my father shouted my name, I slid off the couch in a panic, hitting my head on the TV tray set up in front of it. Rubbing my head, I sat on the floor and scowled up at my father. "Daddy, I'm not a recruit. Please don't ever do that to me again."

"Sorry, sweetpea." He smiled apologetically, offering me his hand. "I guess I'm a little out of practice. And I was a little too excited to wait for you to wake up on your own."

Feeling my own excitement, I let him pull me up and sat on the couch. "What did you find out?"

I noticed the humidor tucked under his arm and watched as he placed it on the table. "Mr. Sconiers was able to develop the roll of film while I waited—probably because there were only three photographs exposed on the entire film." He opened the lid and withdrew three black-and-white two-and-one-quarter-inch-square photographs, just like the ones I'd seen in Louisa's albums. He handed them to me. "Tell me what you think."

The first photo was of the fountain. The grass was shorter in front, the Roman numerals plain to see behind the clipped grass. "The only thing I'm noticing about the fountain is that there's no water in it. It was dry when I came to see Mr. Vanderhorst, too, and my plumber can't seem to get it to work." I met my father's eyes. "Maybe that means something."

My dad pulled out a pocket-sized spiral notebook. "I'm writing down everything we find out. Even if nothing makes sense now, we might find something once we get it all together."

"Good," I said, flipping to the next photograph of the grandfather clock, the growth chart on the wall beside it barely visible. I looked at the clock face, noticing that it wasn't the same one that was on the clock now. Feeling disappointed, I said, "Well, we've already figured that one out—Robert replaced the face with one that has some sort of code that Jack's been trying to solve. I hope the third picture is something new."

I flipped to the next photograph and paused. It was a portrait of a beautiful young woman, with light brown skin and pale eyes, seated on a piano bench. She was looking somberly at the photographer, a sad smile on her full lips. "Who do you think this is?"

My dad took the picture. "She's got a copy of sheet music for 'Oh, Susannah' on her lap. I wonder if that means anything."

"I think it might." I reached into the back of my jeans pocket—the first pair of jeans I'd ever owned and purchased at the urging of Sophie, and Jack who were tired of my Lily Pulitzer capris—and pulled out the torn envelope.

"'Susannah Barnsley,'" my dad read. "The name doesn't ring a bell for me at all, and I've gone through all of the archived papers on this house and am pretty sure I haven't seen that name." He continued to stare at the photograph, humming a few bars to the song.

"Jack has a friend at the library. He's gone to see today if she can find out anything in the archives." I must have put an emphasis on the word "friend" because my dad looked at me carefully.

"Friend, huh? I'm assuming it's a girl, then."

I shrugged. "Don't know. Don't care." To change the subject, I said,

"Let me hang on to the letter written to Nevin, too. I'd like to go over it again, see if there's anything we're missing."

My dad took the letter from the humidor and handed it to me. Before he could say anything else, my cell phone rang and I picked it up when I saw it was Sophie. "Hey, Soph."

"Hi, Melanie. You sound better. How are you feeling?"

"Fine." I heard a baby crying in the background. "Where are you?"

"I'm at the health clinic here on campus. I'm getting a shot that should help me with my dog allergies."

"But you don't own a dog."

There was a pause. "No, but you do, Melanie, and we spend an awful lot of time together."

I thought for a moment. "But General Lee has spent maybe thirty minutes in my company in the last five months."

Sophie didn't answer right away, and when she did, it was about another subject entirely. "I found out about your rose. My friend would need to do more scientific tests to be absolutely positive, but looking at the structure of the petals, he's pretty sure it's a Louisa rose. Does that help you at all?"

"I'm not sure. We seem to have a lot of pieces right now but none of them really fit together."

"How's the house?"

I could hear the apprehension in Sophie's voice. "It's fine. The kitchen's gone, but the rest of the house will be fine after a good airing. And thank you."

"For what?"

"For continuing to work on the house while I was having my little pity party. It looked beautiful."

There was an edge to Sophie's voice. "Why are you speaking in the past tense?"

"Well, there's soot over everything right now. Give it a few days before you come back over, all right?"

"Sure. Is there anything else I can do for you in the meantime?"

"Yeah, you can tell Chad that I've lined up four more condos for him to see and that I need him to call me back." I was about to say goodbye when I thought of something else. I figured it was a long shot, but Sophie Wallen was often full of surprises. "One more thing—have you ever heard of a Susannah Barnsley?"

She didn't even pause before answering. "Of course. Or at least I know her house. It's on one of the architecture tours I give."

I felt a little thrum of excitement flare in my chest. "Her house? Where is it?"

"On Chalmers—in one of those completely renovated neighborhoods. She was a mixed-race woman who was put up in a nice house by her white benefactor."

My heart sank. *Robert had a mistress?* "Does she still live there?"

"No—the house and the whole neighborhood were pretty much abandoned by the nineteen fifties. It's only because of the Historic Preservation Society that they didn't fall under the wrecking ball." I heard the outrage in Sophie's voice and, for the first time in my adult life, could almost identify with it. "Did I help you at all?"

"You might have. I'll let you know after I speak with Jack."

A muffled name was shouted out in the waiting room. "They just called me, so I've got to go. I'll call you later."

"Bye, Soph," I said, but she'd already hung up the phone.

"Jack's here," my dad said as he looked out the window that faced the side of the house. "What's all that stuff he's bringing with him?"

I moved to stand by my father, and peered out the window as Jack removed two suitcases, a box of books, and most surprising, a large potted orchid.

"How did he know that's my favorite flower?" I muttered.

"Is it?" my dad asked, and we both stared at each other as we let the implications pass.

"He must have called Nancy," I said as I admired the play of muscles as Jack lifted both suitcases with minimal effort and managed to balance the orchid, too.

"Looks like he's moving back in," my dad observed.

I didn't answer but turned to jog down the stairs in time to throw open the door before Jack could open it himself. I stopped in the threshold with my mouth poised to speak. Marc stood next to Jack on the porch, holding an identical potted orchid.

When I eventually found my voice, I greeted them both before stepping back to allow them inside.

Without a word, Jack placed his orchid on the hall table, then made his way up the stairs toward his old bedroom, his suitcases knocking the treads every few steps.

Marc placed his orchid in front of Jack's, then kissed me on both cheeks. "I heard about last night and thought your favorite flower might cheer you up. I was so worried, but Nancy told me that you would be fine." He sniffed the air. "It was an electrical fire?"

I nodded. "Yes. Luckily only the kitchen was destroyed. The rest of the house is okay."

He grinned. "As beautiful as this house is, having it burn to the ground wouldn't have been such a bad thing for you, would it?"

I remembered the sense of outrage in Sophie's voice when she'd spoken earlier, and I had to work hard not to duplicate it in my own. "Actually, I think I would have been pretty devastated."

Marc looked at me with surprise. "Ah, so that's the way it is now. I've been told that these old houses can be contagious."

"What's contagious?" My dad was coming down the stairs, the humidor under his arm.

"Old houses," said Marc. "I think Melanie here has caught the bug."

My dad reached the bottom of the stairs and stood in front of us. "Well, that would make sense, wouldn't it, Melanie?"

I sent my dad a warning glance but obviously knowing my favorite flower wasn't the only blip on my personal radar that he had overlooked.

"Really?" Marc seemed genuinely interested.

"Yes. Melanie spent a lot of time in her grandmother's house on Legare. Guess that's where her love of old houses comes from."

I wasn't sure if I needed to defend myself or just agree, so I remained silent.

My dad eyed Marc for a moment. "You're a Charleston native, aren't you? Maybe you've heard the name Susannah Barnesly."

Marc wrinkled his brow in concentration for a long moment. "No, it's not ringing a bell with me. Is this somebody I should know?"

"No, actually," said my father as I kept my eyes on Marc. "Although it might be somebody my father used to know. I found what we're guessing to be her picture in a box of my father's things."

Marc shook his head. "I'm sorry. Don't think I can help you." He paused for a moment. "Wasn't your father good friends with Robert Vanderhorst—one of the former owners of this house?"

"Yes. They were best friends and business partners for a long time."

"I thought I remembered that correctly. Can't remember what I ate for breakfast most days, but I always seem to remember pieces of trivia I've picked up along the way."

My dad laughed. "Ain't that the truth! And just wait until you get older—it gets much worse."

Their shared laughter was interrupted by Jack tramping down the stairs before approaching our group in the foyer. Marc appraised Jack with a dismissive glance. "I might be mistaken, Jack, but it looked like you were moving in."

"Well, Matt, your powers of observation would then be almost as strong as your cologne."

I admired Marc's restraint when he said nothing and turned to me instead. "They're having fireworks tonight at Patriot's Point for Veterans' Day, and I thought you might like to go."

"I'd love to," I said, meaning it. We hadn't spent a lot of time together since I'd canceled our trip to Isle of Palms. If what we had was supposed to be called a relationship, then we needed to go watch fireworks or anything else that would bring us together to move our relationship along. Regardless of how many times I found myself recalling Jack's almost kisses and how I had almost wanted him to. Or how the truth about Emily hadn't changed anything, really. He was still Jack—too irreverent, too comfortable in his own skin, too easy on the eyes, and way too hard on the heart.

"Great," he said, kissing me on the lips, and I wondered how it was possible to not even feel a kiss. "How about we do dinner first at Jestine's? I'm craving coconut cream pie. I can pick you up at seven."

"Sounds perfect," I said, walking him to the door. He kissed me again, lingering longer this time, then left.

I walked back toward Jack and my dad in time to hear Jack mimicking Marc, "'I'm craving coconut cream pie.' Come on, who uses the word 'craving' anymore?"

"Grow up," I said, crossing my arms over my chest. "What were the suitcases for?"

"I'm moving back in to my old room. After last night, I figured you needed the protection."

Not only did I completely agree with him, but I also knew it was useless arguing, so I just put my hands on my hips and said, "All right, but I expect you to follow my rules. First, keep—"

Jack interrupted. "I know, I know. Keep the toilet seat down, and no girls in the house after ten p.m. Got it."

I had to force myself not to smile back at him. "Good. Glad you remembered."

"I only need to be told once, Mellie." He grinned. "So, did you find out anything new?"

"Sophie called and confirmed that the rose in the box was most likely a Louisa rose. What it means, I have no idea. And my dad was able to get the pictures developed."

My dad opened the box and took out the pictures before handing them to Jack, who stared at them for a long time. "What do you think is the purpose of the picture of the clock?"

"I'm not sure, but I'm thinking it's to draw attention to the different face—but we've already figured that one out. And I'm not sure about the one of the fountain, either, other than the fact that it's dry. But look at the other picture. What do you make of that?"

Jack studied the photograph of the woman closely. "Any idea who this is?"

"We're not sure. But my dad pointed out that on her lap there's a copy of 'Oh, Susannah.'" Very carefully, I added, "Somebody once told me that there's no such thing as coincidences, so I'm taking a leap here and guessing that the woman's name is Susannah."

Jack looked at me sharply. "Glad to know that I've been rubbing off on you." He glanced over at my father. "And I mean that very respectfully, sir."

My dad gave him a mock salute, then continued watching us.

Jack continued. "So this might be the elusive Susannah Barnsley?"

I nodded. "It's certainly possible, I guess. And the best part is that Susannah Barnsley had a house on Chalmers—it's on one of Sophie's architectural tours, which is how I found out. That might be a place to start. What about you?" I asked. "Did you find out anything at the library?"

Jack shook his head. "I haven't been there, yet. I needed to pack and move my stuff over first. I was thinking that you could come with me, and then we could head over to my place so I could show you my etchings."

"He means the wax rubbing he made of the clock face, Daddy."

My dad shook his head. "Watching the two of you is like watching a tennis match. I'm going to head back home and see if there's anything else in my father's stuff that might shed some more light on this muddle. I'll get back to you later."

Jack and I followed my father out, making sure to first dead-bolt the door. Then we returned to Jack's car. I pulled out the letter Robert had written to Nevin and read it again out loud, concentrating on the last paragraph. *Be vigilant in all that you do, and be secure in the knowledge always that you were greatly loved by both of your parents and all who knew you. Remember what your mother used to call you, and never have any doubt.* Cerca Trova.

"Cerca trova," Jack repeated.

"You've plugged that one into the ciphers right?" I asked.

He raised an eyebrow but didn't say anything.

"Right?" I repeated.

"Maybe," he said, looking annoyed. I laughed as he stepped down harder on the pedal, making my stomach jump.

"I still haven't forgiven you for lying, you know."

"I know," he said, taking a corner sharply and sending me into his side. "But Emily would have wanted me to keep trying."

I faced him, the long afternoon shadows shooting orange light into the car. "Emily would?"

He remained focused on the road in front of him. "Yeah. That's why she came back, I think. For forgiveness. For both of us."

I sat back in the leather seat and closed my eyes, realizing that I hadn't felt Emily's presence around Jack since I'd told him the truth in the car. The heavy scent of camellias, the harbinger of autumn in the Lowcountry and what I would bet money on had been Emily's favorite flower, floated into the car and wrapped the air around us before it slowly disappeared. I smiled to myself, knowing he was right.

CHAPTER 22

Jack's condo was on Queen Street in an area known as the French Quarter due to the fact that it had historically been the location of a high concentration of French merchants. It was also known for how close it had come to falling under the wrecking ball in the nineteen seventies, and it might have except for the efforts of the Save Charleston Foundation and the donations of Americans from around the country. Sophie, and many others of her preservationist ilk, spoke with reverence when mentioning the entire incident. As Jack and I took a left at Vendue Range, I cringed a little, remembering something I'd once said to Sophie about how a wrecking ball might have solved a lot of the parking issues in the area.

As we walked toward the elevator in the converted nineteenth-century rice warehouse, I caught myself admiring the restoration work that had been done to sensitively convert old warehouse space to hip new condominiums. I caught Jack watching me with a knowing grin, and I quickly averted my gaze to focus on the functional metal elevator.

Jack threw the door open to his unit, and I paused in the entryway, wondering if he had mistakenly let me into his neighbor's condo. The space had all the exposed brick, tall windows, and soaring ceilings with wood beams that made converted condos such a hot commodity in the real estate market. But the beautiful art and furniture—an eclectic mix of urban sleekness and rich antiques—almost made me do a double take to see if I was an inadvertent guest on a reality TV show.

"What's the matter?" Jack asked, his keys dangling in his hand.

"I'm just . . . surprised." I looked around and saw the typical piles of mail on the kitchen bar, old newspapers scattered under a glass-and-chrome coffee table, and a spread of open sports magazines on the leather sofa that made me itch to go straighten them, and figured that I had to be in the right place.

"Surprised?"

"Yeah," I said, facing him. "Did your mother do all of your decorating?"

He tossed his keys in what looked like a Herend bowl on a Beidemeier chest in the entranceway. "No, actually. I did it myself. She helped me make a few purchases at auctions, but besides that it was just me." He moved into the open kitchen and went to the stainless steel refrigerator. Taking out a nonalcoholic beer, he held one up to me, but I shook my head.

I moved to a wall in the living area and looked at what appeared to be a Degas ballerina pencil drawing. "Are you sure you aren't gay?"

He stood next to me and took a long draw on his longneck bottle. "Pretty sure. I've just always known where to place the stray ottoman or how to mix Chippendale with Craftsman. Must be in the genes."

I remembered his silent perusal of my own condo, and I shook my head, trying to erase the memory. "Let's look at those ciphers," I said, eager to focus on business instead of my lack of decorating finesse and Jack's apparent knack for it.

He led the way into a partitioned space separated from the living area with a Japanese screen. The large mahogany partner's desk, with a Mac computer perched in the middle of a mound of paper, took up most of the area, the brick walls covered in modern steel bookshelves filled with books. A muted Persian rug covered the wood floor, warming the space and making it the perfect writer's retreat. A suede camelback couch was pushed against one wall, and I assumed this must be his napping spot when he had writer's block—assuming he ever did. The Jack Trenholm I knew never seemed to be at a loss for words.

"Over here," he said, indicating the couch. He picked up a roll of art paper and unfurled it before placing it on the floor. He kneeled on one side and held down two corners, and I did the same on the other side. "This is the actual rubbing I did of the clock—and, as you saw before, none of it makes sense."

I looked at the crinkled paper at the top and the black crayonlike marks of various letters in no apparent order: *IFANKRNGM-FEFIVEEMNROQNPDKNIASRKE.*

"As you can see, at the top here I placed the letters in columns according to the order they appeared on the face. Starting at twelve o'clock—which is logical, considering it's the beginning of the day."

I examined the paper, noticing this time that at the very bottom was the actual alphabet written from beginning to end across the width of the paper. The paper beneath these letters was nearly rubbed through with erasing from, I assumed, Jack's attempts to find a workable keyword.

"How does this work?" I asked, thinking it looked familiar. My grandmother had loved puzzles of all kinds, and she'd enjoyed making up her own for me to solve. My room in her house had been filled with puzzle books, and I had missed them for a long time after I'd gone to live with my father. I assumed my puzzle books were either somewhere in a box in the attic in the house on Legare or they'd been thrown away long ago.

"If you know the keyword, you simply write it below the alphabet, starting with the letter 'A' so that each letter of the key word has a corresponding letter in the alphabet. Then, after you write the keyword, you start the alphabet right after it—skipping the letters already found in the keyword."

I watched as he picked up a pencil from his desk and wrote "*CERCA TROVA*" beneath the alphabet, being careful to line up the letters in each column. "You're not supposed to have any repeating letters in the key word, but I've seen it done where you just eliminate the repeating letter the second time it appears." He crossed off the "*A*" at the end of "*TROVA*" since it had already appeared in the first word, "*CERCA*," and wrote the rest of the alphabet following it, making sure not to repeat any of the letters used in the keyword. When he was done, he looked up at me expectantly. "All right, read out the letters from the clock to me slowly, one at a time."

I glanced at the top of the art paper, where Jack had written the jumbled letters and read them out loud to him. "I, F, A, N, K, R, N, G . . ."

"Hang on, let me catch up." He began to transpose the letters into the cipher by finding the letter in the actual alphabet, and then finding its corresponding letter in the new alphabet he'd created using the keyword "*CERCA TROVA*." I bent over his shoulder to see if I could make out any words. *BTCIFMIO* stared up from the page. Jack tossed the pencil down. "Damn. It's not the right code word. None of these letter combinations make a single word."

"Maybe Mr. Vanderhorst scrambled the letters so that after the cipher was solved, whoever had solved it had to unscramble it to get the real answer."

"That could be it, but this message is too long and without any spaces between words, which would make it almost impossible. And this was meant for his son—to keep it from prying eyes and not trip up a cryptologist." He scratched his head. "I'll finish the rest of the letters in the cipher just in case we have to come back to it and see if we need to do some jumbling."

"Scootch over," I said, moving books to the corners to hold down the paper and sitting down next to Jack. "Let's just sit here and think of as many words or phrases as we can that Robert Vanderhorst might have used. We're bound to turn up something."

"Fine. Let me get another beer first. Can I get you one? There's no alcohol in them, but they're pretty good."

"Might as well, but just one. I can't imagine this will take very long."

He raised an eyebrow but didn't say anything, just left to go to the kitchen and grab a couple of beers.

Three hours and three beers later, Jack and I had scribbled on every notepad in the office, using every possible keyword we could think of up to and including "piazza," "Civil War," "Magnolia Ridge," "Louisa," "Nevin," and even "General Lee."

Jack sat on the floor, his back against the bookshelves, and threw his pencil across the room. "We're bound to turn up something, huh?"

I rubbed my tired eyes with the heels of my hands. "Maybe we do need to unscramble the letters we got when we used *cerca trova*."

Jack shook his head, then closed his eyes. "Where did I see those words before? It's driving me nuts." He looked at his watch. "It's getting late, and the Historical Society library closes at four. Let's head out and maybe something else will pop out at us."

"Sounds good to me," I said, allowing him to pull me up. I wasn't excited about meeting his library friend, and my brain was beginning to hurt, but I continued to see Mr. Vanderhorst's face from that last time I'd seen him, and I felt an urgency that had eluded me until now.

"Where are we going?" I asked a short while later as he pulled the car up to the curb on Market, nowhere near the vicinity of the Historical Society.

"I've got to get flowers. Yvonne loves them and will be disappointed if I show up empty-handed. I'll be right back." He winked at me before stepping out of his car.

I crossed my arms over my chest and mimicked the name "Yvonne" silently in the privacy of the car.

Jack brought back a bouquet of yellow roses and asked me to hold them. "Yellow's her favorite color," he added helpfully.

I held the flowers on my lap until we reached the Fireproof Building on Meeting Street, where the South Carolina Historical Society was located. Jack's luck at always finding a parking spot at the curb ran out, and we had to park in a garage. I was still carrying the roses as we approached the Palladian-style building with the imposing Doric porticoes. We were halfway up the steps before I realized it and pushed the flowers at Jack to take.

The interior was hushed, and smelled of polish and old books. A cantilevered three-story stone staircase dominated the oval stair hall and was lit by a cupola at the top. I silently applauded myself for not only recognizing but knowing what "cantilevered" and "cupola" meant, thanks to Sophie's books. It also didn't pass my notice that I was actually admiring the beauty of the architecture in a structure that was built prior to the twenty-first century.

"There she is," said Jack, and I waited and watched as he approached a woman with her hair held back in a bun sitting at a long table, studying a large, open book. "Yvonne," he said as he reached her. She turned to him and smiled one of those genuine smiles you rarely get when you surprise an acquaintance in a place you wouldn't expect to see them. He handed her the flowers, and she pressed her nose into them.

Jack pulled back her chair and helped her stand, then beckoned for me. I nearly stumbled as I made my way over, noticing for the first time the cane leaning against the table within arm's reach. "Yvonne Craig, I'd like you to meet Melanie Middleton."

Yvonne stuck out her hand and I took it, amazed at the strength of her grip. She was petite and beautifully dressed, and she had sparkling, intelligent brown eyes. She was also about eighty years old. She smiled, displaying perfect white dentures. "So you're the lucky one who inherited Nevin's house. I always wondered what he would do with it after he passed on. Middleton, did you say?"

"Yes," I said, eager to avoid the next inevitable questions regarding my parents. "It's a pleasure to meet you," I said. "Jack's told me so much about you."

Yvonne surprised me by snorting. "Ha! I bet he led you to believe I was some young thing after his affections. Not that I wouldn't jump at the chance, of course, but I think his energy would kill me, if you know what I mean." She winked and I couldn't help but laugh. "Hand me my cane, will you, sweet boy?"

As Jack handed her the cane, I mouthed behind her shoulder to him, *Sweet boy?* He just waggled his eyebrows.

"Yvonne likes to pretend she's an old woman, but everyone who knows her agrees that there's a feisty twenty-year-old lurking very near the surface. I've been waiting for years to get my chance, but the throng of suitors is too much competition for me."

Yvonne swiped at his leg with her cane. "Remember, young man, that flattery will get you everywhere."

"Yes, ma'am," Jack said. "So, were you able to find out anything about Susannah Barnsley?"

"Yes, actually, I was. And I'm sorry it took me so long but somebody came in this morning and used the book I needed and then shelved it themselves—which they're not supposed to do," she said to me with a sidelong glance. "And the ignorant person shelved it in the completely wrong place—just pure laziness, if you ask me. I found it by some miracle as I was looking up something else for another patron. And there it was, stuck in between bound eighteenth-century maps, of all things."

"Probably some kid," said Jack, absently.

Yvonne shrugged. "I have no idea since I wasn't here this morning. I only know somebody was here looking at it because Priscilla told me when I asked her if she'd seen it.

"This way," she said, indicating a table in the corner of the room with several thick leather-bound volumes stacked on top. We made our way over and waited until she'd opened up the book on top. "You're very lucky, you know. Some kind soul about seventy-five years ago decided he wanted to find the descendants of all the slaves who once lived at Barnsley Hall plantation down by Dauphuskie. He was the grandson of the blacksmith, and I suppose he wanted to find out if he had any relations still living. Because of Susannah's last name, I figured this would be the first place I should look." She winked. "And, as usual, I was right." She gently opened what appeared to be a ledger book, and we found ourselves staring at impossibly tiny handwriting filling every line in the book.

"Don't panic, dear," she said to me. "I already found the information you needed and photocopied it for Jack's file. It's not really detailed—just who her grandparents and parents were—most notably that her grandfather was white. She grew up in North Charleston, where her mother was a laundress. That's all we know about her childhood. The last bit of information was the most relevant, I believe, as it stated that at the age of nineteen she moved to Charleston and lived in a house on Chalmers. A nice house, considering she was a woman with no education and little means."

Yvonne pursed her lips. "Since you'd already given me her last known address, I didn't have any trouble searching the ownership records for the house. And this bit of information might be a little . . . titillating if I do say so myself."

She slid a manila folder across the table to me. "I think that Miss Middleton should be the one to see this first."

I looked at Jack, and he nodded. I flipped open the cover and saw within photocopied pages filled with laborious handwriting.

"It's the one on top, I believe," said Yvonne.

I picked up the top page and studied the document. "It's a lease agreement," I said, scanning down to the bottom, where the lines for signatures were. And there, in thick black ink, was the signature for Augustus Middleton.

I jerked back and Jack took the paper from me. "That's . . . that's my grandfather. Why would he be signing a lease for Susannah Barnsley's house?"

Both Yvonne and Jack looked at me with identical expressions of surprise mixed with amusement. I blinked as the reason dawned on me. "Oh. He. Oh, I see." My first reaction was one of relief—relief that Robert Vanderhorst hadn't had a mistress. On the other hand, I hadn't known my grandfather and felt neither embarrassment nor surprise to learn that he'd had at least one vice.

"They were apparently together for ten years—that was when the house was leased to somebody else, at any rate. She moved out in September of nineteen thirty."

Jack placed the paper back inside the folder. "Any idea where she might have gone?"

Yvonne smiled brightly. "I knew you were going to ask me that—so I already did a little bit of research on my own to see what I could find out." She smiled like a Cheshire cat, and I knew that she'd hit the mother lode. She picked up the folder and began to flip through the pages. "Just because we're all about South Carolina here at the Historical Society, doesn't mean there haven't been plenty of times that we've had to ask for information—and likewise—from our sister societies around the country. And it's a good thing, too."

"Why is that?" Jack prodded.

"Well, first I checked the post office records for any forwarding address. Nothing there—which in itself is interesting. Made me think she was trying to hide or something. Anyway, I thought that most places require a security deposit and that you get it back when you move out. It was worth a try, anyway, to see if a check was mailed after Susannah moved out. Chances are it was sent to Augustus, since he paid for the place. But what if it wasn't? She'd lived there for ten years. Maybe the landlord thought the money belonged to her."

"So, what did you find out?" Jack sat on the corner of the table, his impatience visible only by the tick in his jaw.

"Lucky for you, the landlord kept meticulous records—including the addresses where he sent any correspondence to former tenants." She gave us a self-satisfied smile as she riffled through the pages in the folder, and pulled out a plain piece of copy paper with a handwritten address. "I thought you might like to have it for easy reference, so I copied it down for you. While I was waiting for you to come, I went online and looked up her phone number. I took the liberty of calling it and asking for Susannah. The woman who answered must be a nurse or companion or something because she told me that Susannah was taking a nap but could call me back later. I told her no, thank you, and hung up." Her eyes sparkled brightly. "I guess that means she's still alive."

Jack took the paper from her and looked at it. "Susannah Barnsley, one-oh-two Orchard Lane, Colchester, Vermont." Our eyes met, and I knew we were both remembering the piece of envelope we'd found in the picture frame, the part of the envelope that had Susannah's name but only the words "Orchard Lane" on it.

Still clutching the piece of paper, Jack slid off the table and enveloped the old woman in a huge hug—something she apparently liked, judging by her soft smile and the way her fragile hand patted his shoulder. "You're amazing, Yvonne. It would have taken me weeks to find any of this information." Jack settled her back down on her feet.

"You just need to know where to look, sweet boy." She glanced up at him and actually fluttered her eyelashes. "I think this means you owe me dinner."

"Blossom again or would you like to try something new?"

"Blossom, it is. I'll call you with my schedule." She winked at me. "And Miss Middleton is more than welcome to join us."

"I'd like that," I said, taking her hand in both of mine and squeezing. My cell phone began ringing in my purse, and I excused myself so Jack and Yvonne could say goodbye, and left the building to answer it.

By the time I got outside, the call had switched to voice mail. I hit the button to replay and listened to Marc's voice as he asked for a rain check for our date later that night because of a last-minute out-of-town trip that had come up. His smooth voice was so different from Jack's. Much more controlled and sexy, but almost deliberately so. I snapped the phone shut, wondering why in the world I was comparing their voices.

As I was putting my phone back into my purse, Jack emerged from the building. "Marc just called," I said. "He has to go out of town and had to cancel our plans for tonight."

"What a shame," said Jack, his voice and expression saying anything but. "I guess that gives us more time to work on the cipher. And to make plans for our trip to Vermont."

"We're going to Vermont?"

"Well, I guess you could stay here, but you might find it more interesting meeting Susannah in person than hearing me telling you all about it later."

"True, but can't we just call her on the phone?"

"We could, but my years of research have taught me that you learn a whole lot more visiting your source. It's up to you if you want to come with me, but I'm definitely going."

I thought for a moment, recalling that I didn't have any pressing business and that Marc would be out of town, too. "Sure," I said as I followed him down the steps toward the street, realizing that the thought of solving the cipher and meeting somebody who might have known Louisa and Robert, and who had definitely known my grandfather, was a whole lot more exciting to me than having dinner and watching fireworks with Marc. "I hear the foliage is lovely this time of year in New England."

Jack winked at me. "That's my girl. Now let's go back to my condo and get busy."

I raised my eyebrow as he opened the passenger-side door for me.

He shook his head in mock indignation. "To work on the cipher, of course. Get your mind out of the gutter, Mellie."

"I think I'm going to have to ask for dinner at Jestine's in return for my help, though."

"Have you been talking to Yvonne behind my back?"

"Not at all," I said, concentrating on the street in front of us. "I've just developed a sudden craving for coconut cream pie."

He snorted. "Me, too," he said, and I laughed as he headed down the road back to Queen Street.

CHAPTER 23

Have you tried 'Holy City'?" I asked Jack as we sat in a Delta jet on a runway at Charleston International. Before and after our artery-clogging meal at Jestine's the night before—which included a basket of fried chicken and corn bread covered with honey butter—we had worked on the clock's cipher, once again plugging in every word or phrase we could think of. For a break, we'd played with the Roman numerals on the fountain and had reached the same result: nothing.

"Yep. And Saint Michael's, Saint Philip's, and the Battery. Next I'm going to try Jihad, Hussein, and Iraq."

I looked at him, completely perplexed. "Whatever for?"

"Because I think those are the only words in the dictionary that we haven't tried yet." He sent a sidelong glance at me. "I'm kidding, you know."

"I knew that," I said, returning my focus to the notepad in front of me as I plugged "White Point Gardens" into the cipher.

We spent the next five and a half hours of our trip—with the exclusion of our connection in Atlanta—alternating between working on the cipher and sleeping. We arrived in Burlington, Vermont, around nine o'clock in the evening, rented a car, and booked two rooms in a nearby motel, figuring we could drive the short distance to Colchester in the morning before catching our return flight to Charleston.

I slept fitfully, kept awake by working codes in my head and wondering if Jack was also thinking about tomorrow's meeting with Susannah Barnsley. Jack had spoken to her briefly on the phone, explaining who we were and asking if we could come see her. She seemed reluctant at first until he explained that I was Augustus Middleton's granddaughter.

She'd agreed to the meeting but hadn't said anything more, and I was filled with doubts that she had anything to add and that our trip had been a waste of time.

I felt grumpy and rumpled the next morning as we grabbed a fast-food breakfast and coffee before heading north to Colchester. Jack was chipper and looked well-rested, which made me offer him nothing more than a grunt when he wished me good morning.

We plugged Susannah's address into the rental car's GPS and followed its directions through the chilly Vermont countryside. I was pretty confident that the scenery was lovely and colorful but I was unable to appreciate any of it through my puffy and irritated eyes. Jack had the good sense to keep quiet.

The house we pulled up to wasn't at all what I had expected. I had supposed Susannah would have wanted a traditional Southern home like the one in which she'd lived in Charleston, and not the neat and brilliant white Cape Code Colonial with the white picket fence and black shutters that I now stood in front of. I knew, however, that we were in the right place when I saw the walled garden in the back. Being Vermont in late autumn, the bushes and beds were stripped bare of color, but the sheer extensiveness of it made me think that a Charlestonian must live there.

We stood on the neatly swept brick step, and Jack rang the doorbell. Quick footsteps sounded from inside before a neatly dressed woman in her midfifties answered the door.

"Hello," she greeted us. "I'm Mrs. Marston. I look after Miss Barnsley." She opened the door wider. "Come on in. We've been expecting you."

The house was furnished with antiques—but not the sparse utilitarian Ethan Allen style one would expect of a Vermont country house. Instead, these were elegant pieces that would have been completely at home in the house on Tradd Street.

A roaring fire greeted us as we entered the front drawing room, and I nearly missed seeing the diminutive woman propped up with pillows in a huge winged-back chair near the fire. Despite her age, which I had calculated as being ninety, I recognized her immediately from her photograph. She had few wrinkles in her light brown skin, as if she'd spent a lifetime taking care of it, and her green eyes were wide and vibrant, belying her years.

"You look just like your grandfather, you know," she said, her voice strong and still carrying with it the soft consonants and gentle cadence of Charleston. It made me feel at home.

"Do I?" I asked, as I moved forward to take her offered hand. Her grip was strong as I shook it before introducing her to Jack. I could see by the brightening of her eyes that Jack's charms weren't lost on her. Remembering Yvonne's similar reaction to Jack, I made a note to myself to tell him that if his writing career didn't pick up, he could always be the social director at a nursing home. Or a gigolo.

Mrs. Marston took our jackets before Jack and I sat down on a love seat facing Susannah, the warmth of the fire permeating my chilled body. Because I'm a native South Carolinian, anything under sixty degrees Fahrenheit is too cold for me. Mrs. Marston left to get a tea tray, leaving us to talk in private.

Jack spoke first. "Thank you, Miss Barnsley, for allowing us to come visit. It must have seemed odd to you to get a call from Charleston from out of the blue."

"Not so odd, actually. Yours was the third in as many days."

"Really?" I asked. "Anybody you knew?"

"Well, the first two Mrs. Marston told me were just hang-ups, so I don't know for sure. She recognized the Charleston area code, though, which is how we knew. When you called, I figured the first two times had been you as well."

I remembered Yvonne telling us that she had called to see if Susannah was still living and I assumed that she had called twice and just forgot to mention it to us.

Jack leaned forward, his elbows on his knees. "Well, I'm glad you had some warning beforehand, since I'm sure seeing Melanie brings back some memories for you."

"Yes, indeed. It sure does. Mostly good, though." She smiled, but her eyes seemed turned inward toward another time and place. I felt dizzy for a moment, as if I traveled with her, and we were both back in Charleston and all that was there in her heart was my grandfather. *She loved him very much,* I thought. She faced me again and her eyes sparkled, and I had a fleeting thought that she had sensed me inside her head. "So what is it you would like to know?"

I opened my purse and pulled out the photograph of her that I'd kept between two pieces of cardboard. "Is this you?" I asked.

She held it in her hands, the nails neatly trimmed with clear polish. Her hand shook a little as she examined it. "Yes," she said quietly. "That's me. Or it was me, I should say. Gus had that taken. I only saw it once—he said he liked to keep it with him."

"So, as far as you knew, it was always in Gus's possession," Jack interjected.

Susannah nodded. "As far as I know, it was."

I watched Jack as he nodded, presumably ascertaining that Robert and Augustus must have collaborated on the contents of the box.

Jack continued. "How well did you know Robert Vanderhorst?"

"Not very well at all. Of course, times were different back then. Now folks of all colors are free to walk in any social circles. But back then, my place was not where the Vanderhorsts and Middletons were."

"But you were Gus Middleton's mistress, correct?"

She didn't appear taken aback or disturbed by Jack's bluntness. Instead, she smiled at him. "Yes, I was. He even wanted to marry me but I knew that was foolishness, and not just because I was eighteen years younger than he. I knew how he felt about me, and I didn't need a ring to prove it. He would have had to give up everything—his friends, his law career, his social standing—to marry me. And that would have been our undoing. One day he would have realized that he missed all those other things, and there would be no way to get them back." She shook her head. "No, no. We were content with the way things were. For a time, anyway."

"So why did you leave?" I asked, wondering how my grandmother Middleton had felt about all this. But she had been much younger than my grandfather, and it occurred to me now that they hadn't been married until nineteen forty or forty-one—about ten years after Susannah had left Charleston forever.

Susannah looked down at her small hands, neatly folded on top of the knitted blanket on her lap. "Because Gus asked me to."

Her words lingered in the still room for a moment. "Do you mind if I ask you why?" I felt a tinge of excitement. Her departure coincided closely with Louisa's disappearance, and I thought for the first time since I'd been trying to solve the mystery of what happened to Nevin's mother that I was the closest I had ever been to finding out the truth.

Mrs. Marston entered the room with the tray filled with small sandwiches, pastries, and tea. Susannah poured for us, her hands remarkably steady, considering how thin and frail her wrists were. After ensuring that we had everything we needed, Mrs. Marston again left the room, closing the door behind her.

I placed several pastries and a sandwich on my plate and began eating, stopping myself in midchew when I noticed Susannah watching me with a half smile. "Your grandfather loved his sweets, too. Yessirree. He sure did love his sweets. It's good to see a young girl these days with a healthy appetite."

I heard Jack snicker but I wasn't sure if it was the comment about my appetite or me being called a "young girl" that he found amusing.

Susannah dabbed daintily at her mouth. "Before I answer your question, I hope you don't mind if I ask a few of my own first."

I noticed that Jack was staring at my leg, and I watched in horror as it bounced up and down in uncontrolled impatience. I pressed my folded hands against my calf to make it stop, then smiled at Susannah. "Absolutely. We'll answer any questions you have."

The old woman took a slow sip of her tea, and I pressed my hands harder against my agitated leg. "How did you find me?"

Jack motioned for me to answer. "My father, James Middleton—Gus's son—found your picture in a humidor, along with a letter for Robert's son, Nevin, and a roll of film." I grimaced. "It's all a bit of a mystery, I'm afraid. We're hoping all of these clues will lead us to Robert's wife, Louisa. And . . ." I looked at Jack for confirmation, and he gave me a quick nod. "And maybe even a clue as to what happened to six flawless diamonds rumored to have been in the possession of the Vanderhorst family."

"Ah, so that's what this is all about." She sounded disappointed.

"Actually, no. It isn't." I thought for a moment, trying to remember when my last few months had stopped being about restoring an old house to make money from its sale and had instead become all about finding a young boy's missing mother to tell the world that she hadn't abandoned him. I realized with a small start that that was really what it had been about for me from the very beginning, when I'd read Nevin's letter to me. It was almost as if I had challenged myself to prove to the world that not every mother who abandoned her child did so willingly. I thought of the words of his letter that I had long since memorized: *Maybe fate put you in my life to bring the truth to the surface so that she might finally find peace after all these years.* I cleared my throat and met Susannah's eyes. "Mr. Vanderhorst—Nevin—died without ever knowing the truth about what happened to his mother. I aim to find out and clear her name so that they can both rest in peace. Because I know with all certainty that Louisa loved her husband and her son. She wouldn't have left them willingly."

Susannah's face drooped a little. "So Nevin is gone. It seems wrong, somehow, that he would be gone before me." She shook her head. "As far as Louisa ever deserting her son, though, never. He was her life."

I looked at her hopefully. "So you knew her?"

"Not socially, no. But I knew of her from the society pages and from Gus. She was what we called 'real quality' in the old days. A true lady. And I didn't for one minute believe what the papers were saying about her running off with that no-good Joseph Longo."

"So . . . you don't know what happened to her?" I felt my shoulders slumping. The coincidence of the date of Susannah's departure with Louisa's disappearance had me hoping they had both gone north together.

Susannah shook her head. "I'm sorry, dear, but I don't know. Gus knew, but he wouldn't tell me. He said that the fewer people who knew the better off we'd all be. He said it was the kind of knowledge that could get a person killed." Her bright eyes lighted on me and then Jack. "I guess that means it's my turn to answer your questions."

She sat back and rang a small bell sitting on a low chest by the side of her chair. Mrs. Marston appeared immediately, almost as if she'd been waiting outside the door. Susannah gave her a small nod and Mrs. Marston abruptly left the room. I put another pastry in my mouth and listened.

Susannah continued. "I don't know all the details—just what I heard from Gus—but I think it will be enough to answer your questions." Jack and I waited while she took another sip of her tea. My foot gave a little kick of impatience, but I reined it in with my clasped hands.

"The night Louisa disappeared, Gus came to see me. He told me that something bad had happened—he wouldn't tell me what but that I needed to leave town right away. I didn't want to go, of course. I didn't want to leave him. I loved him more than my own heart, you see." She glanced away for a moment. I watched as the pearls on her sweater rose and fell like the vagaries of time, and waited until she was ready to speak again.

"Gus told me that he needed to give me something to take with me, and that nobody must ever find it. Not ever. He knew that whoever wanted it wouldn't think of me at first, and if they did, I would be long gone. Gus told me that if this . . . thing that he was to give me was discovered, it would mean certain death for him and for Robert. And even little Nevin."

She gave us a shaky smile, and Jack stood to get a clean napkin from the tea tray for her. She touched the corners of her eyes and took a shaky breath. "He promised me that he would take care of me, that he would make sure I had a beautiful house to live in for as long as I liked and unlimited funds in a local bank. I would never want for anything if I agreed." Her face crumpled like a drying rose. "But he was wrong, you see, because all I ever wanted was him."

"But you said yes," Jack promptly softly.

She nodded. "Yes. I knew Gus wouldn't ask me if it wasn't a life-and-death situation. For ten years he had given me everything, and I'd had nothing but my love to give him in return. I thought that I could at least do this one thing for him."

There was a brief tap on the door, and Mrs. Marston entered the room again, but this time she held something in her hand. I stood when I recognized my grandfather's humidor. Jack stood, too, then motioned for me to sit down again. "It's not the same one, Melly. Look, the lock is still there."

Jack held out his hand for the box, and when Susannah nodded, Mrs. Marston gave it to him. We both sat down again and waited for Susannah to speak. "Gus helped me pack my things, then took me to the train station. He bought my ticket and waited with me until the train arrived. And then . . . he kissed me goodbye and gave me that box. Gus told me that he had a business associate who would meet me at the train station in Atlanta and purchase my next ticket and send me up north. Gus didn't want to know my final destination in case . . . well, in case whoever it was he was afraid of would want to come after me. He said this associate—I never learned his name—would take care of my finances and travel with me to help me procure a house. Gus gave me a small package to give to him, explaining to me that his payment for assisting me was inside. I assumed it was money, but I can't be sure."

I felt a lump in my throat. "Did you ever see him again?"

Her eyes were cloudy as she regarded me. "No, dear. I never did." The room was silent except for the gentle crackling of the fire. "He loved me—I knew that. But he loved his friend and his godson, too. He did the only thing he could think of that would keep us all safe, and I understood that." She shrugged. "And I knew, too, that our time together was coming to an end. You see, family was so important to him. One day soon he'd be wanting a wife and some children, and I couldn't help him with either one of those things. And he was such a man of principles that he never would have considered continuing his relationship with me while marrying another woman. Other men would, but not Augustus Middleton."

Her chest rose, as if filled with pride. "No, I never saw him again. So that was my parting gift to him: not only to help him save the lives of those he loved, but also in helping him say goodbye to me."

Jack's fingers were white against the box. "And you have no idea who Gus was afraid of."

Susannah shook her head. "No. And he made me promise to never show this box to anybody except for Nevin. Not anybody. He said that when Nevin was older, he would be told the truth, or at least be led to the truth, and he would find me here. I suppose what you found in Gus's box was supposed to lead Nevin to me."

Jack nodded. "Yes. We're guessing that Augustus held the box for safekeeping for Nevin, in case something happened to his father before Robert decided it was safe to tell Nevin the truth. But Robert and Gus died only a few days apart without Nevin ever knowing anything. And then the first box sat in Gus's effects until one day last month when Mellie's father found it."

The old woman's head drooped so that her chin nearly rested on her chest. "I didn't find out about Robert dying until later, but I knew about Gus. I received a newspaper clipping of his obituary that was in the Charleston paper. The envelope had an Atlanta postmark, so I assumed it was from his business associate. I remembered that I cried all day but it wasn't all from sadness. Oh, no—there's lots more people like me that have a great deal more to cry about. And I had ten good years with him." She glanced up and our eyes met. "I think I was crying because of all the years I'd missed him and how I'd always pretended he was dead. And then he was, and I had to miss him all over again."

"How difficult for you," said Jack.

Susannah surprised us by smiling. "Not really. You see, I feel him here, in this house. With me. When I go to sleep, I see him. It's like he's waiting for me."

I looked away, afraid that I might cry if I didn't. "So the clues have been here all this time, and Nevin never knew. He died without ever knowing."

"That's not true, dear," Susannah said gently. "He knew his mother loved him. And he knew enough to leave his house to you. He must have been pretty sure that you would continue searching for his mother." She smiled. "And that's why I decided to give the box to you and not that other fellow."

Jack sat up straight. "There was somebody else here asking about Louisa?"

Susannah wrinkled her forehead. "Yes—late yesterday afternoon. He was only here briefly, which is probably why I forgot about it until now." She shook her head. "I'm sorry—my memory isn't what is used to be, I'm afraid."

Something cold and heavy gripped my gut. "Do you remember his name?" My voice sounded strangled, as if I were struggling to get the words out from my tightening neck. I recalled Marc canceling our date because of a sudden out-of-town trip, and the person at the Historical Society's library who'd misfiled the book we needed that would lead us to Susannah Barnsley. And the hang-up phone calls Miss Barnsley had received from Charleston that weren't from us. I felt Jack's eyes on me, but I didn't look at him.

Susannah tapped her fingernails against the arm of her chair. "It will come to me, just a moment." She continued tapping her fingers, her brows creased in a deep frown.

Jack cleared his throat. "What did he look like?"

"Oh, that's easy. I always notice a nice-looking man. He was very tall, taller than you. He had very dark hair and dark eyes. And he wore an expensive suit. That's something Gus taught me, you know—how to recognize good tailoring." She chuckled. "It's funny, isn't it, that I can remember things like that from a long time ago but I have trouble remembering what happened yesterday?"

Jack hesitated, and I knew he was going to wait for me to ask the question or not ask it at all. Feeling almost as if my voice was coming from another person, I asked, "Was his name Marc Longo?"

Susannah's frown smoothed and her face brightened. "Yes, that's it exactly. I should have at least remembered the last name. Joseph Longo is who Louisa was supposed to have run away with. Not that I ever believed it, of course."

I opened my mouth to ask the next question and found that I couldn't. Jack spoke instead. "Was he asking about Louisa and Joseph?"

She frowned again. "You know, I'm not sure if he did. But I do remember that he asked me about the diamonds. He asked me several times if Gus had sent me away with them."

"What did you tell him?"

Susannah smiled sweetly. "I told him no, of course. That I had never heard of the diamonds. Which wasn't true—I *had* heard of them, but I didn't know anything about them. Not that I would have told him, anyway. There was something I didn't like about him. Something . . . untrustworthy."

Jack had the decency not to say anything.

I managed to find my voice. "Would you like us to open the box now?"

She appeared to consider my question for a moment, but then shook her head "No. I don't think so. It was never for me, you see. I've kept it and not told anybody but you about it for all of these years, just like I promised Gus. I don't want to break my promise now."

Jack nodded slowly, then stood. "I think we've taken up enough of your time, Miss Barnsley. I can't thank you enough. You've been enormously helpful."

I stood, too, my knees shaky, still not sure if the frozen ball in my stomach was going to be too heavy to walk with. I moved to Susannah's chair and knelt in front of her. "Yes, thank you. Thank you for trusting me with the box."

She touched my hair, and then my cheeks and smiled. "I'm so glad we met. It's nice to see a part of Gus after all these years. You've made an old lady very happy."

I placed her hand between mine. "Then that alone was worth the trip. Is there anything we can send you from home? Anything you need?"

She squeezed my hand. "Gus is gone now, so there's nothing on this earth that I need. But I want you to promise me one thing."

"Sure. Just name it."

"Promise me that you'll set it right—for not just Louisa but for all of them."

"I will, Miss Barnsley. I promise."

"Good," she said, squeezing my hand again before glancing up at Jack. "Is he your beau?"

"Definitely not," I said at the same time Jack said, "I like to think so."

Susannah surprised me by laughing. "I understand. He's a bit like Gus, that one. You'll resist him and you'll resist him, and then one day it'll be like a bucket of water being thrown over your head, and you'll wonder how you ever lived without him."

I stood and grinned wryly. "More likely the bucket will have to hit me in the head hard enough to make me lose my senses."

Jack nudged me with his elbow as he leaned down to kiss Susannah's cheek. "Goodbye, Miss Barnsley. It was a pleasure meeting you. I hope we'll have the chance to meet again."

"Me, too," she said as Mrs. Marston appeared with our coats to escort us to the door.

∞

Wordlessly, Jack and I got into the rental car, and Jack handed me the box. As if in mutual agreement, we maintained the silence until we reached the highway and Jack spoke. "Do you want to talk about it?"

I shook my head.

"Fine." He drew a deep breath. "Any ideas on how we're going to open the box?"

I looked outside the window at the vast countryside passing by, the greens and blues of summer hidden beneath the reds and golds of autumn. "Pull over."

Jack had the good sense not to question me and pulled the car over onto the shoulder of the two-lane highway. I jumped out of the car with the box, and Jack followed me to the edge of a field. "Help me find a big rock."

Realization dawned in his eyes as he turned away from me, and we began combing the edge of the field for anything heavy enough to break the lock. We'd been looking for only about five minutes before Jack called out to me, holding up a chunk of rock a little bigger than his fist. He approached and reached for the box.

"No," I said. "Let me do it."

He didn't argue and handed me the stone. I knelt in the grass beside the box, steadying it with my left hand while I brought the rock up above it with my right. It took me three tries before the metal lock pulled away from the wood.

Jack picked up the box and examined my handiwork. "Hell hath no fury, I guess."

I sent him a warning look. Again exercising good sense, Jack bent to the task of removing the remnants of the lock from the wood before handing the box back to me. "I think you should do the honors."

"Thank you," I said. While he held the box, I slowly opened the lid and peered inside.

"Well?" asked Jack impatiently.

"Oh," I said. "I certainly didn't expect this." I put the box down so we could examine the contents together.

"This is a surprise," said Jack as he reached in and took out a small revolver and began to examine it. "It's a Remington derringer," he said, checking the two barrels. "It can only hold two single rounds and both barrels are empty." Our eyes met for a moment considering the implications before I reached in and pulled out an envelope identical to the one from the other humidor.

"Go ahead and open it," Jack urged.

Nevin's name was scrawled on the front of the envelope in the same handwriting as the first one, but this time I didn't hesitate to open it.

The letter was three pages of neat script, and I cleared my throat before beginning to read.

September 1, 1930

My precious son,

If you are reading this, then I am probably already gone from this world, having never had the chance to tell you the truth of what happened the night your mother disappeared. I regret that this is how you find out, but hope you realize that I had no choice and that every decision I made was made out of love for you and for your mother. I'm hoping also that your own memories of that terrible night will come back after you have read this letter so that you will have corroboration of what I'm writing, and know that it is all true.

On the night your mother disappeared from our lives, we had a visitor to the house—a business associate of mine, Joseph Longo. First, allow me to explain that he was not a business associate by choice. His family was deeply involved in bootlegging and other illegal activities in Charleston at the time and sought to control all avenues of vice in the city.

Never having involved myself in this area before, I was quite naive when I started my own bootlegging enterprise out at Magnolia Ridge in an effort to prevent our family from going bankrupt following the stock market crash of 'twenty-nine. It was quite a profitable venture, allowing us to keep our home and send you to a better school than we could have otherwise afforded. Unfortunately, being profitable meant bringing my enterprise to the attention of Mr. Longo. I knew he was in the pockets of the authorities, and there would have been no purpose in turning him in, but I had no such protection.

He threatened to ruin me both financially and socially by alerting the authorities to my illegal activities unless I agreed to give him something in exchange for his silence. Regrettably, I had unknowingly given him the one weapon he needed to coerce me. You see, many years ago, following the War of Northern Aggression, our family obtained ownership of six very valuable diamonds. These diamonds remained hidden until I accidentally discovered them several years ago. Not guessing at the implications, I had a necklace made for your mother using one of them—a necklace she wore for a photograph that appeared in the newspaper. Longo knew of the diamonds, and thought them legend until he saw the photograph. I was prepared to go to jail rather than let that man have what I'd always considered as your inheritance, and your children's. But he knew of your mother's weakness where you and I were concerned, and played on her conscience by telling her how hard jail would be for me, and how unprotected she and her son would be. Seeing no other choice, she capitulated, and gave him her necklace—since she never knew the location of the other diamonds—and that appeased him, but only for a while. Longo went to Europe and gambled the proceeds, and it wasn't long before he was back asking for more.

On the day your mother disappeared, Joseph Longo—knowing I would be at work, and most likely also knowing that Wednesday was our servants' day off—came to the house to see your mother to demand another diamond. She told him that he would have to talk to me because she didn't know where the diamonds were. He rightly assumed that I would never give him another diamond, so he began to threaten her, assuming she was lying. As she pleaded with him to believe her, you, dear Nevin, must have heard the commotion and entered the room.

Unfortunately for Joseph Longo, I had just returned from my office to retrieve several documents that I had inadvertently left at home. I spotted Mr. Longo's automobile parked outside and knew there would be trouble. Following your mother's cries, I rushed to the drawing room and saw Mr. Longo pointing a revolver at you. My entrance distracted him, and your mother saw her chance to protect you. She ran to you, and as Mr. Longo turned back around, he fired his pistol. I believe the bullet was meant for you, and instead it found your mother.

Your beloved mother died instantly, as the bullet pierced her heart. Do not grieve, dearest Nevin. She would not have survived if you had been harmed. She died as she had lived, loving us both completely, and I am assured by my faith that we will see her again.

I'm not sure of the exact order in which things happened next. I was in a fury such as I had never experienced before. I threw myself at Longo, and he could not protect himself from my rage. I wrested the pistol from his grasp and shot him once in the chest without thinking twice about the consequences. He, alas, did not die immediately. And I watched him die a long and agonizing death. I was glad of it; he deserved to die for what he had done. But I knew the truth of this scene could never be told.

Mr. Longo's business associates and relatives were numerous and well connected. I feared that if the truth should be discovered not only would my life be in peril, but yours would, as well. They are merciless, and would not think twice about killing a child. Since your mother gave her life that you should survive, I could not let her death be in vain.

I called my good friend and law partner, and your godfather, Augustus Middleton, for assistance. I was a wreck by then because of my grief at losing your mother and almost losing you, and he had to be the one to think, as I was incapable. He helped me hide the bodies so that they couldn't be found unless you knew where to look. He also orchestrated the idea behind the two humidors to keep our secret from prying eyes, but to allow you access in the event that something happened to both myself and Gus before we'd had a chance to explain everything to you. And, as you know now, he gave this last box to Miss Barnsley for safekeeping.

Augustus also thought it best to send to the newspapers an anonymous tip stating that your mother had run away with Mr. Longo. It killed me to think of such slander being directed at your mother, but I also knew that it was the only way we could keep you safe. I also believe that your dear mother would agree with anything to protect you.

The only piece of the puzzle that wouldn't conveniently fit was you, dear son. The events of that tragic night wounded you in a way I had not anticipated—a way that was both a blessing and a curse. You woke up the following morning asking for your mama, not having remembered the incident of the previous night. I believe this is how your mind is dealing with this tragedy, by blocking it from your conscious memory, and for that, I am grateful.

Be assured, dear Nevin, that you were always deeply loved by both of your parents. As you are reading this letter, you will look back on your life and know this is true.

Until we meet again, dear son,

Your loving father.
Robert Nevin Vanderhorst

I slowly folded the letter and placed it inside the envelope. "Poor

Louisa," I said, fighting back tears. "And poor Nevin. She died saving his life, yet he grew up believing she'd abandoned him. How very sad."

Jack placed his arm around my shoulder, and I let him because I needed a place to hide my tears. "But at least we know the truth now. And we can let the rest of the world know. That should make us both feel better." I nodded, knowing he was right, but I couldn't quite stop seeing the forlorn look on Mr. Vanderhorst's face as I said goodbye to him in the doorway of his house. An unsettled feeling lingered, as if we weren't completely finished with the story of Louisa and Nevin.

Jack rubbed my back. "There's still so much that needs to be answered. Like where were Louisa and Joseph buried? And where are the rest of the diamonds—assuming any are left?"

I pulled away, rubbing my eyes and staring everywhere but at Jack. There was one last object in the box, and he reached inside and pulled out a faded red velvet pouch closed at the top with a gold drawstring, a fringed tassel that had long lost its gold coloring dangling from the string. A tingling sensation erupted down my back, and I shivered. I remembered my mother once telling me that the feeling was similar to what ghosts felt when somebody walked on their grave, and I shivered again, trying to focus on Jack. He loosened up the top of the pouch, and I felt compelled to hold out my hand, the palm turned upward in a small cup. He tilted the small bag over my hand, and we watched in surprise as a large, seemingly flawless diamond slipped effortlessly into my hand.

CHAPTER 24

The sun hit the brilliant-cut stone, prisms of light exploding from the gem like a shout of freedom. "Well, that answers part of your question," I said, my fingers closing over the diamond as if still wanting to guard Robert Vanderhorst's secret.

"Sort of. But we're still missing three diamonds. We know about three others: Louisa's necklace that was sold and gambled away, we have this one here, and I would bet Marc Longo's Italian suit collection that a third diamond was sold to finance Susannah Barnsley's abrupt departure from Charleston."

My jaw twitched at the mention of Marc's name. "So those three remaining diamonds were either sold long ago, or they're still hidden where Robert put them."

"Exactly."

I looked down at the diamond in my hand. "But at least we know that Louisa and Joseph are dead, and that Louisa didn't abandon her son. You have no idea how relieved I am to say that."

Jack gave me a half smile. "I have a pretty good idea." He opened the pouch, and I reluctantly slipped the diamond inside it.

"I wish I knew where Louisa is buried. I think we need to find that out before she can rest in peace."

Jack nodded. "We'll need to work harder on those ciphers." He replaced the pouch and the gun into the box, but I kept the letter with me, not yet ready to part with it. We walked back up the shallow embankment and got into the car.

Jack started the engine. "We'll have to stop at a Wal-mart or something so we'll have a suitcase to check on the plane. We won't be able to bring the gun in our carry-ons, and I don't want to have to explain that diamond."

"We can't check that—what if it's stolen?"

Jack pulled out onto the highway. "It won't be. We'll buy a Dora the Explorer bag so it looks like it belongs to a child, and some clothes to wrap around it. Trust me—no one will touch it."

"Really?" I asked, still feeling uneasy.

"Really," he assured me. "Have I ever led you wrong?"

I wasn't sure if he was referring to my lack of judgment where Marc was concerned, so I just looked away without answering. "Who's Dora the Explorer?"

"Just a cartoon character who's popular with the preschool crowd these days—a little more educational than the Scooby-Doo cartoons we used to watch."

"I never watched Scooby-Doo, remember? And how do you know about Dora the Explorer?"

Jack shrugged. "Sometimes I watch Yvonne's grandkids when she's doing research for me."

I couldn't reconcile the playboy image I had of Jack with that of him sitting on the floor with little children, so I turned the conversation back to where it had begun. "I'm thinking the whole break in Robert and Gus's relationship was manufactured to distract the Longos from looking closer at Gus and his associates for answers."

"Good deduction, Dr. Watson," Jack said, his trademark killer grin on his face. "You know, we work so well together, we should do this again."

I sent him what I hoped was a scathing look of disbelief. "I think I would almost rather slice off an appendage with a pocket knife and without anesthesia than suffer through the agony of these last months again."

He looked genuinely hurt. "Was it really all that bad?"

I thought back to all that had happened since we'd first met, and knew that I couldn't honestly say that it had been. If I were to be completely up front with him, I would have to tell him that I hadn't laughed as much in my whole life as I had in the last few months, and that seeing my hard work on the restoration of the house come to fruition had been one of the big highlights of my life so far. Even being forced to face my ghosts had been an illuminating experience, and most likely something that wouldn't have happened if I hadn't met Jack Trenholm. I smiled to myself. Either I'd had a rather sheltered life, or I really had been enjoying life for the first time—and I had Jack to thank for most of it. But then again, he had lied to me, and if I didn't think too hard about it, I could also blame him for me being so determined to go after Marc Longo. So I hedged my answer.

"Not all of it, of course."

He pursed his lips and nodded. "I'm assuming you're not blaming me for the Marc Longo fiasco, too."

"I told you that I didn't want to talk about it."

He flipped on his blinker and changed lanes in front of an SUV filled with children in soccer uniforms and driven by a harried mom drinking from a Starbucks cup. "I know. I'm sorry. All that I'm going to say about the whole disaster is that at least you didn't sleep with him."

I remained silent but felt my cheeks flood with warmth.

He looked at me with an expression that was a confused mix of horror and surprise. Somebody honked, and Jack jerked the car back into the middle of his lane. "That sonuvabitch," he muttered under his breath.

We spent the rest of the trip in a strained silence punctuated briefly by polite conversation and potential words for our ciphers, all endeavors turning up nothing more than frustration. We arrived back at the house on Tradd Street a little past ten o'clock that night. All of the lights were off, and I was pretty positive I wouldn't have considered going into the house if Jack hadn't been with me, although I would never tell him that.

As we walked through the garden gate, Jack stopped me with a hand on my arm. "Do you hear that?"

I listened to the quiet night, and there amid the hum of distant traffic was the distinct sound of a rope swing creaking against tree bark. I smiled in the darkness. "Yes, I hear it. It's Louisa and Nevin. They're letting us know that they're there."

"Oh," he said, and I thought I felt him shudder next to me.

"They won't hurt you, you know. They know we're trying to help them. Besides . . ." I hesitated, trying to remember what Nevin Vanderhorst had told me.

"Besides what?"

"Well, Louisa only appears to those she approves of. So far, that would be me, General Lee, the plumber, and you."

"The plumber?" he asked.

"Yeah. He's seen her, too."

"I'm honored," Jack said as he climbed the steps to the piazza before pausing by the front door. "Do you feel that?" he asked.

I nodded, my teeth chattering. The temperature had dropped about twenty degrees between the time we'd entered the gate and climbed the piazza steps. "I think we've got company."

"The good kind of company?" he asked nervously.

I shook my head. "No. If it were Louisa, we'd smell her roses. If you just feel cold and nervous, it's . . . the other entity I've seen several times. He's not very nice."

His white teeth glowed eerily in the moonlight. "Great. So what do we do?"

"You just keep telling yourself that you're stronger than he is, and that works most of the time."

"Most of the time? What about the rest of the time?"

"Then he sets the house on fire and traps you inside."

There was a long pause. "So why are we standing here, trying to get in instead of getting the hell out of here?"

I took a deep breath. "Because now I know his strength. Before, I was trying to ignore him and Louisa no matter how much they tried to get my attention. That's been my MO for a long time—ignore them and eventually they'll go away. But now it's personal—I need to listen to them. And right now the bad guy is telling me to leave. Which means, of course, that we need to go inside. There's something in there he doesn't want us to find." I straightened my shoulders. "We just need to pay attention and not get separated. And if you smell roses, that's good—it means Louisa's there and the bad guy can't hurt us."

"Do you know who he is?"

"I thought at first that it might be Robert. But Robert wasn't evil, and this guy is definitely a bad SOB. Now that I know that Joseph Longo was killed in this house, I think I can make a pretty good guess that it's him."

"Ah, well, that makes it easier, then."

"It does?"

"Yeah. Picturing how you're going to pulverize a guy who tried to kill an innocent little boy makes your adversary a little easier to deal with—ghost or not. It all comes down to: I'm the good guy and he's the bad guy. And that's all I need to know."

I held up the door key, the glint of streetlight on the metal like a hypnotist's pendulum. "Are you ready?"

"Let's roll," he said quietly as I found the keyhole and turned the key.

To our surprise, the door opened without resistance. I quickly walked inside and slid my hands over the wall until they hit the light switch. I was grateful for the glow of yellow light that fell on us. I glanced around in surprise. Apparently Mrs. Houlihan had been very busy in my absence. The grit and dust that had coated every surface had been removed, leaving sparkling wood and glass and the distinct smell of floor polish.

"It's not cold anymore," Jack remarked.

"I think he knows that we're not afraid of him. And that Louisa is near."

We both gravitated into the drawing room, where the grandfather clock chimed the half hour. We turned on all the lights we passed to erase the eerie darkness. I moved to the side window and peered out into the night to where the oak tree stood, and saw nothing. But I knew they were there, felt them watching and waiting. For what, I wasn't sure.

"Cerca Trova," Jack said. He stood in front of the clock, the glass door over the face opened. "I knew I'd seen those words before. They're here—written on one of the signal flags. I probably forgot where I'd seen it because it's not always visible."

I moved to stand by his side. "Those were the words in the first letter to Nevin. Seek and ye shall find."

"But we've examined every inch of this clock, and I've found the secret compartment." Jack thought for a moment. "Does that mean that they're gone, that the three missing diamonds were gone before Robert ever found the hiding place?"

"I don't know. And we won't know unless we can figure out the ciphers."

Jack continued staring at the clock face, his brow furrowed in concentration. I was about to suggest that we go upstairs to bed when I heard a scratching sound, like pencil on paper. Or fingernails on plastic.

"Do you hear that?" I asked.

Jack nodded. "Mice?"

I shook my head. "No. Termites, yes. Rodents, no." I moved to where the sound seemed to be getting louder. It was coming from the wall next to the clock, where the long draperies had once covered Nevin's growth chart. It was now protected by a thin sheet of Plexiglas, and as I kneeled in front of it, the scratching stopped. I carefully examined all the measurements written on the chart, looking for something unusual, as my gaze traveled upward until I'd reached the top and I stopped, my breath stuck in the back of my throat. There, in Louisa's careful handwriting were the initials *MBG. My best guy.*

I straightened, my heart pounding rapidly. "Jack, what did Robert say in that first letter to Nevin, something about his mother. Something about what she called him."

"Yeah, yeah: 'Remember what your mother called you.' Why? Are you thinking of something?"

"My best guy—that's what she called him, remember? It's written right here on the wall." I knelt on the floor and pulled out the notebook, which I'd almost filled with failed keywords, and opened to a fresh page. Quickly, I wrote down the letters of the alphabet and then below it the words "MY BEST GUY" directly under it, omitting the last "Y" and following the phrase with the alphabet starting with the letter "A" and moving on toward "Z" without repeating any letters.

Jack knelt next to me and began to repeat to me the string of thirty-two letters we had both memorized by sheer repetition from the clock's cipher. After I'd written them down in a line, I took a deep breath before looking back at the pad of paper. Slowly, I began filling in the letters from the new keyword alphabet: *A,T,M,I,D,N,I,G,H,T,S,T, A,R,S,S,H,I,N,E,L,I,K,E,D,I,A,M,O,N,D,S.* I looked down at what I'd written and read it out loud. "At midnight, stars shine like diamonds." Our eyes met. "Oh, my gosh," I said as we scrambled up together to go examine the clock.

Jack opened the clock face again. "At midnight . . ." He turned to me. "Remember the photos from the film roll? The one of the grandfather clock shows both hands pointing to twelve."

"But we've both been in this room at midnight more than once, and nothing happened." I fought back my disappointment. "Do you think we can move the hands now to force them both on the twelve and see what happens?"

Jack glanced at his watch. "It's a little past eleven o'clock now. I don't want to do anything that might alter whatever is supposed to happen. Why don't we get ready for bed and meet back down here at midnight?"

I nodded, understanding his caution but not being able to completely override my impatience. We grabbed our bags, and Jack allowed me to carry the Dora the Explorer overnight bag. I assumed he thought it was because it contained the diamond, but it was more to do with the letters, and the last words of a father to his son that were never read. The tragedy of their story weighed heavily on me and finding out the truth had not ended their story. I felt their hidden presence in the house now, watching us as we climbed the stairs. I stopped at the top, feeling as if I could touch the anticipation that seemed to swell and pulsate around us.

"Do you feel that?" I whispered.

Jack shook his head. "Feel what?"

I frowned, trying to identify the sensations that were brushing against me and rubbing my skin. "They're watching us. Waiting."

"Who's they?" he asked, impressing me with the firmness of his voice.

I listened to the whispers that were growing stronger now. "Louisa. Nevin." I paused, feeling the flesh crawl down my back. "And Joseph."

The lights flickered and dimmed, then flicked back on again. "I'm stronger than you. I'm stronger than you," I muttered under my breath.

Jack put his hand on my elbow and guided me down the hall to my room. "Keep saying that, okay? It makes me feel better." He pushed my door open and flipped on the switch. "I'll stay here while you get ready for bed, and then we'll go downstairs together to wait."

I was too relieved to argue with him about my privacy and the house rules that included him never being allowed to step foot in my room. I went into the bathroom and washed my face and brushed my teeth before throwing on a pair of sweats and my bathrobe. I avoided looking in the mirror, afraid of what I might see behind me.

When I came out of the bathroom, Jack was sitting on my bed, a large book opened on the bedspread in front of him. At first, I thought it was one of Louisa's albums, but when I got closer I saw that it wasn't.

"Where did this come from?" he asked, showing me the cover. I read the title: *Ciphers and Codes of the Ancient World.*

I shook my head. "I've never seen it before."

"But it was on your bed."

My eyes widened. "But I didn't put it there."

"Then how did it get here? I'm pretty positive it wasn't with the rest of the cipher books in the attic, because I've gone through all of those and this one wasn't with them."

"Welcome to my world," I said as I sat down on the bed on the other side of the book. "From past experience, I would have to say that somebody wants us to see it." We looked at each other, and I became aware that we were alone in my bedroom and on my bed. I watched a small flicker pass through his eyes and thought he might be thinking the same thing.

Abruptly, I stood and pulled the desk chair over beside the bed. "Have you found anything yet that looks promising?"

His eyes took in my robe and sweats before returning to the book and flipping a page. "Not yet, but I only just started. Maybe it'll give us another way to decipher the word 'midnight,' just in case . . ." His hands froze on the opened page.

"What is it?" I asked, standing to look over his shoulder.

He held the book up. "This," he said, pointing to a picture of a grid that consisted of five columns and five rows. Outside the top row and beside the far-left column were the numbers one to five, in order, and inside the grid, starting in the top left box, was each letter of the alphabet, with "Y" and "Z" sharing the last box. "It's called a polybius checkerboard. I saw it before, in one of the other cipher books, but I dismissed it as being too easy." He sent me an apologetic look. "I forgot what you said about the ciphers being used to keep the secrets away from prying eyes—and not to stump Nevin."

"But how does this work, Jack? If we're trying to find another meaning for the word 'midnight,' it will transpose into a number, not another word."

He took a pen out of his jacket while shaking his head. "Wrong cipher, Mellie. This is a substitution cipher that transposes numbers into letters. In other words, the code is a series of numbers that, when solved, becomes a word."

"Oh, right—the fountain!"

"Exactly," he said. "Do you remember the numbers?"

I nodded. "Yes—but not in any particular sequence."

"Not a problem—there's only three of them, and we can sort them out if we need to."

I closed my eyes, recalling the Roman numerals etched into the side of the fountain. "Forty-one, forty-three, and twenty-four."

I watched as he solved the first number, XLI, by finding the number-four row first, then moving across to the number-one column and writing down the letter in the corresponding box—"P." He continued this same pattern for the other two letters, coming up with the letters "R" and "I."

"P-R-I?" I asked.

Jack stared at the letters he'd written down, understanding clear on his face. "You have to move the only consonant in the middle for it to make sense."

I looked at the letters again, instantly eliminating the first word I came up with and finally settling on "RIP." I sat back down on the bed. "Rest in peace," I said quietly. "That's what you usually find on a tombstone."

"Yes, it is," Jack said, placing his pen down on the book. "I guess we know where Robert and Gus put the bodies, then."

"And why the fountain's never worked—it's probably not even hooked up. Robert built the fountain as a monument to his wife, but was afraid of workmen finding the bodies if they ever dug deep enough to install water pipes." I shook my head, remembering the times I'd been in the garden and felt Louisa's presence. And now I knew why.

"We'll need to call the police," Jack said.

"I know." I frowned, uncomfortable with the peace of the garden being destroyed, even if just temporarily. "Can we wait until morning? I think Louisa likes it there. I'd like to give her one more night in her garden."

"Sure." Jack turned his head. "Hey, do you smell that?"

The pungent odor of fresh roses enveloped the room, filling our nostrils with their sweet scent. "Yes," I said, smiling. "I think Louisa's saying thank you."

The clock began chiming downstairs and Jack stood. "It's a quarter till. I think we should go downstairs now so we don't miss anything."

I nodded and followed him to the door. We had almost reached it when it slammed shut in front of us. Jack leapt for it and tried to turn the handle. "I think it's locked. Do you have the key?"

"No," I said, smelling that other odor now as it mixed with that of the roses.

"God, where is that smell coming from?" Jack asked, scrunching up his nose. "I've smelled it before, and I never expected to smell it again in my lifetime."

"What is it?" I asked, almost gagging as the scent of the roses was completely obliterated by the foul odor.

He stared hard at me for a long time, and I recalled what I'd read about his military service, and I wished I hadn't asked. "It smells like dead bodies that have been left out in the sun. It's a smell you don't easily forget."

I turned away and closed my eyes to make them stop stinging. "He's trying to scare us. Don't let him or he'll win. And remember that Louisa is on our side." It was scant comfort, but it was all I had to offer.

Jack turned the handle and tugged on the door. At first it wouldn't budge, and then suddenly the force holding it shut let go, sending Jack flying backward into me as the door gave way. The lights flickered again and Jack reached for my hand. "Don't let go of my hand, Mellie. He wants us separated."

I wasn't about to argue and clutched Jack's hand like a drowning person would grab a piece of floating wood. The lights all began to turn brighter and brighter, the house filled with the sound of humming until one by one we heard the *pop-pop* of lightbulbs shattering. A blast of cold air engulfed us, frigid enough to make my fingers and nose numb. I shivered and Jack squeezed my hand as the last lightbulb burst and we were thrown into complete darkness.

"Close your eyes, Mellie—that way you'll rely on your other senses until your night vision kicks in."

I nodded and shut my eyes, envisioning the upstairs hallway as I began to follow Jack toward the stairs. As he headed toward the top step, I tugged on his arm. "He tried to push me down them before, remember? Sit down and let's work our way to the bottom that way."

"Good idea," he said as he sat, pulling me down next to him. Slowly we made our way down, step by step. We were near the bottom when Jack let out a muffled cry, and I felt him yank on my hand.

I stopped. "What's wrong?"

He was breathing heavily and trying hard not to gag on the odor, which was stronger now, and which, in the dark with our eyes closed, made me think of an old grave. "Something just kicked me hard in the back. I'm okay. It just took my breath away. Keep moving."

We made it down one more step. As I turned to Jack to ask if I could open my eyes yet, icy fingers wrapped themselves around my throat and began to squeeze. I let go of Jack's hand and reached for my neck, feeling nothing but empty, cold air. I struggled to breathe; even the fetid air would have been welcome if I could just open my airways to let it in.

"Mellie, are you all right?"

I felt Jack's warm breath on my face, and I thawed slightly. Something guttural erupted from my mouth, and then Jack's hands closed over mine as he struggled to pull them from my neck.

"Remember—you're stronger than he is. Keep saying that, Mellie. Mellie, can you hear me?"

I kicked my foot out, striking nothing. Spots formed behind my eyelids, and heat seared my lungs. Jack's voice sounded very far away. "Mellie, you're stronger than he is—say it! Come on, Mellie, come back to me."

I latched on to Jack's voice and his breath on my cheeks. And then I saw my mother's face, and she was telling me that I was strong, that no spirit could hurt me unless I let them. *Mama,* I thought, and she was there, touching my hair, telling me that she loved me. I opened my eyes in shock at the memory and gasped a lungful of air, bringing me back to the present. *I'm stronger than you,* I shouted in my head. "I'm stronger than you," exploded from my mouth as I broke the hold on my throat before throwing myself down the remaining four steps.

The clock chimed. "Hurry, Jack. It's almost midnight."

He came from behind me, grabbing my hand and pulling me into the drawing room in time to hear the third chime. Hazy light spilled into the room from the streetlamp and the full moon, highlighting the dark bulk of the clock and the filmy haze that seemed to float in the air around it like the old hopes of a small boy.

We stood in front of the clock, our hands still clasped together, as a cold wind passed through us. I began to smell the roses now, slowly obliterating the putrid smell of decay and death. The clock chimed again and then again, for the eighth time.

"Listen," said Jack as he opened up the casing. The clock chimed nine and then ten times as we stared into the darkened hollow of the clock, the brass pendulum ticking away the minutes, reflecting the hazy light. "Do you hear that?"

I knelt next to Jack and listened carefully. I heard the sound of the clock's chime mechanism, but there was something else, a faint clicking noise coming from inside the clock. "It's in the secret compartment," I said, my voice high-pitched and raspy. With a shaking hand, I reached inside and fumbled for the secret button and pushed. Nothing happened. The clock chimed for the eleventh time, and I pushed harder on the button, hearing the click as the hidden panel opened. Jack moved his head back to allow the outside light to shine in just in time for me to see a small wooden box begin to raise itself like a small elevator into the clock. I jabbed my hand inside and closed my fist around something soft and bulky.

Yanking my hand out, I watched as the little box slowly raised itself into the top of the clock, until the bottom of it made a false top to the secret compartment. The whirring and clicking stopped, the clock silenced until the next midnight started the show all over again.

I sat back on my heels, feeling dizzy.

"Did you find anything?" Jack's voice was hushed although we were alone now. Even the spirits had gone, leaving only the fading scent of roses.

I opened my hand so we could see a pouch identical to the one we'd found in Gus's humidor. I looked at Jack and he smiled. "I think my next book is going to have a happy ending."

As we'd done before, Jack took the pouch from me and unfastened it, then tilted it over my cupped hands. We watched as three large diamonds fell into my palms, winking at us in the light from the windows.

A crack of thunder shook the foundation as a sudden wind gust pushed at the house, making the eaves howl. A loud crash brought us rushing to the side window to peer out into the midnight garden. A flash of lightning illuminated the side yard for a moment, showing a branch from the oak tree that had fallen on the fountain, neatly splitting it in two. A dark hole appeared beside the fountain like spilled ink, and a shapeless form emerged from the blackness, terrifying in its opaqueness.

The wind moved the leaves and branches of the tree, but the form stood still, as if waiting for something. Then another dark form appeared from beneath the fountain and I recognized the man with the hat I'd seen peering at me from the upstairs window. *Joseph.* The howling began again, but this time I realized it wasn't coming from the wind. The shapeless form seemed to be absorbing Joseph, like two funnel clouds merging into one. Lightning crashed nearby, traveling through the ground and up through my legs, making my bones tingle. The garden was illuminated for a brief moment, long enough for us to see the hole close in on itself, leaving only the broken fountain and the old oak tree to guard the garden's secrets.

The house sighed, and I leaned into Jack. "It's over," I said and I began to weep. Not for me, but for a mother who had never stopped loving her son, and for the son who finally knew the truth.

That night, Jack and I slept on the floor by the clock, the diamonds crushed between us, finally waking from dreamless sleep when dawn pierced the sky and the Charleston sun streamed into the windows of the house on Tradd Street.

CHAPTER 25

When Sophie and Chad along with General Lee appeared later that morning, they were greeted with yellow police tape encircling the garden and a county coroner's ambulance waiting at the curb.

"Whoa, dudette," Chad said as I met them at the garden gate. "Did you do something to Jack?"

"No," I replied with a half grin. "Although now that I know how to hide a body for almost eighty years, I might consider it."

Sophie touched my arm. "So you found her?"

Her nose was red and swollen, and I tried not to stare as I answered. "Yes. It's a long story, but both Louisa and Joseph were buried in the garden. I'll tell you the specifics later—things are kind of hectic right now."

Sophie blinked at me through exceptionally unattractive John Lennon glasses. "I guess your trip to Vermont was a success, then."

"In more ways than one. We found the diamonds, too."

Sophie tightened her rainbow scarf—the one that matched her Mork suspenders currently attached to a pair of oversized painter's pants. "That's great, isn't it? That means we'll be able to finish the restoration."

I watched as my dad tried to guide the police excavation to spare as much of his garden as possible. From my vantage point it appeared the police shovels were winning. "I hope so. I'm hiring a lawyer to make sure that I get to keep them, but from what Jack tells me, I own the house, so technically they're mine. I'm thinking that I'll send a large donation to the Daughters of the Confederacy, seeing as how Jefferson Davis wanted the funds to go to the widows and orphans of soldiers. But not to worry. There will be plenty left over for the restoration."

Chad raised his hand and high-fived Sophie. "Great," she said as she took General Lee's leash off of her wrist and handed it to me. "Now you can afford to hire a dog sitter."

I looked at Chad in confusion and he shrugged. "Soph here is allergic and the Leester can't come with me when I move into Sophie's house."

"You're moving in with Sophie?"

Sophie patted my arm again. "It's only temporary—and just as roommates. I'm trying to help him out because his current lease expires at the end of the month, and you haven't found him the right house yet."

I wanted to point out that the reason I hadn't found the right house for him yet was because he kept canceling our appointments to go see one. But I still had visions of being godmother to their firstborn so I didn't mention it. Instead I asked, "But what do I do with a dog?"

"It's easy," said Chad, thrusting a bag of dog food at me. "He'll let you know what he needs."

"Great," I said, looking down at soulful brown eyes and a wagging tail. "Maybe Jack wants a dog."

General Lee looked up at me, and I could have sworn he frowned before giving a little bark.

Sophie sneezed. "We're going to be late for yoga—I'll call you later. Maybe we can try breakfast at that new place, City Lights, and you can fill me in on everything, and I can tell you what my next projects will be for the house."

"Fine," I said. "But the first thing we're going to do is repair the fountain and garden. I think my dad might cry if it stays like that for too long."

"Fair enough," said Sophie. "I'll talk to you later, then."

I watched them walk away, with Sophie hitching up her pants every few steps as Chad guided her away from sidewalk cracks and other obstacles.

My smile faded as I recognized Marc's car pulling up to the curb. I considered turning and running in the opposite direction, but then I remembered Louisa facing down a gun, and it gave me the courage to stand my ground.

Marc's face became serious as he approached. He must have seen from my expression that I wasn't happy to see him. He glanced over at the police activity in the garden. "Are you all right? What's going on here?"

"We're digging up your grandfather and Louisa Vanderhorst. The police can fill you in. Right now, I'm going to go walk my dog." I placed the bag of dog food on the sidewalk next to the gate and wrapped the leash around my hand.

General Lee had begun to snarl at Marc, doing his best to seem ferocious and managing to look like nothing more than a furball with teeth.

Marc reached for my arm to stop me, and I pulled back. "What's wrong, Melanie?"

I pasted a smile on my face. "How was Vermont, Marc? Did you do any sightseeing while you were there, or was it all about trying to see if Susannah Barnsley had the diamonds?"

He dropped his hand. "Oh. So you know."

"Yes, Marc. I know. I know that you've been lying to me since we first met. At least Jack had the decency to admit it when I confronted him. But you continued to lie to me." My voice remained surprisingly strong, and I was able to keep the tears at bay.

He looked convincingly remorseful. "I'm sorry. You don't know how sorry I am." He took a step forward, then stopped. "I do care for you, Melanie. I care deeply. Please . . . can you let me explain?"

General Lee continued to snarl, so I picked him up. "You have two minutes, and then you need to leave."

He looked like he was about to argue for more time but decided against it. "Fine. About a year ago, I came across a safe-deposit box that had belonged to my grandfather. In it was an old newspaper article about the Confederate diamonds and a later newspaper announcement of Nevin Vanderhorst's christening. There was a picture with the announcement of Nevin's mother wearing a diamond necklace. I put two and two together and figured that somehow Robert Vanderhorst must have had access to the diamonds." He scratched the back of his neck. "I've been having a few financial difficulties lately, and I thought if I could find those diamonds, I could pay back some loans and get back on my feet."

"And that's when you bought Magnolia Ridge since this house was still privately owned. Unfortunately, all that was left at Magnolia Ridge was the remnants of an old still. Then Vanderhorst died and left me the house, and you saw your opportunity."

A stricken expression crossed his face, and it made me feel a little better. "But that's not the whole story, Melanie. Yes, initially, I was just after the diamonds. Then I got to know you better, and everything changed."

A new realization dawned on me. "And the vandalism and break-ins—that was all you, wasn't it?"

He closed his eyes. "They weren't going to hurt anybody. And you weren't supposed to be home the time you surprised the intruder. Look, it was stupid but I was desperate. But I'm not that guy anymore. You've changed me."

Out of the corner of my eye, I saw Jack emerge from the front door and spot Marc and me on the sidewalk. With a tight expression on his face, he approached through the garden, avoiding the police activity.

"Matt, it's great to see you again. How was Vermont?"

Marc narrowed his eyes. "If you don't mind, Melanie and I are having a private conversation."

"Actually," I said, "I think we're done here." I put General Lee down and began to cross the street.

"Wait, Melanie, please. Let me make it up to you." Marc grabbed my arm, and when I tried to pull away, he didn't let go.

"If you know what's good for you, Matt, you'll let go of the lady's arm." Jack's voice had a hard edge to it that I hadn't heard before.

Marc continued to hold me back. "Please, Melanie, give me another chance."

Jack stared patiently at the sky. "I'm warning you. I'm not going to ask you again. Now let go of the lady's arm."

Marc didn't let go. "Melanie?" he pleaded.

"Don't say I didn't warn you." Jack pulled back his arm, and in one quick motion, he slammed his fist into Marc's jaw. Marc lost his balance and fell to the ground. He sat where he landed, rubbing his jaw, but didn't get up.

General Lee had begun to bark in earnest now, and I saw that one of the policemen was straining to see what was causing the commotion. Jack took General Lee's leash. "Come on, Mellie. I have something to show you that I think you need to see."

Without a backward glance, I followed Jack into the house. Already, the atmosphere inside seemed lighter, the sunlight in the windows brighter as if a dark veil had been removed. The whispering had stopped, and I welcomed the silence. I followed Jack into the drawing room, where he stopped in front of the wall beside the grandfather clock.

"Last night, while we were sleeping, I heard more scratching on the wall. It only lasted less than a minute, and I guess I dozed off and forgot about it when we woke up this morning. About an hour ago I remembered it, and came to take a look."

He stepped back so I could see. I squatted down on my haunches to be at eye level with the chart behind the Plexiglas. I was about to ask Jack what it was I was supposed to be looking at, when I saw the words scrawled at the top, above the *MBG* in a childish hand. *Thank you.*

My eyes stung and I reached up to touch the words. I looked at it oddly. "But it's under Plexiglas."

Jack nodded. "This is one of those 'welcome to your world' moments again, isn't it?"

I sniffed and brushed my hand across my eyes before standing. "Well, if you ever want to work with me again to solve an old mystery, you're going to have to get used to it."

"Oh, so you've changed your mind?" A single eyebrow went up.

"Not at all. Just giving you another reason why you wouldn't want to."

Jack flashed his back-cover grin again, and I had to turn away. "Maybe I think talking to dead people is sexy."

It was my turn to send him a raised eyebrow. A shadow passed across the window that looked into the garden, compelling me to move toward it. Jack followed, his hand lightly on my back. My gaze traveled beyond the ruined fountain to the ancient oak, its leaves fluttering in the wind like a child's laughter. The wooden rope swing hung empty, swaying gently as if someone had just gotten off. Behind it stood Louisa and Nevin, staring intently at us.

"Do you see them?" I whispered.

Jack nodded. "Why do you think they're here?"

"They're saying goodbye." Alternating grief and joy flooded the space where my heart beat as I said a silent goodbye. "There's nothing holding them here anymore."

We watched as they turned around and began walking toward the gate, where I'd first seen them, fading gently like the colors of the earth at sunset, until the wind enfolded them in a gust of air and nothing remained except the faint scent of roses.

We were quiet for a long time, staring at the spot where mother and child had vanished. Eventually, Jack turned to me, his face very close to mine. "So, what's next?"

I shrugged, pretending to be nonchalant. "I guess I'm going to move in here full-time. It's silly to be paying rent for a condo I'm not living in. Plus my condo association doesn't allow dogs."

We both eyed General Lee, who had collapsed at our feet and was now looking up at us innocently.

Jack reached down and scratched General Lee behind the ears. "Yeah, a dog's a good reason to move."

"What about you? What are you going to do now?"

"Well, now that I've completed all my research on the Confederate diamonds, I need to finish writing the book. I'll probably need to come back to the house and maybe get together with you a few times for more details. If that's all right with you, of course."

I tried to hide my relief. Jack had become such a large part of my life that I was having a hard time imagining it without him. Even if he was annoying and bigheaded most of the time. "Sure. I don't mind."

He smiled. "Guess you wouldn't be interested in finding another ghost or two who know a few secrets, hmm? I'm always thinking about my next book."

"Running naked through glass sounds more fun. I think I've had enough mystery solving and ghost talking to last me a lifetime. You'll have to do your research the old-fashioned way in the future. It was a short-lived career, but I'm retiring."

Jack laughed. "Gee, Mellie, tell me how you really feel about it." His face sobered. "But I understand. None of this could have been easy for you." He looked past me, toward the men working in the garden. "I'm going to go outside now and see where they are in the excavation. I'll keep you posted."

"Thanks," I said, his face hovering very close to mine. "And thanks for defending my honor today."

His eyes crinkled at the corners. "It was the least I could do, seeing as how my own behavior wasn't exactly exemplary in the gentleman department." He continued to stare into my eyes, not moving back.

"No, it wasn't," I agreed, my eyes half closed as he began to close the distance between us.

His lips hadn't even made contact when my cell phone rang, and he drew back. I dug into the back pocket of my jeans and pulled out my phone, not recognizing the area code or the number.

"Hello?" I said.

"Hello, Mellie."

I froze. Only one person besides Jack ever called me that. "Hello, Mother."

"I realized that if I waited for you to call me back, I'd never talk to you. So I asked your father for your cell phone number."

I couldn't think of anything to say.

"I learned that your grandmother's house on Legare is for sale, and I want you to be my Realtor and help me purchase it." There was a brief pause. "I'm coming home, Mellie. I'm moving back to Charleston."

I held the phone close to my ear, hearing the rushing of my blood thundering through my head. "Don't, Mother. Please don't. I've been fine for so long without you. Please don't come back."

She spoke in a rush, as if she knew I wasn't going to give her enough time to say everything she wanted to. "I don't blame you for saying that. But there are things you need to know before it's too late, Mellie—about your grandmother. About her house and why I had to let it go. There are secrets in our family you should know. . . ."

I cut her off, having had enough family secrets in the last four months to last a lifetime. In light of my recent experiences, which included being nearly choked by a ghost, I was surprised at the fear and angst I felt at merely hearing my mother's voice. But, I reasoned, ghosts couldn't hurt me because I was stronger than they were. I'd proven that. But mothers always could.

"No, Mother. I'm sorry. I just can't." Before she could answer, I closed my phone and turned it off.

Jack raised his eyebrows. "Not good news?"

I took my time sticking my cell phone back in my pocket. "She wants to move back to Charleston and buy my grandmother's house. She claims there are family secrets I should know about. Something about my grandmother."

"And?" he prompted.

"I told her I wasn't interested."

"Uh-huh," he said. "Or maybe my next book is about to write itself for me again."

"Don't bet on it," I snorted, trying to hide how shaken I really was by my mother's phone call.

Jack picked up General Lee's leash and led him outside, with me following close behind.

Without turning to look at me, Jack said, "I believe that was near-kiss number three. If we keep this up, we might have a world record or something."

He headed down into the garden before I could think of something clever to say. I remained on the top step, surveying Louisa's wounded garden and wondering again if it could ever be put right. I crossed my arms, recalling my conversation with my mother with the same uncertainty I considered the garden. Weeds could be pulled and new seeds planted, hardened soil tilled and watered to make a fertile bed. Water could be piped in to make an old fountain cascade for the first time. Perhaps my relationship with my mother could be tended in the same way, with care and patience used to rebuild the bedrock of a mother-child bond that had been broken nearly thirty-three years before.

Or not, I thought as I watched a small bulldozer take a chunk out of the newly bricked path that encircled the fountain. The cherub seemed to wink at me, and I blinked, wondering if it had been a trick of the light.

I turned around and crossed the piazza to the front door. *I'm home.* The thought struck me from nowhere, and when I considered it, I realized how very true it was. I turned the handle of the magnificent door with the Tiffany windows and pushed it open, noticing how nothing barred my way this time. I breathed in the smell of beeswax and polish, and smiled to myself as I gently closed the door behind me.

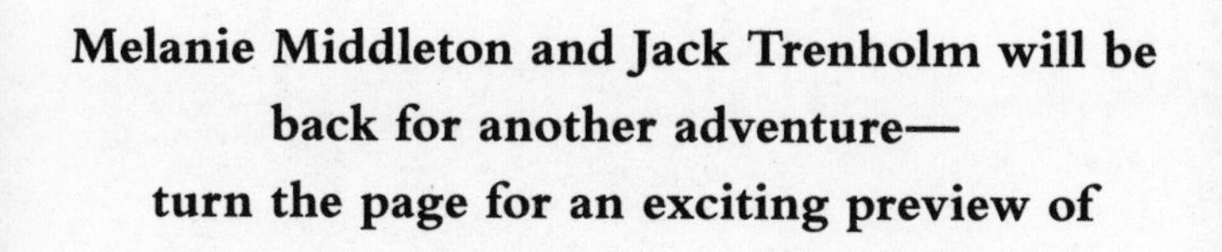

Melanie Middleton and Jack Trenholm will be back for another adventure—turn the page for an exciting preview of

THE GIRL ON LEGARE STREET

Available now from New American Library

The milky glow of winter sun behind a sky rubbed the color of an old nickel failed in its feeble attempt to warm the December morning. I shuddered in my wool coat, my Charleston blood unaccustomed to the infrequent blasts of frigid air that descend on our city from time to time to send yet another reminder of why we chose to live in this beautiful city where its inhabitants, both living and dead, coexist like light and shadow.

I yanked open the door to the City Lights coffee bar, the wind behind me threatening to close it again before I'd gone through it. Glancing around, I spotted Jack at a table by the front window, a latte with extra whipped cream and a large cinnamon roll already sitting on the table across from him. Immediately suspicious, I approached the table with caution.

"What do you want?" I asked, indicating the latte and cinnamon roll.

He looked up at me with a pair of killer blue eyes that I'd spent the last six months of my life trying not to notice. His look of innocence would have made me smile and roll my eyes if I didn't still have the lingering aura of dread that had dogged me all the way from my house on Tradd Street to Market. It had been a strong enough feeling to make me linger outside the café for a moment longer than necessary, hoping to identify whatever it was. I wanted to think it was grogginess caused by a phone call at two o'clock in the morning, after which I'd been unable to fall asleep. That would have been an acceptable explanation, but in my world, where phone calls from people long dead weren't as unusual an occurrence as most people would expect, I wasn't satisfied.

"Good morning, Melanie," Jack said cheerfully. "Can't a guy just want to buy breakfast for a beautiful woman without expecting anything in return?"

I pretended to think for a moment. "No." I unbuttoned my coat and folded it neatly on the back of my chair before sitting down, noticing that all of the women in the restaurant, including the gray-haired woman with a walker at a table by the ladies' room, were staring at Jack and regarding me with narrowed eyes. Yes, Jack Trenholm was way too good-looking for a writer, especially a writer of historical true-crime mysteries. He should have been bald with a gray beard, wearing thick turtlenecks that protruded over his paunch, his teeth tobacco-stained from his ubiquitous pipe. Unfortunately, like so much about Jack, he didn't even try to fit the stereotype.

"So, what do you want?" I asked again as I took out the bottle of hand sanitizer from my purse and squirted a dollop on my palm. I offered the bottle to Jack, but he shook his head before taking a sip of his black coffee. Emptying two packets of sugar into my latte I looked up at him again, then wished I hadn't. His eyes were certainly bluer than they should be, their intensity not needing the help from the navy blue sweater he wore. But something flickered in his eyes as he regarded me, something that I thought looked a lot like concern, and it made me squirm in my seat.

"How's General Lee?" he asked, ignoring my question and glancing out the front window, then down at his watch.

I swallowed a bite of my cinnamon roll. "He's fine," I said, referring to the small black-and-white dog I'd reluctantly inherited along with my historic home on Tradd Street.

"Are you still keeping him in the kitchen at night?"

I avoided his gaze. "Um, no. Not exactly."

A wide grin spread over Jack's face. "He sleeps in your room now, doesn't he?"

I took a huge bite of my roll to avoid answering, annoyed again at how astute Jack could be where I was concerned. After having failed at foisting General Lee off on my best friend, Dr. Sophie Warren—who'd turned out to be allergic—I'd sworn to all who would listen that I wasn't a dog person and had no intention of actually keeping the dog.

"He's sleeping at the foot of your bed now, isn't he?" Jack couldn't keep the glee from his voice.

I took a long sip of my latte, studiously avoiding looking at him.

Jack crossed his arms over his chest and slid back in his chair, a smug look on his face. "He's on the pillow next to you, isn't he?"

"Fine," I said, slamming down my coffee mug. "He wouldn't sleep anywhere else, okay? He'd cry if I left him in the kitchen, and when I brought him up to my room, he'd sit next to the bed staring up at me all night until I brought him up there with me. Sleeping on my pillow was his idea." I slid the mug away from me. "It's not like I actually like him or anything. He just seemed . . . lonely."

Jack leaned forward, his elbows on the table. "Maybe I should pretend I'm lonely and look up at you with sad-puppy eyes and see what happens."

I stared at him for a moment, suppressing the unwanted trill of excitement that settled somewhere near my stomach. "You'd end up in a crate in the kitchen." I pushed my empty plate away and signaled the waitress for another.

Jack laughed, then shook his head. "You know, one day those calories are actually going to stick to you, and you'll have to watch what you eat like the rest of us mortals."

I shrugged. "I can't help it. It's hereditary. My maternal grandmother was as slim as a reed until the day she died, and she ate like a linebacker."

"Is your mother the same way?"

My eyes met Jack's, and I saw he wasn't smiling anymore. "I wouldn't know, would I? I haven't seen her in more than thirty years." This wasn't precisely the truth, as I'd accidentally spotted the famous soprano Ginette Prioleau several times while flipping channels on the television, the remote control in my hand unable to flip quickly enough from the PBS station broadcasting a production of the Metropolitan Opera. The exact truth was that my mother was still as slender and as beautiful as she'd been when she'd abandoned her seven-year-old daughter without a backward glance.

The darkness that had been hovering over me all morning seemed to descend on our corner table, obscuring the light as if someone had hit a dimmer switch. I fought a wave of nausea as the hairs on the back of my neck rose, and I looked at Jack in panic to see if he'd noticed a change, too. But he was too busy staring past my shoulder to notice anything else.

"You resemble her a lot, you know." Jack's eyes slid back to mine, and I saw the look of concern quickly switch to one of apology.

"Oh, God, Jack, you didn't!" I made a move to stand, but he placed a hand on my arm.

"Melanie, she said it was a matter of life or death and that you wouldn't see her or return her phone calls. I was her last resort."

I looked around blindly, searching for an exit other than the door through which I'd entered, and wondered if I could run through the kitchen before anybody noticed me. A small, gloved hand gripped my shoulder as a bright light seemed to pop in front of me like a curtain being pulled back from the window to reveal a sunny day. The darkness dispelled as she squeezed my shoulder and dropped her hand, but the light remained, leaving me to wonder if the sigh and whisper I'd heard as the darkness left had been only in my imagination.

I looked up into the face of the woman who'd once been the world to me, when I was too small to understand the vagaries of human nature and that calling somebody "Mother" didn't always mean what you wanted it to.

"Hello, Mellie," she said in a soft, melodious voice that had haunted my dreams for years until I'd grown old enough to believe that I didn't need to hear my mother's voice anymore.

I winced at the sound of the nickname she'd given me—the nickname I'd never let anybody call me until I'd met Jack and he persisted in calling me Mellie regardless of whether I wanted him to.

I faced Jack, my fury easily turned on him. "You set this up, didn't you? You knew I didn't want to see her or talk to her, but you set this up anyway. How dare you? How dare you involve yourself uninvited, I might add, in something that has nothing to do with you and something I explicitly made clear to you that I wanted nothing to do with?" I paused just for a second to catch my breath, ignoring my mother's presence completely since that was the only way I could remain relatively calm. "I don't want to see you again. Ever."

He raised his eyebrow, and I knew we were both remembering another time when I'd said the exact same words. I leaned forward and pressed my finger into his sweater-covered chest. "And I really mean it this time."

I stood, intending to make a graceful exit, but managed instead to bump the table and spill the remainder of my latte in addition to two tall glasses of water. I slid to the next chair to escape the deluge, and while a busboy and our waitress were cleaning up the mess, my mother used the opportunity to slide into my vacated chair, effectively holding me hostage between her and the window.

She faced the side of my head because I refused to look at her. "Please don't be angry with Jack. I'll admit to using my friendship with his mother to coerce him into helping me. It's hard to say no to Amelia Trenholm, especially if you're her son."

I knew Amelia, and even liked her, but it didn't stop the need I had to get out of that café and away from my mother as fast as I could. Staring down at the laminated tabletop, I said, "I haven't had anything to say to you for over thirty years, Mother. And I don't think anything has changed. So if you'll excuse me, I need to go. I'm meeting clients at nine to show them houses in the Old Village and I don't want to be late."

She didn't move, and I was forced to continue staring at the bright yellow, green and blue specs of the linoleum tabletop, because I didn't want to look across from me and see the reproach in Jack's eyes.

Still wearing her gloves, my mother folded her hands on top of the table, and I wondered if she did it out of habit now or out of necessity.

"I need your help, Mellie. Your grandmother's house on Legare is for sale again, and I need your professional help in purchasing it. Everyone says that you're the best Realtor in Charleston."

Finally, I faced her for the first time, seeing the dark hair swept back in a low ponytail, her flawless skin and high cheekbones, the green eyes that I had always wanted instead of my father's hazel ones, and only the hint of fine lines at the corners of her eyes and around her mouth to show that she had aged at all since the night she'd said good night to me when she really should have said goodbye.

"There are hundreds of other Realtors in Charleston, Mother, all as qualified as I am—and a hell of a lot more willing—to help you purchase a home. In other words, no, thank you. I don't need to make a buck that bad."

To my surprise, she smiled. "You haven't really changed all that much."

"How would you know?" I asked, needing to wipe the smile from her face.

I heard Jack suck in a breath. "Mellie, I know you're hurt, and I wouldn't have had any part in this if I thought your mother was here just to make you feel worse. But there's more, and I think you need to listen to her. She believes you might be in danger."

I resisted the urge to roll my eyes. "Right. Well, tell her that I can take care of myself. I've been doing it for more than thirty years, after all. And I'm not speaking to you, remember?"

My mother spoke quietly beside me. "I've been having dreams. Every night. Dreams about a boat at the bottom of the ocean rising to the surface after many years. There's something . . . evil about it." Her eyes met mine and darkened. "And it's looking for you."

My throat tightened as a lungful of air escaped through my mouth. I recalled the phone call I'd received the night before and the feeling of dread that had followed me all morning, and I had the odd sensation that I had just fallen through thin ice into freezing water. I swallowed, giving my voice time to find me.

"It was a dream, Mother. Only a dream." I slid on my coat and fumbled with the buttons with shaking fingers before giving up on them. "And I really must go. If you need a recommendation for a good Realtor, call our receptionist, Nancy Flaherty, and she'll put you through to somebody."

To my surprise, my mother slid out of her chair and stood, a printed card held out to me between two gloved fingers. "Take my card. You're going to need it. This isn't the first time it's sought you out, you know. But it is the first time you're old enough to fight it." She paused. "We are not as we seem, Mellie."

Again, I was consumed with the feeling of plunging into icy water, and I couldn't speak. I stared at her without making a move to take the card. After a brief moment, she laid it on the table, and with a brief goodbye to Jack, she walked away, leaving behind the lingering scent of orchids and stale grief.

I turned to Jack again, but he held up his hand. "I know, you don't want to speak to me or see me again. I get it. But I think you need to listen to your mother. Her psychic abilities are well-known, and she knows what she's talking about. Sure, she could be wrong—after all, you have the gift, too, right? And you're not seeing anything. But what if she's right? What if you're in some kind of danger—don't you think you should know?"

"Why would you care?" I began to move away, but he grabbed my wrist.

"I care a lot more than you'd like to think."

Our eyes met briefly, but I found I couldn't hold his gaze. He dropped my arm, and I turned around and headed for the door. I didn't have to look back to know that he'd picked up my mother's card and was now carefully placing it inside his wallet.

Photo by Picture Perfect Photography

Karen White is the author of eight previous books. She lives with her family near Atlanta, Georgia. Visit her Web site at www.karen-white.com.